PRAISE FOR

The Devil in the Junior League

"Despite Frede's haughtiness, she is an endearing character who is just a product of her environment, as is the genuine and likable Nikki. . . . Hilarious." —*Library Journal*

"Lee, a former debutante, certainly knows her material."—*Publishers Weekly*

"[A] warm and funny novel that pokes fun at the sometimes myopic world of the socially elite . . . [A] superbly plotted novel. It has rich characterizations and plenty of laugh-out-loud humor." —*Romantic Times*

"I giggled out loud at this wickedly funny peek into the back-stabbing socialite-eat-socialite world of the rich and catty."

—Karen Quinn, author of *The Ivy Chronicles*

"Fresh and funny, original and outrageous, this novel is fabulous from start to finish." —Kristin Hannah, author of *Magic Hour*

"A book you'll sneak off early to lunch with just to get in a few extra pages." —*Pages* magazine

"[A] witty and provocative look at the lives of Texas high-society bluebloods." —*El Paso Times*

"Readers will love Lee's tale of back-stabbing proper ladies, revenge, the quest for popularity, and finding the truth about oneself."

—*News and Sentinel* (Parkersburg, WV)

"A mighty fun ride." —*SRQ* magazine

"Linda Francis Lee has written a brazenly funny novel full of tongue-in-cheek humor. . . . If you like laughs mixed into your love stories, *The Devil in the Junior League* is a must-read." —RomanceJunkies.com

ALSO BY LINDA FRANCIS LEE

Simply Sexy

Sinfully Sexy

Suddenly Sexy

The Wedding Diaries

Looking for Lacey

The Ways of Grace

Nightingale's Gate

Swan's Grace

Dove's Way

Crimson Lace

Emerald Rain

Blue Waltz

The Devil in the Junior League

LINDA FRANCIS LEE

ST. MARTIN'S GRIFFIN
NEW YORK

FOR AMY BERKOWER

This is a work of fiction. All of the characters, organizations, and events portrayed in this novel are either products of the author's imagination or are used fictitiously.

www.stmartins.com

Book design by Gretchen Achilles

LIBRARY OF CONGRESS CATALOGING-IN-PUBLICATION DATA

Lee, Linda Francis.
The Devil in the Junior League / Linda Francis Lee.
p. cm.
ISBN-13: 978-0-312-35497-8
ISBN-10: 0-312-35497-5
1. Women—Texas—Societies and clubs—Fiction. 2. Rich people—Texas—Fiction. 3. Texas—Fiction. I. Title.

PS3612.E225 D48 2006
813'.6—dc22

2006047523

First St. Martin's Griffin Edition: August 2007

10 9 8 7 6 5 4 3 2 1

ACKNOWLEDGMENTS

EVERYTHING ABOUT THIS BOOK has been a gift to me, including the many people who have believed in Frede Ware and helped me bring her to life. My deepest gratitude goes to . . .

From Writers House, Amy Berkower, for the gift of an idea, her guidance, and her deep caring. I am extremely fortunate to have her in my corner. Jodi Reamer, for fortunes told in Chinatown and a crazy subway ride uptown where she did a remarkably good job of pretending I wasn't crazy. Genevieve Gagne-Hawes, for returning from France in the nick of time. Maja Nikolic, for her grace and kindness. And Matthew Caselli, for his quick professionalism.

From St. Martin's Press, Jennifer Weis, who found Frede Ware early, loved her immediately, and helped me make her shine. Stefanie Lindskog, who always makes things easy. Lisa Senz, for her dedication to the book. Sally Richardson, George Witte, Matthew Shear, John Murphy, and Dori Weintraub, for their enthusiasm from the beginning.

My sister, Carilyn Francis Johnson, who reads everything I send her and is never shy about telling me how she feels. (This is a good thing, really.) My brother, Brian Francis, and nephew, Tyler Francis, who were always willing to talk shop whenever I wanted to discuss the crazy world I was creating. (And sometimes we even talked about my book.) My brother-in-law, Tim Johnson, who, along with Mick Ginnings, helped with certain tricky parts of the plot. My sister-in-law, Ginger Francis, who is my biggest cheerleader. And my parents, Marilyn and Larry Francis, who still, after being together since junior high, make each other laugh.

My friends Gloria Skinner, Mark and Roberta Raffalof, and Sean Whitson, for reading early drafts.

And to Michael, who makes everything possible, not to mention, worthwhile.

Dear Reader,

Having grown up managing the byways of Texas polite society, when I moved to New York City, I learned just how different states, and states of mind, can be. I could dress in black, flatten my hair, and stop saying things like *Aren't you sweet* on the subway, but still New Yorkers asked where I was from.

Suddenly I wasn't a bone-deep Texan anymore, but I wasn't a New Yorker either. And that's when it hit me. I should write a book about the secret handshakes of life we learn to prove we fit in.

As the setting for my novel, I chose the 106-year-old Junior League, with past members Eleanor Roosevelt, Katharine Hepburn, and Laura Bush, because the women of the Junior League work together to make significant contributions to their communities, overcoming the challenges caused by the sorts of women who love nothing more than causing trouble. And my novel is filled with women who love to cause trouble!

In *The Devil in the Junior League,* Frede has to teach the flashy Nikki how to be a lady in order to fit in. What I hope readers take away from the book is that yes, manners and etiquette play a part in our lives. But in truth, it is confidence, strength, and a certain amount of fearlessness that gets us places in life.

I've had a wonderful response to the book, and love talking to readers. If you have a group that would like me to speak by phone, please let me know at lfranlee@aol.com.

Enjoy!

Linda

Linda Francis Lee

Photo: Tess Steinkoik

Reading Group Guide available online at **www.readinggroupgold.com**

Visit Linda Lee at **www.lindafrancislee.com**

The Devil in the Junior League

Chapter One

THE JUNIOR LEAGUE of Willow Creek, Texas, is *très* exclusive, one of the oldest and most elite women's societies in the country. And we work hard to keep it that way. Outsiders need not apply.

I know it sounds terrible. But really, if I don't explain everything exactly, in all its unvarnished truth, how will you ever understand how it was possible that I got myself into what I now call the "unfortunate situation" and how all the gossip about *moi* got started.

So yes, it's true that we at the Junior League of Willow Creek are all about being made up of the crème de la crème of society. Do you believe the richest of the rich in Texas would donate money, weeks on their sprawling ranches, or lunches in their elegant mansions to just anyone? I think not. And how do you think we raise all those bundles of money that we turn around and give away to the needy?

From the above-mentioned rich.

I am Fredericka Mercedes Hildebrand Ware, and despite the antiquated sound of my name, I'm only twenty-eight years old. My friends call me Frede—pronounced *Freddy*. My husband calls me "Fred."

I like to think of the collective members of the JLWC as a sort of female Robin Hood (though better dressed since, God knows, not one of us would be caught dead in tights) who cajoles money out of her rich husband and indirectly out of his rich company as she lies in bed at night rubbing her perfectly manicured toes up against his leg.

It goes something like this:

Laying the groundwork.

"Sweetie, if Basco, Branden, and Battle donates a trip on their private jet for the League's Christmas Fair Silent Auction, whisking the lucky winner away to Aspen for a week of skiing, I'm sure it would be one of the top money earners, if not the top earner at the Fair."

Framing the competition.

"Of course you heard, didn't you, that Robert Melman has offered up his company yacht for a Caribbean cruise? Mindy Melman, bless her heart, gloated all through the last General Meeting when she got to announce the news."

Closing the deal.

"You know it's tax deductible, sugar. And after Basco got in that tiny little tiff with the State Bar Ethics Committee last month, I'm certain if the firm donates to a charity of our stature it will certainly give Basco a big gold star. Besides, you remember, don't you, that the Ethics Committee chairman is Jim Wyman, Cecelia Wyman's husband?"

Sex follows some of the time, though the donation is guaranteed.

To be completely honest, not every member is married, and certainly not every member of the JLWC is fabulously wealthy. Mind you, no one is headed for the poorhouse—well, maybe a few are who invested badly, pretended they had more than they did, or got tangled up with nasty habits that cost *beaucoup* amounts of m-o-n-e-y to support. And really, who wants that sort of member anyway, so the sooner they get to the poorhouse and can't pay their dues, the better. Why prolong their misery, I say.

I know, I sound even worse than terrible now, but truly, it's the charitable thing to do to give a gentle nudge out the door so they don't keep spending what they no longer have in an ill-fated attempt to save face.

As I mentioned, the JLWC is made up of the crème de la crème of Willow Creek society, no question, but within the League, there are different tiers.

Tier One: Wealthy members with socially prominent names, which trumps . . .

Tier Two: Members with socially prominent names but no significant wealth, which trumps . . .

Tier Three: Members with m-o-n-e-y but no name.

To secure a place at any level in the JLWC, a woman's reputation must be beyond reproach, she must gain the full endorsement of six members in good standing who have known her for a minimum of five years—be they active members or "retired" members called "sustainers"—and pass the interview process with the membership committee. It's not so unlike the president of the United States trying to get an appointee approved by Congress.

You are probably wondering where I fit into this caste system. It just so happens that I'm one of the few members with my own wealth and my own good name, which is how I get away with having a j-o-b and no one blinks an eye.

Yes, a job.

You see I own an amazing art gallery with a full-time staff that thankfully does most of the work. I provide the good taste and the (endless stream of) funding. I feel it's my duty to support poor starving artists (as long as their art is fabulously chic and never tacky), plus the write-off makes my husband and accountant beyond happy.

To put me in an even higher stratum, my husband is Gordon Ware, the youngest son of the Milburn Smythe Ware family. You may have heard of him.

The Wares have a fine old Texas name, even if they no longer have the fine old Texas wealth their patriarch gained when he struck black gold in his backyard at the turn of the last century. Sometimes I think Gordon has never gotten over this, and if everyone didn't say that I was the most beautiful woman in Willow Creek—which isn't entirely true since Anne Watson is a former Miss Texas . . . though she is in her thirties now—I would fear my husband married me for my bank account.

Even though the wealth is mine, Gordon manages it, which means I still do the toe dance to convince him that "our money," as he now calls it, is put to good use.

Not that anyone I know ever discusses the toe dance. How could we since we at the JLWC never talk about sex. Instead, my friends and I talk about the usual:

1. Their kids because their husbands never listen

2. Trends in hair, clothes, and household staff

3. Who is losing or has lost their m-o-n-e-y

We have a few other topics that we discuss regularly, which need a bit more explanation:

1. Anna—the type of anorexic woman who swears she eats everything in sight, but darn it all, just can't gain weight. I say it would help if she stopped sticking her finger down her throat so she can maintain her size-four figure.

2. Blue Light Special—having nothing to do with Kmart. In this case, BLS would be those unfortunate souls who bleach their teeth so white they look blue. This sort of woman is usually seen with a cup of coffee in her hand at all times, only drinks red wine, and more often than not comes from places like California.

3. BJ—stands for "breast job," not "blow job," since Junior Leaguers really aren't the blow job sorts. Too messy.

4. Jolie—fake lips.

5. NC—a person with No Class, pronounced *Nancy*. Using it in a sentence would go something like this: "There's a Nancy with a Blue Light Special, a really bad BJ, and Jolies the size of inner tubes."

Next comes our favorite topic, Categories of Men. There are three varieties:

1. Rich, good-looking men—otherwise known as "Pay Dirt," because just about every rich man in Texas has made his money from oil, land, or cattle

2. Poor, good-looking men—commonly referred to as "A Shame"—for the waste of good looks

3. Poor ugly men—well, frankly, why bother giving them a name

I can just hear all those feminists in the blue states having a fit over the things we talk about, not to mention the *modus operandi* of using our wiles to get donations from our husbands. As it turns out, it was some of those feminist types who threw very public fits, forcing the Junior League's national office to establish democratic guidelines for admission.

Texas has not succumbed, with varying degrees of success, and still fights against weakening our exclusive ramparts just as our ancestors fought against the Spanish, the French, and eventually the Union Army. In the Lone Star State it is still easier to gain entrance to the Governor's Mansion than it is to gain membership to the Junior League of Willow Creek.

Now, rest assured, the Junior Leagues in Texas, and even the JLWC, have complied to the letter of the new law by removing the age-old blackballing process, and applying "democratic" standards for admission. Perhaps those standards are a tad on the high side (see above) and only the most prominent women in town can meet them. However, if standards are met, she's in. I swear.

It's all very democratic. How can we be blamed if a woman hasn't known six JLWC members for a minimum of five years who would be willing to put their reputations on the line to get her in?

I've ruffled feathers, I know. But really, I had to give you a little background so you can fully appreciate how the Junior League of Willow Creek works and how the "unfortunate situation" got started.

What amazes me is that on the day my life went awry, I woke up in the most *fabu* mood. I got out of bed early and all of the sudden I realized I felt queasy. Sick! Me!

Excited, I dashed to my marble bathroom—a luscious room that I dare say is bigger than most every home on the wrong side of the Willow Creek railroad tracks—leaned over the commode and managed to gag a time or two. Okay, I didn't actually get sick, but it was close and I was elated. Morning sickness!

As further proof of my delicate condition, my always flat stomach was puffy—from pregnancy, I was certain, not from the five pieces of double chocolate fudge cake I'd had the night before due to serious depression over my lack of *petit* Fredericks or *petite* Frederickas.

I didn't need any other proof. After six long years of trying, six long years of, first, spontaneous sex, then charted sex, followed by every sort of fertility treatment known to man, I was pregnant. The toe dance had finally worked for more than a donation.

Which was why I was distracted that day at JLWC headquarters when I was attending the New Projects Committee meeting. Only the executive members of the committee were in attendance that day as we tried to determine which new project we should select for the coming fiscal year. I'm not sure I could have taken the entire group of eight and their gossip disguised as important news. While I'm all for gossip, it can make meetings drag on for ages, and that day—chop, chop—I was in a hurry.

"Frede, how many applications for funding have we received?"

This from Pilar Bass, head of our committee.

I had known Pilar most of my life. In first grade she and I started a little group of best friends. We swore we would be friends to the end. But schoolgirl promises have little to do with reality—at least that was what Pilar said, a realist, I realize now, even back then at the ripe old age of six.

As it turned out, she was right. She and our devoted little group fell apart our sophomore year of high school. Every time we see each other now we pretend we didn't spend every Friday night sleeping over at each other's houses, freezing each other's training bras, sharing secrets and clothes, or pricking fingers to become lifelong blood sisters.

In high school Pilar was voted Best New Debater. I was voted Most Beautiful. By the end of our tenure at Willow Creek High, she was president of the Debate Team, I our Homecoming Queen. After high school, she made the mistake of going up north to college, then took a job in New York City. By the time she returned to Texas they had managed to take quite a bit of the *Texas* out of the girl.

She came back to town wearing boxy black clothes and glasses. Out with the contact lenses, in with the horn-rimmed, thick-framed spectacles that . . . well . . . by Texas beauty standards turned her into a spectacle. And the hair. Does anyone in New York really think all that flat hair is attractive?

But I digress.

As an adult, Pilar had become an ambitious Leaguer, approaching every issue like a savage corporate warrior and trying everyone's last nerve. She had forgotten that it was possible, and decidedly more desirable, to wrap one's true feelings up in "bless your hearts" and "aren't you sweets." She'd forgotten that ferreting out true meaning from words swathed in smiles was an art form—Texas girls learning the skill just like they learned the waltz for their debutante balls. She had become direct, forgetting the rules of acceptable behavior that were learned like secret handshakes, passed down from generation to generation.

Now, don't misunderstand, it's not that Texas women don't have opinions or share them. We do. It's just that we wrap them up in honey and smiles and hugs until a sharp rebuke can feel like a compliment, the true meaning not sinking in until later, hitting like a left hook to the jaw. As the saying goes, a Texas woman can tell you to go to hell, and make you think you're going to enjoy the trip.

"Frede, are you listening?" Pilar asked, her tone grating, her perfectly straight, blunt-cut black hair swinging militantly across her shoulders.

No didn't seem like the perfect answer. (See above reference to rules on acceptable communication.) Besides, truly I was distracted. While I was certain I was pregnant I had no official confirmation. The second I could slip away from the meeting I would, skipping the practically required after-meeting lunch at Brightlee, the Junior League tearoom. Everyone would expect me to be there for the rest of the afternoon. By leaving early, I would be free of interference, phone calls, or demands on my attention. I could go home to use the Clear Blue pregnancy test I'd picked up at the drugstore on my way to the meeting.

Not willing to share any of that, I scrambled around in my brain for some snippets of the conversation that might have sunk in.

Pilar sighed. "I asked how many applications for new projects we've received."

"Oh, yes, of course." I adjusted the cream-colored cashmere sweater that draped elegantly across my shoulders, then pulled out my personalized FREDE WARE notepad and scanned it. "We've received twenty applications, only sixteen of which included a detailed proposal. When it was all said and done, I narrowed the running down to five."

An ominous moment of silence passed.

"You narrowed it down?"

Her tone was imperious and the other girls of the New Projects Executive Committee came to attention then pressed back in their straight-backed chairs. Gathering myself, I glanced from face to face of our little group. There was Lizabeth Mortimer, who was thirty-two if she was a day, though she swore to anyone who would listen that she was twenty-eight. Unfortunately for her, she had been a senior at Willow Creek High School when I was a freshman, and I knew for a fact she wasn't twenty-anything. But the thing was, she had been dating that cute Ramsey boy who was only twenty-six, and really, what woman wants to be older than her beau. That is, unless she's forty and catches a twenty-six-year-old, in which case I say, *Brava!*

The other woman present, besides yours truly, Pilar, and Lizabeth, was Gwen Hansen. Actually it was Gwendolyn Moore-Bentley-Baker-Hansen. She'd been married and divorced three times, was approaching forty and the Sustainer years, when members of the JLWC are forced from an active role to one that is more supervisory. We all knew she had slept her way through Willow Creek and never would have gotten into the JLWC if she hadn't already been a member when she decided to turn sex into a sport. Just as with those Supreme Court Justices, it's *très difficile* to get a woman out once she's in, short of having her head for the poorhouse.

Unfortunately for the JLWC, Gwen had more money than even *moi*, so we had resorted to trying to get her married for a fourth time in hopes that she would settle down.

As to Pilar and her ominous glare, she didn't make me nervous. What was she going to do? Kick me out? Me, Frede Ware?

She might be ambitious, but everyone who was anyone knew that I would no doubt follow in my own mother's footsteps and one day become president of the Junior League.

I smiled at her with the patience of a saint. "Pilar, sugar, if you want to take the applications and go through them yourself, fine by me." I retrieved the Louis Vuitton messenger bag I had bought especially for this committee, and retrieved the stack of official forms and thick stacks of detailed proposals.

When I extended them to her, she sniffed. "Fine, we'll consider the five."

I swear I didn't gloat. I simply began my little talk with a graceful smile.

"Maurice Trudeaux's wife sent in a form requesting we start a sculpture garden around Maurice's work."

A heavy sigh of boredom shimmered through the group, and Lizabeth and Gwen resumed their glossed-over stares.

Maurice Trudeaux might be one of Texas's finest sculptors, having trained in Europe, but he was short and not particularly blessed in the looks department. It didn't matter that Trudeaux's *Pietà* was one of the most exquisite, and had been on loan to the Metropolitan Museum of Art. At least, it didn't matter to the other members of the committee. I, on the other hand, cared a great deal, and as president and owner of Hildebrand Galleries (not to mention with my degree in art history from Willow Creek University), I felt it my duty to give opinions on all things art related.

"His work is simply perfection. A true Texas gift. His wife says we could get the garden started with a hundred thousand dollars and ten to twelve volunteers."

Pilar was scribbling as fast as she could on her own (boring spiral) notepad.

"Next on the list," I went on, "is a horse camp for autistic children. Ten thousand. While I love the idea of helping autistic children, I don't think we could get the twenty volunteers needed to staff it from within our membership. All that mucking out of stalls."

The women murmured their agreement.

"Project number three is an after-school tutoring program for underprivileged children in South Willow Creek which needs thirty thousand and eight volunteers.

"Number four is a physical fitness program for a senior citizens' community that needs sixty thousand and ten volunteers.

"Lastly, we have a request for two fabulous, brand-new neonatal machines for St. Bethany Hospital, and five volunteers. Each machine costs a hundred thousand dollars. It fits our profile best, plus, Margaret James has been hounding me every day since she's the one who is ringleading the project. If the League agrees to the proposal, she and her husband will match our funds."

At the mention of Margaret's name, the not-so-young-but-sweet Lizabeth stifled a laugh (barely), Pilar pressed her lips closed in distaste, and our very own Gets-around Gwen got a superior look in her eye. Margaret's reputation was worse than Gwen's, though it had nothing to do with sexcapades. Also unlike Gwen, Margaret was bending over backward to redeem her sullied reputation after her husband had gotten crossways with the law.

Fortunately, all had been straightened out and he had gotten little more than a slap on the wrist. *Un*fortunately, he had done the most NC sort of thing by hiring the infamously vulgar attorney Howard Grout. I had never seen the lawyer and I hoped I never would, but I heard he was the worst sort of hound dog, was said to be wild, wore gold chains and tasteless clothes, and had *beaucoup* amounts of new m-o-n-e-y. In short, he was the worst sort of cliché.

He was also my neighbor.

I lived in The Willows of Willow Creek, an exclusive gated community. About two years earlier, Howard and his flashy wife bought the old DuPont place next to mine, which was bad enough. But then they immediately tore it down and proceeded to build the most disreputable foreign-looking, palacelike structure, which had outraged the neighborhood.

"Enough, ladies," Pilar said, breaking into the gossip that had erupted in our ranks. "While I think all the projects are worthy of attention, each one is similar to something we are already doing. Frede, I want to go over the entire group of applications, after all. In fact," she added, with not a little smugness, "I have an idea of my own that I think we should pursue."

Lizabeth and Gwen sucked in their breaths. I went very still as Pilar considered me through her horn-rimmed glasses, but I wasn't about to be undone by a blue-state convert. I simply smiled and handed over the stack.

"You are so completely right, sugar. You should go through the files." I gave Pilar a sympathetic look. "I'm sure you have plenty of time to do your work and mine too. And no doubt you have a fabulous idea."

Or not. Everyone knew that Pilar was not an idea woman.

I stood and blew kisses all around. "Ciao, girls. I have to dash."

"What about lunch?" Lizabeth asked, recovering from her shock.

"Sorry, sugar. I have some unexpected business to take care of."

I made my escape and my heart beat in time with the click of my Manolo flats (stilettos are *très* NC and no one would be caught dead wearing them to a committee meeting) as I hurried across the parking lot to my white S Class Mercedes. Soon I would be getting my very own mommy car, a top-of-the-line Chevrolet Suburban, so I could careen through the streets with my progeny chatting amiably to one another in the backseat as I chauffeured them from one activity to the next. At least on the nanny's day off.

The nearly spring Texas weather was glorious, not yet hot and no rain, the sky wide open and clear. I turned the ignition and headed for The Willows feeling gloriously optimistic with visions of polite, exceedingly well-behaved little children dancing in my head. My emerald-cut pink diamond ring flashed in the sun, the Clear Blue pregnancy kit sitting in its plastic bag on the seat next to me, as I hurried away. Without braking at the intersection that led out of headquarters, I waved at Blake, the policeman who regularly patrolled the area, and smiled at him when he shook his head at me for running the Stop sign.

I raced through the curving, narrow, tree-lined streets of Willow Creek, driving past Willow Creek Square and the quaint shops, the courthouse in all its sandstone and Doric-columned glory, then the university campus and the college students whom I told myself I couldn't run over.

Minutes later, I pulled up to the guard station at The Willows.

I sat patiently as I waited for the guard to swing the electric gate open. Oddly, the man just stared at me while his mouth opened and closed like a fish out of water.

I buzzed down my window. "Juan, sweetie." (I'm always sweet as pie to service personnel.) "I'm in a hurry. Please open the gate."

"But, but . . ." The buts trailed off and he said something that sounded like *"Madre mía,"* before he pressed the button.

I didn't ask questions or give it much thought as I flew up the cobbled length of Blue Willow Lane to my sprawling mansion and the bathroom so I could pee on the stick.

I pulled into the driveway lined with neatly trimmed shrubbery, then bypassed the long brick path that would have taken me back to the garage. I veered right, curving around as I headed for the front door. The minute I crested the ridge (the satisfying sight of my whitewashed, redbrick, formal Georgian home coming into view) I saw a faded brown car of indeterminate origins that I had never seen before.

My live-in maid used a cute-as-a-button Ford Focus we had purchased for her—plus, Wednesday was her day off.

The gardener drove a truck.

Gordon played golf at the Willow Creek Country Club on Wednesdays.

Which meant the drive should have been empty.

My heartbeat sped up in a way that I rarely felt, and to make it worse, there was a foreign urgency mixed in that made the world shift into slow motion. Call me a drama queen, but that was really how it felt, fast and slow at the same time in a way that I didn't like at all.

With a calm I had perfected over the years, I parked nose to nose with the unfortunate vehicle. Pulling out my house keys, I had the sudden vision of myself opening the door and stepping into the two-story foyer, then heading up the long, curving staircase to Gordon's and my bedroom. I had a sinking feeling I knew what I would find. But when I pushed into the house, it was to voices and hysteria.

Two women were there. My maid, Nina (dressed in street clothes rather than her uniform, a 1950s-era handbag swinging on her wrist), and a strange woman, whom, like the car, I had never seen before.

It took a second for the occupants to notice I was there. When they did, silence reigned for one blissful moment before Nina started carrying on in Spanish. I only made out bits and pieces, but it was enough to understand that my maid had forgotten her grandson's birthday present, had returned to get it, found this . . . this . . . woman in the cheap department-store suit, and I should call the police because the woman wouldn't leave.

I can't tell you the relief I felt. You probably guessed what I had thought—that Gordon was upstairs having an affair with another woman, in our house, in our bed, on my nine-hundred-ninety-thread-count French sheets. But this mousy plain Jane could not be a mistress, at least not my husband's mistress.

"Nina, sugar, calm down."

I walked over to the stranger with all my elegant grace, then I extended my hand.

"I'm Fredericka Ware. Can I help you?"

The mouse stood up from the mahogany bench with its damask seat cushion where she had planted herself, and didn't offer her hand. For the life of me, I couldn't imagine what she wanted as she stared at me defiantly, especially since I could see she was shaking.

"My name is Janet Lambert," she said, "and I am pregnant with your husband's child."

Chapter Two

BEFORE I SAY ANYTHING ELSE, I should tell you a few things that were true about my husband on that day I found Miss Mouse in my foyer.

1. I hated him. Oops, bad me. I'm getting ahead of myself. That came later.

2. His full name was Gordon Lidicott Ware and he was thirty-eight years old.

3. He had blond hair and blue eyes, and was just shy of six feet tall.

4. He was the youngest of five children in the Ware family. The first four siblings were girls, then along came Gordon, as if Mr. and Mrs. Ware just kept their monthly tryst going until they got their boy, then quit after Mr. Ware proved he had what it took to produce a male of the species.

5. Gordon was the best-looking member of the Ware family, far prettier than his sisters, not to mention he looked nothing like a single one of them. All golden blond to the far less stellar browns of the rest of the clan. Several people around town had speculated that his father actually didn't have what it took, so instead went out and secretly "made arrangements" to get the boy he so

desperately felt he needed to prove his manliness when he feared his wife could give him nothing but girls.

6. His parents still lived in the same house where Gordon was raised just north of town. I had yet to understand how Gordon's parents support themselves since Papa Ware (a former judge) hadn't worked since I met him. Mama Ware was a past JLWC Volunteer Extraordinaire. She believed in the sanctity of ladies wearing hats to church on Sunday, the box-Pleat dust ruffle on all beds, and every proper home having a deviled-egg plate.

7. Every one of Gordon's siblings had moved (far, far) away with the exception of his sister Edith, a former member of JLWC (and determined spinster), who still lived with their parents.

8. Even though we grew up in the same city, I had never seen him before my senior year at Willow Creek University. I was studying at the always quiet law library before finals when I met him. He was a practicing attorney, not a student, who had just finished teaching some sort of torts class. Being ten years older than *moi,* he seemed to have everything that was missing in the callow youths I was used to dating. When he sat down and declared that he was madly in love with me, I didn't think he was some desperate loser. Instead I thought he was the most romantic and honest man I had ever met. Really, what sensible man wouldn't fall in love with me on sight?

9. He had a wandering eye, was the biggest flirt in town, and wasn't shy about offering compliments to a pretty lady. Which made him the most popular man at Junior League social functions.

10. He knew that my father—a true Texan who believed in protecting what was his—would kill him with a double-barreled shotgun if more of him wandered than his eye.

11. He was a huge disappointment to my mother, because: (a) she'd had high hopes that I would marry an oil baron or real estate heir—or at the very least, she had wanted me to marry someone

with enough money of his own so he wouldn't work so hard to spend mine; and (b) my own siblings had also moved (far, far) away, and Gordon hadn't done even the most basic thing of providing her with grandchildren who lived in Willow Creek.

12. Because Gordon was the youngest, the only son, and the best-looking member of the bunch, he was pampered by his sisters, coddled by his mother, spoiled by his father, and he thought he could do no wrong. Though to his credit, he had always been smart enough to be afraid of my father, and very much afraid of my mother.
13. He wanted to be the Most Important Man About Town, though that tended to be a little *difficile* since the money was mine and everyone knew it. But he persevered. In fact, the only competition I had for attention among the better half of Willow Creek came from my husband.

Based on everything I knew about Gordon Ware and the world we lived in, I wasn't particularly worried when I came face-to-face with the woman in my foyer. Surprised by her declaration, yes. Worried, no, because as I stood in my entry hall, its curving rotund walls disappearing up into the heights and the mosaic ceiling I'd had commissioned the year before, I didn't believe a word the woman said.

If she'd had bigger, better-styled hair and enviable clothes, or if anything about her had suggested she lived more than a hand-to-mouth existence, I might have felt a quiver of concern. I was nothing if not susceptible (since at that very moment I was holding a Clear Blue pregnancy test in a plastic bag at my side) to a declaration of someone else's delicate condition, purportedly caused by my husband. But I knew none of it could be true because rich is rich, and we recognize our own . . . and the people who could conceivably cavort within our elite ranks. This woman was not from (nor could ever be a part of) Gordon's and my world.

Why was I so sure?

There are three possible looks for people of wealth:

1. Tasteful clothes made of expensive materials, which are always distinguishable to someone in the know. Think St. John knits—conservative, but with enough flair to keep a Texas woman happy. (JLWC acceptable.)

2. High-quality clothes that are so old and so worn that an outsider would think they were cheap. Think decades-old Pendleton wool or old wealthy men on golf courses wearing green plaid pants and bright yellow shirts. (JLWC acceptable.)

3. Expensive clothes that scream bad taste. Think of those Euro and Latin sorts who wear everything feathered, bangled, and/or wildly colored. (*Not* JLWC acceptable—and not so unlike an East Texas woman who shops at Sack o' Suds in her rhinestone-studded warm-up suit.)

Miss Mouse, with her polyester skirt and jacket, shiny faux leather shoes, and nondescript coiffure, didn't fall into any of these acceptable or even nonacceptable categories. Which put her very firmly in:

4. Cheap clothes that are atrociously tasteless, scream NC, not to mention bleat "No m-o-n-e-y." (Very much *not* JLWC acceptable.)

Like minds understood the difference with a mere glance. My husband knew this, and was an unapologetic snob.

I can't begin to tell you how the woman looked planted on my highly polished white Carrara marble floor. She was framed in the archway that led from the entry hall to the living room, looking dreadfully out of place in all her NCness.

Trying to get my head around the situation, I focused on the trees and greenery I could see through the floor-to-ceiling windows in my cathedral-ceilinged Grand Room. The Willows was surrounded by a nature preserve that circled the neighborhood like a lush green moat, separating us from the masses. At least that was how it had been until Howard Grout gained entrée using the Trojan horse of his very unclean money.

But Howard Grout wasn't my problem just then. Miss Mouse was.

And standing there with the woman staring at me, I was secure in the knowledge that Gordon loved me and the life we had built together, not this stranger.

"Nina," I said with my usual calm, "call security."

No doubt she would have since she hated Gordon as much as he hated her. My husband would have fired her long ago if he could have. But she was more nanny than maid, had been with me since I was born, when my own mother was heavily involved doing her own good works at the Junior League. Nina was like silverware, handed down from generation to generation, moving to this house when I got married. She knew more about me and my life than my husband, or even my mother.

With her handbag swinging on her wrist, she headed for the phone. But she didn't get very far since Gordon chose that second to breeze in through the west hallway, which led from the kitchen, clearly having driven straight back to the garage to park when he returned home. He was whistling as if he didn't have a care in the world. Though that changed the minute he saw me.

"Fred!" he barked, his happy tune cut off, his smile disappearing. "What are you doing here?"

Before I could answer, he saw our visitor.

I had heard the expression "blanching white" before, but I had never witnessed it. FYI, it's more like going gray, but the effect is the same. Shock. Gordon was shocked and anxious at the sight of her.

The certainty I had felt seconds before started to nosedive into the entry hall floor.

"Janet!" he yelped.

Crash and burn. Nosedive complete. He knew her.

Given the high ceilings and all that exquisite marble, her name echoed, the warbling sound making my spine stiffen.

"What are you doing here?" he demanded, this time of her.

Minnie's own spine restarched itself and she looked him in the eye. "You haven't returned my phone calls all week. We need to talk."

A fine sheen of sweat had broken out on Gordon's forehead (I assumed he was thinking of my father and his double-barreled shotgun). He ran his hand through his hair with such agitation that his head was left with the look of a freshly plowed field with furrows just waiting for a planting.

"Yes, Gordon," I added. "We need to talk. Miss—" I glanced at her in question.

"Lambert," Nina supplied.

Nina and I smiled politely at each other.

"Miss Lambert says she's pregnant with your child."

I said the words straight-out, and if possible his shock shifted and grew. I might have hoped I felt queasy that morning, but I definitely did then. As I've already established, my husband is a lawyer. What I haven't explained is that he didn't practice law. He practiced golf and tennis and exercising five days a week, and when he wasn't at the country club or on our tennis court or in our pool, he was off to parts of the world unknown, engaging in "extreme sports." Jumping out of helicopters to ski unreachable mountaintops. Rappelling down sheer rock cliffs. Conquering the Himalayas. Deep-sea diving. If it was dangerous, he did it. Or that's what he told me he did when he disappeared and was "unreachable" for weeks at a time. Right then, I wasn't so sure.

My husband couldn't seem to move. Janet Lambert took a step forward. "Gordy," she said with a soft intimacy that felt like a punch to my midsection. "I'm pregnant with your child. Our child," she added, with all the melodrama of a beleaguered B-list actress in a sappy Lifetime Movie of the Week.

I felt light-headed.

"That's a lie!" he blurted out to me, before he turned back to Miss Lambert. "You can't be pregnant. I swear. It's impossible. I had a vasectomy ten years ago."

And the hits just kept on rolling.

Silence rushed through the house as if the volume had been turned off on news footage of a nuclear explosion, before sound erupted again. Voices exploded at once, arguing, people pointing fingers, screeching—that is, everyone but me. I don't do hysterical.

Nina, on the other hand, is an expert at hysterical. Miss Mouse, despite her accountantish, numbers-crunching suit, was verging on hysterical, her mouth gaping, what must have been her plan to extort money blowing apart like a straw house in the face of the big bad wolf and his big bad terrible huff of breath.

Then there was my husband, with all his blond-haired, blue-eyed, pretty-boy good looks, as he realized what he had just said.

"A vasectomy," I said, heat burning my cheeks as my stomach roiled—and not with morning sickness, apparently.

I wanted to yell, an act that would ruin the ice-queen persona I had worked so hard to master. In that second, all the years I had spent chiseling and molding myself into a woman to be reckoned with fell away. And that was unacceptable. I don't fall apart any more than I do hysterical.

"Frede," he said, rushing forward.

As I mentioned before, he never calls me Frede—unless he is in some kind of trouble.

"What do you mean you've had a vasectomy?"

This from Janet, though I was wondering the same thing.

Nina rattled on in rapid-fire Spanish, continuing in a less-than-complimentary mode regarding our unexpected guest and my husband. Miss Mouse wasn't fazed; that, or she didn't understand she was being maligned. My husband never listened to Nina anyway.

"You said you loved me!" Minnie said. "You said you were going to divorce your wife and we'd have our own family. You promised me this life!" she added, sweeping her arm around to encompass my home.

The slow-motion effect returned and I glanced between my husband and the woman. Had he really said those things? Had he meant them?

I couldn't tell anything from the expression on his face, though I knew he was panicked. Not to harp on a point, but it was *my* money, and he did sign a prenuptial agreement. Did I mention that Gordon Ware had very expensive tastes? I doubted that Miss Lambert had more than a few pennies to rub together, certainly not enough to keep my husband in the style to which he had become accustomed.

"Frede," he said, "you've got to listen to me. I hardly know the woman. I don't know what she's talking about."

Minnie made all sorts of rumbling noise before it congealed into a single word. "Liar!" Her body shook. "You know everything about me, just like I know everything about you. I know all about your swanky wife with tons of money." She skewered me with a look. "I know all about your fancy bed since I've spent every Wednesday afternoon there for the last three months, on my back, making love to your husband."

Now here was a woman who could benefit from an etiquette lesson or two—namely a session where one learns that one should never, ever discuss private matters with anyone other than a doctor, lawyer, or priest.

"Miss Lambert, I suggest you leave my house before I have you arrested for trespassing."

Janet narrowed her eyes and smiled, then whipped out a key. Yes, a key. To my house. A lesser woman would have been fazed.

"I don't think anyone is going to arrest me when I was given a key and permission to enter. Just ask the guard. My name's on the list."

That would be the permanent list kept at the guardhouse naming all those guests who are allowed to enter without calling ahead. Each resident of The Willows has their own list.

I remembered Juan's gaping surprise (and horror, no doubt, since I'm the one who brings his end-of-the-year bonus check) when I pulled up to the gate unexpectedly on a Wednesday before lunch. The memory made me realize the woman wasn't lying. Though really, all I had to do was look at my husband to know she wasn't.

I know it's dramatic, but my world tilted. As I stood in the foyer, my free hand curled around the single strand of pearls I wore around my neck, and I felt everything shift. My husband had had or was having an affair with a woman who couldn't come close to competing with me in any way.

Which meant what?

I didn't have a clue and wasn't willing to think about it just then. There was always tomorrow.

"Out," I said with quiet force, my dignity still intact as I dropped my hand to my side.

Thankfully, everyone stopped cold. The ice queen hadn't melted entirely.

"Frede," Gordon interjected, coming toward me.

"I said out."

Janet looked mutinous, as if she wasn't about to leave. But Nina took care of that. My maid started carrying on, her Spanish ricocheting off the walls. Janet leaped out of the way when Nina took a swipe at her with the handbag. When Gordon didn't step in to defend or protect her, his mistress looked at him, then sighed dramatically. "I know you love me. I know we'll straighten this out." Then she left.

Clearly Miss Mouse had more of a flare for drama than I would have guessed.

"Fred," Gordon repeated, regaining his footing. "We should talk. It's not what it seems."

If ladylike behavior hadn't been drummed into me since birth, I would have snorted. As it was, I headed for the stairs that curved up the rotunda walls. "There is nothing to talk about."

At least not until I could get my head around what had just happened.

"Fred—"

Whatever he was going to say was cut off when I heard Nina take a swipe at *him* this time.

"Hey!"

Nina let out a barrage of castigating Spanish, and he flew up the stairs behind me.

"Estúpido!" Nina fired after him.

Very true. Though right then I felt like the stupid one for having been betrayed by my husband in a way that I could hardly absorb. It wasn't about the other woman, which was bad enough. It was about the fact that he'd had a vasectomy without ever mentioning it.

A vasectomy, for mercy's sake, I thought, as if repeating the word would make its meaning clearer.

I had been jumping through hoops to get pregnant for six years, all with his blessing, and it had never been a possibility if what he had blurted was true.

The fertility drugs, the testing, the charted sex, were all for naught. The depression and the feeling that I was failing at something for the first time in my life every month when I started another period had been a waste of energy because he'd had a vasectomy before he ever met me based on the "ten years ago" he had tossed out.

When I reached the second floor, I walked carefully along the Oriental runner that covered just the right amount of hardwood floor as I headed for our bedroom. Gordon still followed.

"Fred, I didn't mean it," he said.

Call me a fool, but a surge of hope shot through me. Had he lied to the woman?

My hope was short-lived because the truth was that while I had never suspected he had surgically removed the possibility of children, I had known deep down that something wasn't right.

I still held the plastic bag, and needing to be sure, I walked into our bedroom, then continued on into my bathroom. In a matter of two minutes any trace of stubborn hope that I was pregnant was gone. After I tossed the stick with its single blue line into the trash, I stared at my reflection in the mirror, at my perfectly highlighted, just-past-my-shoulders blond hair, the blue-green eyes, the flawless skin. My father always called me the most beautiful girl in the world—told me that the world was mine for the taking.

I closed my eyes and willed myself to remain calm. But calm seemed impossible. Plus there was something else happening, something I hardly recognized.

A lifetime of lessons surfaced. A lady should never:

1. sweat,
2. raise her voice,
3. throw things.

And most especially, a true lady never:

4. gets angry.

That was what I felt. Anger.

When I came out of the bathroom, flinging the double doors open like an A-list actress in a Broadway play, Gordon jumped.

"Fred, what I said to Janet isn't true."

I didn't bother to answer. I strode over to his walk-in closet and pulled out a single piece of his luggage. I noticed that for someone who traveled the world for weeks at a time, the bag was in damn good shape.

I forgot:

5. a lady never uses profanity.

Without a word, I yanked open his drawers and started pulling out anything I could get my hands on. Colored silk undergarments, designer socks, carefully folded button-down shirts. Like a crazed woman, I started shoving things inside the soft-sided bag.

"What the hell are you doing?"

"Packing your things."

"Fred." His tone was stern, as if he could intimidate me. "Stop acting like a child."

Me, acting like a child? Unforgivably hysterical, yes. But a child? I don't think so.

I barely managed to hold back what I really wanted to say, and only with the aid of all those years of training.

He tried to take a stack of shirts away from me, but I jerked aside.

"Stop acting like a lunatic," he said. "Let's talk about this like adults."

I felt the hair rise on the back of my neck and I whirled around to face him. "Have you or have you not had a vasectomy?"

"I said I hadn't."

"Then prove it. Let's go to the doctor and get a test. Prove that you haven't been lying to me since the day I met you."

"I don't have to prove anything. Besides, you know I've gotten several tests since you haven't been able to get pregnant."

His forehead was lined with deep furrows, and he shifted his weight from foot to foot.

"So you've said. But strangely enough, you've never let me go with you for the test, and you've never let me see the results. Each time you have your doctor—your little brother from your college fraternity, I might add—call up my doctor and read off numbers and counts."

I set the suitcase down and yanked up the phone. "In fact, why don't I call your doctor right now and tell him what I suspect he has done."

I started to dial the number I knew by heart.

"Okay, okay. So I had a vasectomy. What's the big deal? I can have it reversed."

I choked on my unladylike rage. I felt myself gasping and wheezing as I fought to regain acceptable behavior. My jaw throbbed as I clenched my teeth, sucking in breath through my nose.

"Fred, calm down."

That was just it. I couldn't. It was as if six years of rage had built up, and when he tugged the phone away from me, set it down, then picked up the suitcase and started to return it to the closet, I surprised even myself.

"Get out, Gordon," I said, my jaw clenched.

He paused and turned around. The look on his face wasn't sweet and easygoing, or even nervous.

"What did you say?" he asked.

"You heard me. Get out."

He raised a brow, then he started to laugh. "Fine, I'm leaving. Happy to go. I should have left months ago."

My head snapped back. I wanted to kill him, and I very nearly did when I grabbed the small brass bedside clock and threw it. At him. While yelling. I could even feel the sweat bead on my forehead as I added profanity.

That got Gordon's attention. He had to jump to get out of the way. Not that it did him a whole lot of good. I wasn't finished.

I grabbed a porcelain dish, noticed that it was a Hildebrand family heirloom so I quickly set it down then found another piece, this time a gift from his family. Crash against the wall. I couldn't seem to stop myself. I screamed and threw whatever I could afford to live without.

"You're crazy!" he yelled as he ducked.

I was. Crazy and angry. God, it felt good. It felt even better when he finally fled the bedroom, then left the house. It felt great. *I* felt great. More than that, I felt free.

Gordon didn't deserve me.

I pulled out my library of photo albums that were filled with pictures of Gordon and me from the *Willow Creek Times* society columns.

"Nina!" I called out. "Bring me the scissors."

Chapter Three

IT WAS HARDER than I imagined it would be to cut my husband out of my life.

After a short confab with Nina, it was decided that scissors wouldn't do. Ten minutes later, I sat at my beautiful, antique Queen Anne desk that I kept for daily correspondence, my head bent in concentration. The newspaper photographs where Gordon stood in the middle of a group tested my fledgling X-Acto knife capabilities, but I was determined.

I had gotten as far as our third year of marriage, more specifically up to our third Boots and Belles black-tie charity ball, when the anger that had gotten me that far started to die. More's the pity, because once that was gone, I started thinking about other things—like my husband not wanting me. The smile on his face when he said he should have left months ago had proved as much.

How could he not want me—me, Frede Ware, the most beautiful, most sought-after, most envied woman in town? What was wrong with him?

I didn't get much chance to dwell on it because the phone started ringing with people wanting to know if we were free for X, Y, and Z nights for our usual rounds of social engagements.

With the piles of cut-out, newsprint photographs of Gordon growing steadily, I felt a surge of non–morning sickness at the thought of having to tell my friends that my perfect marriage wasn't so perfect. I've learned that in my world one's reputation is based on perception, rarely on fact. It was the perception of my fabulous life that made it fabulous, at least in my friends' eyes. The minute a perceived weakness reared its ugly head all bets were off. That was when I realized I had to navigate the new waters carefully, which meant I probably should glue Gordon back into the albums—at least for the time being.

"Richard, sugar," I told one of my husband's friends when he called, "Gordon just stepped out. He'll be back in an hour or two, though we have plans for later. Magnificent plans, and I know we'll be out late. Why don't I have him give you a call when he has a minute in the next day or two?"

Which was how I got myself into the precarious position of pretending my husband was still living at home when he wasn't.

For hours that Wednesday, I assumed he would return. Nina stayed with me until late afternoon. She clucked around my desk, provided glass after glass of sweet tea, and wouldn't leave my side. I finally had to insist she take the rest of her day off.

"Nina, really. I'm fine. Go see your grandson. It's his birthday."

She studied me. Ninety-nine percent of the time she pretended not to speak English—despite the fact that she sat at the kitchen table every morning reading the *Willow Creek Times*. It worked out fine for both of us because we had no trouble ignoring each other when the mood struck.

"Bueno, me voy," she said. *"Pero regresaré mañana."*

She continued gabbing away as she retrieved her handbag and straightened her attire, muttering about how I shouldn't be by myself after my husband betrayed me in such a horrible manner.

I appreciated the concern, but quite frankly, I was ready to be alone.

My entire life I had lived a fairy-tale existence. I believed, and it came true. It never occurred to me that Gordon wouldn't come to his senses, return, and beg me to forgive him. How could he not? Remember, it was me he had left.

It wasn't hard to explain why I wanted him to return. There's another word that only bears mentioning in the spelling form. D-i-v-o-r-c-e. Call Gloria Steinem on me, but the truth is, once the anger had died away I wasn't ready to give up on my marriage so easily. He might have lied and cheated, but I was an old-fashioned, proper girl and I knew I would rather figure out a way to fix my marriage than have to admit I had failed at it. And that included not letting anyone know that Gordon and I had been, for any length of time, separated.

That was why when the next day arrived and I found my husband still missing, I came up with the idea to keep his (unfortunate but not insurmountable) betrayal a secret.

It seemed easy enough. *Au contraire.*

I dressed in a hurry while it was still dark outside, then raced downstairs. Thankfully, Nina would return at seven-thirty. I had a plan, and I needed her help.

While I waited for her, I hurried out to the three-bay garage. It was only five-thirty A.M. when I pulled the Mercedes through the portico that stretched between the house and the garage, then glided down the drive. That early the guard wasn't yet on duty. Juan would arrive at seven. For the hours that the guardhouse wasn't manned, there was an intercom system that connected to each home in The Willows. Though anyone wanting to depart the enclave only had to drive up to the gate and it opened like magic.

I pulled up to the gate to leave and the electronic arm swept up. Willow Creek is a wealthy enclave, its winding streets and lanes built with satisfying picturesqueness into the rolling hills covered with willow, cedar, pecan, and live oak trees draped in Spanish moss. We're as sophisticated as Dallas, but maintain the lovely charm of Austin—at least that was the case before the state capital filled with those pocket-protector types who clogged their roads when the tech craze happened in the nineties.

Willow Creek Square stands at the center of town, the country club to the north, the university to the east, The Willows to the west, and South Willow Creek, well, to the south beyond the railroad tracks. Everything else, from JLWC headquarters to Symphony Hall, the Municipal Courthouse to Hildebrand Galleries, is nestled between the lanes, streets, and avenues that sprawl out in all directions from the main square.

I zipped out of The Willows and raced to the nearby market to get the newspaper. Despite my husband's laissez-faire allure, he was a stickler for schedules. Every morning he got up and jogged, then stopped at the market and retrieved two local newspapers on his way back to the house. He dropped one off for Juan, so that it was waiting when the man came on duty, before continuing on home where he sat in our sunroom drinking coffee while reading his own copy.

With my two newspapers in hand, I hurried back to The Willows, tossed one in front of the locked guardhouse door, swiped my card key, and then raced to my postcard-perfect mansion. There was still much to do before Nina got there and I could put my plan into action.

On Mondays and Thursdays, Gordon played tennis on our court just below our swimming pool. The high green hedges blocked any view, but the hollow sound of tennis balls could be heard two doors down. My neighbor Caryn Kramer, another League member, had told me that she could count on Gordon and tennis as surely as she could count on the sun rising.

Did I mention it was Thursday?

As soon as it was a somewhat reasonable hour, I called Gordon's tennis partner, mentioned something about the flu, still in bed, rain check, and so forth. I could tell the man was still half asleep and probably was happy to roll back over and catch another hour.

At seven twenty-eight, Nina walked in the back door and I was waiting for her, dressed in tennis whites (a white sweater tied stylishly around my shoulders) with my hair pulled back in a ponytail. She stopped in her tracks.

"Missy Ware, wha you doing?"

When I was growing up, she called me "Missy" whenever she was unhappy with me. Since I had become an adult, she called me "Missy Ware" when she was disgruntled—which seemed to be most of the time.

In answer, I shoved a bright orange velour warm-up suit at her. "Go change. We're going to play tennis."

It was no surprise when the Spanish erupted, but I herded her back to her quarters and didn't move away until she reappeared, grumbling, looking like a short, squat, very round jack-o'-lantern wearing sensible maid's shoes. Not perfect, but it would have to do.

I gathered up the old rackets I had found in the storeroom, then pulled her out the sunroom's sliding glass door, down the flagstone steps that curved through the perfectly manicured gardens then alongside the pool that glistened from its twice-a-week cleaning by the most delicious pool boy I had ever seen. (Not that I would ever dream of doing anything about it, delicious or no. I have never even said hello.)

We hurried down another level to the courts. I had already set up the ball machine Gordon used with the zeal of a religious convert.

"Wha you doing?" Nina repeated, giving me the evil eye.

"I thought it was high time you and I spent some quality time together."

She made a lot of those gagging noises, then said, "You no want neighbors to find out that Meester Gordon is no here."

Did I mention that she's smart as a whip?

"Nina, that's ridiculous."

She snorted. "Gemme dat thing." She swiped one of the rackets away from me.

She planted herself on the baseline like a linebacker in a professional football game. "Turn on da matcheen."

Which I did.

She whelped when the first ball struck her in the shoulder. She cursed in Spanish, then started whacking away at the yellow balls that came out far faster than she could respond. She might be smart, but she's not particularly agile.

"Shhh," I hissed at her. "It's supposed to sound like Gordon and Bernie Brown are practicing."

She stopped and raised an I-told-you-so brow. Thankfully, another ball struck her in the opposite shoulder and she got back to work.

After about two dozen balls (and what promised to be a colorful black eye the following morning) she actually got the hang of it, and the very satisfying sound of tennis-ball whacks could be heard echoing through the neighborhood.

Once the machine was through, we each took a bright green hopper and started gathering balls. When we were done and had the machine reloaded, Nina smiled at me.

"You turn, *Bernie*."

She flipped the switch and the balls shot out at me like a cannon.

I screeched, much as Nina had.

"Shhh," she hissed at me.

I scowled at her and barely had time to leap out of the way when the balls started coming faster. Fortunately, unlike my maid, I had played tennis once upon a time. I wheeled back and forth and smacked the balls.

Nina whistled. "You good."

"Would . . . you . . . expect . . . anything . . . less?" I asked between whacks.

Never pleased with what she believed was my lack of humility, she sent up a despairing snort into the early morning air. She had been raised with the Latin sensibility that the fairer sex should be retiring and self-deprecating. (Not that she showed the qualities herself with her hard, squat body and hint of mustache.)

When I was done, we attempted to volley the ball back and forth across the net. But this exceeded Nina's fledgling abilities, so we called it a day.

I retreated upstairs and showered, then dressed in a cashmere short-sleeved sweater tucked into a beautiful pair of bone-colored pants. I put pearls around my neck, and flats on my stocking feet before I returned downstairs. Generally after tennis Gordon showered, ate breakfast, then went to the office he kept in our home. Thank God, I didn't have to worry about fooling some secretary or office personnel. That might have exceeded even my imaginative skills.

Golf would be problematic that weekend, but surely Gordon would have returned by then. If not, it wasn't uncommon for my husband to head out on some unexpected adventure. Or had it always been a liaison?

My newfound anger tried to flare and my fingers curled until my nails bit into my palm. I would not get angry. Not again.

NINA AND I MANAGED to make everyone believe my husband was either at home and busy, or had just stepped out, with relative ease until Friday afternoon.

The doorbell rang, which was never good since very few people had access to my front door. Juan called for visitors.

It could have been a neighbor, but I'd never had a neighbor come to my door unannounced before. I assumed it was someone on our permanent list kept in the guardhouse, that list Miss Mouse mentioned. Aside from her, the list consisted of a few friends and family.

"Dear God, please not my parents."

God was listening, but he was laughing just the same.

"Edith!" I said with an enthusiasm I didn't feel when I pulled open the front door and found my sister-in-law.

Edith Ware was older than her brother, and nearly as tall. She wore prim, sensible clothes—pleated pants, sweater sets, and low-heeled shoes. Not a surprise on a Sustaining member of the Junior League, but with her the cut and cloth had no style. She was all about earth tones and functionality, which was all well and good in some things, but not, in my opinion, in fashion. Edith just looked dowdy.

That said, she still would have been a handsome, if not pretty, woman if she had bothered to color her hair. She had started going gray early, and unfortunately for her she didn't have that beautiful dark hair that could actually look good going gray. Edith was a dirty-blonde, and her hair just looked dirtier as it lost its color in fits and starts. She was turning forty-two next month, a fact I knew because I was in charge of remembering all birthdays of friends and family. Gordon just signed the cards I put in front of him. Though when it came to his own family, he personally delivered the gifts that I purchased. His mother still didn't realize that he forgot her birthday every year.

"Is Gordon here?" Edith asked without a word of greeting.

"Hello to you too." I smiled at my sister-in-law with a calm I didn't feel. Edith was always looking for some excuse to make me look bad. She had never quite accepted the fact that I had taken her precious brother away. Little did I know he wasn't much of a catch.

"I'm sorry, Frede, that was rude of me. Is everything all right?" she asked. "I've been worried. I heard you left headquarters early on Wednesday."

It was a wonder I hadn't heard before that my husband was having an affair, given that nothing of consequence in Willow Creek went unnoticed in this town. But Gordon was nothing if not cautious, not to mention private, so I felt confident that no one knew. Yet. I would have to walk a very fine line if I didn't want to become the Number One Topic of Discussion.

"I had some business to take care of, is all," I said.

Edith glanced around the foyer. "Where is Gordon? I've been calling but Nina has been evasive and keeps saying he just stepped out. I've called his cell phone. I've called everywhere I can think of, but no one has seen hide nor hair of him." She looked at me closely. "Are you sure everything is all right?"

"Aren't you the dramatic one today, Sister Edith?"

She hated it when I called her that. And it wasn't an entirely accurate description of her since while Gordon's sister might lead the sexual lifestyle of a nun she was anything but merciful.

"Now, Edith," I continued, turning up my accent a notch, "you know as well as I do that Gordon had a trip planned." This was a lie, but it wouldn't be the first time my husband had left town unexpectedly.

"I knew no such thing."

"I'm sure he told you. Besides, how often does he leave without a word to anyone?"

She sighed at the truth of this. "When is he scheduled to return?"

"He won't be back for"—my brain spun—"three to four weeks."

Her sigh turned into a groan. "Not another of those long ones."

"Why are you so concerned?" I asked. She never had been before.

She debated, then finally said, "There are some bills he normally pays that are overdue."

I must have looked confused.

"He uses his money," she stated, her tone defensive.

After six years of marriage, I finally understood why Papa Ware didn't have to work. Gordon was supporting him. Not that there is anything wrong with a man supporting his family. But I had to bite my tongue to keep from saying that Gordon didn't earn a red cent. Technically, *I* was paying the bills.

However, it wasn't the time or place to get into something else I hadn't known about my husband. All I needed to do for the time being was keep my world turning as it always had. I realized then that it was only wise to call my banker and cut Gordon off from access to my accounts until we could get everything straightened out.

First I had to get rid of his sister.

"As soon as I talk to him I'll let him know you stopped by."

"Gordon has never been late with a payment before. This isn't like him." She studied me. "He hasn't been himself lately."

That got my attention. "How so?"

"Well, for starters, he has become . . . careless. A little angry, even. Are you making him unhappy?"

More than once Sister Edith had told her brother that he would regret marrying a spoiled daddy's girl, as she loved to call me. I probably didn't do a lot to make it better. If she lamented that she saw someone wearing a flashy pink sweater, I'd say, "Do you think it was me? I just bought a *fabu* pink *ensemble* with an amazing fur collar just the other day."

Her lips would purse, and rightfully so, since we both knew that no JLWC member who wanted to keep her reputation would wear something so flashy. Every time it happened, though, I couldn't seem to help myself.

"Edith, sugar, you know that Gordon loves me just as much as I love him."

Which didn't really answer the question, but it wasn't a lie.

Edith left, and as soon as the door shut behind her I raced to my study. Ripping the phone out of its cradle, I jammed in the number for Ned Reed at the Bank of Willow Creek. But instead of getting through to him immediately, his secretary said two words she had never said to me before.

Chapter Four

"WHAT DO YOU MEAN, he's unavailable?" I asked with ice-queen politeness.

"Ah, well, he can't take your call right now, Mrs. Ware."

I told her I would wait.

"Wait?"

"Yes. Tell Ned I'm not getting off the phone until I've spoken to him. And if he won't come to the phone, I'll come down to the bank to see him in person."

I was put on hold, and a long series of minutes passed before Ned got on the line. "Frede. How are you?"

"I'm doing fine, Ned."

We exchanged pleasantries as if indeed everything were fine. When finally the tidbits of life wound down, he said, "What can I do for you?"

"Ned, I need to cut off Gordon's access to my accounts. It's temporary, of course, and only a precaution. But a precaution I feel is necessary since he's off on one of his adventures in faraway lands and I've been terribly concerned about . . . identity theft and whatnot." I hadn't a clue if any of that made sense, but I hoped it was enough to get him off the scent of marital problems.

The banker sat on the other end of the phone and couldn't seem to find words. "Frede," he finally began in a voice I didn't like. "I don't know what to say other than you no longer have accounts here at the bank. I thought you knew."

"What are you talking about?"

"Gordon moved y'all's money out of here almost a month ago. You signed the papers yourself."

"I didn't sign anything about moving my money!"

The muffled sound of his hand over the mouthpiece didn't block out his voice when he called out, "Abigail, pull up the Ware file."

"Ned, what is going on?"

"You need to ask Gordon that. You put him in charge—"

Much to my father's dismay. And even more dismaying was that I had a rush of memories of Gordon approaching me at my perfect Queen Anne desk and setting a stack of papers in front of me. He would give me a brief summary of what each was, and I signed without reading. It was easier that way. I was busy doing all that good.

I felt my stomach launch up to my throat.

"Frede, all I know is that your accounts are closed. I don't know what else to tell you."

Heat flashed in my face because deep down I sensed the truth in what Ned was saying. My money had gone MIA.

I replaced the receiver and knew that my husband easily could have stolen every penny of mine and I would have been blissfully unaware. That's when I knew there was no saving my marriage. I could deal with lying. I could overlook cheating. But no man was going to steal my money and get away with it.

My heart rate was through the roof when I called our lawyer, Jim Wooten.

"Oh, hi, Mrs. Ware," his secretary said. "Let me put you through to him."

When the phone clicked again, it wasn't our lawyer who came on the line.

"I'm sorry," the woman said awkwardly. "I didn't realize he had just stepped out."

My palms got sweaty. Not to be deterred, I called back repeatedly.

"Oh, ah, Mrs. Ware, I've told you, Mr. Wooten isn't available."

It wasn't until she realized that I wasn't going to leave her alone that she got huffy. "Please hold, Mrs. Ware. I'll see if he's available now."

Long seconds passed before a click sounded and Jim Wooten got on the line. "Frede! How are you?" His voice boomed with congeniality, as if he hadn't been avoiding me for the last two hours.

"I am divorcing Gordon and I need you to file whatever it is you need to file for me in order to get it done first . . . I mean, fast."

I could hear his chair creak as he sighed and leaned back. "Well, hell, I wish it hadn't come to this."

A shiver ran down my spine because I realized he wasn't in the least surprised, as if he had already spoken to my husband about the state of our marriage.

"Frede, I wish I could help you. But . . ." The chair squeaked some more.

"But what, Jim?" My ice-queen abilities were in fine form.

He sighed with gratifying nervousness, then said, "Look, you know Gordon and I went through UT together, then law school after that. As much as I wish I could, Frede, I can't represent you. My firm already represents Gordon in all sorts of business. It would be a conflict of interest. You understand."

Actually I didn't, not really. Though it had nothing to do with me not understanding conflict of interest. I realized in that second that just about every lawyer in town did some sort of business with Gordon (I had assumed on my behalf) or with someone in his family. Plus there was the whole issue of Papa Ware being a retired judge.

My head ached.

"Frede, go out and find yourself a good lawyer." He hesitated. "I'm sorry, really I am."

I had barely hung up when the phone rang and I jumped. I snatched up the receiver. "Gordon?"

"Fredericka, this is your mother."

My mother never says things like "Hi, honey," or "It's me." Such common language is beneath her.

"Hello, Mother."

"I can tell by your voice that something is wrong."

"Nothing's wrong."

"Then why did you snatch up the phone and blurt 'Gordon,'" she asked, though didn't wait for an answer. "What has he done? I've always said that man was no good."

Many times.

"Thurmond," she called out. "Your daughter has gotten herself into some kind of trouble. No doubt it's related to Gordon."

Blythe Hildebrand was a tiny woman, five feet tall, and couldn't weigh more than a hundred pounds soaking wet, but she could put the fear of God into a man twice her size. Gordon avoided her like the plague.

"Trouble?" I heard my father respond in the background, then he yanked up the second phone line. "What has that son of a bitch done to my little girl?"

Where my mother was tiny, my father was a big bear of a man and his voice about blew out my eardrum.

Texas men came in many forms. One of the most successful types was the man who sounded like an illiterate lunatic. Think George W. Bush or H. Ross Perot spouting things like, "Ya can't put a boot in the oven and expect to get brisket."

However, as long as they had money and a socially prominent name, the crazier the better . . . with the tiny little caveat that they come from fine old families or, at the very least, have created fine "old" families.

My daddy was one of the finest, spewing out lunacy with the best of them—hence the shotgun remark of earlier and Gordon's real-life need to be wary of his father-in-law. Though I realized with regret that my husband's concern hadn't gone deep enough.

"I'm gonna kill that son of a bitch if he's hurt so much as a hair on your head."

I believe I mentioned I was a daddy's girl.

"Thurmond, quit making such a ruckus. Let Fredericka tell us what she has done now."

I don't think I need to add that I wasn't a mama's girl.

There had always been a kind of competition between my mother and me for my father's attention, and more often than not I won. I'm sure this was the reason for my mother's condescending certainty that I couldn't handle my own life. She believed I'd had the world handed to me on a silver platter, which was true. Regardless, I steadfastly refused to believe she was right about my abilities, despite the whole issue of my missing money. But if I told her one word about my predicament I would never hear the end of it. There was also the concern that my daddy would spend the rest of his days in jail after he filled Gordon Ware full of buckshot.

I decided to keep my problems to myself.

"Mother, really, everything is fine. Better than fine," I added for good measure. "I'm having a glorious day."

I could practically hear the wheels in her brain spinning.

"You're sure?" my father asked.

"Yes, Daddy. Things are great."

No question, all I would have to do was say a single word and not only would my father hunt Gordon down, but he would find the best lawyer in all of Texas to make my errant husband pay. That certainty might have outweighed the headache of my mother holding the debacle over my head for the rest of my life if, in my rapidly growing closet of secrets, there hadn't already been the very big secret I had recently learned that my daddy's oil fields were running dry and the price a man could get for a head of cattle just wasn't what it used to be.

Not that either of my parents would admit such a thing. But I knew it because Gordon had been keeping track and had filled me in. At the time, I had been thankful that my husband was investing here and there to keep my trust fund shored up. Who knew he was siphoning it off, sending it who knew where?

The long and short was that my parent's fortune was dwindling, and I wasn't about to add to the decline.

"All right, if you insist everything is fine," my mother said.

"I do."

"Then you're coming for dinner on Sunday? With Gordon?"

Devious little thing.

"Of course I'll be there, but don't count on Gordon. He's off on another of his adventures. I don't expect him back for three to four weeks." It was my story and I was sticking to it.

My dainty mother snorted, which was interesting because I had noticed recently that all the manners and acceptable forms of behavior she drummed into me, and had always followed herself, were going by the wayside—as if she had come to a place where she started thinking that life was too short to waste time with the sorts of games she taught me to play. This could have been great, but the minute I stepped out of bounds she was still quick to point out the error of my ways.

"Well, at least you're coming," my mother said. "I just wanted to check. I'm having Cook make your father's favorite. A rib roast with potatoes and creamed spinach."

"If you're sure you're all right," my father pressed.

"Daddy, I'm fine. Really."

I had every intention of making sure it wasn't a lie.

To that end, as soon as we hung up, I looked for Janet Lambert's address in the phone book. It seemed like the only prudent thing to do was sit down with the woman and find out what was what. But she wasn't listed.

I finally found her through directory services, two towns over. Afraid she'd hang up on me if I called, I drove to the address in a low-income part of Twin Rivers, Texas. There wasn't a car in the drive or a light on in the house when I arrived.

When I walked to the door a neighbor stuck her head out the window. "Janet isn't there, honey," the woman called out in a thick Texas accent. "She left town with that fancy boyfriend of hers."

"Boyfriend?" I asked, the word sticking in my throat.

"Yeah, Gordon something."

Instantly I wondered two things:

1. Had my husband forgiven his mistress for getting pregnant by what clearly could only be accomplished by another man?

2. Or had she, like me, been mistaken about her delicate condition and hadn't been pregnant after all?

For all my wondering mattered. If it was true that he had gone off with the woman, they had forgiven each other a great many things.

The Mouse's neighbor shot me a narrow-eyed gaze of accusation as she looked me up and down. "You don't look like any friend of Janet's."

It must have been my lack of cheap polyester that gave me away. Not that I cared. My only coherent thought at the time was, how on earth was I going to keep this tidbit of news from my friends.

I decided then and there that the only thing to do was go home, crawl into bed, and pretend it was all a bad dream.

• • •

FOR THE NEXT FEW DAYS, I didn't allow Juan to send anyone up to the house and I didn't take calls. I had Nina tell anyone who would listen that Gordon's three-to-four-week trip was to New Guinea. I felt certain that New Guinea was filled with all kinds of adventurous sports. But more importantly, it sounded far away and relatively phoneless.

On Sunday, I went to my parents' house for dinner, and pushed my A-list acting abilities to their limits.

By Wednesday, a week after the unfortunate incident, Pilar Bass rang the house. I didn't take the call, but Nina swore the woman was worried. I didn't doubt she was since I had missed the New Projects Committee meeting that morning, making clear to the no-nonsense woman that she was truly going to have to do both of our jobs. That would teach her to doubt me in public ever again.

As unacceptable as it was, I lived in an old pair of pajamas that I had saved from college, had the barest contact with soap and water, and contemplated throwing myself out the window. This might have worked fine had I lived in a high-rise. My house had only two floors and I doubted I would do more than break an arm, and there was just no good way to make a cast look fashionable.

Since the day I found Miss Mouse in my foyer, not only had I missed the New Projects Committee meeting and the monthly General Meeting, but I had missed my weekly volunteer Placement hours as well. Instead, I sat in bed with the Yellow Pages going through the Attorney listings, wondering who could fight against my husband and stand a chance of winning when between my husband and his father they were friends with just about every lawyer and judge in town, not to mention well-connected across the state?

It was when I hit the *G*s that my brows narrowed. "Howard Grout, Attorney at Law," I practically whispered.

I turned toward the side window, and looked through the lush trees and leaves to make out a hint of the tacky palacelike structure next door. Pulling back the sheets, I walked closer to the window to get a better look.

Howard Grout. My neighbor.

He was a lawyer who didn't know anyone in my husband's family, and I was willing to bet that he was one of the few people in town who wouldn't be intimidated by the Ware name. How could he be if he was willing to move into The Willows despite the neighborhood's machinations to keep him out, all of it led by my husband. In fact, he might be in the mood to have a little payback.

I disregarded the thought that he might want a little payback toward me, because I had no doubt I could charm him. Granted, I couldn't turn on too much charm since the man was a notorious letch. But letch or no, he was the one person who could help me get the revenge I had every intention of obtaining. Hell hath no fury, and all that.

With renewed purpose, I strode to the bathroom and had my first real bath since Sunday dinner. Nina came flying in, probably afraid I was trying to drown myself. When she saw that I was only taking a giant bubble bath, she nodded.

"Finally," she said in gruff Spanish.

"Nina, sugar, I need you to pull out my clothes."

There are rules that are crucial to follow when a highly thought-of member of the JLWC, or any respectable Texas woman for that matter, leaves the house—for any reason.

1. One must be fully made up at all times no matter if she is going to the gym, grocery store, or a dinner party
2. Always dress with understated elegance
3. Never wear warm-ups, even the expensive kind made out of cashmere—unless she is on her way to the country club to play tennis or golf
4. Never show cleavage unless it is at night in formal attire, and even then, only a tiny amount can be shown
5. Never, *ever* show the midriff
6. Low-cut pants are for high school girls of lesser families

"Pull out my single-pleat cream pants," I instructed from beneath the mounds of bubbles. "Also, the cream silk blouse, the café au lait cashmere sweater to tie around my shoulders. And the little bone Ferragamo pumps with the clip-on bows." For the first time in days I felt a glimmer of my old self. "I have a visit to make and I want to look my best."

Chapter Five

NINA WAS THRILLED, muttering her cantankerous joy that I was getting out of the house. The sun and fresh air would do me good, or so she said. I worked hard to keep my twenty-eight-year-old skin out of the harsh Texas sun, but it didn't seem like the moment to mention that, especially since I had done the whole "outdoor" tennis thing so recently.

By the time I was bathed, coiffed, and manicured, my bedroom was sparkling clean, the bed made, my clothes laid out on the exquisite duvet that had arrived from France two weeks before, after a three-month wait.

Nina had arranged the attire I requested in the shape it would take when worn. As I studied the *ensemble* with its neutral palette of colors, a novel thought struck me. Neutral probably wouldn't appeal to the sort of man who was rumored to wear more gold than Anna Nicole Smith in all her NCed and BJed glory.

I debated a possible new course of action, but I only debated for half a second before I strode to my walk-in closet and put away my pearls. My maid looked at me oddly since I always wore my pearls during the day. Her enthusiasm waned even more when I pulled out a light blue chiffon dress that, despite its high, respectable collar, showed off my figure—a very big no-no for eleven o'clock in the morning.

"What are you doing, Missy Ware," she demanded in Spanish.

"I'm going to get myself a lawyer, sugar."

"What kinda lawyer wants to see you in clothes like that?"

I smiled at her. "The kind who can make Gordon regret that he didn't actually play golf on Wednesdays."

Nina wasn't happy, but she was a woman who could appreciate revenge as well as the next.

She put away the first outfit as I finished dressing in the new one. I added nude stockings that held a tiny hint of shimmer (bad me), a bone slingback pump that was satisfyingly sexy for a shoe with only an inch worth of heel, and a wide-brimmed straw hat adorned with a beautiful, barely blue and white muted floral chiffon scarf that floated down the back.

I asked Nina for a basket of fresh baked goods that she always kept on hand. She looked at me with narrow-eyed suspicion (who took muffins to a lawyer's office?) but did as I asked without further comment.

Her stoic silence didn't last long when I let it slip that I was on my way to visit not just any lawyer, but the lawyer next door. She made a big choking gasp and restarted her rapid-fire Spanish. She said a great many things that I won't repeat here. Suffice it to say that a lesser woman would have melted under her heated attack.

I ignored her.

I hooked the basket over my forearm like a good Texas belle on her way to a Sunday picnic, strode to the garage under a nearly painful blue sky, got into my car, fastened the seat belt, checked the mirrors, then pulled down the long drive. I turned left and drove to the estate next door, then made my way up to the front of my neighbor's home.

It was the first time I had seen it up close. Lord have mercy, I can't begin to tell you what a tasteless sort of place it was. Palm trees imported from God knows where. A gilded cupola so large that when the sun hit it just so it must send false signals up to satellites. If you live anywhere close to central Texas and your weatherman's predictions are consistently wrong, blame it on Howard Grout's tacky home.

I got out of my car with the basket and strode to the front door. As I understood it, Howard Grout worked from his home office. Not exactly an arrangement most lawyers in town preferred, but Mr. Grout, apparently, didn't care. He did things his way, it was said, and quite frankly, he could, since rumor had it that he had made so much money he now only took on a select few cases despite a laundry list of people desperate to get even an hour of his time.

Not that this worried me. I was Frede Ware, after all.

Assuming the man and his wife were home, I planned to make my welcome speech, never doubting that the man would be so thrilled that I had come at all that he wouldn't give a thought to the fact that I had come two years late. After my speech, I would muck through a short visit with the lawyer and his wife, regardless of how ill-bred they were. I would dazzle them with my famed charm and good manners, then I would say, "By the by, Mr. Grout, I'm in need of a lawyer. Could you make a recommendation?"

Of course he would fall all over himself wanting the job, and I would then kindly bestow the honor on him. Remember, I'm nothing if not gracious.

Feeling *fabu* with my plan, I rang the bell. I waited a bit before finally I heard a voice coming from inside.

"Where the hell is everyone?"

A Texas accent without an ounce of cultivation boomed through the house.

Texas accents vary greatly, from virtually none to the sweetest melodic sound. Betwixt the two is every sort of cruelty to the ear. The sound coming from inside was an Appalachian *Deliverance* sort of voice that made me think of Ned Beatty squealing like a pig.

I would have gone back to the Yellow Pages if the door hadn't burst open just then. This time I was the one whose mouth opened and shut wordlessly.

The man who appeared looked put out. His wiry reddish-brown hair was askew, his cheeks ruddy with impatience. He wore faded Wrangler jeans partially tucked into a disreputable pair of cowboy boots, as if he had been dragged away from a horse-breaking session with a bucking bronco out back in his corral. However, I knew for a fact that he didn't have a corral any more than he had horses—at least out back. The Willows' bylaws prohibited such things.

But that wasn't the worst of it. He was a short plug of a man with hair all over his naked (yes, naked) chest. I can't tell you the last time I saw a man's bare chest in broad daylight. Naked chests are reserved for the worst sort of NC man who doesn't know better, youngsters at the Willow Creek Country Club swimming pool, or, well . . . my pool boy.

If I hadn't known for a fact that this man had won an astounding number of supposedly unwinnable cases, I never would have believed he could spell "courtroom" much less know how to work his wiles in one.

The man's impatience evaporated. He studied me, his big paw of a hand running down his chest to his rounded stomach, which he gave a good slap.

"Well, well, if it isn't Frede Ware."

My photograph really did appear in the local paper with far more frequency than my mother would have liked. Always at the best parties, always doing some sort of good, always wearing the perfect clothes. More than one woman in town aspired to be just like me.

I ignored his unwarranted familiarity when he called me by the name reserved for my friends. I smiled.

"Hello, Mr. Grout. I've come to welcome you and your wife to the neighborhood."

I extended the basket.

He didn't take it.

He narrowed his eyes. "Aren't you a couple years late, darlin'?"

Had everyone in my world gone mad and begun to think that being direct was appealing? Of course, Howard Grout was not of my world.

I lowered the basket to my side, but before I could think how possibly to respond to this lout of a man, he laughed. He had a big booming laugh that echoed in what I could just make out was the largest entry hall I had ever seen. The space was large and filled with a treasure trove of gaudy knickknacks and gilded baubles.

He reached out and took the basket. "Kinda got you there, didn't I, Frede. Glad you're here. Better late than never, I always say."

He anchored the basket between his elbow and his waist, and all I could see was his flesh pressing up against one of Nina's famous blueberry and sour cream muffins. I doubted I would ever eat another in my life.

"Come on in, darlin'."

I really, really didn't want to.

I reminded myself of my goal (Gordon speaking *a voce alta* begging for my forgiveness), and reminded myself as well that this NC was a lawyer who could exact my revenge.

"Why, thank you, Mr. Grout."

"Call me Howard."

"Thank you, Howard."

He laughed again and walked inside, neither holding the door for me nor gesturing for me to follow. Though truth to tell, bad manners seemed far better than the thought of this man touching me, even if it was a polite gesture of hand to elbow as he guided me inside.

Not knowing what else to do I entered, and when I didn't see any sort of servant, I closed the door myself. After a second, I pulled off my hat, fluffed my hair in the extravagantly large entry hall mirror, then decided there was nothing to do but follow his voice.

I made my way down a long hall absolutely crammed with artwork. I was surprised by the mix. Tasteful watercolors and an impressively textured oil by an artist that had recently burst onto the scene, plus two black velvet Elvis paintings, as if Howard Grout were saying, *I have taste, I know art, but I'll hang whatever the hell I want.* If he'd had a pedigree he would have been adored. Without one, he was just plain offensive.

I had nearly made it to the end of the hall when I saw the sculpture—a nude male figure carved in marble. Despite the fact that on the whole I don't believe in naked art (it's nearly impossible to decorate with), it was a truly spectacular piece that both provoked and made the breath come a little faster. If it hadn't been so masterfully done, I swear it would have been pornographic.

I looked closer and found SAWYER JACKSON carved into the base of the piece. I had heard of the artist before, didn't know any dealer who hadn't. Most every gallery in Texas and even New York, from what I had heard, had tried to get the man to show his work. But he was as elusive as smoke, and no one could pin him down for an exhibition. I had never tried; who needs a temperamental artist on their hands. Though I have to admit, until that moment I had never seen his work.

When I finally found Howard I would have asked him about the artist, but my mind was distracted because I found him in the kitchen. Yes, the kitchen. I'm sure I don't have to point out that no one ever takes a guest into the kitchen unless they have known them forever and are the closest of friends.

Howard was riffling through the basket of Nina's goodies when I entered.

"Mmm-mmm," he said. "These look mighty fine." He took a bite. "I'm impressed," he added with muffin in his mouth. "You're some kinda cook."

"They are my maid's specialty," I clarified, then looked around. "Is Mrs. Grout here?"

"Nikki?"

"Are there any others?"

He blinked, then laughed that eardrum-rupturing laugh. "That's a good one. Nope, there's just the one. Ya surprised me, is all. I haven't heard anyone call my Nikki 'Mrs. Grout.' Has a nice ring to it, though, don't you think?"

What I thought was that I was very angry at Gordon for putting me in the position of having to deal with this man.

"To answer your question, no. Nikki isn't home. She's out shoppin', spendin' all my money. It's just you and me, darlin'. We got a maid or two, just like you. Don't know where any of them are though."

I couldn't imagine what he was getting at. Or couldn't I? The house did sound very empty. There was no distant sound of laundry going. No dusting, vacuuming, spring-bulb planting. No subtle sounds of industriousness. Which meant I was alone with a half-naked letch.

Did I think this man would attack me? No.

Did I think he would force his affections on me? Certainly not.

But from the considering look on his face, I could very easily see him testing the waters of my interest in him. When I said no in as oblique a way as I could, my answer wouldn't put him in the best frame of mind to help me.

"I'm so sad that Mrs. Grout isn't here. I look forward to seeing her. Perhaps one day soon she can come over for tea."

The man chuckled. "She'd like that."

He tossed the half-eaten muffin back in the basket then took a step closer. I mentally groaned. Suddenly I realized that no matter how much I wanted revenge, I couldn't go through with this attempt to befriend Howard Grout. I cursed my shimmering hose and stunning dress that made me even more irresistible than usual. I would have to try my best to take his mind off my beauty, and perhaps the damsel-in-distress façade would derail his fantasy train before it left the station.

"In truth," I blurted out, "I'm here because I need your assistance."

That stopped him.

"Really? You need me?"

"Yes." I clasped my hands. "I need a lawyer."

He gaped at me. "You know every lawyer in town. Why the hell would you need me?"

In a gush of words, I told him all that had happened. Despite my personal religion of privacy at all costs, I spilled every sordid detail. The words didn't stop until he cut me off.

"I'll help you."

Had it really been that easy? "You will?"

"Yep. And you have my word that Gordon Ware will rue the day he did you wrong."

"Oh, then, thank you."

"Don't be thankin' me yet, little darlin'. There's a price."

"I thought I made it clear that I am a bit strapped for m-o-, um, well, money right now."

"I don't want your money, Mrs. Ware."

Not a good sign. Why call me "Mrs. Ware" this late in the game?

The man looked me up and down and I realized that I hadn't stopped any fantasy train, after all. He would demand sex. Sex with the prestigious Fredericka Mercedes Hildebrand Ware, wife of Gordon Ware.

Gasp your indignant outrage over my arrogance all you want. But I know what I know.

The thought of sex with this squealing pig of a man made me want to do a little screaming myself. And not the good kind—not that there was a good kind of screaming, mind you. And not, quite frankly, that I would mind some sex either. After the aforementioned unimaginative sex I'd been having with my soon-to-be-ex-husband, I had a very unladylike itch that was desperate for a good scratch.

(A secret: for all my manners, I was raised on a ranch. I know about wild animal sex even if I pretend not to. Though I truly have never had the good fortune to engage in any.)

But with this man staring at me, ready to:

1. represent me,

2. find my husband,

3. and put the screws to him in a way that would make *him* scream,

I had to wonder if I could pay the price I felt sure he was about to demand.

"What price is that, Mr. Grout?"

His lips hitched at one corner, and those lecherous eyes looked at me with challenge.

"I'll represent you," he said, "if you get my Nikki into the Junior League."

Chapter Six

I WAS GETTING *TRÈS* tired of surprises.

Get Nikki Grout into the Junior League?

Most any Junior League in the South would be hard enough, but Howard Grout had made it clear he wanted her in the Junior League of Willow Creek. The idea was insane.

But that surprise was mild compared to what I felt a few seconds later when none other than Nikki herself came bursting into the kitchen from outside.

"Sweetie doll, I'm home!"

When she saw me instead of her "sweetie doll," whom I could only assume was her husband, she stopped dead in her high-heeled tracks. If I had been making any sort of forward progress myself, I would have frozen on the spot as well. Her attire was enough to stop traffic on every main street in better parts of Texas.

Nikki Grout was a tiny woman, made taller by her four-inch stiletto heels—and we know what Leaguers think about stilettos (unacceptable), not to mention stilettos worn in the daytime (VERY unacceptable). I glanced at the clock, though I didn't need to. It was eleven-thirty in the morning.

But if stilettos weren't enough to send shock waves through conservative Willow Creek, she wore hot-pink leopard-print spandex tights with a hot-pink top, the neckline and cuffs lined with pink ostrich feathers that floated around her shoulders and wrists like puffs of cotton candy. She looked as if she belonged in a strip club or a Mötley Crüe video. Either way, her attire screamed, *I charge by the hour because I'm desperate and needy,* not, *Let's cajole money out of our rich husbands and give it away to the needy.*

The irony didn't escape me.

But surprises weren't done with me yet.

"Frede!" Nikki squealed in delight.

She raced—with surprising swiftness considering her footwear—across the terra-cotta tiled kitchen floor and wrapped me in a cloud of feathers that stuck to my tastefully muted *light* pink lip color, nearly crushing the hat I held in my hands.

"I knew you would come!"

I could see Howard out of the corner of my eye as I pulled a strand of fluff from my mouth. He stared in shock as well.

"You know each other?" he asked in disbelief.

Well, that was the thing. I actually did know Nikki, had since I was in first grade. Remember the little group of friends I mentioned that I had formed with Pilar? Nikki was included.

"Frede was my very first friend," Nikki explained.

She stepped back and beamed at me, her hair big (acceptable) and wild (unacceptable), her bejeweled ears, throat, and fingers making her look like a flashing neon sign on the Las Vegas Strip.

"Why didn't you tell me?" her husband asked in a sputter of syllables and flying saliva.

She laughed with a twinkle in her eye, completely unintimidated by her husband's bluster. "I wanted to surprise you when she finally came over to welcome us. I knew she would."

You'd think Howard would simply be thrilled. Instead he shot me a glower over his wife's head. As if I had done something wrong. NC Howard Grout chastising me, me Frede Ware? It felt a little strange, but mainly I was not pleased.

"Oh!" Nikki suddenly said, for the first time seeming to notice her husband's attire, or lack thereof. "Where's your shirt, sweetie?" She glanced back at me. "And tea! Let me get you some tea."

She did two things right:

1. She knew that her husband's state of dress mattered.
2. She offered me the only acceptable casual-social-call beverage. Tea. Preferably sweetened and iced, though hot was acceptable.

Unfortunately, the above facts were negated by:

1. She had a husband who would stand there shirtless at all, but worse, he was in the kitchen with two females sans shirt.
2. She made her offer of tea with overblown enthusiasm. A lady of the Junior League should never appear to be trying too hard.

"No, really, I can't stay—"

"Mrs. Ware." Howard Grout cut me off, his shock gone, signs of the man who won unwinnable cases appearing like magic. "You'll have tea."

I bristled even more at the additional proof that I didn't belong in this ill-mannered household, and I wanted to leave. But there was the whole pesky problem of my needing a lawyer.

"Howie, stop." I guess I don't have to explain who said that—not *moi.* "Be nice."

He glowered at me.

I smiled back and said, "Yes, Howie, be nice."

Which was crazy since I needed a favor. Though it was no crazier than his thinking I could get his feather-clad wife into the JLWC. But I stayed, at least long enough to think through my predicament.

While Nikki fluttered around the kitchen, gabbing the entire time, fixing me tea as though I were visiting royalty—it really was embarrassing—I didn't see how Howard Grout and his "payment plan" that was set out before me could work. A lesser woman would have felt sheer, utter depression knocking just south of sanity.

I smiled. "Good Lord, look at the time. I've got to go."

Nikki stopped abruptly, flying feathers deflating around her, her smiling visage doing much the same, two teacups held out on either side of her as if she were the Scales of Justice gone bordello. "Oh," she said.

"So sorry. But I'm late for an appointment."

"Mrs. Ware," Howard repeated.

"Really, I can't stay. I would love to, but I have to dash."

"Does this mean you don't need my help?"

It all came back to that. I did need help, and Howard Grout was considered the best of the best. Even better, he had no ties to my husband or his family. On top of that, there was no way I could start asking around for the name of a good lawyer in, say, San Antonio. Talk about raising a red flag.

"Help? What help?" Nikki asked.

He looked at me rather than his wife, and said, "Your friend and I were discussing some business before you walked in. Nothing to worry your little head over, muffin."

Did I mention the list of Things Not to Do? Just below "No public displays of affection" and "Only fast girls shave their legs above the knee," is "Do not call anyone 'muffin,' or for that matter, 'sweetie doll.'"

Money or no, the Grouts would be the bane of any Junior League.

But what to do about it?

I wanted to say, Absolument pas, *I don't need your help.* But I couldn't seem to get the words out of my mouth. Nor could I get a *oui* pried from my lips.

"Let me get back to you on that, Mr. Grout." I replaced my hat with a flourish. "I really am running late."

I got out of the house as quickly as I could without looking as though I were fleeing. I slid into the plush leather seat of my car with a relieved sigh and an unacceptable curse, my determination to make my husband pay growing exponentially for putting me in this position as I sped down the Grouts' long, sweeping drive.

FRIENDS FOREVER.

Damn Gordon Ware and his lying self.

The thoughts drummed in my head as I pulled away from Palace Grout, then drove along the narrow, curving streets of The Willows, the impressive homes spread apart like individual jewels set in rolling hills covered in thick green trees. The truth was, Nikki and I met at Willow Creek Elementary School when we were both assigned to Miss Lait's first-grade class. There were three of us in our little clique that bonded together that year. Pilar, Nikki, and *moi*.

I arrived at Miss Lait's class first that day since my daddy had driven me into town before he began work at the ranch. Between raising longhorn cattle, running several oil-producing wells on our property, not to mention seeing to whatever his latest investment was, he had his work cut out for him. He wasn't a man to turn the details over to anyone else.

Every day after that, Daddy designated Rado, a ranch hand Daddy trusted, to drive his little girl the five miles into town to go to school, then back after the final bell rang. But that first day, Daddy saw me off in style.

I would have cried, despite the fact that my mother had threatened me with my life if I did such an NC sort of thing, if my big bear of a daddy hadn't looked me in the eye and said, "You're my girl, and my girl doesn't cry." Well, how could I shed so much as a single tear then? I would have done just about anything for the only man I loved, even not cry when he was taking me to a world so foreign and hostile (already a little boy had made fun of my dress), and intending to leave me there for who knew how long.

So I did the only thing I knew how. I smiled beautifully for my father as he left the tiny grade-school grounds, then found the mean-mouthed boy and punched him in the nose. The redheaded, freckle-faced child steered a wide berth around me for our next twelve Willow Creek school years.

I was inside the classroom that first day, in the middle of fending off attention (the good kind I was used to), when Pilar arrived. Her mother brought her in, holding tight to the dark-haired girl's hand, walked right up to Miss Lait and told her who knows what. Whatever it was, Miss Lait was always half afraid of Mrs. Bass after that.

Pilar was instructed to be a good girl and get good grades. I knew all about the good-girl lecture, but although I had been privately tutored on the ranch until that year, no one had bothered to tell me what grades were. Already something new that I could be "good" at. School was looking better by the second.

Once Mrs. Bass was gone, Pilar marched up to me, stubborn, mulish, and announced that I was her best friend. Then she sat down next to me. I wasn't sure if I wanted to be her friend, but I figured she had a jump start on the whole get-good-grades thing, so I decided not to tell her to go away just yet.

Pilar pulled out a whole slew of pencils, fat, dull-tipped soldiers that she lined up in perfect order. Next came a writing tablet and a ruler. I couldn't imagine what she was going to do with all this, but I was fascinated. I was even more fascinated when she turned to me and said, "You look rich."

Another new concept.

"What is rich?"

"Having lots of money."

I knew nothing about money. "Money?"

Pilar sighed her impatience, precocious even back then. "Do you have lots of toys?"

"Yes."

"Lots of clothes?"

"Not like my mother."

"Does she have lots of clothes?"

"Oh, yes. Closets and closets full."

"Then you're rich."

When I arrived home from school that day and my mother asked me what I had learned, I proudly announced, "That I'm rich."

I was spanked, sent to bed without supper, and told to never say that again. But my mother didn't deny it. Clearly Pilar knew what she was talking about, and I wanted to learn.

With only seconds before school was supposed to begin that day, Nikki came racing in sans mother or father, all wild golden-brown hair that looked as if it hadn't seen a brush for the better part of her life. To Pilar and me, with our privileged, ordered worlds, Nikki was an exotic creature, unembarrassed by her tangled hair or wrinkled, mismatched clothes. And she was confident enough to speak to us when we went out to the playground. All the other kids watched us but didn't approach. (My guess is that by the time recess rolled around, word had gotten out about my run-in with the mean little boy and his newly bloodied nose.)

"We're best friends," Pilar stated to Nikki, gesturing to herself and me. "Who are you?"

Nikki got big-eyed and clasped her hands together. "I want to be best friends too."

Pilar considered her. "Are you smart?"

"I don't know."

"Are you rich?"

"I don't know."

"What *do* you know?"

"I don't know."

Pilar wasn't pleased, but she had already told me that we needed a minimum of three people to have a clique. "Well, at least you're not pretty like Frede. And not nearly as smart as me. Okay, you can be our friend."

So we were formed.

Nikki—the dreamer.

Pilar—the realist.

And me—the princess.

All these years later I see that Pilar had been headed toward the life of a too-direct liberal since first grade if not birth. No doubt she was one of those who felt she had been born to the wrong family in the wrong state. But the fact remained, even though she had gone up North, she had returned, proving that once you were born and raised with Texas in your blood it was always there despite left leanings, flat hair, and ugly glasses. How could she not come home?

As for Nikki, if I agreed to Howard's payment plan of getting her into the League, it could be said that her dreams had come true and once and for all she would be a permanent part of the biggest clique in town.

As for my being a princess, I had never felt less like one in all my life, since suddenly I found myself on the verge of becoming a pauper. Which was completely unacceptable and needed to be remedied.

I headed out of The Willows complex, waving at Juan in his limestone-brick guardhouse as I slid through the exit. I needed time to sort through my options. I didn't want to be saved by men. Pampered, adored, put on a pedestal? Yes. But saved? *Non.*

But if I were to stand a chance of keeping my throne, I would need Howard Grout's help. The thought didn't sit well, especially since the price I would have to pay could very easily ruin me socially for life.

The proverbial between a rock and a hard place.

But it was as I drove through town, bypassed Willow Creek Park on the east side of the main square, the thick copse of live oak trees and wild bluebonnets spread out like a carpet of color everywhere, that I realized if anyone could pull off getting Nikki Grout into the JLWC it was *moi*. I was a genius at pulling off the impossible. Besides, if I didn't gain Howard's help to get my money back, I would be ruined in the JLWC anyway. At that point, the reality was that I had nothing to lose by going to Howard Grout. And everything to gain.

Decision made.

I found the cell phone I kept in the glove compartment and dialed information. I was surprised that the Grouts were listed, but relieved that I wouldn't have to go back and face them, at least not yet.

"Mrs. Ware," Howard said.

Caller ID was so NC.

"Yes, it's me."

"You accept."

The words I had prepared froze on my lips, and I could all but feel the tension that came over the airwaves. I couldn't get my mouth to work. But just when he cursed and would have hung up, I said, "I accept."

He hesitated. "Good."

"You'll get my husband?"

"Mrs. Ware, if you get my Nikki into the freakin' Willow Creek Junior League thing, I'll personally make sure that all that bastard has left is earnings from the job he'll have to get flipping burgers at Sonic Happy Eating."

Cold, shallow, completely unladylike delight slid through me.

"Well, fine. We have a deal."

"I'll tell Nikki the good news that she's going to be in the club."

"The only news you need to tell your wife at this point is that I will start by introducing her to a few of the Junior League of Willow Creek members. This is a process, Mr. Grout, not an instantaneous in."

"Fine. Though maybe you should come over and talk to Nikki about it yourself. That way you can tell her what she should do. Besides, you and I need to talk. I need every bit of information you have on your husband's affairs."

"I only know about the one."

"Work affairs, Mrs. Ware."

"Ah, of course. You want bank information and such."

"ASAP."

"When would you like to get together?" I asked.

"Tomorrow's good."

"So soon?"

"If he's really stolen your money we don't have a second to lose. If I didn't want to look into a few things myself, I'd say get your pretty little butt back over here today."

The more I talked to him the more I was convinced that everyone in town was right. He was an unmannered thug. But what was a girl to do? Nothing but deal with it. Which was why I pulled back into his driveway the following day loaded with files pertaining to my husband and plans for my new lawyer's wife.

Chapter Seven

I AM NOTHING if not organized, and it would require organization to get Nikki Grout into the JLWC. That and a miracle. Which meant I had plans to make, people to see, places to go. And it wouldn't hurt to pray.

By the next morning, I had my game plan mapped out. I was even encouraged when I arrived at my neighbors' home and a uniformed maid (good start) answered the door.

"Is Mrs. Grout—"

"Frede!"

I heard Nikki's voice, and what could only be the rat-a-tat-tat of her stilettos on tile. (Good start ruined.)

The maid stepped aside to let me in. Nikki threw her arms wide and embraced me and my Louis Vuitton messenger bag, which was now doing double duty.

"I'm so excited you're here!" she enthused.

While the presence of a maid was a good sign and interrupting the maid could be dealt with, Nikki's attire had not improved. She looked as if she were trying out for a Dolly Parton look-alike contest. Her hair was big (too big, and yes, there is such a thing), and she wore more tight, spandex clothes, with heels so high and thin that I didn't know how they supported the sheer volume of her bustline, which was shockingly noticeable today since her top was tight and low cut.

For this visit I had chosen to wear a white, cotton sateen long-sleeved blouse, tucked into a mid-calf-length skirt, made from a cream, pale yellow, and tan floral silk. I had my pearls around my neck and at my ears, with a cotton and silk cream-colored sweater hanging beautifully on my shoulders.

"Come in, come in," Nikki enthused, grabbing my free hand (the maid had to catch my falling sweater) and pulling me across the entry hall. We catapulted through a set of French doors and into a living room that was an astonishing palette of neutral colors and tasteful furniture. I was as pleased as I was surprised. While the entry hall was all gilded gold, it could be seen as acceptable as long as the rest of the house blended with this sort of tasteful style.

However, in the blink of an eye, we left good taste behind and entered what must be called the "Safari Room." All leather and leopard prints, and paintings of exotic animals mounted on the walls.

I suspected that the designer the Grouts had hired had insisted that the living room, at least, be done in her taste, rather than theirs. I wondered what magic words the designer had used to get her way.

"This is Howard's study."

"Ah, it's—" I couldn't think what to say.

"And out here is the pool."

I immediately smelled chlorine. No one had a pool so close to the house that people inside would know it was there—that is, unless you lived in L.A. and used pools as works of art cascading into nothingness. We were not in L.A.

Worse, the pool wasn't even outside. We came through another set of double doors into a huge atrium that housed a not-insignificant pool, surrounded by Doric columns, Greek statues, and completely out-of-place palm trees that shot through openings in the glass ceiling. We had obviously come to the theme part of the house. *This is the Jungle Room, and this is our Greco-Roman Harem Room gone tropical.*

A good decorator could, and should, mix design elements, colors, and styles. But this mishmash of things was a shock to the senses.

Finally we made it to what must be our destination, a sunroom at the back of the house. Just beyond, through the picture window, I could make out a guest cottage. No question, it had the look of a minipalace, but somehow it managed to look tasteful. Yet again, I was soothed and relieved by the sight of normalcy. The sunroom was filled with pale yellows and greens, white and airy fabrics that felt casual and classic at the same time. I wondered if two designers had battled it out in this house, each finally dividing and conquering what they could.

When we entered the sunroom, Howard was there, reading the newspaper and drinking coffee. He didn't bother to stand when we entered.

"Maria," Nikki called out loudly.

The maid rushed in.

"Bring tea for my friend."

I cringed. And Howard was watching. Oops.

Nikki didn't notice. She directed me to a chair, then hurried to another and pulled up close next to me. "I can't tell you how excited I am about getting into the Junior League of Willow Creek! Me! Imagine!"

I couldn't.

"Now, tell me every little thing I need to do."

"As your husband might have mentioned, to start the process—and this will be a process—I want to introduce you to a few women in the League."

"I can't wait!"

"Good, because we don't have time to waste since new members are selected at the end of May. We'll have to work fast. I thought I'd start by hosting an intimate tea for you at my home next week. It will be short notice since the clock is ticking, but I'll call each guest personally and invite them."

"I've always dreamed of having a party for ladies." Her eyes got wide and she leaned forward, grasping my hands. "Oh, Frede, let me have the tea here at my house."

"Here?"

"Please. It will be great, I promise. A real classy ladies' tea. With fancy china and silver. I swear." She crossed her heart.

"Nikki, I'm not sure."

Howard set his coffee mug down with a clunk. "What's not to be sure about? Have the damn tea here. Don't think I don't know that half of Willow Creek wants to see this place." He snorted. "Plus, then they can see proof that I have a pantload of money."

True. Half of Willow Creek did want to see "Palace Grout," as I called my neighbors' home. And while it was completely NC to mention his wealth, I couldn't deny that people were interested in just how much Howard Grout really had.

Against my better judgment, I started seeing the wisdom of the change in venue. Surely it would be easy enough to keep guests out of the poolroom and office. No Junior Leaguer in good standing would ever ask to be given a tour of anyone's home. It was a known rule of etiquette that if the hostess wanted to show someone around, she would offer. I would make sure that Nikki didn't offer.

The maid brought me a cup of tea.

"So, we'll have the little party here?" Nikki persisted.

"Fine. Plan on having it next Tuesday morning at eleven-thirty."

"Oh, my gosh! So soon?"

"We have to get six women to sponsor you, Nikki. I, of course, will be one of those sponsors. But we still need five more."

"Oh, my," she said a little breathlessly.

"Exactly." I took a sip of tea, hot, not my preference.

"Okay, Tuesday'll be great! This is going to be so much fun!"

No question Texas women by and large are enthusiastic and cheerful. But Junior Leaguers in Willow Creek maintained a refined cheerfulness. Nikki's was overdone, like her clothes.

"What should I serve?" she asked.

I think I might have blinked. "It's a tea."

Nikki laughed. "Silly me! But that seems kind of boring. How about champagne?"

I stared at her for a second. "As I said, the tea is at eleven-thirty in the morning."

She looked confused.

"Too early for champagne," I supplied.

"You're right! What was I thinking? I should serve morning drinks! Like mimosas and Bloody Marys."

"No! I mean, no. Just tea—sweetened and iced—plus some that is hot. Maybe a little coffee. Also, fresh-squeezed orange juice. Perhaps some finger sandwiches. Cucumber with a little mayonnaise would be wonderful. Crusts cut off."

Nikki wrinkled her nose. "You want me to make sandwiches out of cucumber and Miracle Whip?"

If you are keeping track of the list of Things Not to Do, add "Never, ever use Miracle Whip." Mayonnaise, preferably homemade, should be real. If homemade is not feasible, then it must be Hellmann's.

I explained this as politely as I could.

"She'll take care of it," Howard interjected. "What else?"

"Petits fours would be nice. Maggie's Bakery on Willow Square makes the best. Serve them on your best china, and the sweet tea in your best crystal. Cloth napkins are a must. Something appropriate for daytime as opposed to dinner. I'll start making calls as soon as I get home. Plan on a party of seven to eight or so women, including you."

"Okay," she said, her blue eyes going wide with excitement. "I'll get it right. And I'll serve everyone at tables around the pool."

"No!" Yet again, my poise escaped me. "I mean, no, that isn't necessary. I think it would be absolutely lovely to serve tea in your beautiful living room, and didn't I see a lovely receiving room just beyond that?"

"But that's so boring."

"Well, boring is probably best for this sort of thing."

"Are you sure?"

"I'm sure."

I went over a few more details. And I hadn't even gotten to the most difficult part yet. But there was no help for it, so I plunged ahead.

"Also, Nikki, it would be, well, a good idea if you wore something . . . less . . ." I searched my brain for the words. Flashy. Slutty. NC. "Less grand."

"What do you mean?"

"Something more in keeping with the mood of a Junior League morning tea."

"You don't like my clothes?"

"What's not to love? It's just that the girls in the League don't get so . . . dressed up that early in the day."

"What do you want her to wear?" Howard asked.

He sounded suspicious, and I felt like saying that if he didn't like what they wore to Junior League teas perhaps he should reconsider having his wife become a member. But of course I didn't. I have learned that being direct gives far more truth than most people can handle. Besides, there was still that detail of my needing a lawyer.

"Oh, anything really." Or not. "Something feminine, dainty. Bows and pearls are always good."

Howard scoffed. "Bows and pearls. Hell."

"Think Jackie Kennedy."

"She's freakin' dead."

"Howie!" Nikki scowled at her husband, then turned to me. "Like a pretty dress with a bow, and a pearl necklace?"

"That sounds lovely."

"Okay." She absorbed the words. "Okay!" she repeated, this time with conviction.

I hated this, really, really hated this untenable spot. I sent up a silent curse at my husband's head—wherever his head might be. But then I consoled myself with the image of him dressed in a Sonic Happy Eating uniform, writhing in utter embarrassment when all of his school friends and fraternity brothers came in for a burger. I might have been in a sort of purgatory sitting there with Nikki and Howard, but soon enough, Gordon would be in a hell of Howard Grout's making.

The maid returned and refilled my tea with grace, and I felt my misgivings ease a bit. I also wondered if it might be easier to get the maid into the JLWC than Nikki. But if Nikki Grout could have tea served to me this morning with something approaching class, surely she could put together a small gathering that wouldn't curl my friends' hair.

"Did you bring the information I need?" Howard asked.

It was a relief to move on to something else, which is saying a lot since the last thing I wanted to move on to was my husband and any discussion of money.

Once a month, at my father's insistence, my husband went over our accounts with me. He provided an itemized list of all our holdings. I had brought those statements, along with the set of books Gordon kept on Hildebrand Galleries.

I handed over everything I had, then sat back gracefully, and picked up my cup and saucer.

"What files?" Nikki wanted to know.

"Nothing to concern your pretty little head over," he said to her. "We're going to talk business now. Why don't you go get started planning?"

"I can't just leave."

"It's business, muffin."

"Lawyer stuff that I can't hear, I suppose." She sighed, then pushed up from her chair. "I'll see you at the tea?"

"Yes, next Tuesday. I'll call with the guest list and I'll come over early in case you need some help. Though don't hesitate to phone if you have any questions."

She perked back up and hurried from the room, hollering out to the maid.

Howard took thirty minutes and two cups of coffee to get through everything I brought him.

"Who all knows about this?" he asked.

"No one." I hoped.

"You haven't told anyone?"

"No." Other than Nina who I knew wouldn't tell a soul.

"Good. We'll use that as leverage when I find him. If he doesn't come to heel right away, then we'll threaten to go public with his affair."

"No! You can't!"

"Sorry, but I have to tell you, we don't have anything else on him. At least not yet. We've got to prove he stole your money. Technically, right now, it's just missing."

"I don't mean that, I mean we can't go public with anything!"

"Why the hell not?"

"Mr. Grout, I am relying on your discretion. I can't have all of Willow Creek knowing that my husband . . . did whatever he did with my money and ran off with some woman."

"I hate to break the news to you, darlin', but I'm sure that's just what he's expecting from you. He probably figures you'll want to keep everything quiet, which makes it easier for him to get away with things. We'll try it your way first. But if you want your money back, I'm telling you now, it ain't gonna be pretty."

I admit it. I felt dizzy.

"All right," he said, "this is enough for me to get started." He stood, making it clear I should leave. But at the last minute he looked back at me and held up one of the files. "While I'm working, I suggest you make this crazy-ass art gallery of yours start turning a profit. Or at least break even."

I straightened in my chair. "What do you mean?"

"That place is a money guzzler you can't afford. And no one in their right mind would buy it at this point. Plus, any sort of sale would just complicate matters. So spend some time making it work."

I must have looked as confused as Nikki had when I started discussing appropriate beverages for a tea.

"Get an artist, Mrs. Ware. Put on a show. Do something to bring in some income. You can't afford a tax write-off anymore."

"I have artists."

"Yeah, ones that don't sell for squat."

True.

"Find someone worth a crap." He thought for a second, then hollered out. "Nikki! Who the hell did that statue you made me pay a fortune for? That fairy artist with the faggot name."

She peeked back in. "Sawyer Jackson?"

I remembered the sculpture in the hallway.

"Yeah, that's the one," Howard said. "Where's his studio?"

Nikki mentioned an address on the wrong side of town. "But he doesn't like visitors, he likes his privacy. Besides, he doesn't do shows. In fact, I think he's mostly building things these days."

"Building what?" Howard asked.

"I don't know. Last time I saw him, he spent more time talking about construction than art. Plus, you've got to stop calling him a fairy, Howard. It's not nice."

"Muffin, just give Frede here his phone number and address." He looked at me. "Seems to me if you can convince someone who doesn't show his work to put on a show with you, it would go a long way toward causing a stir—just the kind of art exhibit that could stop the hemorrhaging going on over there at Hildebrand Galleries."

Nikki planted her fists on her hips. "But, Howard—"

"Nikki, doll, don't you worry about it. I can't imagine Frede Ware being anything but super nice to your little fairy friend." He grinned at me. "No scaring him, no being snippy."

Scaring him indeed.

His grin turned to a chuckle. "And if anyone can convince someone to do what she wants, I'd say it was you."

Well, what can I say, the man was smart.

Sawyer Jackson might say no to everyone else, but as Howard recognized, I'm not everyone else. I had no doubt that the artist would clear his schedule once I called. After the seed was planted, and having seen the man's work, I had every intention of calling.

"Just find the number, Nikki," he said, before skewering me with a look. "Call him, set something up, then go talk to him. See what kind of moneymaking show you can pull together. In the meantime, I'll be working on this."

When I stood, Howard smiled at me. "Sounds like you have some work to do for a change."

I leveled a gaze at him and finally his snide smile faltered. But that was all I did since I wasn't about to lower myself to his level. "I appreciate your help, Mr. Grout," I said simply. "I look forward to an update once you've made progress."

Then I walked out of his partially fabulous mansion, got into my car, and curled my perfectly manicured nails around the steering wheel, wondering what (the hell, as Howard Grout would say) I had gotten myself into.

Chapter Eight

THE FIRST THING I did when I got home was put a call in to the artist to arrange a viewing of his work.

After seeing the piece in the Grouts' hallway, I had no doubt his portfolio would be impressive. But as far as I was concerned, art alone does not a successful artist make. I would need to meet the man, see what he looked like, and assess how he presented himself.

He didn't need to be handsome, per se. And I could work with gay as long as he had the ability to charm Willow Creek's wealthier residents into buying *beaucoup* amounts of his work. Granted, if we were going to put a stop to the money hemorrhage, as Howard called it, going on at Hildebrand Galleries, the artist wouldn't be able to act too gay. Though a little gay went a long way toward pulling in the ladies. Especially when it was someone as infamously elusive as Sawyer Jackson.

Setting aside the sweater I had retrieved from the maid, I went to my desk and dialed the number Nikki provided. The other end rang repeatedly. It took a second to realize that no one was going to answer, not even an answering machine. Not that I'm a fan of answering machines, but who in this day and age didn't have a maid or at the very least a machine to take messages?

Thinking I had dialed incorrectly, I called again. This time an answering machine picked up after little more than two rings. I had the distinct impression that someone had turned the machine on in the time it took me to redial.

Whatever the case, a prerecorded voice came over the line. *"I'm working. Leave a message. If I can, I'll call back."*

So much for the hope that he was charming.

If the man was as rude as his message, I doubted I'd be able to sell a single piece of art—at least at a show where he was in attendance—and I couldn't imagine how Howard Grout could think this was the man to put Hildebrand Galleries in the black. Not that Howard would recognize good manners, or lack thereof, if they jumped up and bit him in the face.

But still, I couldn't forget the lifelike detail found in each curve of flesh carved in Sawyer Jackson's marble sculpture.

The machine beeped. "This is Fredericka Hildebrand Ware, of Hildebrand Galleries. I was given your name for a possible show I am putting together at my gallery. I'd like to speak to you at your earliest convenience. Please call."

I barely had time to give my phone number before the machine cut me off.

But that was the least of my concerns. The more pressing problem was the fast-approaching tea and finding a handful of Junior Leaguers willing to attend.

To that end, the first person I called was my mother as I started to plan Nikki's initial, intimate launch with a few of my closest friends. Actually, maybe I wouldn't invite my *closest* friends, but a few (lower-level) ladies who would serve as guinea pigs. If I was going to pull off a miracle, I would need to get the lay of the land, see how the women responded to my foray into *l'impossible.*

My mother would be far from easy to win over, but she had given birth to me, so you'd think she'd be more inclined to help. Plus if anyone could help me put a patina of respectability on the affair it was Blythe Hildebrand.

I dialed the number.

"Mother?"

"Is that you, Fredericka?"

"Does anyone else call you 'Mother'?"

"Sarcasm is not only unbecoming in a lady, but it is completely uncalled-for. Myrna is here doing my hair, and she was giving me a quick spray when I picked up the phone so I could barely hear."

A "quick spray" was, one, a lie (there was nothing quick about it), and two, the term my mother used when her hairstylist lacquered her hair with Aqua Net. Blythe Hildebrand was one of the few remaining women in Texas who still had their hair done once a week. It was the Net that held the style in place the entire seven days. That, and keeping her head still while she slept. I was convinced my mother hadn't had a good night's sleep in all her adult life.

The first thing she said after I told her about the tea for Nikki was, "She's not our kind, dear. Of course we can't let her in."

My mother isn't exactly a believer in the "all men are created equal" idea.

"Mother, really. Nikki was always sweet."

"The JLWC isn't interested in sweet, Fredericka. We are interested in the sort of good breeding that will benefit the group as a whole. Good families, good connections, bring in good donations, which puts us in a position to do plenty of good work."

A variation of my own speech, but not what I wanted to hear.

"Then do it for me, Mother."

That surprised her, an appeal to sentiment.

"Come to her party," I cajoled. "You don't have to approve, but it would be nice if you supported your own daughter."

"Support my daughter in her folly?" She sighed heavily into the phone. "Why are you doing this?"

I'm nothing if not cool under pressure and wasn't about to tell her the truth. "I think the League could use some new blood."

My mother actually laughed.

"That, I doubt," she said. "But fine. I'll be there."

My mother never pressed for the truth if she thought she wasn't going to like it, at least where I was concerned. She frequently operated under the "Don't ask, Don't tell" motto so that she didn't have to feel obligated to do anything about whatever she assumed she would find displeasing. It had worked far better for my mother than the military.

"If nothing else," she continued, "it's an excuse to see that god-awful monstrosity they call a home."

My mother was a snob—more specifically, an unapologetic snob. You'd think (as did most everyone in town) that she was from a fine old family with piles of money. You would be wrong. It was my father who had come with the fine old family money. Which just goes to show that the worst sort of snob is frequently a new snob.

My mother's version of how she and my father met goes something like this:

"The minute he saw me, your father had to have me. I was in the WCU cafeteria"—*she leaves out that she was serving food, not eating it*—"and the minute he said hello it was love at first sight."

When asked about meeting my father's family, she goes on about how much they loved her. His parents are now dead, so it's hard to refute. Unfortunately for my mother, my father's sister is still alive, and tells a different tale.

As Aunt Cordelia explains it, the Hildebrand family disliked my mother on sight. They let her know in myriad ways that they didn't approve, which, my aunt said, amused my father in equal measure to how much it made my mother crazy.

On the day my mother met the Hildebrand family, my father took her to the family's city house just off Hildebrand Square, east of the main road into Willow Creek. The house was a sprawling Victorian, with a wraparound front porch, and green lawns graced with willow trees.

My mother had taken great pains with her appearance that day. She had bought a dress especially for the occasion at JCPenney. It was a bright shout of billowing material, cinched by a belt at the waist, a full skirt that would swirl, all of it covered with lush red roses. She had bought high-heeled shoes in red (a color reserved for the lowest level of women), a matching handbag, brand-new gloves, and a white hat with a faux red rose in the band.

Not only did her attire scream tacky, but it was the extreme opposite of the Hildebrand women's simple attire made of fine materials and given luster by demure pearls, tasteful brooches, or ivory cameos. My mother's flowered dress floated around her calves with the stench of flamboyant inappropriateness, like the smell of burned eggs hanging on hours after the skillet has been pulled from the range.

My aunt never should have told me the story, as she readily admitted. But that didn't stop her from telling me that and more. My aunt gave my mother credit for being a quick study since she never wore a wildly colorful dress with flowers on it again. Over the years, my mother became known for her prim suits, low heels, and expensive, though tasteful, jewels—the very picture of old money. But I digress.

My grandmother Hildebrand was a formidable woman, and she ran her family with an iron fist—with the exception of my daddy, the only Hildebrand who wasn't intimidated by her steely personality.

That day, my grandmother led who she thought was just another of my daddy's flings to a front receiving room. She was in for the surprise of her life.

Aunt Cordelia and my uncle Robbie and his wife joined them for tea. The small group sat in the elegant room with high ceilings, fine draperies, and more furniture than should be allowed in any one room. A uniformed maid brought in a tray, and much to my mother's surprise, Felicia Hildebrand poured.

"Tell us, dear," Felicia said, after handing over a delicate cup that my aunt swore shook in my mother's hand. "Where in Texas are you from?"

"Dallas."

"Highland Park?"

If only that had been the case. Highland Park was an old-money enclave in the big city, and one of the few addresses Felicia Hildebrand deemed acceptable.

"No, ma'am. I'm actually from a little place outside of Dallas called Burserville."

Not a popular response and a sniff of unsuitability drifted through the room. My mother has always been perceptive, and I can imagine the embarrassment she felt. I'm sure her cheeks were as bright as the roses on her JCPenney dress.

"Well then, who is your family, dear?"

I'm surprised my mother didn't just out-and-out lie at that point. Though maybe she would have if, just before she got to the Hildebrand house, my daddy hadn't cupped her face in his strong hands and sworn his family was going to love her as much as he did. To this day, she sticks staunchly to the story that they did.

So my mother told the Hildebrands about her family, about Daisy Jane and Wilmont Pruitt and their eight kids. It sounds like something out of a bad Depression-era movie, but it's true.

Sitting in that receiving room must have gotten more uncomfortable by the second. But finally tea was done, and my mother might have gotten away thinking things hadn't gone too badly. But that would have been too easy.

My father couldn't seem to leave well enough alone, and had to tell the story of how they met. (I swear he married my mother just to make his own mother crazy.) My mother tried to stop him, but no one was having any of that. Thurmond Hildebrand plunged ahead, my mother dying a thousand deaths at the mention of her position as a server at the university.

His mother appeared unfazed by the news. She stood and thanked my mother for coming. Everyone started to leave, though my aunt hung back so that just when my mother was about to make her escape, she heard Felicia Hildebrand say, "You're mistaken if you think you can walk in and trick my son into keeping you."

At that point in the story, Aunt Cordelia always remembered who she was talking to and had the good sense to reach out, clasp my hand, and say, "Though God was watching over us that day, since how else would we have gotten our sweet little Fredericka."

After my aunt assured me of the Hildebrand love—something my very stern grandmother always made me feel regardless of how she felt about my mother—she came to the most cringeworthy part of the story. She would tell how Felicia Hildebrand went out into the hall where my father waited and told him she had seated him next to Roslyn Lindsay at the dinner she was giving that Saturday night. She added that she expected him to pick up the daughter from the socially prominent family and bring her to the event. The words were said without a question, as if her son would undoubtedly do exactly what she stated.

That's when my father told them of his big news.

"Mother, I won't be picking Roslyn up for the party, and I won't be sitting next to her."

"Thurmond, there will be no discussion on this."

Apparently this got my grandmother stirred up in a tiff of grand proportions, so sudden and quick that everyone, except my daddy, took a step back.

"You will pick up Roslyn, and there will be no further discussion of the matter."

"Mother, mother, mother," he said with a smile, proof that my father was enjoying himself. "I thought you were one to avoid controversy at all costs."

"What is that supposed to mean?"

"Mama, darlin' "—she hated it when he called her that—"what will all your proper friends in the Junior League say when I escort one woman to your dinner party when I'm already married to another?"

Aunt Cordelia swore that her mother nearly had a stroke right then and there on the beautiful hardwood floor. But Felicia Hildebrand did nothing so weak. She didn't even reach out and grab a chair. From well-bred stock, she stood and turned that glacial gaze on my mother, assessing. Finally she turned back to my father.

"You are neither Catholic nor without means. Either you find a way to dissolve this marriage that disgraces not only yourself but your family heritage, or you are no longer welcome in this home." She glanced one last time at my mother. "The choice is yours."

My aunt always ended her tale with a sniff of woe, and then added that my father made his choice, and in the end his mother—"A saint, I tell you," she always added—backed down. At least she did on the surface. To the end of my grandmother's days, she and my mother never got along, no matter how respectable Daisy Jane and Wilmont Pruitt's daughter became, or even how high up in the Junior League she went.

Blythe Pruitt Hildebrand grew to be just as well mannered and uppity as my aunt and grandmother, until she was an outcast in her own family back in Burserville. In fact my mother had become so respectable that there were days when I wonder if she had completely rewritten her history in her head until she believed the fiction.

Whatever the case, I just hoped my mother would support me in my quest to get Nikki Grout into the Junior League of Willow Creek and not end up becoming my biggest opponent.

Chapter Nine

OVER THE NEXT couple of days, I put in several calls to the artist, none of which were returned until one morning while Nina and I were out working in the garden. I came back inside to a message on my machine that said simply, *"This is Sawyer Jackson. I'm not interested in a show, so stop calling."*

The *très* rude artist turned me down. I couldn't believe it.

I was used to men and women alike interested in me for my money. When a girl was raised with wealth, she got used to that sort of attention. Then you add my good looks and inarguable charm, and I was a veritable man magnet. You add to the mix my spectacular personality that made people think I cared about them, and I was a woman magnet as well. I didn't have a lot of experience with gay men, but really, who wouldn't love me? At least, who wouldn't love me who wasn't a lying, cheating husband?

Which was the only reason I could come up with for why I woke up first thing the next morning and dressed in a pale peach *ensemble* that highlighted my peaches-and-cream complexion, found the address Nikki had given me, then headed for the garage.

"Where you going?" Nina wanted to know.

I kicked my accent up a notch and turned on my very best Scarlett O'Hara charm, and said, "To get me an artist, sugar."

I already knew he lived in the wrong part of Willow Creek, but I hadn't known that he lived on the very outskirts of that part of town. After I crested the railroad tracks that marked the entrance to South Willow Creek, I nearly ran into a group of protestors, waving signs that said BIG MONEY GO HOME.

For a second I thought they were waving their signs at me, but then realized they were protesting a construction site where bulldozers were making short work of demolishing several blocks that I would have to say deserved to be torn down.

I skirted the crowd and continued on through the narrow streets lined with faded Easter-egg-colored houses, getting more looks than Miss Texas during the bathing suit competition. South Willow Creek was like many wrong parts of towns—filled with rundown buildings, peeling paint, unmowed yards, and boarded-up windows. I finally found the address and pulled up to what I could only call a minihacienda. There was a tall adobe wall that surrounded a small complex, and a gate to keep out the rest of the world. Fortunately for me the gate stood open, and it was like driving into a completely different world.

The inner courtyard was a mix of terra-cotta brick and newly green grass with a fountain bubbling in the middle. The complex was quite nice in an 1800s sort of way. The antiquated motif was only skewed by several large pieces of artwork placed here and there. The more I saw of the man's work, the more I was intrigued.

I got out of the car and walked to the front door. There was no official doorbell, just an old bell on a rope. I pulled, the clang echoing against the walls, and I waited. When no one appeared, I rang again.

It was early March by then, and the heat had already begun to drum against the earth, the air filled with the pungent scents of marigolds, honeysuckle, and burning wood somewhere in the distance. Central Texas is known for the mesquite trees that are used to make all sorts of *fabu* mesquite-grilled fare. If anyone ever offers you a mesquite-grilled lobster tail, plop yourself down and get ready to sing hallelujah. It is divine.

I would like to say it was the thought of a potential mesquite-grilled meal that sent me around to the back of the house, but I'm afraid it had more to do with my being stubborn. I admit it, it's an unbecoming quality that I try to conceal.

I came around the side of the house and entered the backyard. The area was an explosion of color created by the brilliant blue sky, green grass, rows of perfectly manicured flower beds, stone walls, and statuary. It looked like a sculpture garden of both traditional and modern art. I was even more impressed.

Just beyond the gardens was another building. The door stood open and it didn't sound like any work was going on. I tiptoed through the grass (not because I was having a Nancy Drew moment, but because I was trying to keep what remained of the morning dew off my silk pant cuffs), and peered inside the building. It took a second for my eyes to adjust. Then I saw him.

Yes, it was as dramatic as that.

He was standing at a wooden drafting table, his hands planted on the rough surface, his head bowed as if he were praying or exhausted or doing some sort of meditation. I didn't see anything in the way of work anywhere near, and I figured that barking rude messages into phone machines must be tiring work.

"Hello!" I called out. "Mr. Jackson?"

He straightened and turned to face me.

Let me start by making one thing verra verra clear. This man fell solidly under the "A Shame" category of men for the sheer waste of good looks. He was a perfect specimen—tall, dark, and yes, handsome in a rugged, oh-so-not-gay kind of way. He looked to be in his early thirties, and words like "little," "fairy," and "scare" didn't seem to apply. Though what did I know. I had never met a gay man in my life—at least that I was aware of.

If his A Shame status wasn't bad enough, as much as I was reluctant to admit it, I felt what I can only term lusting impulses at the sight of him. But better to lust after a gay man than a straight one, I realized, since there was the whole "I'm still married" problem. Which, when I thought about it, surely made the lusting oh-so-safe.

Interesting.

"Sawyer Jackson?" I added when he didn't respond.

Still nothing.

He looked me up and down (lessons in etiquette would have served the man well), then leaned one of his broad shoulders against a post as if he were auditioning to be the next Marlboro man. His jeans were hanging low on his hips, his shirt unbuttoned over a beautifully carved, naked (so much to learn, so little time) chest, and I had to remind myself that he was inclined toward men.

Whatever he was, while he might have been rude to me on the answering machine, I anticipated the moment he finally realized who exactly I was and took in all my . . . well, Frede Ware–ness. I knew he was considered elusive, but really, who could hold out against *moi*? I nearly smiled at the thought of this arrogant man suddenly bending over backward to please me.

"Who the hell are you?"

All right, no bending yet, but I was nothing if not confident in my abilities to win anyone over.

I opened my mouth to answer, but he cut me off.

"Don't tell me. You're Fredericka Hildebrand Ware."

He didn't say it in the exclamation sort of way I would have expected. It was more riddled with disdain. For me. Fredericka Hildebrand Ware.

"Yes, that's me. I've been calling—"

"Ten times. Didn't you get my message?"

"Well, yes."

"What did I say?"

It wasn't like me to fidget but I shifted on my feet. "That you weren't interested."

He pushed away from the post in a way that I can only term aggressive. My heart flipped in my chest, but I stood my ground.

"What part of 'I'm not interested' didn't you get?"

Before I ever arrived at his house I had known I loved his art. I had been almost entirely certain that convincing him to show with me could save my gallery. Now, watching the way he carried himself, knowing that the arrogance combined with his good looks would intrigue art buyers even more, I knew I had to have him.

"I don't understand," I said. "How can you not want a show?"

"I just don't. Not with you or anyone else. Got it?"

"Actually, I only get the 'or anyone else' part. Maybe you could expand a little on the 'not with you' part."

Imagine dark brows slamming together.

I scrambled around in my brain for just the right words to convince him to let me put on an exhibition of his work. A Sawyer Jackson show would introduce him to the world and provide me with a whole lot of that money I was so in need of. "I don't think you realize what I can do for your career, Mr. Jackson. And truly, what's the point of being an artist if you're going to be elusive?"

He didn't look happy, though this time when he started to speak I cut him off.

"I can transform you from a man with a sculpture standing next to a black velvet Elvis painting in Howard Grout's hallway into an artist whose works are admired around the country."

He started to say something again, but I wasn't finished.

"I will put on the type of show that will get you noticed by the most important people in the art world. I'll invite art critics, art reporters; I'll even invite senators, congressmen, and businessmen." A thought occurred to me. I hesitated, but plunged ahead because I wanted at least to appear progressive and open-minded. "You can even invite whoever you'd like. A friend, a date . . . a boyfriend, whatever." Granted, the man of the hour with another man at his side might be a bit much for my friends (gay was one thing, but two homosexual gentlemen on a date was something else altogether), but I could make something up when he was out of earshot. They were brothers. Cousins. Or better yet, I'd say they were client and agent. Perfect!

Please, God, don't let them hold hands.

Standing on the threshold of the small building, I was so lost to the idea of what a triumphant coup it would be if I snagged the mysterious Sawyer Jackson, that it was a second before I realized the artist was headed toward me. In little more than a handful of steps he got to the entrance and stopped.

His expression could hardly be termed friendly, but I smiled grandly anyway. "It will be perfect, Mr. Jackson. What do you say? Do we have a deal?"

He slammed the door in my face.

I stared at the weathered wooden plank, hardly able to understand what had just happened.

"I take it you want to think about it," I called out through the door.

His reply was muffled, but I heard it all the same. "Go away."

I blinked. Even after I had gone over to his house (on the wrong side of town, I might add), and introduced myself, even after I explained all I could do for him, he still wasn't interested . . . in me, me Frede Ware.

What was wrong with everyone these days?

Chapter Ten

WHATEVER MY EXPECTATIONS were for Nikki's *petite soirée,* let me just say I was in for a surprise.

The tea got off to a tricky start when I arrived at Palace Grout and found Nikki dressed just as I suggested.

I must have looked confused.

"You said bows and pearls," she reminded me.

I should have been more specific, adding words like "understated," "tasteful," or even just plain "small." Nikki wore:

1. a white dress covered with big red flowers (not so unlike my mother's flowered debacle of decades earlier) and the largest red bow I'd ever seen that wasn't on the hood of a new car parked in the driveway Christmas morning, displayed in a 1980s Linda Evans *Dynasty* sort of way on her left hip,
2. several ropes of hail-sized pearls circling her throat that appeared to be choking her,
3. fake eyelashes with Tammy Faye Bakker–style mascara clumped, not combed, on,
4. bright clown spots of blush, which was bad enough, but the color had a (suitable-at-evening-events-only) shimmer to it,

5. no stockings (I can't begin to explain all that is wrong with this),

6. another pair of strappy sandals (True, Central Texas is warmer than many places in early March, but sandals are for very late spring and summer. The only exception to this rule is a satin, over-the-toe, strapped—absolutely no thongs—evening sandal to wear with the most formal of evening wear),

7. more specifically, *white* sandals. (How was it possible that there was anyone left in the country who did not know that white could only be worn between Easter and Labor Day. To this rule there are no, zero, zilch exceptions. It might as well be a law in Texas, and it certainly was one in the JLWC, punishable, I was afraid, by rejection on first sight.)

"Well, ah, don't you look . . . just like you," I stated with an enthusiasm I didn't feel.

Nikki beamed and twirled. "Let me tell you, it was hard to come up with an outfit with bows and pearls that could be amazing, but I managed. Can you believe it?"

It is difficult to manage the byways of indirect speech when you have someone asking direct questions, even when it is a simple "Can you believe it?" that can easily be ignored as rhetorical. I experienced the very real desire to tell her just exactly what I thought of her attire. (*You look like a party cake at a fifteen-year-old South Willow Creek girl's* quinceañera). But years of training in the Right Sort of Behavior prevailed and I swallowed the impulse (my mother would have been proud) and said, "No, I can hardly believe it."

"I know!" She ran her hands over the bow. "I've come a long way since my mama made me wear hand-me-downs and thrift-store rejects."

I started to ask about her mother, then stopped myself because I really didn't want to know. I had only seen Marlene Bishop a handful of times. Once, when I was ten, I went over to the Bishops' house, our family driver taking me through the dirt roads to the ramshackle trailer park in the wrong part of Willow Creek. When I saw the kind of neighborhood Nikki lived in I was astounded. Our livestock lived in better conditions than Nikki.

I was in the big black Cadillac Rado used to take my mother to town instead of the truck he normally used to drop me off at school. Immensely insightful even back then, I told Rado to drop me off a block away and wait for me at the 7-Eleven convenience store instead of in front of Nikki's house as my mother had instructed. When he said no, swearing my mother would have his hide on a stretcher before the day was out if he did as asked, I just smiled my trademark smile and mentioned (ever so innocently) the pint of whiskey he kept stored in the truck's glove compartment that I couldn't imagine he would want my daddy to know about.

He dropped me off at the 7-Eleven.

For all the good it did me.

My surprise visit was not well received. Marlene Bishop didn't need another kid to take care of (clearly she hadn't been raised with my mother's school of thought that the child should wait on the mother, not the other way around) and sent me back down the rickety wooden steps. Nikki caught up to me, apologizing, explaining how she didn't have a daddy to help out her mom, which made her mom tired and crabby and . . . But I just kept walking. I was so confused by the whole incident that I forgot that Rado was waiting for me in the Cadillac. When we got to the parking lot, Rado leaning up against the car sipping a Slurpee, Nikki took one look at the car and the man in a driver's cap, then turned around and ran away as fast as she could, her heels kicking up her stained and wrinkled dress.

The next week at school we didn't say a word about it. But the ease she'd always had around me and even Pilar disappeared.

DESPITE NIKKI'S RED-BOW-AND-PEARLS ATTIRE, as soon as we walked farther into Palace Grout, I was relieved to see the butler dressed in tails and white gloves, and ecstatic when I saw two maids attired in black uniforms with white aprons, their hair pulled back in neat buns. The place looked picture perfect even if Nikki did not.

Just off the living room, we proceeded into a white-tiled receiving room where a Louis XIV server was covered with beautifully prepared cucumber sandwiches, pastel-colored petits fours (I chose to ignore the unfortunate *G*s iced onto the top), and a silver coffee urn. Bone-china coffee cups and saucers were lined up with perfect precision.

But the *pièce de résistance* was the lovely silver punch bowl filled with the Texas requisite, sweetened iced tea, mint sprigs floating on top. A silver ladle and etched crystal (not china) cups with saucers stood to the side.

I know my silver, and I knew on sight that Nikki Grout was serving tea from a Grand Baroque silver bowl by Wallace.

A Texas lady began her training at an early age, learning to walk, talk, and sit properly, then moving on to dancing and etiquette. She learned about stationery, linens, and most importantly, the use of china and silver. A girl from a truly good family had silver that was handed down to her. Though if no one had died yet and the silver was still in use by a preceding generation, then a pattern could be bought, one that went well with the one that would one day be passed down.

Francis I by Reed and Barton was one of the most popular patterns, its ornate design of fruit and leaves speaking to the lady who had high expectations for all that she deserved. The Texas girl learned things like the fact that Francis I should never be mixed with Chantilly by Gorham, a sweet pattern that would look plain in comparison. And anyone who was anyone knew that you never mixed Strasbourg by Gorham with Buttercup by the same maker. Not even the names were compatible.

There were more patterns, and I knew them all, but just then I only cared that Nikki was serving tea with one of the finest silver patterns of them all. Moreover, she was using true silver and not silver plate. Silver plate would have been a deal breaker.

Next to the bowl, the china cups were set out. They were a lovely, white bone set with finely painted flowers, by Tiffany I knew without upending a single dish.

The crystal was beautifully cut. The napkins were white linen. I was feeling better about the chances of this tea working by the second.

"Nikki, this is lovely."

"Yeah, I did like you said. No mimosas or champagne." She looked disappointed, but then the doorbell rang.

"It's time!" Nikki fiddled with her pearls and looked like an actor trying to get into a part. "Okay, I'm not going to mess this up. I'm ready."

Though no one in the JLWC was ready for Nikki Grout's foray into the *soirée intime*, including *moi*.

THE FIRST FIVE women I had invited arrived promptly, each wearing a variation of my cream clothes with single strands of pearls. Each of the ladies experienced a moment of shock over the sight of Nikki's attire, but like me, they were too polite to mention it.

There were the Twins, as they were fondly called, Deena and Deandra Ducette.

"Aren't you two the cutest things!" Nikki enthused. "You match!"

More accurately, they coordinated (a plus in home decorating, but not when applied to two grown women who should have stopped matching or even coordinating after they graduated from first grade).

I had invited the Twins because I knew if I had included only one of them, they would have talked about everything anyway, so why not use them both for my trial run. Plus, the Twins were the sweetest (and most naïve) members; they loved everyone.

Mara Burke arrived next. She was a year younger than me, was pretty (in a plain way), smart (hid it well), and never tried too hard to fit in. I'd be able to gather a lot from the way she dealt with Nikki.

Olivia Mortimer followed, joined by Leticia Godwin. Both were Sustainers who spent most of the year traveling with their retired husbands. If things went terribly wrong they wouldn't be around often enough to do much damage.

My mother had yet to arrive.

For half a second I had considered inviting Pilar, but I hadn't a clue how she felt about Nikki anymore. Besides, as we know, I'm not her favorite person. I'd like to say that it started with our little battle over the new project, but it went deeper . . . or should I say, farther back than that, building through the years. It started in high school when I tried out for cheerleader and she did not. I became even more popular, surrounded by friends, and she started spending her lunches in the debate room. Even later, at our debutante ball, which should have been no competition, I managed to trump her there as well. Though only because she had just started college in that blue state up North by then, and had come back for the winter ball looking, well, not so Texas-debutantish. Her father had sighed (he was, after all, the one who had to present her), saying, "Why can't you be more like Frede Hildebrand?"

The bottom line is I didn't think it would be the best idea to ask Pilar to do me anything that might be perceived as a favor.

At the tea, I made introductions all around, doing my best to promote conversation between Nikki and the members. At first, there was more sound coming from the rustle of Nikki's taffeta bow than her mouth, as if she were afraid to say a single word.

"You have nothing to worry about," I told her quietly. "Just relax."

I would have told her to be herself, but I wasn't exactly sure what that was other than overly cheerful and gaudily dressed. Maybe "nervous" was better.

The ladies seemed more interested in the house than in the woman they were there to meet, but they were too polite to ask for a tour. I had already told Nikki that she shouldn't offer a tour under any circumstance, and she had reluctantly agreed. I didn't dare risk an excursion that might take us to the Tropical Greek Island or the African Safari Room and the man who did his business in it.

By noon, things were no better. Realistically, this sort of tea would last an hour. We were barely halfway through and already conversation was growing more strained. Worse yet, my mother still hadn't arrived and I was worried that she was sending a message by consciously snubbing the event.

"Frede," Nikki whispered frantically. "This is horrible. I can tell that everyone wants to leave. You have to do something!"

What was I going to do? I had talked more and smiled more in thirty minutes than I had in my life. Though I wasn't a quitter . . . especially since I still needed five more sponsors.

"Fine, let me see what I can do."

"Thank you! I'll go out and get Maria to bring in more tea and cucumber sandwiches."

"Good idea."

I went over to Leticia and asked about the roses she entered in the Garden Club's annual rose contest. The response was lackluster. I tried to discuss a new china pattern I had heard Tiffany & Co. was launching with Olivia and Leticia. I got only a grumble of displeasure. I even offered up dubious compliments about the Twins' attire. But no one was taking the bait and running with conversation.

It was Nikki who finally got them to talk when she returned, the maids following in her wake like ladies-in-waiting. She asked Mara about her child. One simple question. "Do you have kids?"

Next thing I knew, Mara was going on about her son who had just been admitted into the prestigious Brookdale Preschool honors program. The Twins were all ears because they were hoping their children would soon be gaining *entrée* to the exclusive school. And who knew that both Olivia's and Leticia's children had walked those same hallowed halls?

A single question about a woman's precocious toddler and the group was off and running as if they were long-lost friends.

Then the unthinkable happened. Olivia asked if they could have a tour of the house. She just asked. Point-blank. As though that were *normal*.

"Here, here!" Leticia agreed, raising her crystal cup of sweet tea. "A tour."

I was so stunned I felt light-headed. Nikki had found a way to get them to open up, then practically turn them into her best friends. All by talking about children.

"If you're sure," Nikki said.

I tried to wave her off, but the women were already on their way. I didn't know what else to do but follow along, my brain already scrambling for possible explanations for the tackiness that lay ahead.

What happened, however, was that after only a room or two, I threw in the towel. I stopped caring about what they saw or that the party could easily turn out to be the social disaster of the season. I, who had always been the center of attention, the one who had plotted and planned for the perfect party, was no longer concerned about what the ladies of the League would find in Palace Grout. I ate my finger sandwich and sipped my tea and followed along like a visitor to the Dallas Metropolitan Museum of Art with Nikki as our guide.

The girls saw it all. The African Safari Room, replete with a cigar-smoking, phone-bellowing Howard (wearing a Western-cut suit and even a tie, no doubt meant to impress in his own gauche way) giving a quick wave of welcome before he bellowed something else into the receiver.

The maids followed after us, offering more sandwiches and more tea in each room where we stopped. The girls were laughing, chatting, and having a great time. The potential social disaster had turned into a social coup. And amazingly, the farther along we went the more relieved I became. Walking through Nikki's house, I couldn't remember a party going so well. Suddenly I was glad that my mother had decided not to attend.

After covering the entire first floor, then proceeding upstairs, we ended up in Nikki's bedroom, where she threw open the doors to her closet.

We all gaped at the size.

I have a lot of clothes, but Nikki Grout's closet could have passed for a medium-sized boutique. A crystal chandelier hung from the ceiling and the walls were painted pink with matching pink carpet. I had a glimmer of a thought, something about being caught up in the swirl of a cotton-candy machine, but it was gone before it settled.

The ladies gasped and walked inside as if drawn into a foreign world filled with clothes purchased from what had to be places like Wild Wear, My Spicy Treasure, or even Bizarre Bazaar, because there wasn't a lady in the Junior League of Willow Creek who would have clothes like those. Everything was feathered, bangled, or beaded with plenty of sparkle thrown in for good measure. Rack after rack of boas, animal prints, sequined tops, and jeweled bottoms.

It was as if Nikki couldn't help herself when she wrapped a black and brown boa around her neck. She kicked off her plain white sandals and put on a pair of leopard-print mules. Even I laughed. And even I joined in with the group when they started adding feather boas and sequined shawls to their own demure attire.

I can't begin to explain the change that came over me, the feeling of those hot-pink feathers sliding across my neck, the tickle on my face. All I could think was it was delicious. My vocabulary is *très* gigantic, but "delicious" isn't one of my words. But that's what I felt. My mother and Gordon weren't a thought or a worry. I kicked off my own tasteful shoes and found a pair of four-inch stilettos.

I pulled on a giant floppy hat with a glittery band, and barely recognized my reflection in one of the full-length mirrors that stood between the racks of shimmery clothes. Getting Nikki into the League seemed like the smartest thing I had ever done.

Smart. Bold. Daring.

And very, very wrong, I realized a few minutes later when two things happened. First, and amazingly the lesser of the two unfolding disasters, was that one of the Twins pulled out a tiny piece of material.

"Lord have mercy, Nikki, what is this? A scarf, or . . ." Deandra's words trailed off since there wasn't enough material to wrap around anything, not to mention the odd straps that made it look more like a face mask than anything else.

Nikki laughed and took a playful air swipe at Deandra. "That's no scarf, silly! It's a bathing suit bottom."

You'd think she had produced a flawless, fifty-five-karat diamond for the sudden oohing interest the little group had. We all leaned in to have a look.

"But how do you . . . well, keep from showing . . ." Deandra's words trailed off.

Nikki wasn't so inhibited. "How to keep from showing any hair down there?"

From the startled look on Deandra's face, it was a safe bet she hadn't been thinking hair.

But Nikki didn't notice. "It's easy! You get a Brazilian."

There would have been more shock, I assure you, if anyone in the room but Nikki and *moi* had known what a Brazilian was.

"What is that?" Deandra wanted to know, thinking, erroneously, that she was on safer ground.

"A wax. And Lordy, does it hurt. They just slather wax on your unmentionables and rip, hair gone. Smooth as a peach."

This time the girls were shocked, embarrassed . . . and mortified to be caught in such a conversation. The good mood evaporated in the room. But not before none other than my mother walked into the little dress-up party like a queen making an entrance. Everyone froze as Blythe Hildebrand took in the scene.

"Good Lord, Fredericka. I smell alcohol. Have you been drinking?"

Chapter Eleven

If at first you fall on your face the only acceptable response is to pick yourself up, refluff your hair, and go on bigger and better than ever. Wallowing in self-pity, or, worse yet, apologizing, is unacceptable. Even acknowledging that you bungled something is beaucoup *unacceptable. It shows weakness, and being weak is far far worse than making a mistake. Moreover, if you hold your head high and you navigate a blunder carefully, most people will forget that you ever made one.*

I LIVED MY ENTIRE LIFE by this philosophy. Which was why when my mother entered the extravagant dressing room, her still tastefully colored, dark blond hair swept back, curling perfectly just below her jaw, her barely gray sweater set and matching skirt making her look steely, I did little more than blink at the shock of what she said, stiffen at the realization that it was true—the suddenly happy ladies were caused by spiked tea, not Nikki's magnetic personality.

"Heavens, Mother, aren't you the dramatic one today."

Another tip: if at all possible, deny, deny, deny.

"Bless your heart, we haven't been drinking," I added.

Of course the other ladies were suddenly looking around as if for the first time noticing they were in someone's closet draped and swathed in items that were not JLWC acceptable. But they weren't without brains.

"Uh, drinking, Blythe?" Olivia said. "Nonsense."

"Utter nonsense," Leticia added for support.

I threw the hot-pink boa more firmly around my shoulders. "Nikki, a masquerade ball will be just the thing come fall. How great of you to think of it."

It helped to be able to think on your feet when you needed to get out of a sticky situation. Fortunately the other guests had enough sense to agree. "Yes, a masquerade!"

Pathetic, yes, that a group of grown women could be reduced to the stance of guilty grade-schoolers. But my mother had a way about her—and far too much power within the Junior League to ignore.

The minute a hint of doubt crept into my mother's perfectly made-up face, the group took advantage of the moment. You've never seen five proper ladies shed clothing so fast and flee from the room without so much as a thank-you tossed over the shoulder.

It didn't take long before it was just me, my mother, and Nikki Grout facing one another. Doubt had been replaced by suspicion on my mother's face, so I reminded her of the time she was sure Daddy had been drinking and it turned out he had been in the barn dealing with the breech birth of a calf. "Your nose isn't known to be the most reliable."

"Humph," was all she said, then turned with the flourish of a disgruntled despot, retraced her steps, and left the palace.

A complete disaster had been avoided. Not that I wasn't totally angry with Nikki. Spiking the tea was bad enough, but what respectable sort of woman gets a Brazilian wax, much less talks about it?

If "No shaving above the knee" ranks high on the list of Things Not to Do, you can imagine how "No waxing of intimate parts" ranks. It was so out of bounds that a proper woman wouldn't even think about it in order to put it on the list.

"This isn't working," I said simply, then headed for the stairs.

"Frede! I'm sorry!" She ran after me. "I was nervous and wasn't thinking. I shouldn't have spiked the tea."

I kept going. She didn't even know that the tea was only part of the problem.

"I just wanted them to like me!"

That stopped me and I turned back. "Nikki, when are you going to learn that the harder you try the less people *will* like you? You always tried too hard." My head snapped back at the directness of what I had just said. I could only blame it on the tea.

"I'm not perfect like you, Frede. I just want to fit in."

Thankfully I had gotten ahold of my wayward tongue and bit back the fact that she would never fit in, at least not in my world. And I was through trying to make it happen.

I headed down the stairs and found a very dangerous-looking (if spluttering) Howard Grout standing in the foyer.

"Where the hell did everyone go?" he bellowed. Then he saw his wife's tear-streaked face. "What the hell did you do to my Nikki?"

There it was again, the protectiveness that did strange things to me, made me feel wistful and empty. "I didn't do anything, Mr. Grout. I suggest you ask your wife what she did."

Then I was gone, out the door, back to my house to concentrate on refluffing my hair.

"QUÉ PASÓ?" Nina inquired when she found me in my bedroom a few hours later.

"I'm hungover."

She screeched a number of things, but my brain wasn't translating as quickly as it normally did. I only managed to gather, "In the middle of the day?"

"My thoughts exactly."

My other thought was that I hadn't a clue what I was going to do about my current situation. I didn't know how I would find my husband or my money without Howard's help, or without all of Willow Creek knowing the true state of my affairs. But it didn't matter. I was done trying to get Nikki into the League.

I thought about going to the police, but that made my head hurt all the more. "I need some coffee."

"How did theese happen?"

It was as I told the tale (Nina clucking her combination of sympathy and outrage) that the doorbell rang.

"I'm not here," I told my maid.

As soon as I got home I had changed into an elegant peignoir set of white cotton, ruffled high collar, with a pretty pink satin bow (of an acceptable size). I curled down into my exquisite sheets and waited for Nina to send whoever it was on their way.

Unfortunately, it was Howard, and he wasn't one to take no for an answer. Even Nina was no match for the man, that or he didn't speak Spanish and had no clue she was badgering him to leave.

"I know you're up there," he bellowed into my foyer, the sound echoing up the stairs. If he had just yelled *Stella!* it would have been a regular *Streetcar Named Desire* moment, sans, of course, any outraged desire.

Nina unloaded a satisfying barrage of truly despicable Spanish, which only made Howard laugh.

"You're a feisty one, little lady."

By then I had come to the top of the stairs, wrapper held securely at my neck, and was in time to see Nina blush. I kid you not.

When he saw me, he started up the stairs. He still wore the suit, but the tie was loosened, and I noticed he wore a flashy pair of alligator-skin cowboy boots.

"Stop right there," I said.

It didn't look like he wanted to, but he held up his hands. "Fine, have it your way. You've got me by the short hairs and we both know it."

Short hairs? I grimaced.

"Mr. Grout, as I said to your wife, this isn't working."

"I know, she told me. That's why I'm here. I want you to reconsider. She didn't mean any harm."

"I know that she didn't, but the fact is, she's . . . just not right for the JLWC."

Clearly the alcohol hadn't worn off completely.

I expected him to get all dangerous-looking again. Instead he surprised me. "Maybe not on the outside," he conceded, "but underneath all her feathers, my Nikki has a heart of gold. And isn't the Junior League all about helping people and doing good?"

Well, yes, but—

"Hell, Frede. Don't turn your back on her now. Give her another chance." He studied me in a way that actually made it easy to imagine how this ruddy-faced, wiry-haired, barrel-chested Texan managed to win so many unwinnable cases. "For old time's sake," he added.

An appeal to sentiment. It had worked on my mother, sort of, and I felt it working on me. He must have sensed it because he smiled and went for the kill.

"She mighta made some mistakes, but she can do better. And if anyone can help her get in, it's you. We both know that."

An appeal to vanity. He was getting closer.

"You can get my Nikki into the club. Then she'll donate time and money and whatever the hell you gals want."

He was smarter than he looked because he seemed to sense that time, money, and "whatever the hell we gals want" wasn't enough, so he added, "And I've gotten a lead on that flaky husband of yours. You don't want me to stop now, do you?"

Check and mate.

"Well, we would have to do some work on things like . . . not spiking the sweet tea."

He chuckled, then caught himself. "You name it, she'll do it."

"I'd have to coach her in how to carry herself."

"Done."

"Coach her" was an understatement. Nikki would need to be razed to her trailer-park roots, stripped of her nouveau riche trappings, and rebuilt as a lady.

"And just so you know," he added, "because of how much I appreciate all you're doing, I am paying the private investigator's fees and such out of my own pocket."

I shuddered. It kept coming back to that. Me and my lack of means.

He considered for a second, then added, "And if you need any cash until we get this straightened out, I'm happy to dole out a few grand. All you have to do is ask."

Money. No spelling, just straightforward need of cold hard cash. The worst of the worst. This ill-bred man offering me money.

I looked him in the eye and smiled. "Why, Mr. Grout, aren't you the sweetest thing. But I'm fine. Really. In fact, I'm close to having my big show set up at the gallery, and I'm sure it's going to be a huge success."

"Then you got everything set up with that fairy artist fella?"

Actually, no. "We spoke the other day when I visited his studio." This wasn't a lie. "I'll be sure the girls at the gallery send you and Nikki the details when I have everything arranged." I wanted him out of my house. "Tell Nikki that I'll call her to set up a time when we can talk about a few things."

"I think you should come over now."

"What?"

Everything about my neighbor changed. He shifted his weight uncomfortably, then he let loose with a surge of words, saying things like "she's upset," "doesn't even want to eat." An impression started to form that he was implying I, me, *moi*, was responsible for putting her off eating.

"Howard, I haven't a clue what you're talking about."

"Nikki, damn it! She's depressed and I can't stand to sit by with her upset and all." Then his tone settled and got surprisingly soft. It hardly seemed possible. "If you just came over and talked to her, told her that it's going to be all right, I'm sure she'll perk right up."

"Me? Why me?"

His exasperated sigh shuddered up the staircase. "Because you're her friend."

Can you say *très* awkward?

Of course I wasn't her friend, but all my subtle excuses that really meant N-O weren't sinking in with the thickheaded man. And I'd had all the being direct I could stomach for a while.

"Fine. Let me get presentable, then I'll be over."

I could tell he wanted me to come running right then, but he must have had a tiny bit of savvy and realized I wasn't a woman to go anywhere without being properly attired.

"How long?"

I raised a brow. "About an hour or so."

"Hell, woman, you're not going to a ball at the governor's mansion."

As if I could get ready for a ball in an hour.

"If that's too long, then perhaps you should find someone else."

"Damnation. Just hurry."

He marched back down the stairs and banged out the front door. Nina still stood there, and, I swear, she had a look of true concern on her face.

"You going, yes?" she said.

This meant I had better go or else. I had heard the tone my entire life, though I only paid attention to it when it suited me. I told myself it suited me because it kept my lawyer hunting down my missing husband.

"Of course I'm going. I've always been a good neighbor."

I think she might have snorted as she disappeared down the hallway to the kitchen.

I dressed in a light pink miniherringbone blouse, tucked into pink, light-wool gabardine trousers, with a pale mint silk cotton cardigan draped over my shoulders. I went with three strands of pearls (always worn in odd numbers) that skimmed my collarbone and a pair of bone leather Ferragamos. It was my version of cheerful dressing, and I looked lovely.

I had Nina put together another basket of goodies, then I was off. What I found when I arrived at Palace Grout was enough to put me off lunch for a week.

"Thank God, you're here," Howard said, taking the basket in one hand, without regard for the precariously placed baked goods, and my arm in the other. "She's up here."

He set the basket on the floor, dragged me up the stairs to their bedroom, then nudged me inside. Howard, however, didn't follow.

It couldn't have been more than four or five hours since I'd been there earlier for the infamous tea, but now the room was a mess. The giant bed was unmade, and Nikki was curled up in the sheets, wrapped in a rhinestone-studded warm-up suit. Crying.

I think I've made it clear I don't do emotion, most especially crying.

Her hair was askew and she looked wretched. I would have turned around and left, but as much as I didn't want to admit it, she reminded me of me just after I found out that Gordon had run away with Miss Mouse.

I walked over and, after a moment's hesitation, I sat down on the edge of the bed.

"Nikki, sugar, can I get you some tea?"

I didn't ask her what was wrong because I didn't want to know. My only mission was to cheer her up.

"What do you think of my new *ensemble*?" I asked.

I gave the rolling *ble* like a true Parisian, and it got a look from Nikki.

"What?" she asked, as if I were speaking gibberish.

I gestured to myself. "My outfit. I just got it. What do you think?"

She started crying again. "I can't dress right. They think I'm white trash. They don't want me in the Junior League."

True. True. Very true.

"That's not true, sugar."

"My tea was a disaster. Everyone pretty much ignored me when they left, but Olivia and Leticia were hateful."

And they had been. Flying out the door, Olivia had let it be known we wouldn't be getting her support. Leticia had agreed.

It was very awkward, all that truth lying out before me. Then I surprised myself when I took her hand. "Olivia and Leticia don't have the sense God gave a chicken. And after we polish you up a bit, we'll find plenty more women in the Junior League who will adore you."

Then something worse happened. She looked at me with those big Bambi eyes of hers, all glistening with leftover tears. "Do you think? Howie said you're going to fix me up. Do you think it'll work?"

Before I could answer, she started gushing like a burst water faucet. I don't mean gushing over me and my new outfit. She started talking and talking, acting as if we were still back in junior high.

"Oh, Frede, I'm so glad you're here. I don't have anyone to talk to, not really. I love my Howard, but he's a guy and he doesn't understand when I tell him it's like I'm afraid everything around me isn't real. Like I'm going to wake up one morning and it'll all turn out to be a dream. I'll be back in South Willow Creek in that trailer without two pennies to rub together. And it isn't the money I love about my Howie. I swear to God, it isn't. He's the sweetest, kindest man in all of Texas. And I love him." She got this sort of shy look on her face, then added, "And he loves me too. Can you believe it? Someone as great as Howard Grout loves me."

The whole conversation was way too Psych 101 for me. I didn't want to know about Nikki or her feelings. But Nikki couldn't be turned off, and believe it or not, I'm not so self-absorbed that I didn't realize that to do such a thing and leave, as I wanted to, would have crushed her.

"You know," I said as politely as I could, "talking is really overrated. Why don't you get up and take a bath. I'm sure you'll feel better after that."

"Frede." She grabbed my hand. "I've got to get into the Junior League. I've just got to."

"Nikki—"

"It's weird to have money but not be able to be friends with other people around here who have money too." With a jerk, she yanked her legs up Indian style on the bed, then dashed the back of her hand across her face, her gaze intent. "The first week of April we're having a big fancy dinner party with a bunch of important guests. I know they're only coming because of Howard's money, which means they'll get here and be real stiff. But if I were in the Junior League, I just know they'd be nicer to me."

It was pathetic and I didn't want to hear another word. But then she said something else, all that intense energy hissing out of her like air out of a helium balloon.

"It's like I'm stuck between two places and don't fit into either one. The people I knew in South Willow Creek don't like me anymore because I'm rich now. They say I put on airs."

She sighed, and rude or not, I wanted out of there because somehow, at some level, I knew what was coming next.

"And then fine-mannered people like you won't give me the time of day because I'm still considered white trash."

Hearing the words said out loud was beyond unacceptable. Not that they weren't true, it's just that harsh truths should be avoided, or at the very least, candy coated. But there was something else as well. It was during our last month of junior high. Pilar, Nikki, and I were still best friends. We walked into Jimbo's, the Willow Creek Junior High crowd's favorite hangout. It was going to be our final hurrah since we were sure that no respectable ninth-grader would go to an ice-cream parlor. It just wasn't done.

The three of us walked in as usual, and headed for Our Table—the popular one. But instead of Betty, our usual waitress, none other than Nikki's mother, Marlene, appeared, replete with apron, paper hat, and order pad. "What can I get you girls?"

It was a shock that was felt around the world, or at least around our table, which at the time really did seem like our whole world.

"Mama, what are you doing here?" Nikki could barely get the words out of her mouth.

"Today's my first day. Jimbo himself hired me." Marlene leaned closer. "He's paying me a full twenty-five cents an hour more than he normally pays his waitresses." She preened her short, curly hair.

It was hard enough that Marlene acted more like a teenager than Nikki, but Marlene working at Jimbo's and announcing to the world that she was impressed by twenty-five cents more an hour (not to mention maybe doing a little extracurricular work for Jimbo after hours since he had given her such a deal) was more than Nikki could take, I guess.

"I hate you," Nikki breathed, then she scrambled out of the booth and fled the shop.

Pilar and I exchanged a glance. Talk about an awkward moment. We grimaced uncomfortably, then placed our orders. We didn't follow Nikki since we both knew that there was nothing to say about this horror. A mother who acted like Marlene, went through boyfriends like my mother went through maids (Nina notwithstanding), and now had to get a job at Jimbo's for all her friends to see? It was hugely embarrassing.

When Marlene returned with our orders and a heavy sigh, I didn't have a clue what to say. Pilar didn't have the same problem.

"Hello," she said with a snort, "where are my sprinkles?"

Pilar, Miss Sensitive.

The day Nikki saw my daddy's limousine had started the strain, but looking back, the day at Jimbo's had made a break inevitable. Somehow, I had started to realize, our worlds didn't work together—and Nikki was coming out the loser.

Sitting next to Nikki so many years later, I shook myself out of my thoughts and surprised myself when I offered her the only thing I could. "Starting tomorrow at noon, over lunch at my house, we're going to turn you into the classiest lady in Willow Creek." We didn't have a minute to lose. "On the night of your big dinner party, you are going to be the picture of elegance and everyone in Willow Creek is going to be amazed at Nikki Grout. After that, we'll have members lining up to sponsor you for the League."

"Really?" She sniffed and wiped her nose again.

"Yes, really."

"You think I can do it?"

"Of course you can." She would have me as her teacher.

Nikki threw her arms around me. "Oh, Frede, you're the best."

"Yes, well."

I pulled away, already wondering how I was going to turn this flashy duck into a fabulous swan.

Chapter Twelve

I KNEW IMMEDIATELY that I would rue the day I agreed to play Henry Higgins and turn Nikki into a lady. But how else was I going to get her into the Junior League?

With one single tea she had proven that she didn't know the first thing about any sort of proper behavior for a lady of quality—at least a lady in Texas. Botswana, maybe. Or even Newark, New Jersey. But I couldn't imagine getting the support Nikki would need to join the JLWC as she was.

In the plus column, thankfully, I had one thing going for me: technically it wouldn't be hard to find five more women who had known her for the requisite five years because she had gone to school with many of us since grade school and had lived in Willow Creek her whole life. However, getting five more women willing to risk their reputations for her was another matter altogether.

To get it done, I would have to take on the *comportement* of a general plotting to win a war. And let me tell you, a war it would be. But there were three reasons I was willing to take on the job:

1. Quite frankly, I didn't have much choice. What lawyer out there, at least what lawyer with talent and the—excuse my French—balls to go up against Gordon's family, would take me on sans m-o-n-e-y? (I was back to spelling, which reassured me that I was

getting back to being myself.) And even if those other lawyers did have talent and were willing to take me on for some sort of payment at the back end, they would no doubt be publicity hounds who would drag my good name and beautifully perfect photo through the newspapers on a daily basis to get attention for themselves. I'd rather make over Nikki Grout and get her into the Junior League.

2. I had a secret. I was bored. Fabulous clothes, gads (albeit now missing gads) of money, and night after night of all the right parties were losing their appeal. Sure, it sounded *fabu* on paper, but in reality, it was a lot of work. You had to wear the perfect clothes, the right jewelry (impressive but not too flashy—with the exception of diamond engagement rings), and keep track of who was doing what to make sure you didn't RSVP *oui* to a party given by someone who was in the process of desperately trying to save face. (A list I was doing my best to stay off.) It was exhausting work, not for the faint of heart.

3. I never could resist a challenge. My mother always said it was because I had to have everything my way. I say, What's wrong with having everything my way? As I see it, it's not my job to make anything anyone else's way.

Given my predicament, I developed a three-part plan:

1. teach Nikki how to act like a lady,
2. find five other women willing to sponsor her,
3. have her ready in time for the night of her big party to launch her into Willow Creek Society.

When I felt a quiver of "I can't do this" regret (which in itself was so disturbingly unlike me) I did the only reasonable thing I could. I shopped. Who doesn't? It's a known mood elevator, and one that is acceptable to most any woman of the JLWC, unlike all those nonnatural mood elevators like yoga and meditation.

I had every intention of shopping madly as I drove straight to the better stores in Willow Creek Square, just off Hildebrand Avenue, and tried to concentrate on new summer fashions. But my heart wasn't in it and I was heading back to The Willows in under an hour.

On the way home I decided to check on any progress Howard might have made with "the lead" he had gotten. It had been two weeks since my husband left the house and hadn't returned. If I had been the desperate type I would have been swallowing back anxiety like a cowboy throwing back tequila shots. Given that it was me we were talking about, I just called my lawyer to ask the status.

He answered on the first ring.

"What can I do for ya, baby doll?"

"Any progress on that lead you mentioned?" I asked brightly.

He muttered and cursed. "He's a slippery son of a gun, but I've got a whole army of high-paid people searching. So far, we've traced him to the Caribbean. Listen, that's my other line. I'll call when I've narrowed it down even more."

He hung up on me, me Frede . . . You know the rest.

I hadn't flipped the phone shut before it rang. "Hello?"

"Fredericka, this is your mother."

"Bonjour, maman."

"You and your French."

I really am a trial to my mother, even when I'm not trying to be.

"Good morning, Mother," I amended.

"Are you sober yet?"

Ah, so I hadn't fooled her after all. "Mother," I cajoled.

"Don't 'mother' me. I know funny business when I see it. And I hope you've finally seen the light and are done with Nikki Grout. I had a call earlier, and there is talk among the powers that be (read: my mother and her friends) about you becoming president-elect of the League next year."

A thrill shot through me. I had dreamed of being president since I was young. My mother expected it. I anticipated it. But even better, if I became president-elect next year, I would become the youngest president in JLWC history.

"Don't do anything to ruin that, Fredericka."

My excitement froze. But then I assured myself that given my standing in the League, no one could undermine my bid at this point.

I didn't mention any of that, just as I didn't think it was such a good time to tell my mother I was about to get more involved with Nikki than ever.

"But that's not why I'm calling," she said.

Thank God.

"What is going on with Gordon?"

"Nothing, Mother." My free hand tightened on the steering wheel. "He's traveling. We've been over this."

"Yes, we have. And didn't you mention to Susan Davies that he was in New Mexico or some heathen place like that?"

Sometimes conversing with my mother was like playing chess. You had to anticipate her moves, and I had a distinct feeling this was going somewhere I wasn't going to like. "New Guinea."

She humphed her success. "New *Wherever.* I had lunch with Marg Chadwick and she swears she saw Gordon at the Ritz in Grand Cayman."

Howard Grout and all his well-paid minions had nothing on my mother and her network of spies.

"Grand Cayman? Of course he's in Grand Cayman." As ever, quick on my feet. "You don't think our Gordon could stay in any one place for an entire month, do you?"

"He isn't *my* anything, unless 'my greatest lament' counts as a possession. And didn't you say he'd be gone for three weeks?"

"Three to four weeks." It was time to put the shoe on the other foot. "What is wrong, Mother? Why are you all worked up about Gordon? You're acting positively overwrought."

A good Junior Leaguer in Texas could be ever so slightly dramatic as long as she had the old-family pedigree that allowed it, but no respectable woman would ever be thought of as *over*wrought. Saying that to my mother was a low blow, but I was desperate.

"Well, I never . . ."

Blythe Hildebrand sniffed her insult and hung up. I quickly redialed my phone.

"Frede, doll, I know I'm irresistible, but—"

"Howard, I have a lead on my husband. Try the Ritz in Grand Cayman." Then I flipped the phone closed. It felt good to hang up on him for a change.

I drove the rest of the way home with visions of revenge dancing in my head. Serving burgers at Sonic Happy Eating wasn't good enough, I realized. Good manners or not, when I found Gordon's lying, cheating hide and had recaptured my wealth, I would call in a favor. A reporter I knew owed me after I had gotten him an exclusive, one-on-one interview with Barbara Bush the last time she was in town signing books at the Junior League Christmas Fair. I'd get Beau Bracken to write a front-page article in the *Willow Creek Times* to let the town know just what a lying, cheating, thieving man my husband truly was. Once my future was secured, I could afford to be a little on the eccentric side.

Feeling better knowing that my husband would squirm soon enough, I pulled into the drive, curving around to the front door, and found yet another unknown car parked on my masterly laid red bricks. Though this one was a Lexus, and since Gordon seemed to have a preference for women of a lesser sort, I wasn't too worried that another *amour* of my husband's had landed on my front step.

I pushed in through the doorway.

"Frede! In here!"

Believe it or not, all that cheer was coming from the boxy, black-clad, unsmiling Pilar Bass. Which made me grimace. Not because of the cheer, but because her being there reminded me of what day it was. Wednesday. New Projects Committee meeting day. I had forgotten again.

"Nina let me in. I hope you don't mind, but I had to see you."

I'll bet. She might not like me anymore, but it wasn't difficult to figure out that she was there to grovel after having questioned my judgment regarding the list of potential New Projects candidates. The big smile and sunshiny cheer gave her away.

Pilar knew as well as I did that no one in the League got anywhere without Frede Ware's say-so. It drove her crazy that money and looks meant more than brains. That was why, I swear, she loved living in the Northeast. From everything I could tell, up there in Flailing-elbowville it appeared that the only time looks mattered was if you were a runway model. Brains trumped all. Well, brains and any sort of money (new or old) since a person could do very well in New York City without an old-moneyed name . . . and/or manners. (Think Donald Trump or that Behar woman on the television show *The View*—pretty now that she's all Botoxed up, but the mouth on her? My mother would be appalled.) But that wasn't the case in Willow Creek, Texas. And now that my money had gone missing, for the first time I wondered if perhaps a place like New York might have something to offer after all. Anonymity. Not that I would need it, mind you. I was getting my money back, I was certain. I had to, because all it would take was for word to get out that my wealth had gone missing and no more groveling from people like Pilar. I wasn't sure I could get used to people not groveling.

"Don't you look chic in all your black," I said with my own luminous smile.

She didn't know how to take that and her brows furrowed.

"So tell me, Pilar, what brings you to my neck of the woods?"

"Ah, well"—the smile returned—"I just wanted to tell you that I was wrong to question your decision. Plus, after reading your notes, I realized that the idea I mentioned actually goes well with your *amazing* expertise in art!"

Exclamation marks *and* flattery from Pilar? She must be desperate to get back in my good graces.

"You see, I'm calling my idea 'Art Stars.' We get Texas artists to give art classes to underprivileged children. Stars of the art world turning kids into Art Stars!" Then she got ahold of her excitement. "Though it's just an idea, and we can't do any project without you. So whatever new project we end up doing, I hope you'll come back to the group. Everyone was there today, our entire committee, and it just wasn't the same without you. I hope you aren't upset."

I waved my hand as if waving the words away, my pink diamond engagement ring catching beautifully in the sun that streamed in through my windows. "Pilar, sugar, I never gave it another thought."

We both knew that wasn't true. But true or not, my superior smile froze when the doorbell rang.

I glanced at the clock. Five minutes until noon. I had forgotten all about Nikki.

Nina generally wasn't all that fast about responding to the bell, but that day she seemed to move at lightning speed, whipping open the front door as if she were expecting a long-lost friend.

"Nina!"

I heard Nikki exclaim my maid's name from the front steps, the chipper sound of her voice reassuring me there would be no more of yesterday's emotional display.

"Don't you look pretty wearing that brooch?" she said.

"Ah, thank you, Missy Grout. I love eet."

I could see Nina, and yet again she was acting like a schoolgirl. And what was this about a brooch?

On closer inspection, I noticed that indeed attached to the top of my maid's black and white uniform was a gaudily jeweled daisy displayed proudly.

"That was just the sweetest thing," Nikki added, "for you to bring over that other basket of goodies. I do swear, you are the best baker in all of Willow Creek."

Nina glanced back at me and I raised a questioning brow. My maid looked part defiant, part nervous that I would take the brooch away, or reprimand her for clearly taking goodies over herself. Then she hurried off, mumbling something about someone having to be nice to the poor lady. Like I wasn't. Like I wasn't the one risking my reputation. All Nina was doing was baking muffins.

Nikki stepped inside and instantly saw my other guest.

"Oh, my Lord," Nikki breathed. "Is that you, Pilar?"

The two women stood on opposite sides of my foyer, Pilar in all her dour black and Nikki in her usual shock of color. She wore multicolored cigarette pants that looked like they had been painted on. A bright yellow Lycra top with a bow at the center of the neckline. Plenty of pearls at her neck. Hot-pink stiletto heels with matching hot-pink toe polish. And a lime-green tote bag swinging from her shoulder, so big that it looked like one of the small square states.

Pilar was as shocked as Nikki, though she recovered quickly. "Yes, it's me. And you are?"

Who knew Pilar had it in her to be a snob?

"Oh, my stars! It's me, Nikki Bishop! Nikki Grout now!"

Pilar absorbed the news, not to mention the new last name, with the same sort of shock I had when I learned of Nikki's marriage. It was a relief to realize that New York City hadn't taken all of the *Texas* out of Pilar.

"This is such a surprise," Nikki added, then trotted herself across the marble floor to give Pilar the same sort of all-encompassing hug she had given me that first day. Thankfully she wasn't armed with a feather boa this time.

Pilar looked from Nikki to me, then back again. And all that fake cheer disappeared, replaced with speculation. "I didn't realize the two of you were still friends."

"We are!"

I'm sure I don't have to spell out who said that.

One of Pilar's (painful-to-look-at unplucked) brows rose.

"We are having a ball!" Nikki continued, her knees dipping for emphasis. "It's just like old times. In fact, Frede is going to teach me a few things to help get me into the Junior League!"

Silence shuddered up to my mosaic ceiling as one side of Pilar's unlipsticked mouth crooked.

"You're kidding, right?" Pilar said to me.

"No! It's the truth!" Not answered by yours truly.

Pilar eyed me. "I heard you were putting together a group for a prospective new member."

"Yes, well," I said noncommittally.

Nikki's blue eyes went as wide as cornflowers. "Oh, Pilar! It could be even more like old times if you were one of my sponsors! Say you'll do it! Say you'll sponsor me!"

Now both Pilar and I were in shock. But mine lasted longer since in a few seconds Pilar gave a firm nod of her head. "Frede, if you're spearheading Nikki, then I'd be happy to join the group. In fact, you know Eloise Fleming, don't you? I'm sure I can get her to join us as well."

Pilar *and* Eloise? This was way too easy.

I had to wonder if news was getting out that I was being considered for next year's position of president-elect. Certainly that would explain why Pilar was suddenly bending over backward to get in my good graces. Frede Ware was powerful, but President Frede Ware would be unstoppable. No doubt Pilar had to wonder if supporting my cause would wipe out the insult to me during the New Projects meeting?

Not really, but I didn't say that. I've never gotten over grudges all that easily. I know, I know, bad me.

"How great of you, sugar," I said.

We engaged in the requisite small talk until Pilar left once I had promised I would call her with details.

"Isn't this the best," Nikki enthused once the door shut.

"It's absolutely fabulous," I said.

"It's going to be just like old times. The three of us together again."

Tears actually welled in her eyes.

"Yes, great, let's get started."

I was ready with my plan of action to "reinvent" Nikki. I had made a list of all that I would go over with her—an outline from my days at Little Miss Debutante just off Willow Creek Square.

We'd start with the basics:

1. Etiquette

2. Voice

3. Posture

4. Poise

And then, yes, we'd have to deal with:

5. Style—the most difficult concept, I suspected, given Nikki's taste in apparel.

With just over two months before the new members would be decided on, the clock was ticking. And let's not forget that I had less than three weeks before the Grouts' big dinner party. I wouldn't just have to be Henry Higgins, I would have to be the Miracle Worker as well. But if I could pull it off, that party might very well land me a few more sponsors. Now that Pilar and Eloise were on board, I only needed three more, and I was certain that after the Spiked Tea debacle, no amount of cajoling or reasoning would get any of those ladies to support my cause.

Knowing there was no help for it, I decided I would tackle the most difficult subject first. Style.

"Nikki, I'd like to start by discussing your clothes."

She smiled at me as if she were ahead of the game. "I remembered what you said." She gestured toward herself. "See, bows and pearls."

I was going to be haunted by those words for the rest of my days. Forget SHE WAS FABULOUS written on my tombstone. Instead it would read, SHE LOVED BOWS AND PEARLS.

"Isn't that what you told me to wear?"

"Don't get me wrong, sugar, you look fabulous," I lied enthusiastically. "But maybe a little too fabulous. What with all those pearls, the girls will be green with envy."

Nikki beamed at this.

"Envy," I persevered, "when we are trying to gain support for your bid into the Junior League, probably isn't the best way to go."

"What do you mean?"

"Maybe the bow is *too* extraordinary for our little group. And the pearls are just too impressive. You want the girls to love you—though I swear, what's not to love?—not be jealous of you."

"Of me?" she asked, looking as though I had just awarded her the Maid of Cotton crown. "Oh, I never thought of it that way! I can't believe it. Jealous! Of me!"

"But remember, jealous isn't good."

Which wasn't altogether true.

Certainly, you could never predict what a jealous woman might do. But as long as you held the power, another woman's jealousy could be hugely helpful in getting things done. The woman who was jealous of another was instantly in the weaker position. While in my day-to-day life I was surrounded by jealous women, I didn't need them to be jealous of Howard Grout's Too-Tacky Wife. I needed them to help me help her get into the JLWC. Though in truth, not a woman I knew would be jealous of Nikki's pearls or bow.

"Why don't we go upstairs to my dressing room, and I'll show you the sorts of clothes I think you should start wearing," I suggested.

"Really? You'd do that for me?"

"Of course."

Nikki stopped every few feet on the way upstairs to gawk at this or that. A vase. A painting. Hildebrand family heirlooms.

I herded her into my bedroom suite.

"Wow, this is so . . ."

I was expecting "lovely," "amazing," "beautiful"—a whole thesaurus of words that could correctly describe my living quarters.

"It's so beige," was what she came up with.

"Yes, well . . ." What do you say to that?

I directed her into my dressing room, and while she didn't do the "beige" thing again, she was even more creative. "It's so plain in here."

Boring, beige, plain. And she was talking about me.

She walked over to the built-in shelves and cabinets that were covered by individual doors with see-through glass inserts. Opening one, she ran her hands over the stacks of cashmere sweaters (only wearable a few months a year in Central Texas and had yet to be put away for spring). "They're as soft as soft can be," she purred, rubbing one against her cheek.

When she finished, she shoved it back in place (unfolded) and turned to me. "Okay, I'm ready. I told Howie I would do what you say. So tell me what sorts of things I should wear."

"A general rule to keep in mind is that a ladylike appearance should be subdued, modest, and demure. Take jewelry, for example."

She looked worried.

"Have you ever heard the expression 'No diamonds before dinner'?" I asked.

Her eyes squinted as her brain searched for an answer.

I didn't want her to wear herself out so early. "It means that diamonds—with the exception of a diamond engagement ring—shouldn't be worn during the day, specifically before six in the evening."

Her hands came up and felt her gigantic diamond earrings. "I can't wear my diamonds?"

You'd have thought I told her she couldn't wear clothes at all, though that might not have gotten the same distress from Nikki.

I forged ahead. "In addition, a lady never wears a watch *after* six in the evening when people of . . . let's say, a certain class aren't supposed to be keeping track of time."

Her hand flew to her wrist. "If I can't wear diamonds before six, and I can't wear a watch after six, then when can I wear this?" She thrust out her diamond-encrusted timepiece.

I tried to look apologetic and shrugged. "Never?"

"Oh, my gawd! I can't *not* wear my watch. I love my watch. It's my very favorite thing."

"And lovely," in an over-the-top extravagant way. "Unfortunately, a diamond watch exists in a no-man's-land and can't be worn at all."

She did a lot of blinking.

I hurried on. "Ankle bracelets."

She glanced down at hers. She wrinkled her nose and I could tell she knew something was wrong, she just didn't know what it was. "You want me to wear it with hose?"

I held back a shudder. "No, not with stockings. The only appropriate place for an ankle bracelet is on the wrist."

Her eyes narrowed. "Wouldn't it just be a bracelet then?"

"Exactly!"

More blinking.

Before she could respond, I said, "Let's move on to clothes."

She didn't look like she wanted to, but then she drew a deep bracing breath. "Maybe I could try on some of your stuff, see how it looks, and all."

"Oh, well . . . fine."

I thumbed through several outfits searching for just the thing that would get the concept of "demure" across. I found the ideal piece, a beige shirtdress with a respectable grosgrain belt. I had never worn it because as it turned out the bustline was not at all flattering on me. While my breasts are fabulous, they aren't particularly large and the sheath did nothing to accent my shape. But it would be heaven on Nikki.

"Voilà," I said, pulling it out. "This is perfect."

Her face fell. "You want me to wear that ratty ol' thing?"

Chapter Thirteen

"JUST TRY IT ON," I cajoled.

"But it's beige."

"What do you have against beige?"

"Can we start with 'boring'?"

"Sarcasm is unbecoming in a lady." Had I really said that, words straight out of my mother's mouth?

"Beige is hardly boring, Nikki. It can be fabulous." On the right woman, in the right cut and cloth.

She didn't look convinced, so I plunged ahead. "The problem with bold anything—color or cut—when it comes to style is that then the clothes wear the woman, not the other way around. After someone has met Nikki Grout, it's you they should remember, not your attire."

I couldn't bring myself to spell out the fact that to some women, clothes become an armor, be it wild spandex tights or black boxy pantsuits and ugly glasses. I say a woman's glowing charm should tell the world who she is, not her attire. Though if a woman has no charm, I guess she has no choice but to buy personality with a credit card.

"Now, for the shoes." I always kept an extra pair of Ferragamo pumps on hand for emergencies. "What size do you wear?"

"Seven and a half."

"Perfect."

I pulled out a box and handed it over. She took it suspiciously, then peeked inside. At the sight, she looked as if I had stabbed her in the heart with one of her stiletto heels.

"Flats. Why am I not surprised?" she said.

She looked down at my feet. Somehow my bone Ferragamos with tailored bows seemed anemic rather than classic when propped next to Nikki's stilettos. Which was ridiculous.

"They are not flats, they have a lovely one-inch heel. You've got to trust me on this, Nikki." I handed over the belted beige cotton next. "I've never worn the dress either. Give it a try."

She seemed to be on the verge of an out-and-out mutiny. But then she sighed, agreed, and stripped down to bra and panties in the amount of time it took a normal woman to take off her coat.

My being shocked hardly covered it. For one: I had meant she should take the dress home and try it all on later, and two: I hadn't seen a female undress since I was in junior high and forced to take gym. However, junior high girls generally lacked Pamela Anderson breasts and the sort of lingerie sold in stores where anyone under eighteen wasn't allowed to venture without a parent.

I turned away. "I'll let you dress," then left as quickly as I could.

A few minutes later Nikki appeared, dressed (unhappily) in the beige dress and pumps—sans stockings, which I would deal with later. Somehow the neutral palette of color muted everything about her, the Tammy Faye Bakker eyelashes, the bright spots of blush, even the breasts.

"Nikki, you look lovely." I actually meant it.

She sulked as we returned downstairs, her own more colorful clothes stuffed into her bright green shoulder bag.

"I just wish I didn't have to dress like such a troll."

"Troll? Impossible. I'm wearing beige and do I look like a troll?"

"Since you asked—"

I cut her off. Given her dislike of all things tasteful, I doubted I would want to hear what she had to say. "Lunch is ready."

"Oh . . ."

I led Nikki to the sunroom where we would move on to basic etiquette. The table was set with a delicate floral-on-white bone china that was appropriate for a casual daytime meal.

"Wow!" Nikki exclaimed, picking up a plate and flipping it over to read the back. "These must have cost you a fortune!"

I took it away and set it down. "You can't pick up a lady's china to have a look. And never, ever mention the cost. Of anything."

"But what if you want to get some of it yourself?"

"How can you be original if you spend your life copying someone else?"

"I don't get it. I thought the whole point of all this fixing was to make me *less* original."

I hate to admit it, but I had the startling (and disturbing) thought that she was right. Then I shook myself out of it, reminding myself that the key to having the sort of Presence that made a woman truly remarkable was taking all that cream and beige and perfectly coiffed hair and combining it with something about her personality that made her stand out. But that something couldn't be anything that flashed like a neon sign. It had to be subtle, but memorable.

Like *moi.*

"Things will start making sense soon enough." I hoped.

Once we were seated, Nina served chicken salad made with almonds and vertically cut seedless grapes cradled in a half of an avocado, along with fresh fruit on a bed of lettuce, drizzled with hints of my maid's homemade dressing. And of course, sweet tea—of the nonspiked variety.

I prayed that my informal luncheon with only a fraction of the rules and silverware needed for a proper place setting would be a manageable step for Nikki.

The first clue that it might be too much was her squeal of delight when Nina delivered my heirloom deviled-egg plate. I am sure Nikki would have turned it over no matter what I had said except there were a dozen deviled eggs perched in the pockets.

As soon as we took the last bite, I launched into my plan of attack. "I've had a chance to observe you as we've been eating, and I have just a few"—*I was being kind*—"comments."

"I'm ready."

She was nothing if not enthusiastic. At first.

"Since you're right-handed, your left hand should remain in your lap while you eat. Your right hand holds the fork or spoon."

"How do you cut anything?"

"You bring up your left hand, like this." I demonstrated. "The fork is transferred to the left hand and your right hand is then used to cut—which is why the knife is sitting right there by your right hand. After the cut is made, the knife is set down on the plate—without a loud clank and never, ever set back on the tablecloth—then the fork is transferred back to the right hand, left hand returned to the lap, and the bite is taken."

"Jesus, Lordy!"

"By the by, things like 'Jesus, Lordy' really don't work in polite settings, and certainly not at the table."

She looked confused. "By the by?"

I moved on.

"Chew with your mouth closed. Never speak when you have food in your mouth. And always wipe your lips between bites. No one wants to sit across from you and be distracted by crumbs on your lips."

She rolled her eyes, but thankfully kept her thoughts to herself.

Next came Conversation, and I provided her with a list of taboo topics:

1. Personal health
2. Politics
3. Religion
4. Questions about another person
5. Personal opinions

She scoffed. "Great, a party where all anyone talks about is the weather and the food."

"See! You're getting it already."

"But—"

As impolite as it is to cut someone off, I couldn't help myself. "Next up: Comportment." There are only so many hours in a day, and it wasn't like I was the one who wanted to teach her. Seemed to me only fair that I shouldn't have to put up with any wildly colored lip.

Comportment is a tricky subject. The things I wanted to warn her away from but didn't because I was much too polite were:

1. Christmas lights on the house year-round is NC.
2. Plastic gnomes or pink flamingos in the yard is worse.
3. Sue or Jo should not be attached to perfectly good names like Betty and Carla.
4. French underarm hair should be left to the French. (If you have to wax, please don't mention it, then wax the underarms. What woman can be considered a lady if she raises her arm and looks like a man?)

Unwilling to share any of that, I launched into the points that my mother and the charming women at Little Miss Debutante had drummed into my head, otherwise known as the Four Nevers:

1. Never dominate a conversation.
2. Never speak in a voice that can be heard more than three feet away.
3. Never *do* anything that anyone would notice if they were more than three feet away.
4. Never boast of your accomplishments.

"The fact is," I continued, "if you do something worth noticing, it will be noticed. As the saying goes, don't toot your own horn."

"That's not what Howard says."

"Really?" I acted surprised.

"Howard says that if you want something in life, you got to grab it by the balls. You've got to go after it, because no one's going to get it for you.

And everybody needs to know how great you are." She smiled fondly. "He always says, The more you toot, the more people get out of your way and let you pass to the head of the line."

Clearly he had been born to the sort of hillbilly existence where sheep sometimes serve as dates.

"And I'm sure Howard knows what he's talking about"—hardly—"in his world. But if you want to secure the remaining three sponsors, you better do it my way."

She debated, then sighed. "Okay, fine. Like I told you, Howie said I have to do what you want."

I just barely held back a *Jesus Lordy, thank God for Howie.*

"Another tip to tuck away: never show your feelings."

"What do you mean?"

"For example, no crying in front of other people."

She snorted. (I thought about starting a list of Things to Correct.) Instead, I sighed then started to say something about it, but I was saved the effort.

"No snorting," she said, surprising me.

I might have smiled. "Exactly."

"Okay, what else?"

Zipping along, I added the Three Don'ts:

1. Don't look at yourself in the mirror while in public.

2. Don't touch any part of your body while in public (or ever, according to my mother).

3. Don't eat anything unless you're sitting at a table.

"Is gum food?" she asked.

"It doesn't matter. A lady never chews gum."

"Ever?" She gaped at me.

"Ever."

"Jesu—" She smiled apologetically. "Okay, let me see if I've got this straight. We've got the Four Nevers and the Three Don'ts. A little like Motown Does Etiquette."

This time I blinked.

She leaped up and belted out the chorus of "I Heard It Through the Grapevine," adding dance steps and finger snaps. I imagined her at the next Boots and Belles Charity Ball and it was all I could do not to drop my head on the linen tablecloth and cry uncle.

"Sorry," she said with a laugh. "I'll be good now. But before we get back to business, I've got to go to the little girl's room. Nothing like sweet tea to go right through you."

I groaned.

"What's wrong now?"

It would probably be easier to make a list. "Mainly, when you leave the table, no matter the reason, just say, 'Excuse me.' Don't explain where you're going."

She just laughed some more. "Yeah, I guess everyone doesn't need to know I'm going to pee."

She disappeared and I wanted to.

As much as I'm reluctant to admit it, when she returned I hurried through the rest. I buzzed through Poise, then Posture, and by the time I got to:

1. entering a room (with quiet composure and dignity),
2. walking (as if a book is balanced on head, with spine straight, stomach in, rear tucked under, shoulders back, head held high), it felt as if the antique grandfather clock were ticking in my head.

The fact was, Nikki Grout wasn't good at doing anything with quiet dignity and she was horrible at walking. At least like a lady. A call girl, maybe. But not a member of the Junior League of Willow Creek.

We dashed through:

1. getting in and out of a car (with knees together sit first, then pull legs in—with knees together put legs out, then stand)

2. gesturing (no wild waving)
3. descending the stairs (hand gently resting on banister, head held high)

Though on the last one, we nearly lost Nikki to a tumble. Thankfully there was a landing of sorts halfway down the curve of steps.

"Why don't you practice at home," I suggested. "Then tomorrow I thought we'd go to Saks Fifth Avenue in San Antonio to get you some new clothes. In fact, we'll get the perfect outfit for you to wear to your big dinner party."

She stared at me. "But I already have something to wear for that. It's dreamy, all gold and glittery—"

In her defense, she cut herself off, grimaced, then nodded her head. "Okay. Shopping it is. But first I have a surprise."

She retrieved her lime-green leather tote and pulled out a book. *"Voilà!"*

"What is that?"

"The Willow Creek Junior High yearbook!" She strode over to me and flipped it open. "Look! Here's where you signed!" She shoved it in my hands.

Even all these years later I recognized my handwriting. Straight up and down, plump, curvy letters. My signature hadn't changed a lot since then, just toned down.

When I didn't say anything, she started reading out loud, clearly having memorized the words.

"Nikki, you don't need to do that."

She couldn't be stopped.

" 'To my good friend Nikki. Frede.' "

Even back then I wasn't inclined toward enthusiastic exaggeration.

She smiled dreamily. "Boy, do you remember that day back in seventh grade when we—"

"Look at the time." I snapped the book shut and returned it. "We'll pick up again tomorrow with shopping."

I didn't have to tell her twice. She might have been disappointed by not getting to tell her story, but she was thrilled to be let out of "school."

Though for all the good my lessons had done her, since she hollered out good-bye to Nina and slammed out the door with a wave and a laugh, as if I hadn't spent the better part of the afternoon teaching her to do just the opposite.

When I heard her car roar down the drive, I reminded myself of the front-page article in the *Willow Creek Times.*

Spent, I went upstairs to take a long, hot bath, but before I walked into my bedroom, I found myself heading instead for my study. My body seemed to work independently of my mind, and I went to a bookshelf and pulled out my own Willow Creek Junior High yearbook. There I was, Class Favorite. Most Beautiful.

I flipped through the pages until I found a photograph of Pilar, not yet anything other than a student. Then Nikki, smiling so wide that she was all teeth and curls and laughter. Finally, I found the signatures. Pilar didn't do signings. But there was Nikki's, messy, scrawling. "You'll always be the sister of my heart."

Melodramatic even back then.

It was a trip down memory lane that I had no interest in taking. I shoved the yearbook back in its spot, then headed for my room, swearing that Nikki Grout and her NC ways were not going to wear off on me.

Chapter Fourteen

BEING FABULOUS TAKES EFFORT. Being Frede Ware Fabulous is an art form. Which was why the next morning I was feeling a teensy bit on the guilty side after having rushed Nikki through the paces. But really, a woman can only take so much.

When I arrived at Palace Grout for our shopping extravaganza, I promised myself I was going to be a picture of patience. My sole job for the day was to convince my little duckling to steer clear of trendy, wildly colored and decorated clothes.

How hard could it be?

The maid led me through the maze of taste and tackiness to the sunroom, though I stopped abruptly when I entered. The maid didn't seem fazed by what we saw—Nikki and Howard engaged in something extremely NC.

I tried to back away from the door, but I was so surprised I must have made a noise because both of the Grouts whipped around to face me.

"Frede!" Nikki exclaimed.

Howard chuckled, the book dropping from the top of his head to the floor when he turned. "Hell, this is harder than it looks."

"I told you," Nikki said. She looked at me. "I've been practicing, but it's so hard."

I should have known that neither Nikki nor her husband would be embarrassed by being caught with Howard walking back and forth across the room balancing a book on his head like a fat, squat wanna-be debutante.

Howard retrieved the book from the floor just as his cell phone rang. He glanced at the readout, grunted, then sent the call to voice mail, as if he had more important things to do than answer.

"Tell me how to do it?" He planted the book back on his head and started off across the room.

"You're moving too fast," I said automatically.

He slowed down.

"Too slow."

"Make up your mind." The book fell from his head, and he caught it with a flourish, then replanted it. "Let's try this again." He took off at a moderate pace.

It was crazy that I was instructing Howard Grout how to walk like a lady. But let me tell you, for all his girth, he was a quicker study than his wife.

"Don't swing your arms."

He plastered them to his sides.

"Too much. You're too stiff. You are supposed to be moving fluidly, with grace."

Which stopped us all dead again.

"I'm a whole lot of things, darlin', but graceful ain't never going to be one of them." To prove his point he started back across the room, attempting to flow. "How'm I doing?"

"Better."

Howard snorted. "Liar."

Tacky but smart.

He tilted his head, and the book fell into his hands, then he extended it to me. "Your turn, baby doll."

I looked over my shoulder in surprise, then back, too confused to instantly grasp that the whole "baby doll" issue was directed at me. "You want me to do it?"

"Yep." He gave a little shake to the not insubstantial latest bestseller. "You must be a pro at this book stuff for all the class you've got."

I can't explain why I did it. I haven't a clue what came over me, other than to say that the man had a certain *je ne sais quoi* in all his inappropriate NCness. Or maybe I did it because when a tasteless man recognized my refinement, I thought he should be rewarded.

Nikki clapped her hands. "Yes, show us!"

Even the maid was watching with interest, and truth to tell, I had never been able to resist an audience. I know, I know, I was being NC, drawing attention to myself. Hadn't I just yesterday told Nikki that it was improper to attract attention? But, well, when in Rome . . .

With the book on my head I started off across the room, shoulders back, arms gracefully at my sides, chin parallel to the floor. Somewhere in my parents' attic there was an award (several, actually) from my days at Little Miss Debutante. I could walk circles around all the other girls, the certificate proclaiming as much.

I had just made my turn (by far the most difficult maneuver in the book walk) when someone barged in unannounced.

"Sawyer!" Nikki said.

This time the book fell from my head.

The artist entered, seeming to suck the air out of every square inch of space. He didn't notice me at the far end of the sunroom. He was bigger than I remembered, and clearly happy in a just-rode-in-from-the-ranch/John Wayne sort of way. I was surprised he even knew how to smile given his phone message and my single run-in with him at his studio.

"How great to see you," Nikki enthused.

His smile tilted at one corner. "The dry spell is over. I'm painting again. One visit from a prissy-ass gal—"

Nikki's eyes went wide. "Sawyer!" she blurted, cutting him off. "We have a visitor!"

The artist took in the rest of the room, first seeing Howard, and he started to say something. But then he saw me, and his head cocked. "Well, look who's here."

Everyone in the room turned to stare, and given that I was smart as well as beautiful, no one had to spell out who exactly the "prissy-ass gal" was. That would be me. My guess was he had been on his way to saying "prissy-ass gallery owner."

I could tell Nikki was uncomfortable, Howard was amused, while the artist's mouth ticked up at one corner. "If it isn't Her Highness herself, Fredericka Hildebrand Ware."

His smile wasn't particularly friendly when directed at me, more of a sneer, which was getting really old, especially from the tall, if idiotically dressed, man. He might be some sort of catch in the art world, and he might have looked hot in his studio, but today he wore cargo pants (should only be worn by teenage boys of ill-bred families) with an army fatigue T-shirt (should only be worn by GI Joe dolls with preformed muscles and plastic guns) and sandals (should never be worn by any male—real or not).

"I should have figured Nikki was the one who gave you my name," he said. "Hell, you should have told me. I might have been nice."

First, my name got sneers from this man, then laughs, while the Grout name could have gotten me invited to the artist's debutante ball. Go figure.

Nikki walked over and playfully swatted the man's arm. "I didn't realize you were coming over today, Sawyer. Frede and I are going shopping. Not that I need clothes! Look at me!" She twirled around. "Frede's teaching me how to look like a real Junior Leaguer, and I'm really getting the hang of it."

I had to look closer to figure out what she meant.

"The beige!" she stated.

Ah, beige. I should have realized. Clearly Nikki was having a hard time grasping the differences between her and me. She wore beige spandex paint-on pants.

"Don't you just love my new sweater set?"

She extended her arms like a fashion model to give her guests a full view of the "sweater set," the quality of which indeed could have come out of my closet, though only if Nina had mistakenly put it in the dryer first. It was skintight cashmere (I didn't know this was possible) that I swear had to have spandex in it too. The outer sweater was trimmed in pearls, as if she had decided, *If I can't accent with glitter, I'll decorate with pearls, and the more the better.* Furthermore, it was March and now past cashmere weather in Texas.

"Yes, sugar, just look at you," I managed.

Nikki preened, then called out to the maid. "Maria, could you bring some tea?" She looked at me. "We have time, don't we?"

The artist made it impossible to answer when he called after the maid. "Could you make mine hot, Maria?"

The next thing I knew everyone was sitting around the small table. Nikki giggled and forgot . . . Sorry, that's incorrect. She still didn't *remember* any of the etiquette rules I taught her the day before. The artist sat down and pushed his chair back, crossing his legs . . . at the knees. I've seen this done by men living in places like, say, New York or Latin America. But last I looked, we were still in Texas where real men preferred the ankle-to-knee thing.

Howard joined us, which I thought was interesting since most redneck Texans steer clear of men with preferences for other men—unless they were hunting buddies called Bubba.

"So, Sawyer," Nikki began, "you said you were painting again—"

He waved the words away with a swish of his hand. Which looked *très* odd on a man of his size. "I came by to tell you that another of those gallery owners had come by wanting to do an exhibition of my work." He glanced at me. "And lo and behold, here she is."

"You should do this one, Sawyer," Nikki said.

"He already said no."

"What?" Howard eyed me. "I thought you said it was in the bag."

I smiled with all the innocence of a First Baptist choir girl. "Did I say that?"

The artist looked at me, just looked. I couldn't tell exactly what he was thinking, but something in the back of my head said he was disgusted. By me. But I couldn't say for certain since I had never encountered disgust before, at least not to my face.

"Who knows," the artist said, a smile surfacing. "Maybe a show with Fredericka Hildebrand Ware would be . . . interesting."

"Does that mean you're saying yes now?" I asked.

He shrugged. "If I do, will you stop leaving messages on my answering machine?"

Howard gave me the eye. Nikki fidgeted. I might have gasped, and while I wouldn't admit this to anyone else, let me just say that I felt a distinct burn in my cheeks.

The artist didn't wait for an answer (thankfully those pesky rhetorical questions never need one); he laughed. "I'll think about it. When do you want to have the show?"

Part of me would have loved to say, *The third of never*. It would have felt so good. But the other part of me thought again about the triumphant coup of catching the elusive artist, even if he was mean and seemed to prefer every other sort of person that wasn't me.

"In a month," I said.

Nikki clapped her hands. "This is wonderful! You've just got to do it, Sawyer. Then this summer, after it's all said and done, we throw a big party to celebrate your very first show and me getting into the Junior League!"

For all the things Nikki does wrong, she does one thing very right. She has a healthy belief in herself, I'll hand her that. Confidence is an integral part of being a true lady.

Sawyer just smiled and sipped his hot tea out of a china cup.

"Look at the time," I said. "Shopping awaits."

The words worked like magic.

TWENTY MINUTES LATER, Nikki and I were on our way to Saks in San Antonio, though not before Howard took my elbow and guided me off to the side. "I've got some news."

I stopped and tried not to let it show that I was holding my breath. *Please, God, let it be good news.*

"That sorry-ass husband of yours was in Grand Cayman, just like you said."

My mother should have been a detective.

"Was?"

His shark eyes bored into me. "Yep, but by the time I got someone there, he was gone. We did find out he's traveling with a woman. A gal named Janet Lambert."

This was no surprise, but it still felt like a punch to my perfectly flat stomach. And that made me even angrier. I would not go weak.

"I pulled some strings"—this said in a way that made him sound like Guido the Enforcer twisting arms or breaking kneecaps—"to get the dirt on what exactly your slimeball husband did with your money after he withdrew it from your bank here in Willow Creek. Turns out he moved the money to a little no-name bank in Austin. Probably didn't want anyone looking over his shoulder since I found out he invested in a bunch of those stupid-ass get-rich-quick schemes. I hate to tell you, darlin', but the SOB lost a pantload of your money before he ever left town."

My heart lodged in my throat. "Is it all gone?" I barely got the words out.

"No."

Had I been inclined toward showy displays, I would have dropped to my knees and offered up thanks. As it was, I simply nodded. "Good. We'll have the account in Austin frozen."

"Not so *good*. He's already moved the money out of Austin."

I put the pieces together and got light-headed. "To Grand Cayman," I surmised.

"Bingo. He closed the Austin account the day he walked out of your house. Must have driven straight to the bank and withdrawn it all in the form of a certified check."

"And the money is still there? In Grand Cayman?" I asked weakly.

"Nah. And those Caymanians make it hard as hell to keep a good sniff on a money trail, what with their sneaky offshore banks, and all."

I must have visibly steadied myself because he added, "But don't you worry. I'll catch him. I have my ways."

I didn't ask about his ways, didn't want to know about his ways, didn't care if they involved broken bones or ever-so-unfashionable cement footwear. All I cared about was getting my money back.

Feeling what I can only call caged, I got into Nikki's car, and we made our way to San Antonio. I would have preferred to take my car since I like control and all. Unfortunately, I had little choice since before Howard ever gave me my bad news, he had given his wife good news. You see, the minute we got up from tea, he had pulled his wife close, kissed her square on the lips, then said, "I have a surprise for my special gal."

No question it was the tackiest of tacky behavior. It got even worse when we trotted outside to find a brand-new fire-engine-red Jaguar, with a big red bow attached to the hood (almost as big as the one Nikki wore to her tea).

Sometime between my arrival and that moment, someone had delivered the new car. I glanced at the artist and saw he and Howard exchange a conspiratorial glance, and I realized that Sawyer Jackson must have brought the car by for the big surprise.

"Oh, my stars!" Nikki breathed. "For me?"

Howard beamed, then laughed and staggered back a few steps when his wife launched herself into his arms.

"I love you, I love you, I love you," she said, planting kisses all over his face.

I made a mental note to discuss "No public displays of affection" with Nikki.

The artist and I glanced at each other. He smiled and shook his head as if he were indulging a small child. I tried not to grimace. I must not have done a good job since he tsked at me. I gave a startled shake of my head and jerked away.

As a result of Howard's gift, there was no way we could take my car—the one that would have driven at respectable speeds. Instead, we left my lawyer smiling proudly in the driveway, flew down I-35 with windows open, Nikki singing along to the radio, hitting the home of the Alamo in record time, thankfully in one piece. However, if I'd had on Lycra tights I would have been mistaken for a hooker when I got out of the car. My hair had been blown wild, my cheeks bright red from the wind.

After a not-so-quick stop in the ladies' lounge to repair my face and hair, I was back in the designer section of Saks.

Oh, and there's one thing I forgot to mention. Sawyer Jackson had made the trip with us.

I ask you, what kind of a man is willing to spend the afternoon shopping with two women, one of whom he doesn't know?

Granted, Nikki had practically begged Sawyer to join us, and I agreed after he said that *if* he decided to do my show it would give him the perfect opportunity to wear the purple sateen suit he had gotten just last week. I hoped he was joking, but couldn't take the risk. I was getting closer to ruin by the day as it was. First Gordon, followed by Nikki, and I certainly would be finished off if I managed to hook up with the only gay artist in America who didn't have a clue about fashion—elusive or not. The thing, truly, about being elusive, is that when people finally see you, you better not disappoint.

So there we were, a regular trio of incongruity, breezing through the store. I can only say that I must have been spending too much time with my neighbor, because as we went through racks of clothes I couldn't find my usual subtly cutting, though sweet-as-pie, remarks. Before I knew it, with each piece of apparel Nikki held out, I was commenting with a directness that would have gotten me kicked out of the better social circles in Texas.

The leopard-print jacket and black pants with rhinestones in place of a tuxedo line: "Sleazy."

The turquoise tube top (do people really still wear those?) that stopped a good five inches from the low-cut hot-pink pants: "Slutty."

The baby-doll minidress: "Spank me, big boy."

Sawyer laughed out loud. Nikki looked less cheerful by the *ensemble*.

A few outfits later, I caught Sawyer studying me, as if he didn't know what to make of me. Was it my fault that Nikki was immune to subtlety and I had taken to being direct?

I decided that the only reasonable thing to do was to pull up my very best and most proper façade. And it was a good thing I did, otherwise I might have said something hugely improper when Nikki shifted gears and started pulling out clothes for *moi*—completely tasteless attire that she oohed and aahed over, but I wouldn't be caught dead in.

"This!" she waxed on about, throwing the "find" over her forearm with a flourish. "You have to have it!"

It was a white silk tunic top with an (admittedly) beautiful design of tiny violet and pale green flowers around the neckline and hem, which wouldn't have been horrible (though still not wearable) if it hadn't been for the fact that it was sheer. Sheer is beyond bad.

"I can't wear that. It's too . . ."

"Revealing?"

"For starters."

"You don't wear it by itself, Frede."

She rummaged around until she found a white camisole. Then she produced a pair of jeans. Flared (bad) and low cut (worse).

"Well," I said, "bless your heart for trying, but that really isn't . . . me."

"It should be!" Nikki breathed. "You'd be beautiful in it."

My artist was looking at me. Again. "And this," he said.

He extended a bracelet, an unseemly thing with jangly crystals and gaudy (not to mention faux) mother-of-pearl droplets.

Before I could think twice, my head spun back to junior high and the day I bought one so similar. I had come home, showed it off at the dinner table. The next day it was gone from my room. When I asked, my mother said she hadn't any idea what I was talking about. Later, I saw it on one of the new maids as she left for her day off. I started to question her, but Nina stopped me from making a scene.

"You mother gave it to her, Missy."

I wasn't sure if I was more stunned by my mother's blatant lie or by the bracelet that I loved going off with the maid.

I shook the thought away.

"Thank you," I said to Nikki and the artist, pulling up a sharp glance, "but we aren't here to shop for me. We're here for the two of you."

I turned and immediately saw an attractive pale yellow (not even beige!) silk blouse with pale yellow cuffed trousers.

"This will look lovely on you, Nikki."

"That?" There wasn't exactly a sneer involved but she wasn't jumping up and down either.

"Yes, this." Okay, so I might have said it kind of tightly, and perhaps I sounded put out that she continually proved she just didn't get it.

"Frede! That won't look good on me! I'll puff that shirt out so big that I'll look like a freakin' puffed-up corn fritter just out of the deep fry."

"You won't look puffy," I snapped. "You'll look sensible for a change."

She got really quiet. "You're saying I'm not sensible?"

"Do you think gold lamé or pink feathers are sensible?"

She gasped.

I glared.

"Ding, ding, ding." Sawyer held up his hands. "Is there going to be scratching involved, or is this just a verbal fight?"

Nikki and I turned to him in unison, like synchronized NC tramps, and blurted, "We aren't fighting!"

He raised a brow.

Oh, dear God, I wasn't making an inch of headway with Nikki, but she really was turning me into a trailer-park wanna-be.

Nikki groaned then smiled apologetically. But I didn't. With my face set firmly, I headed for the St. John knits, leaving Sawyer standing there with an amused smile on his face, and Nikki sighing her disappointment.

Fortunately, St. John had enough in the way of gold buttons to make

Nikki reasonably happy. That or she knew I was at my wit's end. She disappeared into the fitting room with an overly excited saleswoman, leaving the artist and me alone.

It wasn't long before I noticed that he was staring at me again.

"What now?" I demanded.

"Just trying to figure you out."

"There's nothing to figure out, Mr. Jackson. I'm no mystery." Humility ranks right up there with "No cleavage before six in the evening." "I'm exactly what you see." A trashy shrew from what he had witnessed so far.

He laughed again, sort of a snort of disbelief. "I doubt that."

I could tell by the way he said the words that it wasn't a compliment.

"Tell me this," he said, "why are you really helping Nikki?"

What could I say to that? "Because she'll be good for the Junior League," I responded, just as I had said to my mother. "Besides, my husband and I always do what we can for our neighbors." I was impressed with my answer.

"You and your husband, huh? While you were taking forever fixing your hair, I asked about yours. Nikki said she's never met him. Says he doesn't seem to be around a lot."

To think I stepped right into that one.

That caged feeling returned. Too many questions that I couldn't answer. Me acting more common than a fourth wife on a billionaire's yacht. My money gone, being spent on another woman who had slept on my nine-hundred-ninety-nine-thread-count sheets.

Suddenly a front-page article or even broken kneecaps were too good for my husband. I found myself standing in the middle of Saks Fifth Avenue fantasizing about Gordon Ware being broke and dying a painful death in some third-world country.

And that made me feel horrible—not because I would think that about Gordon, but that I would become so common as to have such unacceptably crass thoughts.

Which must be why I then proceeded to wax eloquent about my husband and my marriage. "We have a fabulous relationship. Really. It's just that he travels a lot. But I adore him, and he adores me." What was a few more lies in the scheme of things? Not that the lies mattered since the artist didn't look like he believed a word of it.

Nikki finally reappeared, twirling around in the most glittery of the St. Johns.

"Not bad," the artist said with cool approval.

After that, nothing else was said about me or the state of my marital affairs. But by the end of our shopping excursion, my protégée had eight new *ensembles* and the artist had a Hugo Boss three-button black suit with a deep blue button-down shirt.

It took all three of us to get "the stash," as Nikki kept calling it, to the car. By the time we returned to Willow Creek, I knew the day had been mostly a success. Nikki would be dressed appropriately for any sort of event a Junior Leaguer could throw her way, including her big coming-out party that was fast approaching.

But all I could think about were the three words my artist said just as I started to close my car door.

"I'll do it."

"Do what?"

"Your show."

Chapter Fifteen

EVERY ACTIVE MEMBER of the JLWC has to put in one hundred volunteer hours each Junior League year, generally accomplished in the months from September through May, doing an assigned "job" or Placement in addition to committee work. The day after the shopping extravaganza, with the artist's announcement still swimming gratifyingly in my head (reassurance that no man—homosexual or not—could resist me for long), I made my way to the JLWC headquarters and Brightlee to start putting in make-up time for the Placement hours I had missed. As soon as the lunch hour was over, I would start making arrangements for my big show. I also planned to find out everything Nikki knew about Sawyer Jackson. I would start that afternoon at the hair appointment I had made for her with none other than Eugenie Françoise of Salon Françoise.

But first I had to get through the Placement hours.

When I arrived at Brightlee, I had no choice but to glide by a scowling Margaret Penderwelt (a past Outstanding Volunteer and current head of the volunteer staff at the tearoom) telling her that I hoped I hadn't been missed too much. She knew better than to question me.

Brightlee had gotten its name from Eunice Houston Brightlee, founder of the JLWC back in 1917. The tearoom was a lovely space of verandas, hardwood floors, and antique furnishings, a place where everyone who already was or wanted to be anyone went to be seen for lunch and early afternoon tea.

Once I was dressed in the uniform of floor-length, wraparound royal-blue apron and white blouse, I got to work. I set tables and readied water pitchers. Thankfully we had "real" paid kitchen staff who made some of the best crustless sandwiches in town.

A woman's Placement had the ability to be fabulous or horrendous. Given that you had to spend at least once a week with the same group of volunteers for an entire Junior League year, it was imperative to get assigned to a job that was made up of women worth being around. Most everyone I did my hours with were just the right sort—primarily since I had practically handpicked the girls myself. But there was one woman who had wormed her way into my group who really wasn't my cup of tea.

Her name was Winifred Opal, and just before the doors opened at eleven-thirty, she came up to me at the bread-warming oven where I was filling the warming drawers with buttered dinner rolls and orange-iced sweet rolls that had come straight from the big ovens out back.

"It's a crying shame," she said, reaching for a pair of aluminum steel tongs, "that some people don't have the common courtesy to let a soul know when they aren't going to show up for waitressing."

Was Winifred Opal taking a jab at me?

Winnie was a large woman, tall, not heavy, six feet if she was an inch. She wore her thick hair in a long earth-mother braid and had a fondness for dogs. Her laugh was booming, her manner of dress less than perfect JLWC. The only reason she was a member was because she was a direct descendent of Eunice Houston Brightlee herself.

She was odd, to say the least, which was not unusual in Texas, but not so usual in the JLWC. She was constantly seeking attention from the news media for one of her animal causes. You can't imagine the stink she raised when she went on her antifur rampage a few years back. You haven't seen anything until you've seen Winifred Opal with a squirt bottle of French's (very) yellow (and very staining) mustard. The PETA people with their cans of spray paint could learn a lesson or two from our Winnie. There hasn't been so much as a rabbit's-foot key chain within our city limits since she bought stock in French's Foods.

"What this place needs is some new blood," she added in a
was meant to be insulting.

I went very still, then slowly turned to face her as my thoughts congealed. New blood?

"Why, Winifred Opal. You are so right! Of course we need new blood. I was just telling my mother that very same fact. You're a genius!"

Winifred gaped at me in shock. But odd or not, she had the ability to sponsor someone—namely Nikki Grout.

"You know, Winnie, we don't spend enough time together."

She couldn't seem to move, the long silver tongs holding a drippy sweet roll midair. "Me? With me?"

"Of course, Winnie. We've never had a chance to visit, just you and me. Time to get to know each other. Why don't I give you a call? We'll set up a time to have a good long chat."

We finished up the rolls and I swear Winnie smiled all through the entire seating. She didn't even yell at a single lunch guest, which went down in the JLWC record books as a first.

The tearoom was busy that day, and I didn't get out of Brightlee until nearly three that afternoon. I was home in ten minutes, but still had to hurry if I was going to get cleaned up and make it to Nikki's hair appointment. As soon as I got there, I didn't waste a minute.

"So tell me, sugar, what all do you know about Sawyer Jackson."

I had barely gotten to Salon Françoise in time to meet Nikki. But I made it and we were sipping pink lemonade from (fake) crystal cups while we waited for Eugenie, the owner of the place. Eugenie's real name was Euless Franks, but since she did hair like nobody's business I didn't say a word to anyone about her reinvention. Deep down there was a part of me that was intrigued by anyone who had the courage to reinvent themselves so completely.

"What do you mean, what do I know?"

Nikki's anticipation for her "new look" was written all over her face as she stared at her reflection in the mirror. Everything in Salon Françoise was lacy or fouffy, all of it pink, either satin or velvet. I knew Nikki would love the place, and truth to tell, she couldn't wait to get started.

The problem occurred when Eugenie walked out from the back room with the bowl of color. At the sight, the champagne bubbles of Nikki's personality went flat, as if she had been left out overnight with her cork out.

"Are you sure about this, Frede?" she asked.

"Of course I'm sure. Blond is one thing, bleached blond is something else altogether."

"But it doesn't look like it's going to be blond at all," she said, eyeing the color.

Eugenie took Nikki's lemonade away. "Don't you worry," she said. "I know what I'm doing."

Nikki stared at her reflection like a deer caught in headlights. As I saw it, the only kind thing to do was take her mind off what was happening. Plus I really wanted to know.

"So you were telling me about the artist."

"What?"

"Sawyer Jackson."

"Oh, yeah." Her eyes met mine in the glass. "So, you like him?"

Eugenie's proficient hand hesitated. Currency in any beauty shop is paid as much in gossip as it is in actual dollars, and the potential news that Frede Ware was interested in another man would make Eugenie a small fortune.

I clarified. "He's *très* talented. And despite the fact that he prefers men—"

Eugenie sighed and returned to work.

"—I know his show is going to be a huge success. But I know virtually nothing about him."

"Well, he's the sweetest thing," she said, still staring at her reflection. "And his art is to die for. He's got more talent in his pinky than any other artist I know. But he's real finicky about who he lets see his work. I wasn't surprised that he said no to you."

"Didn't I tell you, he agreed after all."

She swiveled her eyes to look at me in the mirror. "No!"

"Yes."

She shook her head in what must be amazement and Eugenie grumbled. "This is great," she said.

"So what else do you know . . . for publicity's sake, of course?"

"Well, he and his family moved to Willow Creek when I was in fifth grade. He was a freshman."

"He's lived here that long?" How was it possible I hadn't heard of him before? "Where did he live?"

"Same place as now."

Ah, older than me, living in South Willow Creek. Enough said.

Nikki smiled fondly. "Even then everyone knew he was different. He was big and muscular, and didn't shy away from a fight."

I was confused. "This doesn't sound so different from most any guy in South Willow Creek."

"Maybe, but Sawyer was all into art. No guys in our neighborhood were interested in anything arty—at least not that they would admit to. But Sawyer was always drawing, talking about this artist or that. I remember my mother and everyone used to talk about it, about him and his arty ways. Plus, his parents were old, like grandparents old. I think they were professors at WCU, smart, for sure, just like Sawyer. He graduated early from high school and got out of town. He just returned last year. You should have seen that place when he got back. Just a wreck. He's fixed it up, always seems to be doing more to it."

"So who are his friends now?"

"I don't know."

"How about boyfriends?"

"I don't have a clue, Frede. You'd have to ask him."

As if I would ever pry. At least not directly.

I wasn't getting anywhere with my search, and all attempts came to a screeching halt when Eugenie took Nikki back to rinse out the color. My protégée's horror grew in direct proportion to how far along the new hairstyle progressed. When Nikki returned and got a look at herself in the mirror, she about fainted dead away.

"Jesus Lordy!"

And let me just say it wasn't a good "Jesus Lordy."

"My hair is brown!"

"Now, silly, that isn't true." And it wasn't. Once dry, her hair would be very Proper Junior League. A dark blond that toned down her appearance. "Let Eugenie cut it now."

I couldn't get a peep out of Nikki after that about Sawyer or anything else. She sank lower and lower in the chair as Eugenie trimmed the bottom layers off Nikki's layered haircut. It was about as close to a shoulder bob as it was going to get when Eugenie started in with the blow dryer.

That was another reason I kept mum about Eugenie aka Euless. Salon Françoise was the only place in Willow Creek that used a blow dryer. Every place else was a set-and-dry beauty shop that loved their Aqua Net. Until Salon Françoise opened, I had to drive clear to San Antonio to get my hair blown out.

Finally Nikki was finished, and she stood up from her swivel chair looking like everything I had hoped. In a matter of two and a half hours she had gone from trashy and flashy to tasteful and refined.

"Nikki! You look fabulous!"

She looked at me as though I were out of my mind, and I despaired that I would ever get through to her.

We headed back to Palace Grout, and let me just say that the drive was a verra verra quiet one. I think Nikki was in shock from all that demure sophistication and hadn't a clue what to say.

Howard pulled open the front door when we stopped in the drive, as if he had been waiting to see the outcome. He flipped his cell phone shut on a gruff, "I'll call you back."

Nikki sank down a few inches.

"Go on. Show Howard how fabulous you look!"

Her lower lip actually trembled, but like a brave little duck, she got out. I came around to her side just in time to witness Howard getting a good look at his new wife.

To give him credit, he didn't say the words that played across his face. His green-eyed gaze took her in, adjusted, then nodded his head. "Well, muffin, if that's what it takes, then that's what it takes."

Men can be so clueless.

Nikki burst into tears, then raced into the house, nearly tripping on her lovely one-inch heels.

"Yes, well," I said for the umpteenth time that day. "I'll just be heading home."

Howard finally looked away from the now empty front doorway. "Hold on, Frede. I've got another update."

I braced myself.

"Your husband is in the Bahamas now." His brow furrowed. "But he's going through your money faster than a priest goes through leftover communion wine on Sundays."

"What do you mean?"

"For starters, he's staying in expensive hotels. He dropped twenty-five grand a night to stay in the Bridge Suite at Atlantis. And he's throwing parties, lavish parties, like he's trying to impress people. I know you don't want me going to the police here in town, but—"

I must have gotten white in the face.

"Hell, Frede, your money is missing, and your husband—who doesn't make a living in any way I can see—turns up spending money like there's no tomorrow."

I felt hot and cold at the same time. I was rich, but there were limits even to my money.

"We've got to have some police helping us somewhere. So I got the word out with some foreign agencies I've worked with before in hopes of nabbing him." His expression went even harder than usual. "But he's chartering private jets and boats to move around—which makes it hard as hell to keep track of him. He's a wily one. And I still can't find a trace of where that bastard's put your money."

"Then how do you know he's spending it?"

"Because he keeps using his real name. Like I said, he's doing everything he can to impress people with these parties he's throwing. Looks to me like he's trying to make a name for himself."

"But why?"

"That's what I'm going to find out."

I WAS SHAKY as I made my way back home and felt downright sick when I found my sister-in-law Edith's car parked in the back drive by the kitchen door. Edith only came over when there was a problem, or if Gordon specifically invited her. Since I already knew my husband was (hopefully catchable and still) in the Bahamas, I could only assume there was a problem.

The back door was unlocked, though even a lock wouldn't have kept Edith out since Gordon had given her a key. When I entered, Nina was the only person in the kitchen.

"Where is she?" I asked in a whisper.

Nina didn't like Edith any more than I did. She glanced at the door that led to the rest of the house, then back. "She in Meester Gordon's study."

Not one to put off the inevitable, I headed there myself and entered just in time to see her riffling through my husband's things.

"Edith, what a surprise!"

Edith about cut off her hand when she closed the file drawer before she got said appendage out. She whelped, then shook off the pain like a refined, refuses-to-show-emotion woman should. Standing, she didn't dither. "I insist you tell me what has happened to my brother."

A little sisterly love goes a long way when bills aren't being paid. Though perhaps I was being unkind. She appeared genuinely worried. Her clothes were more dowdy than usual, and she had dark circles under her eyes.

"I've been worried sick," she added for good measure.

"As I told you, he is out of town. On one of his adventures. Remember?"

"Yes, I remember that's what you told me. But no, I don't believe it for a second. Gordon Ware is responsible, and well . . . this disappearance is the height of irresponsibility."

True. But what was I going to say?

"If you don't tell me where he is and how I can get ahold of him, I will be forced to go to the police."

Well, that was a song I didn't want sung—at least if they weren't singing to the international sort who couldn't influence Willow Creek social standings.

"Edith, that's ridiculous."

"I'm serious, Frede. Every time I turn around, yet another bill hasn't been paid."

So much for sisterly love.

"Another bill? How many does he pay?" I asked, though my tone probably wasn't sweet as pie, and there might have been an edge to it that would have made Pilar proud.

"Like I said," she told me, her chest puffing up with moral indignation, "Gordon feels an obligation to support his family."

That's when it happened. I blame it on the hours I had spent with Nikki. I became unforgivably direct.

"You know, Edith, have you ever wondered where your magnanimous brother gets his money to pay your bills?" I couldn't believe it any more than I could help it. The words were tumbling out, as if I had been raised in a South Texas barn.

"Gordon is a successful lawyer," she said. "And a highly thought-of money manager, I might add."

"And just where did you hear this?"

She looked a little concerned at that, but she was no pushover. "He told me so himself."

"Ah. And did he mention any cases he has handled in this law practice of his? Or whose money he manages?"

"Well, no."

"That would be mine. My money. Which, as it turns out, has gone missing."

"What?"

"Yes, sweet sister-in-law. My money, the money that has been paying your way, has disappeared—along with your brother."

She sat down so hard that the seat cushion whoofed out a gush of air. "Missing?"

I couldn't tell if she was concerned about her brother or the money that had been supporting her.

"Yes, missing." Then I did the only thing I could do. I told her the whole sordid tale—much as I had told Howard Grout—about finding Miss Mouse, the vasectomy, the missing money, then added the news of the bad investments, Grand Cayman, and the Bahamas.

She stared at me in shock, her lips opened and pursed, sort of warbling with nonsensical sounds. Then her expression hardened. "I can't believe he would do this to Mama and Daddy."

Hello, what about me?

She gave a sharp, bitter laugh. "Though I'm not surprised, as spoiled as he always was."

Nothing like a little money crisis to make true feelings bubble to the surface.

"All he's ever cared about was himself."

"He should have married Pilar." I really can be flip at the most inappropriate times.

She gave me an odd look, then said, "We've got to go to the police."

"Fine by me." Hardly. "Let all of Willow Creek know that Gordon is a lying, cheating scum of the earth, and the rest of us Wares no longer have two nickels to rub together. Hmmm, let's see. That makes us 'those poor Wares.' Perhaps you should run all this by Papa Ware before we zip over to the precinct."

That did the trick, just as I knew it would. As we already know, the last thing any member of good society needs is a scandal . . . or to be considered poor.

I had bought myself some time, but I knew the clock was ticking. I couldn't keep this a secret forever.

Finally Edith was gone and I didn't want to think about anything. Not Nikki and her hair. Not my husband and my missing money. Not Edith and her misdirected anger. Instead, I dove into planning my art show for my artist.

In truth, I had been planning in my head ever since I decided I would get him. I had the sneaking suspicion I had become obsessed with the man. Jesus Lordy, as Nikki would say, it truly was a shame he preferred men.

I had no problem that the man was gay, but I did have a problem lusting after yet another man who was at some level unavailable to me. And let's face it, Gordon had never been available to me. The vasectomy was proof of that.

What I couldn't get out of my head was the way my artist was always studying me. It was like he was sizing me up.

Sure, it could have been done with an artist's eye as he considered painting (and who could blame him) the fabulous Frede Ware. Or maybe he just wanted to sneer at me, disdain me, solve the mystery of why I was helping a woman who even he could see tried my patience.

The confusing part was that I couldn't figure out why I cared what he thought.

I spent the afternoon arranging the exhibition. I spoke to the director of my gallery and gave her the names of my friends who should be on the invitation list for the opening. There were also my acquaintances, my important contacts, and my Rolodex section of media personnel who were musts for any successful event.

My show was going to be the biggest hit since the husbands of the Junior League of Willow Creek put on a production of *Best Little Whorehouse in Texas* to raise money for the Willow Creek pediatric surgery center. You haven't seen legitimate musical theater until you've seen a cast of Willow Creek's most distinguished gentlemen dressed up as hookers.

Everything was in order, I was doing a grand job of pretending everything was fine. But the next morning I woke up in what I could only call a panic.

Me. Panicked.

This is an unheard-of occurrence for me, and it only got worse when the phone rang earlier than was acceptable, at eight-thirty. No one who knows anything calls anyone between the hours of nine P.M. and nine A.M. Calls during those nighttime and early morning hours are for things like being told someone was hurt, dead, or the caller was a truly NC person who didn't know better.

Which meant that either someone was calling with bad news, or Howard and/or his wife were on the phone.

I debated not answering, though there was always the hope that it was news about my missing husband.

I picked up and it was the director of my gallery—a woman who was all about manners, which meant the call couldn't be good.

"What is it, Peggy?"

"I'm sorry to call so early, but we've got a problem."

Chapter Sixteen

"PEGGY, WHAT'S WRONG?"

She hesitated as if she were gathering her wits (or swallowing her distaste) to share some horrible news. "The gallery account is overdrawn."

Peggy didn't like talking about money any more than I did.

"I've left messages for Mr. Ware on his office line, but I haven't heard back and checks are, well, being returned. Including payroll."

A jolt hit my stomach. Call me what you will, but I hadn't given a thought to how bills were paid, either here or at the gallery. Gordon had taken care of that for so long (and my father before that) that I rarely if ever thought about those things. Maintaining "charge" accounts with most local vendors was the only tasteful thing to do. When I made a purchase, all that needed to happen was a quick, *I'll take this, put it on my account,* and I was out the door. Even at the bigger stores in Austin, San Antonio, and Dallas I had accounts. There was just something vulgar about having to whip out my American Express platinum card.

"I hate bothering you with this, Mrs. Ware. If Mr. Ware is available, I could discuss it with him."

Three weeks ago I wouldn't have given a thought to a statement about preferring to talk to my husband about money rather than me. Now, three weeks into this new life, I was half insulted. But only half since the other part of me was worried. With my money still MIA, how was I going to pay bills?

A novel thought. Sue me.

I told her I would get back to her, then started to hang up when she reminded me of the publicity shoot I had scheduled for that afternoon.

When making the arrangements for the artist to have his publicity photo taken for the show, I had thought having the shoot in my home would be a great idea. My artist by the pool, or my artist sitting on the lovely stone wall that curved along my terraced gardens. Plus it would give me control in a way that I wouldn't have had we done the photos at his house or studio. Photos taken at my gallery would have been too plain.

Now my only thought was, how would I pay the photographer?

My artist had insisted on using someone he knew, which had been fine at the time. But not knowing who it was, I hadn't a clue how the person would expect to be paid. I couldn't imagine my artist watching me flail over something as NC as money.

I finally hung up and approached my husband's study with trepidation. Nina always got the mail and delivered it to Gordon's office, who then went through it and dispensed with it as was necessary. When I pushed through the door, the stack of missives sat on the desk. It took me a full thirty minutes to go through it all.

The damage?

An amassed debt of seventy-five thousand dollars since the last statements, which thankfully had been paid. Plus, there was a giant stack of unRSVPed invitations.

I was appallingly late in responding on at least half of them, most of those for the best parties in town.

Putting the cream-colored invitations in order by date of event, I started thinking about what to say to each hostess. Some invitations were for couples, and they would be nos. Others were for women, some of which I would attend to maintain the air of nothing being wrong. And others would be declined since I would never have attended them regardless of my situation.

Then, more importantly, I turned my attention to appropriate party attire. No question I would have to get to the shops ASAP after the RSVPs were handled. Which stopped me cold.

Shopping. Shopping took money. I had no money to pay the bills much less for shopping.

I groaned and went back through the seventy-five thousand dollars' worth of bills.

There were the usual things like groceries and dry cleaning, but the new (and exquisite, if I do say so myself) settee I had purchased to go in my dressing room the week before the unfortunate incident cost ten thousand dollars. I could hardly believe it. And no, I hadn't bothered to ask the price when I told the man I had to have it.

For half a second, I considered returning the settee. But the shop was in town, and word would get out if it was sent back at this point—especially since I had already told the owner of the store how perfectly it had worked out. Plus, finding the perfect piece of furniture to go in that space had taken me two years. Money would have to be found elsewhere to tide me over until Howard found my missing money.

Yet again, I thought about going to my father. And yet again, I ruled it out. Eventually my parents would have to be told, but I couldn't face my mother's knowing scorn, and I wasn't about to let my father bail me out and potentially go down the drain with me.

I even thought about asking my lawyer for a loan. But that was unbearable, so there was only one thing left for a respectable woman of my position to do when faced with a money crunch. I went to my closet and opened the safe kept at the very back. Most of my better pieces that were handed down to me from my family were kept at the bank . . .

The thought had me staggering back and sitting down hard on my ten-thousand-dollar settee. Had Gordon taken my best jewels too?

My head swam and I put my head between my knees, telling myself to breathe.

Someone else would have been embarrassed by the sheer number of things that were occurring to me at this late date. I only got madder at Gordon, which helped me breathe again.

A new lesson:

Panic = difficulty breathing

Anger = plenty of oxygen and feels a whole lot better than panic

And why not get angry? Why bottle it up, as had been pounded into my head since birth? Why should *I* feel bad about myself if my once trusted husband betrayed me? Betrayed Frede Ware!

I retraced my steps to the vault and pulled out my least favorite piece, least favorite because Gordon had had his sister Edith pick it out for me. It was as imaginative as Edith herself. Three strands of cultured pearls with a four-karat diamond pendant. I also chose a dated piece that Gordon had given me for one of our anniversaries which I had meant to have reset. Sapphires and diamonds in a bright gold setting. I might not know the price of a settee on sight, but I do know the cost of jewelry. It would give me enough to pay off the debt, meet the payroll at the gallery, and maybe pick up that *fabu* lightest-of-green Chanel suit I had seen at Saks Fifth Avenue.

While normally it takes me a good two hours to get ready, that morning I was out the door and heading for the San Antonio jewelry broker my family had used for decades in a little under fifty minutes. And still, my attire was impeccable.

I called my former bank on my cell phone while zipping down I-35 only to be told by some minion that indeed my safe-deposit box had been closed. Translation: family heirlooms gone.

I just about wrecked.

Despite that, I made it to San Antonio in record time and had instant entrée to the office of Konrad Kingswell, LLC, jeweler to the wealthiest of wealthy in the Lone Star State. He was a short balding man who always fawned over me despite my usual kind but cool demeanor.

That day I melted just a bit. I smiled extra wide, complimented his tie, and called him "sugar." Unfortunately, it was wasted effort, because Mr. Kingswell set down his loupe and said, "They're fake."

I was beyond being surprised at that point, I just felt cold. Mechanically, knowing the answer before I asked, I extended my pink diamond engagement ring, supposedly worth a great deal.

"Fake," he said apologetically to my mute stupor.

My nonfeeling self had gone through a gamut of emotions during the last three weeks. Anger, stress, panic. And now I felt something else. Hate. I hated Gordon Ware.

I left and returned home. There was only one thing left to do.

Nina helped me take a few of my paintings down from the wall. As a gallery owner, I had been investing in art for years. Selling art was the only solution. Since I had bought them, they couldn't be fakes.

Turning the paintings in to a wholesale dealer my gallery did business with regularly only took minutes. When I was finished, I left with a check for enough money to tide me over for another few weeks.

With a quick glance at my watch I saw there was only an hour and a half before my artist and his photographer were supposed to arrive at my house.

I swung through an NC part of town until I found the kind of bank my friends wouldn't dream of patronizing, in a 1960s-era strip shopping center with a glass front. (It had probably been a Woolworth's five-and-dime back in its day.) Pulling on a pair of Jackie O. sunglasses and a wide-brimmed straw hat, I entered and announced that I wanted to open an account.

Depositing my check in the better part of Willow Creek at my old bank wasn't possible. Even though I knew Ned Reed would keep everything quiet since the last thing he wanted getting around town was that my husband had managed to get my money out of his bank without my knowing about it, I couldn't just all of a sudden start *banking* at the very bank where all my friends' husbands did their own banking. That had always been Gordon's job.

The manager of First National was anxious to accommodate me, all but tripping over himself as he ushered me inside a closet-sized office. "Please, Miz Ware, have a seat."

I could tell that the man was skewered on the twin forks of my beauty and apparent wealth.

"Can I get you some coffee or a soda, ma'am?"

"No, thank you."

Then he just stared at me.

I waited for a second, expecting him to say something, but then I realized he was enamored. I'm all for mood elevators, but I had things to do, people to see.

I waved my hand in front of his face. "I'm in a bit of a hurry."

Blood raced up his neck to his face. "Sorry. Let me tell you about the different types of accounts we have—"

"No need. Just open one up with my name on it."

"Oh, sure." He fumbled around on his desk for a form. "If you'll tell me how much you want to deposit . . . and keep in mind if you deposit more than a thousand dollars you'll get a toaster and free checking—"

I handed the man my check. He glanced at it, then looked as if he would have a coronary right there.

"Please, Mister"—I glanced at his nameplate—"Alston, I am in a terrible hurry. Just open whatever you think is fit."

It took another thirty minutes to open the account, get a set of "temporary" checks, and the toaster (did any bank in the entire United States still give away appliances?) that was easier to take than refuse. Then I dashed home, arriving thirty minutes late for my *rendezvous,* or rather, appointment.

What had to be my artist's car was sitting in the drive—an ancient MG. Think Ryan O'Neal (prehookup with that NC Texan, Farah Fawcett) in that ancient movie *Love Story.* Or was it a Triumph Spitfire? Hmmm. Whatever. Think small, dangerous, and nothing I would be caught dead riding in.

When I entered, the foyer was empty. Which gave me time.

I hurried up the stairs and went into my bath suite.

Looking good for a jewelry broker, an art dealer, and a NC banker was a very different kettle of fish from looking good for a homosexual artist and a photographer of his choosing.

I stripped down to my bra and stockings. I would have bathed again, but it was getting late, so I went instead with a dusting of powder.

I refluffed my hair, reapplied my very light and very tasteful makeup, then dressed in a white blouse, an equestrian-print silk skirt in cream, brown, and a dash of pale orange, and three strands of pearls. I looked lovely enough to make it nearly possible to forget that I had just spent the morning dealing with money. I almost was able to revert to the days of spelling the word. But I was afraid Gordon had stripped that innocence away from me once and for all.

Descending the stairway with my hand barely touching the banister, I expected to find Sawyer Jackson waiting. But the foyer was still empty. I checked the receiving room, the living room, and even the den. All to no avail.

I finally heard voices and found my artist sitting at the kitchen table with Nina, both talking in Spanish as if they were long-lost friends.

This was amazing because there is the whole rule about entertaining in the kitchen. But to compound the faux pas, it was my *maid* who was entertaining in the kitchen. And that wasn't even the biggest surprise. (As you know) Nina hates everyone but me (though she was showing friendly signs toward Nikki). Sitting at the kitchen table, Nina was leaning close and telling the man all about her favorite new reality show that was shown on the single Mexican station she could get in Willow Creek. *Bailar Mejicano,* where once a week, one Don Juan de Tango was dancing his way through a dozen women in order to find his perfect dance partner. On more than one occasion I had gone into the family room to find my maid tangoing along with the show.

"I hate to break up the party, but we have work to do."

I used my haughtiest tone of voice that should have intimidated the two of them. My artist turned to look at me and laughed (yes, laughed) and Nina scoffed at me. "You be nice," she said. "He bring you present."

That got my attention.

"A present? For me?"

My artist laughed again and pulled something out from under the chair next to his. He stood and extended a shiny gray Saks Fifth Avenue shopping bag.

Ridiculously excited, I pulled out a small box and had the package open in record time. What I found shouldn't have been a surprise.

"The bracelet."

"I could tell you liked it."

Foolishly, I did.

"Plus," he added, "I figured I owed you an apology after our shopping trip."

He truly was A Shame. A gift and an apology for being rude to me. Though he was even more of A Shame when I finally noticed his outfit. He wore a white jean jacket, some sort of black shiny shirt, and white jeans. This might work in South Beach or Europe, but it doesn't work in my world. Forget the whole "No white before Easter" thing, a matching white jean *ensemble* is like sandals—should never be worn by a man. Any man.

I sighed. "As sweet as you were to bring it, I can't accept."

"Why not?" he asked.

Nina looked at me with knowing disappointment. She had learned propriety from my mother at the same time I learned it, and she knew as well as anyone that a present from a man other than my husband was just not done.

"Because I'm a man?" he asked.

Nina was too devastated to watch and had to leave the room—as if I made the rules!

Which made me reconsider. The fact was, the whole homosexual territory was new to me, and really, would it be so wrong to accept a gift from a gay man? Besides, it had been ages since Gordon had surprised me with anything but a mistress and I desperately wanted a gift.

"On second thought, it's lovely, and I thank you," I said, accepting. "Though call me a busybody, but I'd love to know why you feel the need to apologize this time. You certainly didn't after you slammed the door in my face."

He shrugged and looked amused. "No question I was rude when you showed up. But what can I say. I'm moody." He reached for the bracelet. "Let me put it on," he said. "And try saying my name for a change."

"What are you talking about?"

"I haven't heard you say it once since you came to my studio, and even then it was a question. Maybe you don't remember it."

"I know your name."

He laughed again. "I know your type. You probably think of me as 'the artist.'"

It was too close for comfort, especially since the real version had shifted to "*my* artist."

I closed the lid on the box, and said, "I'll put it on another time. For now, that's the doorbell—" Thank God. "That must be your photographer."

A few minutes later, the photographer entered.

"Sawyer!" the man called out.

"Reynaldo."

The two men hugged and did that whole double-kiss to the cheek thing. (This ranks right up there with eating a meal while keeping the fork in one hand and the knife in the other without setting either down. I'm all for when in Rome—or Europe—but we weren't either of those places.)

I was introduced, and Reynaldo took my hand and kissed my knuckles. (Hello, we're in America, people.)

"You are a vision," he exclaimed.

Okay, so some men can get away with excessive displays of European charm.

But that was where his charm ended, at least in regard to me. My artist—rather, Sawyer—and Reynaldo immediately got to work, acting as if I weren't even there. Plain and simple, I was ignored.

We went out back and they discussed the best angles for the shoot, the direction of the sun, the composition of the final product, all the while laughing like old friends. I had the thought that this might actually be Sawyer's boyfriend, or at least someone he was dating.

I admit it, I felt uncomfortable. Yes, me. And it wasn't because I was uncomfortable thinking about two men being together. I was oddly uncomfortable thinking about my artist being with another anyone. And it only got worse as the hour progressed.

When they finally got around to the shooting part, I had to watch Sawyer in next to nothing (or as nothing as he agreed to wear) by my pool. He wore jeans with a chambray shirt unbuttoned. I'm not sure who was lusting more, me or Reynaldo.

Sawyer looked so good by the pool that even Nina recovered enough to join me from my vantage point.

"He good-looking," she stated. "Almost as good as Don Juan de Tango."

True, not that I would admit it to Nina. "Certainly his boyfriend thinks so."

"Boyfriend?" Nina looked over at me with one of her evil eyes. "You jealous of Reynaldo?"

I worked up an admirable case of indignation. "I most certainly am not jealous of Reynaldo." I wasn't. Really.

Nina snorted. "You bad, Missy Ware."

Which is when we both noticed that Sawyer was looking at us. With a gleam in his eye, he took the few steps that separated us. But instead of coming to me, he took Nina's hand and danced her in a circle.

"Oh, Meester Sawyer!"

She sounded like a schoolgirl with a crush on the most popular boy at the eighth-grade dance. I was embarrassed for her.

Then she was back by my side, though not for long since next it was my turn. My artist had me out on the deck, dancing me around much as he had Nina.

"Mr. Jackson!"

At least I didn't sound as bad as Nina.

"What are you doing?" I demanded.

He pulled me close while Nina said several *Dios mios*. Sawyer didn't seem to care. He danced me around the pool as if we were ballroom dancing. Swoops and sweeps, and he was singing. Singing the tune we were dancing to. It was strange and exhilarating.

After several turns, he did one final Don Juan–esque dip, arching me over backward. I was rattled, no question, because when someone is holding you bent over like that you can feel . . . well, strength. I don't know how else to say it. All sorts of muscles working to hold you up. If he hadn't been inclined toward men it would have been ultra bad form, my being married and all. Fortunately that wasn't a concern. I decided that having a gay friend was better than having a husband since he was strong, handsome, and I didn't have to worry he would disappoint me.

It was surprisingly wonderful and I gave in to all the safe strength of him. This was what I had needed my whole life and hadn't even known it. A friend who was a man who wouldn't look at me and want me or be jealous of me.

"I could easily adore you," I said.

I felt even more of that power when he swept me back up and pulled me close. This was the beginning of a great, wonderfully platonic friendship with a man who wouldn't threaten my reputation. I felt happier than I had in ages, and I wished I had thought to find a friend like him sooner.

He looked at me and smiled as if he knew exactly what I was thinking—and thought it too. Or so I thought.

"Just so you know," he whispered in my ear, "I'm not gay."

Chapter Seventeen

MY WHOLE LIFE I have been traveling down a single (beautifully landscaped) highway, never veering, never detouring. In my all-time most hated class in college (Psychology 101—surprise!) we were taught that a daughter learned a lot about how to deal with the world from the way her father treated her.

At the end of junior high, the school sponsored a graduation dance for the eight-graders. We were all in a tizzy, what with it being our first dance. Even Pilar in all her no-nonsenseness was excited. Our little clique of three planned every second of the upcoming event with the precision of little generals, so much so that we even practiced what we would say when we were asked to dance. We spent hours deciding how to style our hair, how to get away with putting on makeup, and what we would wear. Pilar and I were getting new dresses, but Nikki was having to make do with something from somewhere we didn't want to ask about. As the dance got closer, Nikki's anticipation diminished in direct proportion to how Pilar's and mine grew. More than once Nikki stood in front of Willow Creek Teens and Tots, staring and wishing for the confection of pink taffeta in the window that cost more than her mother probably made in a month.

"I'm going to look like a dork if I can't wear something great!" she cried with her usual theatrics.

What were we going to say to that because, quite frankly, it was true.

A week before the dance, my father sent me off to bed with the words he always said. "I'm going to give you the world, princess, because I love you that much."

No question it was silly and over-the-top, but it had become a ritual, his version of good night. In his larger-than-life flamboyance, he could get away with just about anything.

But that night I didn't respond with my usual "I love you, too, Daddy." No, instead I asked him to buy Nikki the dress.

Not exactly what he expected.

"Well, I don't know, sweetheart—"

"But a dress isn't half as big as the world, Daddy."

He looked at me closely, then smiled real big and laughed so loud that my mother came into the room. "What are you two up to now?"

"Nothing, love," my father said. "Go back to your book."

He kissed me on the forehead. "Let me see what I can do."

On the night of the big dance, with Pilar and Nikki getting ready at my house, we found three Teens and Tots boxes tied with big fancy bows sitting on my white canopy bed. One for each of us.

Pilar opened hers and just stared. I found the dress I had already told my mother I wanted. I pulled it out, but was more interested in my other friend opening hers. Nikki tugged at the bow on the box as if she were afraid to hope, her breath held. When she pulled off the top, she sucked in her breath. "Oh, my," she whispered, pressing her face to the fluff. "Oh, Frede, you are so wonderful."

Pilar watched, didn't look as happy as I expected her to be, then shoved hers back in the box. "I don't need your dress."

I began to understand then that in the role of my daddy's daughter, as the very proper Fredericka Hildebrand, I could have power—though not everyone would like it. Being held in the suddenly nongay Sawyer Jackson's arms, arched over the pool, I felt as though I had come to a fork in the road— or let's face it, an exit ramp. If I took the exit, changing paths, I knew that there would be no proper knife, spoon, or linen napkin to be found along the way. And, God forbid, no power. This man, with all his strength, was not about anything having to do with the life I knew.

I jerked so hard against the thought—and him—that he nearly dropped me in the pool.

"What do you mean you're not gay?"

Fortunately, as has already been established, he was all about strength and muscles, so he managed to keep me on dry land.

"How can you not be gay?" I continued. "You have to be gay."

I know, I was acting worse than common. But really, how could he not be gay? I had spent the last few hours flirting with him. It had been all right (mostly) when he preferred other men—fun and safe, and while not proper, it was not a horrible sin against acceptable behavior. But if he wasn't gay . . .

"You're upset because I'm *not* gay?" His dark eyes glittered with mischief. "Are you sure you're from Texas?"

"Funny. And of course I'm upset. You should have said something sooner."

"Like before you said you adored me?" His mouth ticked up at the corner.

"I said I could *easily* adore you."

Pushing away, I smoothed my attire and tried to get my head around this man and his lack of gayness. I was devastated. Filled with despair. And hot as Hades in a totally inappropriate lusting sort of way. Me, Frede Ware. Lusting.

You might as well take out a list of every known inappropriate emotion that I had spent a lifetime learning To Not Have and watch me flounder with a bad case of them all.

Sawyer was amused. "If it'll make you feel better, you could keep pretending that I am."

If only. But I had been my mother's daughter for far too long to play pretend. Ignore? Absolutely. But now that I knew he wasn't same-sex oriented it would be impossible to pretend that the strange tingling he made me feel wasn't anything to worry about. When I thought he preferred men, I managed to discount the sensation as a sign of sheer desperation given my lack of relations in the last few weeks. And while I was all about proper, I was female and only twenty-eight years old. I wasn't dead. A good-looking, available, heterosexual male who made my body show signs of life would be hard to ignore any longer.

Thankfully, the photographer approached. "We're done here," he said.

I smiled at him with forced sincerity. "Good, and thank you. I know the pictures will be wonderful. I appreciate your coming to the house."

But the man just stood there. After a second he looked at the artist, then back to me. Finally Sawyer said, "Here, let me get that."

He walked over to his duffel bag and pulled something out. A checkbook. He was going to pay!

My spine went stiff with something I think might have been embarrassment. "Absolutely not," I said. "Let me run to the house and get a check."

I crossed the pool deck, the click of my fabulous Delman flats on the paving stones marking every step as I made my way inside. When I returned a few minutes later I had my "temporary" checkbook out, ready to write.

"How much do I owe you, Reynaldo?" I asked.

"I charge five hundred dollars for the shoot."

It cost five hundred dollars for a simple photograph?

"That doesn't include prints. Those are another five hundred bucks. When I have the proofs, you can come over to my studio and decide which shots you want to use."

A thousand dollars?

My Tiffany blue purse pen shook as I wrote out the check.

My artist looked at me curiously, then gathered his bag, gave me a ruggedly sensual smile that shook me even more, then the two men headed out, through the living room, right past the gaping white wall where the paintings had hung just hours before.

NIKKI'S PARTY WAS fast approaching, as was the new members deadline, and Nikki, bless her heart, just couldn't seem to get the hang of demure, ladylike behavior. I might as well have been teaching her Latin for all the sense it made to her.

On top of that, it seemed as if every day following her appointment at Salon Françoise her newly cut and colored hair got a little wilder—though thankfully it stayed the same respectable shade of dark blond. And for all the proper, subtly colored clothes we had purchased in San Antonio, every time I saw her she had added some bauble or bangle . . . as if I weren't going to notice the disco ball earrings partially hidden by her new coiffure.

With the clock ticking and no help for it, I had to start setting up individual appointments for Nikki to meet members who might sponsor her. Since I didn't dare ask a single woman from the infamous Spiked Tea for support, I set out to find a new set of ladies who might be more receptive to Nikki.

The first person I called was Winifred Opal. After she got over the shock that I was calling her, we scheduled a time to meet. It was for ten on Monday morning, followed by a visit at eleven-fifteen that I got set up with Misti Bladewell, then another at twelve-thirty with Mandi Huff. I had told them all that I would be bringing a friend with me, though I hadn't mentioned names since I didn't want them to say no before I ever got the chance to charm them face-to-face.

I had chosen Winifred, of course, because of our previous conversation. I had chosen Misti and Mandi because their names alone made me think they might be receptive to Nikki. Plus, all three women had attended Willow Creek High at the same time Nikki had, and while I don't think they were ever great friends, no one could deny that everyone knew everyone else when they were there, even if it was just in passing. Technically, they had "known" her for the requisite five years.

When I arrived at Palace Grout the morning of our appointments, Nikki was dressed in a beautiful camel-colored St. John knit top with gold buttons, and matching knit pants. She wore a perfect pair of low-heeled camel leather pumps and matching handbag. She looked like a perfect lady and I was encouraged.

Winifred lived in The Willows, two curving streets over in one of the first homes built in the enclave nearly eighty years ago. Live oaks dripping with Spanish moss extended their branches over the street as we drove, like a green lattice archway, the bright blue sky seeping through. Her house was an old Victorian, with a wraparound porch, white painted wood, and lots of gingerbread detailing. A white picket fence surrounded the front yard, the fence lined with a profusion of roses. White, yellow, pink, red. There was no order or conformity.

I was even more encouraged.

When we got to the front door Nikki was practically dancing with excitement.

"Remember," I told her, "ankles together, hands gracefully in your lap, and all will be fine."

"This is going to be so great!"

As soon as I rang the bell the house exploded with barking dogs. It sounded like bedlam inside, though silence reigned the minute Winnie pulled open the door with a flourish and said, "Sit!"

Nikki almost sat down right there on the wraparound porch.

Our hostess pushed open the screen door. "Frede!" She looked at Nikki, and I couldn't tell what she was thinking.

"Winifred, you remember Nikki Grout from Willow Creek High. Nikki, I bet you didn't know that Winifred is one of the Junior League of Willow Creek's most prestigious members." That was a stretch, but there was the whole founding-member connection and it couldn't hurt to throw a few compliments around.

"It's nice to meet, I mean, see you," Nikki said, and sort of curtsied.

I swear.

Winnie gestured for us to enter. For all the noise the dogs had made, there were only two of them, both miniature poodles. And they were dressed.

The lady of the house made some proper introductions of her own—to the dogs. A white poodle named Renata wore a white satin party dress while a black poodle by the name of Benjamin wore a black tuxedo jacket and bow tie.

It was a safe bet that not many Junior Leaguers had gone to her house when she was gaining her own sponsors, since I doubted that even being a direct descendant of the founding member would have outweighed dressed dogs who sat with us while we had tea.

I declined the cookies Winifred offered after she had served the dogs first on a lovely set of delicate bone china. My mother and Nina would have been appalled, though no doubt Blythe Hildebrand would have made excuses for a fellow Leaguer (at least one who wasn't her daughter) by calling Winnie a character. That was what proper Texas ladies called anyone in their circle who had more than a fleeting acquaintance with crazy.

We talked and Nikki outdid herself, even managing to get Winifred to let loose with a belly laugh. The best news of the day was that the dogs loved Nikki. Renata even trotted over and curled up in her lap. By the time we were leaving, I was sure I could count on Winifred's support.

Nikki was down the steps and standing by my Mercedes while I lingered behind to finalize the deal.

"I wondered if you would agree to become one of Nikki's sponsors to join the League," I said.

Winifred looked surprised. "Oh, dear. I don't know if I could."

I stared at her for what had to be a full five seconds. "Why not? You got along great and you said yourself you thought we needed some new blood."

"We did and I do. But I didn't say anything about new blood coming from Nikki Grout. Besides, did you see the pattern on her stockings?"

I hadn't and I felt a shiver of concern, not just because of her tone of voice, but because stockings should never, ever have a pattern.

"They were animal prints," she clarified.

While this was very bad news, I still had a brain. "Winifred, how can you say no when little Renata absolutely adored Nikki?"

She tilted her head. "There is that," she said, considering. "Okay, I won't say no, but I'm not saying yes either. Who do you have lined up so far?"

"It's me, Pilar Bass, and Eloise Fleming."

"Pilar? I'm surprised the two of you are sponsoring someone together, especially Nikki Grout."

"Why is that?"

"Because we both know Nikki Grout isn't the best political choice for someone to sponsor, and I hear the powers that be want you to be our next president-elect. I also happen to know that Pilar is angling for the same position."

"Pilar?"

I knew she was ambitious, but president?

Rumor had it (and you didn't hear this from me) that the reason she returned to Texas was because she had gotten fired from her job up North after being hired straight out of college as a star. Apparently, the whole New York, liberal, professional-woman thing was beyond her (despite her proclivity for flat hair and black clothes) and supposedly she dug her own grave when her blue-state, hardcore colleagues learned she had secretly voted for George W. Twice. Three times if you count when he ran for governor.

Whatever the cause, getting fired at all went a long way toward explaining why Pilar's whole life these days seemed to revolve around the League and her success in it. Her wanting to be the next president-elect shouldn't have been a surprise. If I had to guess, she had every intention of proving she could make it somewhere. Not that I was worried, mind you. If it came down to a contest between Pilar Bass and me, who do you think would win?

"Let me think about it," Winifred said. "One or the other of you is going to be president someday, and I've always fancied chairing a committee on animal rights."

She smiled at me and I realized that even crazy Winifred was political.

When I got into the car, my neighbor was buoyant. I was not.

"Is she going to sponsor me?" Nikki said with a mix of nervous excitement and trepidation. "She said yes, didn't she?"

"Well, no."

Every drop of buoyancy evaporated through the windshield.

"No?"

"Actually, she didn't say no to sponsoring you. She just didn't say yes. She's going to think about it."

"I don't understand."

I didn't want to mention she had a problem with Nikki in general, so I offered up something fixable, and I offered it as politely as I could. "She wasn't happy about your animal-print stockings."

Nikki practically jackknifed when she glanced down at her ankles. "But you can hardly see them. Besides, why would anyone care about my hose?"

How to explain the intricacies of the concept that what one wears tells a great deal about who she is, where she comes from, and what sort of choices she could potentially make in life? Even a hint of wild-animal print said very clearly that Nikki had high potential for making less than stellar choices and certainly was Not JLWC Acceptable.

I considered taking Nikki home to change. We only had five minutes to get to Misti Bladewell's house, and being more than ten minutes late was totally unacceptable. Which only gave us fifteen minutes. Besides, once upon a time I had seen Misti and Mandi out together for lunch in San Antonio, both of them wearing stiletto heels. I believed they were closeted NCs who sneaked out of town to have their little tacky-clothes flings. Nikki's stockings might be just the thing to get them on board. On the other hand, why risk it?

I drove Nikki to the Palace where she dutifully changed into nude stockings. Then we flew out of The Willows, past Juan, Nikki sinking down in the leather seat as we made our way to the next appointment.

Misti's home was built of a (beautiful) pale limestone brick with one of those extremely expensive (though god-awful) tin roofs. Hers was green. Who in their right mind ruined a perfectly good limestone with a green roof? But let her have her hideous roof if she would support Nikki.

We were let in by a young Swedish nanny, who couldn't have been more than eighteen, though with her hair a mess and a deep furrow between her brows she looked a hundred and eighteen. Everyone in the League knew that Misti Bladewell had five boys, all of them terrors, most of them under the age of seven.

Misti appeared oblivious to it all, which could only mean that she was: (a) dim, or (b) taking something Not JLWC Approved. I voted for the drugs as an answer since Misti—despite her unfortunate name—once was a child psychologist of some renown and had to have at least some brains in that head. Whatever she was taking, her nanny looked as if she could have used a dose or two.

Misti entered the foyer wearing neither stiletto heels nor acceptable flats. Her attire could only be termed nondescript. She also wore a big dreamy smile that instantly put Nikki at ease, though it was hard to maintain said ease with all the screaming and fighting going on in the nether regions of the house. (Winifred could have taught Misti a thing or two about discipline. I had never seen better behaved dogs.)

"Oh, those boys," Misti said cheerfully, waving in the direction of the noise as if she could wave it away.

Somehow the not-so-controlled setting perked Nikki up even more. Nothing like someone else's warts and problems out for all to see to put others at ease (or feel superior). Which goes back to my philosophy of never telling anyone anything personal, and never letting anyone see that anything is wrong. Nikki was proof. One minute she was glum and discouraged, the next she was smiling.

But even the ease that settled between us didn't make it any easier to have a conversation. The yelling. The boys racing through the living room chasing each other. The nanny hot on their trail. Misti ignored it all, though Nikki and I couldn't. But ten minutes after we arrived, even Misti couldn't tune out the excruciating scream that shot through the house.

Next thing I knew there was lots of crying, plenty of blood, and the nanny rushing Misti and the boys off to the emergency room.

Nikki and I let ourselves out.

"I hope the boy is going to be all right," she said.

"The nanny said the emergency room staff knows them all by name because they make so many visits. I'm sure whoever or whatever was wounded will be fine," I assured her.

"Do you think Misti will sponsor me?" She looked like she hated to ask, but had to know.

"Hard to tell. I'm not convinced she'll remember we were here."

"Yeah, she did seem kind of dazed."

That's when we noticed the blood.

"Oh, Lordy, look at me!" she cried, pointing to her camel top. "I can't go to meet anyone else looking like this!"

She had no problem with leopard-print stockings but came undone over a little blood.

I took out a linen handkerchief from my handbag. Nikki took it and started dabbing away at the knit.

"You can hardly see it," I said.

"Are you sure?"

"Absolutely."

By then, every bit of Nikki's optimism was gone. As she got into my car for the third time, her mood sank even more.

"Nikki, really, you have to cheer up."

Talk about opening Pandora's box. She swiveled in the leather seat to face me. "Cheer up? Freakin' A, Frede! How am I supposed to cheer up when everything I do is wrong, or ends up wrong, or doesn't work out?"

I gritted my teeth and smiled. "Nikki, far be it from me to criticize, but one of the worst things a prospective member of the Junior League of Willow Creek could do is use foul language."

"I didn't cuss!"

"You might as well have. It doesn't take a genius to know what *freakin'* is a stand-in for, though I shudder to think what 'A' is referring to, especially when combined with Freakin'. No Junior Leaguer in Willow Creek will sponsor a woman who curses."

Or wears leopard-print stockings.

Or disco ball earrings.

Or is married to Howard Grout.

But I didn't mention any of that, didn't even let them settle into my head, because I refused to accept that what I was attempting to do was impossible. It had to be done, and I was the woman who could do it. End of story.

"This is so hard." She looked truly abashed. "I wear the wrong thing, I say the wrong thing even after all the practicing I've been doing."

I almost smiled at the thought that she was getting it. I had high hopes she would throw out the rest of her regrettable attire the minute she returned home and finally get serious about getting into the JLWC as she swore she wanted. Though, truth to tell, being part of cliques had never been Nikki's strong suit.

It was at the beginning of our freshman year at Willow Creek High School that our little group truly changed. Nikki's mother had been through a slew of jobs, one after the other, each worse than the last. Nikki's clothes got rattier in direct proportion to how the rest of ours got better, not better moneywise but more fashionable.

At thirteen going on fourteen, we were all about the latest styles and we had the money to indulge. Even if Pilar wasn't about trendy, she was all about looking put-together. With the exception of the one pink party dress I had gotten for her, Nikki wasn't fashionable or put-together. I knew it was because she didn't have the money for either, though no one seemed to know that except for me.

It was at lunch one day when it started to fall apart for good. We were sitting in the high school cafeteria, food lines passé, brown bags worse, the cool of the cool buying candy bars and sodas at the concession stand. Nikki always showed up a few minutes later than the rest of the group, our clique now having grown to include more than just the three of us.

She would arrive with her tray from the free hot lunch line. I wonder now if she suffered the indignity because she knew it was the only good meal she would get for the day. Whatever the case, she would arrive, take the seat across from Pilar and next to me, the other girls knowing not to sit there.

It was a Friday, I remember, when Rebecca Milbanks leaned forward before Nikki got there and told us the news.

"You are never going to believe who tried to get a job at my house . . . as a maid!"

None of us would have cared a lick about the topic if it hadn't been for Becca's tone of voice.

"Who?" we all wanted to know.

"Nikki's mom!"

I can't begin to explain the shock we all felt. None of our mothers worked, let alone as a maid. It hardly made sense.

"What do you mean she wanted to be a maid?" Pilar asked, her sharp features getting even harder.

The girls slid down closer to better tell the tale, taking Nikki's seat.

Becca's brown eyes were lit with the promise of scandal. "Nikki's mom came to our house to apply for a job as maid! Can you believe it! Her mother is a total embarrassment."

It wasn't until then that we realized Nikki stood behind us, having arrived with her free-lunch tray, her face a mask of shock. The girls straightened with that peculiarly teenage mix of guilt and pleasure. Though instead of making the other girls move back to their regular seats, Pilar sat for a second, then pointed to the end of the table and said, "Sit down there, Nikki."

A shift ran through us all. Nikki couldn't seem to move. She looked at me. *Moi*. Like I could do something about it. Which of course I could have.

I didn't know what to say or even what I thought. I focused on the diet Coke I had squeezed lime into. I thought of the pink dress she had worn to the dance. Could I keep saving Nikki? Did I want to?

I'm not sure what I would have said, but as with every other time something like that happened, Nikki ran away.

Sitting in my car outside Misti Bladewell's house, I had to wonder why Nikki would put herself through the precarious waters of a clique—again—regardless of her desire to fit in.

"Ready?" I asked.

"Ready."

I put my Mercedes in gear.

• • •

MANDI HUFF LIVED CLOSE TO MISTI, in a nice home in a nice neighborhood populated primarily by dual-income upwardly mobile types. The house was a two-story Mediterranean stucco with a terra-cotta tile roof and a nice-sized yard. A Suburban was parked in the circular drive lined with boxed green shrubbery.

Mandi herself answered the door looking very much like a Madame Alexander doll (so much for my hope that she'd be dressed in a little leopard spandex herself) with her brown hair curled under at the shoulders and held back with a brown velvet headband, her (1980s era) bangs making her look like she was twelve.

"Frede Ware," our hostess said. "How good to see you."

Her smile was a perfect quotient of kindness and welcome, but beneath the good manners, she gave my neighbor a once-over, raised a brow, then added, "And if it isn't Nikki Grout."

Hmmm.

"Please come in," she said.

She led us into the living room where she had a tray of glasses already filled with sweet tea set out with a plate of cookies. I suspected she didn't have a maid to serve us.

She chatted nonstop to me, about the last Boots and Belles Charity Ball, about the last General Meeting, about Wanda Mason's new baby—all topics Nikki couldn't contribute to. A good hostess always makes sure no guest is left out of the conversation.

Double hmmm.

I turned the chat toward the weather and other basic niceties. Nikki, always loud and talkative, couldn't string two words together. She sat perfectly still, a smile frozen on her face, her ankles together and tucked as close to the sofa skirt as was possible, her hands clasped around her tea with such force that I could just make out the faint clink of ice trembling against the glass.

After ignoring Nikki for the first several minutes, Mandi suddenly turned to her overlooked guest, and said, "I'm guessing Frede brought you here because you want to join the League."

Nikki was so surprised (not to mention flustered) that she jerked back, her tea sloshing over the rim of the glass, splashing on her clothes. But while St. John is tasteful, it isn't particularly good at absorption, and the tea kept going, running down before anyone could do anything about it, spilling onto Mandi's (very white) sofa, the brown stain looking like something that should have been left on a ranch.

"Fuck!"

Mandi froze and stared at Nikki who had slapped her hand over her mouth.

"Oh, I'm so sorry!" Nikki breathed.

But sorry wasn't enough.

Before you could name the six flags that had flown over Texas, Nikki and I were on the front steps of the house, the door slammed firmly at our backs.

Nikki was frantic. "I'm sorry! So sorry! It's just that you said no cussing, not even 'freakin',' which as we both know is just a nice way of saying 'fuck,' and all I could do was think, *No fucks!* Then there it was." She practically wilted under the wide blue sky that was already beginning to scorch.

"We should go," I said tightly.

"Oh, God, I'm really sorry."

We drove back to The Willows in silence. I barely waved at Juan before proceeding through the gate. When I pulled up to Nikki's front door, I hadn't even gotten the car into park before she was out and flying inside.

I debated following, but really, what was I going to say? I couldn't even muster a cheerful lie. It was impossible to smooth over a "fuck."

I let her go and I returned to Chez Ware, wondering how on God's green earth I could continue with this charade. The whole thing was like a runaway train that had already left the station, no way to turn back.

Chapter Eighteen

AT THE RISK OF SOUNDING totally not like me, I have to say that when I returned to Chez Ware I felt as if I were on the verge of taking out stock in Winifred Opal's form of crazy. I know, me, Miss Melodrama. Who knew?

But that was the thing. It was like everything around me was changing and I had very little control. How was it possible that everything in my life was going wrong? I hardly knew things could go wrong, and certainly had no experience with it. I felt as if I had been thrown into the deep end of the country club pool without having been taught to swim.

Granted, there was no way Frede Ware was going to sink, that much I knew. And if anyone could survive this with the elegant strokes of Esther Williams in those strange swimming movies it was *moi*. But in the meantime, all the paddling was *très* exhausting.

If that wasn't bad enough, to make matters worse my mother called. I was too tired to use French.

"Hello, Mother."

"What's wrong?"

"Why do you assume something is wrong every time you call?"

"I can hear it in your voice. Though I can't imagine why I bother to ask what is wrong since I already know."

Great. I knew it was too good to be true that no one would find out about my missing husband. And part of me was relieved. Finally it was out there. Finally I didn't have to manage the waters all by myself. Though truly, I couldn't imagine how anyone would learn the truth given the pains to which I had gone to keep it secret.

"I heard from Lucille Sanger this morning, and she says she's certain that despite my warnings, you have forged ahead and are trying to get Nikki Bishop into the League."

My stay of execution had been . . . well . . . stayed.

"Her name is Nikki Grout now."

"As if I don't know that, married to that horrible Howard Grout. It's a crying shame when the likes of that man moves into The Willows."

"Now, Mother—"

"Don't tell me you're going to defend him. How hard did your very own husband fight to keep him out? What is going on with you, Fredericka? And mercy, tell me Lucille is mistaken and you haven't truly persisted in this mad scheme to help Nikki join our ranks. She's not proper Willow Creek, as well you know."

"Mother, just stop."

Yes, I was curt, surprising us both.

A whole lot of silence came over the line, though despite the five-mile distance between us, I could feel the tension as if she were standing next to me.

"Mother, I'm sorry. But really, you have got to be more open to Nikki."

She made a sucking noise—a very bad sign.

"I guess this means it's true you're attending the Grouts' dinner party Tuesday night?"

"How do you know about the party?"

"Alberta Bentley mentioned it."

"Is she going?"

My mother sniffed. "Yes."

"If Alberta goes, why shouldn't I?"

"We both know Alberta's husband is a politician and has no choice but to attend any number of lesser events in the name of raising contributions."

Contributions. Not money.

"Well, I'm going." Just like that. "I've said I would be there, Mother."

She hung up on me.

My whole life my mother and her determination to be a fine lady of the Junior League had guided my life. I had never given much thought to the fact that until I was thirteen we saw my father's family every week for Sunday dinner at the Hildebrand House just off Willow Square, but I only met my maternal grandparents once.

It occurred when I was eight, coming down the stairs at the ranch (think South Fork on *Dallas*) in all my grandeur to find a proud, if poorly dressed, couple standing in the foyer.

The woman stood tall but the man got tears in his eyes at the sight of me.

"You must be little Fredericka?" he said.

"Yes. Who are you?"

I couldn't imagine who they were since The Help always went to the back door, Guests arriving at the front door, but these two weren't dressed like any Guests I had ever seen.

"I'm your grandpa."

"Grandpa?" The word "pa," in any incarnation, was not used in any Hildebrand household.

"He's your grandfather," the woman said.

This, I knew, couldn't be true.

"You're not my grandfather." Grandfather Hildebrand lived in town and every Sunday before dinner I sat with him in his study where he told me about all the generations of great Hildebrands that came before me.

"I'm your mama's papa."

Now this was news. My mother had a father?

Ridiculous, I know. But my mother didn't seem the type to have relations. To me she seemed fully capable of springing to life without the necessity of two living, breathing parents. Sort of like Athena springing to life from Zeus's head, fully grown, dressed in her armor of pearls and tasteful clothes. Which made this man even less of a "father" candidate since he didn't seem anything like Zeus. Grandfather Hildebrand and my own daddy were like Zeus.

Nina came down the stairs a few minutes behind me, back then just as stout and just as ancient, though she couldn't have been more than my age now.

"Señora Ware no está aquí," she said.

"What do you mean?" I started to protest.

Nina gave me the evil eye (one of the few things that could actually keep me quiet—at least back then) then insisted again that my mother wasn't there.

The woman didn't look surprised, but the man claiming to be my "grandpa" got even more tears in his eyes. He was a crier, and I nearly told him he was lucky my mother was pretending she wasn't there because she wouldn't have been nice about the tears. But even back then I knew telling him he shouldn't cry was much too direct regardless that it would have been helpful if he wanted to get in good with my mother.

They went away and I never saw them again.

It wasn't until years later that I truly understood that they were indeed my mother's parents and she hadn't wanted to see them. When I finally figured that out, I assumed they had been mean to her, but that hadn't been the case. It was my aunt Cordelia, my father's sister of indiscreet fame, who told me that my mother was embarrassed of her family. When my aunt told me, it was the first time I had felt embarrassed of my mother.

"Granted," my aunt had added, "despite what Blythe goes to great lengths to make everyone believe, she is from the wrong side of the tracks and it's understandable that she would work hard to keep that a secret, but to turn your back on family . . ."

She didn't say another word about it, but it was as clear as Hildebrand heirloom crystal that my mother had done wrong on top of wrong. Or as Gertie, our cook, used to say, "Your ma just can't win for losin'."

I've often wondered how, when my mother so easily banished her own parents from her life, she could insist on being so much a part of mine.

FOR THE NEXT FEW DAYS leading up to the Grouts' big *soirée,* I helped Nikki practice everything from introductions (which she mangled every time) to descending the stairs (which I finally told her she wasn't allowed to do for fear of breaking her neck in front of Willow Creek's mildly important citizens), then progressed to a quiz on all I had attempted to teach her.

Using paper diagrams and etiquette charts, I reviewed place settings and seating arrangements, dinner menus and topics of conversation. If I had been running a school she would have been demoted and returned to the previous grade.

Unfortunately, invitations had already been sent and the party was charging toward us like a bull heading for a matador's cape. Part of me wanted to have an unexpected trip to Dallas come up, but another part of me was planning my outfit with care. My newly nongay artist had RSVPed *oui* to the party.

Bad, bad me.

I had found out innocently enough about Sawyer when Nikki told me who would be attending. We were working on the seating arrangements, and guess what? The artist was placed next to little ol' *moi.* Not that I had any intention of flirting. I don't flirt—at least with men who have preferences for women. Plus there was still the whole married thing. But the fact remained, my husband was who knew where spending my money like he was a Saudi prince with an oil well bubbling up in his backyard.

The day of the dinner party arrived with a dazzling blue sky. It was warm, but not hot, perfect weather for a party.

I dressed with care, a sheer white organza puffed blouse with high collar and pearl buttons over a white (demure and perfectly proper) camisole, tucked into a black silk skirt that hit just above the ankles. I wore a black satin pump with small rhinestone buckles. My hair was swept up in an elegant French twist.

When I arrived at Palace Grout thirty minutes early, the place was in a panic. The always unflappable Howard was flustered, his ruddy complexion flaming.

"She's gone crazy, I tell ya. Crazy."

"What are you talking about?"

"She's throwing clothes all over the room, tried on everything in the whole state of Texas—"

"But we bought her clothes for tonight."

"Tell her that. She swears she won't come downstairs looking like a frump."

The juxtaposition of killer lawyer and vulnerable husband was disconcerting. Which could be the only reason I surprised myself and actually asked the question that was racing through my head.

"Why do you really want Nikki in the League when you hardly seem to like society women, and you certainly look down your nose at proper behavior?"

He stared at me for a second, that vulnerability getting worse. "Just because," he grumbled.

"Just because?" I said, the words a prompt.

He scowled. "Damn it, because when I married her, I promised myself that I would give her everything she never had. A big house. Lots of clothes. Fancy jewelry."

"You've done that."

"Yeah, I know." He shifted his weight, then glanced up the stairs a little wistfully. "But I haven't been able to give her friends."

Well, that certainly wasn't the answer I expected.

"You think you can buy those too?" I asked with more than a little disbelief.

He didn't like the sound of that, but he didn't back down. "I want her to fit in. But Nikki never feels like she's good enough. It makes me crazy because it's not true. She's the sweetest angel I ever met. Hell, she married me, didn't she?"

For half a second he shook his head and smiled, then refocused. But this time the vulnerability was gone, determination taking its place. "I know if she could just get into your stupid-ass clique of fancy women, they'd fall in love with her in a heartbeat. They'd be clamoring to be her friend. Then maybe, finally, that would prove to her that she's as good as anyone. And if the only way I can get people to meet her is to make a deal with you to get her into the club, so be it."

My head snapped back. I felt several things:

1. Insulted that my friends and I were being called a "stupid-ass clique of fancy women"
2. Annoyed that the bargain I had struck with the man sounded so . . . coarse when spelled out so clearly
3. Unexpected emotion at the thought of the lengths to which he would go to make his wife happy

Not liking any of the things I was feeling, I gathered my skirt in my hands, then dashed (far too quickly) up the stairs to Nikki's bedroom.

I found her standing in the middle of a sea of taffeta, animal prints, feathers, and who knew what all. I didn't see a lick of "demure" in all the mess.

"Nikki, what has happened?"

She whirled to face me, her makeup streaked. "They're going to hate me, just like Mandi and Misti, Olivia and whoever else!"

I think it was in that moment that I realized I cared. I barely let the thought seep through my normal reserve because I really didn't want to feel anything for her other than as a trying obligation. But there it was. She looked so hurt and scared and pathetic—so like she had when I hadn't defended her at the lunch table all those years before.

I strode forward and took her hands. "They are going to love you."

"Yeah, that's what you said before."

"True, but that was before you learned how to fit in with this crowd. Now you know how."

"How can you say that? I have failed at everything you've tried to teach me."

"But it's all in there," I said. "It's in your head." I grabbed a box of tissues that a maid held close by. I pulled out three in rapid succession then put them in Nikki's hand. "You can do this. Stop worrying about what people think, or what they'll say. Think about what you're trying to accomplish. To be a member of the Junior League. To be a part of Society. To fit in. You can do this. You can be whatever you want, just stop undermining yourself."

She looked at me long and hard, no more of flighty Nikki and her glittering smiles.

"Is that what I've been doing all this time? Undermining myself?"

I know, I know, me being direct. "Let's just say you've been making things harder than they need to be. Stop thinking, Nikki. Everything you need is inside you. Get dressed in the clothes we picked out. And remember: attire is the frame that shows off a lady, not the artwork itself."

I could tell she still didn't know what to believe.

"You can do this, Nikki, if you really want to. And if you don't believe my advice, if you feel that you'll be more comfortable doing it your way, then go ahead. It's your choice."

I left her alone and joined her husband downstairs.

The party was supposed to start at seven. At six fifty-eight, Howard started pacing. At six fifty-nine he hollered up the stairs. When the first guests arrived, Nikki still hadn't appeared.

Howard welcomed the arrivals by himself with a strained smile. He didn't slap anyone on the back, though I would have bet money that under normal circumstances he would have. As it was, I had the thought that Nikki's absence was serving her husband well.

The dinner party was comprised of twenty people including me. By seven-fifteen, everyone had arrived but the artist . . . and Nikki.

I stood off to the side, absorbing the surprise on people's faces when they saw me in attendance. But I hardly cared. Even I felt like pacing as I waited for the most important arrival. Though I wasn't sure who I wanted to arrive most, Nikki or my artist.

The decision was taken out of my hands when Nikki appeared at the top of the stairs and everyone turned to stare. The drama queen in me that was rapidly taking hold got light-headed at the sight of her standing there.

"Dear Lord in heaven," was the last thing I heard before she started descending the stairs.

I think the words came from me.

Chapter Nineteen

"GOOD LORD, is that Nikki Grout?"

This from someone standing behind me or beside me or somewhere just far enough away that I could hear them without seeing who it was. All I knew for sure was that my neighbor had done it. She had managed to shock a reasonably respectable Willow Creek crowd—shock that the Queen of Tacky could appear so proper.

She wore the outfit I had picked out at Saks, the pale blue suit with long sleeves, belled at the cuffs with delicate blue velvet bows, the collar high in the back, then plunging down in front, showing nothing, but the effect of high to low seemed more evocative than if she had shown all of her Pamela Anderson breasts. The bottom of the short jacket flared at the waist, giving way to a matching pencil skirt with a pleated, demure ruffle at the bottom. She wore nude hose with a hint of shimmer, with a two-inch heel on stunning Ferragamo slingback taupe pumps instead of the matching blue stilettos she had bought because "How can I not match!"

The subtle elegance of the suit made her newly tamed dark blond hair look striking and demure, her makeup making her look like a porcelain china doll. I couldn't have been more proud if she had been my child coming out at her debutante ball as she descended the curving stairs. I held my breath until she reached the bottom, and I swear the Queen of England couldn't have done a better job.

I must have been going soft, because I thought even better was the look on Howard's face. Sheer awe. Though on closer inspection, I think there was just a little fear. Yes, Howard the Shark was looking a bit guppyish since wild Nikki was one thing—specifically, she was in his league. But perfectly proper Nikki was something else altogether, perhaps out of his reach.

I could see the dawning realization on his face, as if the possibility that she could move out of his world had never occurred to him, and the insecurity that flared as a result. But just as quickly it was gone and loud obnoxious Howard Grout was back, elbowing his way over to the bottom of the stairs to claim his wife.

The couple stood together, and I noticed for the first time that Howard had done some shopping himself. He wore a two-button Hickey-Freeman dark blue suit, suitable for the most proper of Texas men. His shirt was white, his tie a dark blue and silver diagonal stripe, and he wore a pair of black wingtip shoes.

The house buzzed with chatter, and everyone lined up to say hello to their hosts. Senator Dick Bentley headed their way, dressed in a blue blazer instead of a suit as if he expected a summer dinner party out by the pool. But the politician was not easily flummoxed. He took his wife's elbow and guided her toward their hosts. Alberta Bentley (a JLWC Sustainer dressed in a cotton frock suitable for a lot of things but not an elegant dinner party) didn't look nearly as enthusiastic about where they were headed.

I stood on the periphery of the activity watching. It wasn't that I didn't want to be noticed any more than I already had been, really. And it wasn't that my mother's words were playing havoc in my head, telling me that I shouldn't be there at all. I was standing off to the side so Nikki could have the spotlight all to herself.

Unfortunately, I wasn't standing far enough out of sight and a man I had never seen before (and, if there is a God, will never see again) came up next to me.

He was a head shorter than me, and he looked me up and down. "Butter my butt and call me a biscuit, could you be any more beautiful?"

Did I mention that the party was a mix of relatively good society and obnoxiously bad?

A week ago, as discreetly as I could, I mentioned to Nikki that she would be better served if they had two dinners. But Howard had eventually heard of it and would have nothing to do with two separate parties.

"My friends are always welcome in my home, regardless of who all else is here."

A fine sentiment, unless your wife was trying to get into the JLWC.

"So who are you?" the man inquired.

He was short and rugged, as if he had spent his whole life working in the punishing Texas sun. He wore a western-cut suit, bolo tie, and mother-of-pearl snaps running down his shirt. He ogled my breasts like he wanted an introduction. Had I not been Fredericka Mercedes Hildebrand Ware I would have said something crude in response. As it was, I raised my chin and pulled up hauteur.

"I beg your pardon?"

I assume you can hear the disdain in those words. But my letch was not blessed with an ear for subtlety.

"Oh, baby, I could go for a little beggin'."

Then he laughed, big and booming, in a way that made Howard Grout look like he had the manners of Prince Charles.

"Excuse me," I said with cutting reserve, and started to walk away . . . at which point the man slapped me on my silk-clad *derrière*. I kid you not.

After a single second of stunned disbelief, my demeanor went frosty and I slowly pivoted back to face him, then said the most un–Frede Ware thing of my life. "You better get that buttered butt of yours away from me before I have you turned into a biscuit."

Which pretty much shocked us both.

The butt-slapper started to say something, and it didn't look like it was going to be nice. At which point, my artist, as if on cue, made his appearance.

"Keep your hands off the lady," he said—all six feet of tall, dark, dangerous Marlboro man.

The letch sputtered and didn't look like he was about to leave, until he realized that Sawyer was twice his size and might actually be able to turn him into a biscuit.

It was all very knight-in-shining armorish. I loved it. And hated it. As I've said, I'm not interested in being saved.

Fortunately, the little man had a brain in his head, and he made haste in the opposite direction, leaving the other guests circling around Nikki and Howard, and me alone with my artist.

I hadn't spoken to Sawyer since the whole coming-out-of-the-straight-man closet episode. He looked like Mr. Hot, Sexy, In-Total-Control Guy who lived just South of Safe. A thrill ran down my spine, which was ridiculously girly, and ranked very high on the scale of All Things Unacceptable.

Then his expression softened. "Are you okay?" he asked.

I had never experienced this sort of strong, take-charge, take-care-of-me protectiveness—not from anyone other than my father, and even then, it had always been more, *Don't you dare mess with what is mine,* than it was worry about me.

Sawyer Jackson's concern was focused solely on *moi.*

The hairs on my arms stood up.

He looked far too fine in his crisp black suit, white shirt, and silver tie, his dark hair combed back. He might live in the wrong part of town, but he knew how to dress for a proper party. Now that I knew he wasn't gay, I had to reassess. What had simply been model good looks before took on new dimensions. His dark eyes, dark hair, and the strong bone definition in his face became unsettling.

I lifted my chin. "I can handle myself, I assure you, Mr. Jackson."

"So, we're back to formal."

"We never left."

We both knew that wasn't true after the dance around the pool.

Then he noticed something else. "The bracelet looks good."

Why I wore his gift I will never know. At the last second before I left the house, I slipped on the jewelry that was beyond inappropriate for a dinner party. But I figured I had the whole when-in-Rome concept going for me.

Nina about had a fit when she saw me heading out of the door wearing it. Though she let it go since she was half in love with the man herself.

Regardless, had I not worn the bracelet the man gave me, I'm sure things would have turned out differently that night, because the sight of all that NC crystal and gold plate on my wrist proved that I thought more of him than I should or was willing to admit. Mainly, to myself.

He smiled at me, as if he could read my thoughts. "You might have turned Nikki into an elegant swan, but I think she's changed you too."

A curl from my perfect coif had come free and he brushed it back behind my ear. I felt a flush of heat rush through me at the touch, and at the memory of what I had just said to a strange man who had slapped me on the backside. "Changed" seemed a wild understatement.

His fingers lingered at my ear, then trailed lower to the (erratic) pulse in my neck. I easily could have grabbed his hand, dragged him back to the African Safari Room, and thrown myself at him.

"Yes, well . . ."

I didn't know what to say or what to feel except light-headed, so I turned and walked away.

Yes, it was rude, not that he seemed to realize it since I walked away to the sound of his amused laughter. But he threw me. I *was* changing, me, *moi,* whatever, I could feel it, and I hadn't any idea what to do about it.

Everyone was busy talking, so when I remembered that I was supposed to sit next to the man, I discreetly changed the arrangement. I couldn't have taken sitting next to him all night.

Not that sitting across from him was better.

Thirty minutes later when the party of twenty was seated—with my artist across the table—every time I looked up he was studying me with an amused nonchalance that was unnerving. I ignored him.

The dining room was lit with a *fabu* chandelier and sterling silver candelabras marching down the center of the table like sentries. The walls looked like painted gold, the floors like Belgian chocolate surrounding an oriental carpet that must have cost more than Nikki's ancestors could have made in a lifetime.

When ignoring Sawyer proved a challenge, I focused on the three forks to the left of my plate, and the three knives, soup spoon, and oyster fork on the right. At the top of the place setting, another spoon and fork lay perpendicular to the plate.

Glancing at the handwritten menu card, I already knew what I would find. I read every entry regardless.

Baked Oysters En Croûte

Hot Consommé Brunoise

Lobster de Luxe

Fillet of Beef with Marchand de Vin Sauce

Herbed New Potatoes and Green Beans Amandine

Cherry Tomatoes served on Belgian Endive with Vinaigrette

Champagne Sorbet

Assorted Cheese and Fruit

Chocolate Soufflé

Coffee and Tea

Each course was served with a complementing wine or champagne. It was satisfyingly impressive.

Nikki didn't appear nervous, but seemed a little stiff, like Audrey Hepburn at the races in *My Fair Lady*, not yet at ease in her role as a proper lady. She enunciated each syllable so perfectly that at any second I thought she would launch into a rendition of "The Rain in Spain." Though the only other person besides me who seemed to notice was my artist.

I looked across the table and caught Sawyer's eye before I could think better of it. We were both trying not to smile. Not in a mean way, I assure you, but in an indulgent-parent way.

The first three courses went off beautifully. People talked, smiled, laughed politely. Alberta Bentley held court.

"So, Senator," Butt-slapper began. "Have you tried Bennie's BBQ down on State Street yet? Best damn ribs you've ever eaten in your life."

"I love a good rib," the politician replied. "And I bet Bennie's is great. Just great. Which reminds me of the time George W. and I were down on his ranch—before he was president since he's swamped now . . . though I did just get a note from him . . ."

I tuned out, knowing all too well the art of answering a question with a completely unrelated response, one designed to make the person responding look impressive.

Howard Grout was at his best . . . because he said virtually nothing at all. Unfortunately, he eventually found his voice.

"Now, Alberta darlin'," he said to Dick Bentley's wife. Her shoulders stiffened. "It's nice to see a woman who doesn't mind a little sun on her skin, has a healthy appetite [she had a forkful of new potatoes halfway to her mouth], and keeps away from the hair dye."

I swear on a stack of Bibles, that's what he said.

"Plus I hear you like animals."

Liking animals is relative. There is the whole hillbilly fondness we've discussed. There are those people who are partial to pets and dress them. Then there is Alberta Bentley. She raised prize quarter horses on their ranch not far from my parents and loved to tell people about it in a way that sounded very much like, *I spend millions a year on a hobby and you don't.* I would venture to say that she didn't think of herself as "liking" them.

"Do you know Winifred Opal?" he asked.

This time my fork froze halfway to my mouth.

Mrs. Bentley was still gaping over the skin/appetite/hair dye comment and couldn't get a word out. Mr. Bentley stepped in.

"Of course we know Winnie. Lovely woman."

"I haven't met her," Howard said. "My Nikki has though. Had tea with her. And all I can say is I would love to meet her myself. Sounds like my kind of woman."

Not one of us could imagine where this was going, but I think I saw Sawyer cringe.

"No cookie-cutter prima donna, no sir. Can't be, what with those dogs dressed up in fancy clothes, sitting down to tea, even if one of them did fart."

"Howard!"

This from Nikki.

"The dog didn't fart," she said, her ice-queen persona melting under duress.

"You told me one did, darlin'. Little Renata."

"Well, maybe she did." She giggled, the old Nikki trying to break through.

No one else so much as smiled since you can imagine where a discussion of bodily functions (even those of dogs) ranks on the list of Things Never to Do.

I take that back; you can say all you want of that sort if you visit Mr. Butt-slapper, since he started laughing so hard he choked on his fillet of beef.

The night didn't get much better from there. Though other than that single lapse, Nikki was back to her Audrey Hepburn self. Not that it did any good. The mistake had been made, the die cast, and I despaired that I would never find three more women to sponsor Nikki for the League.

The evening wound up, and for a few minutes I actually forgot about the sponsor dilemma when I looked around and found my artist missing. I was so surprised that I flat out asked Howard where he was.

"He's gone, little darlin'. Left as soon as he could, I might add. He ain't much for socializing with the hoity-toity." Howard looked at me carefully. "Are you sweet on that fairy fellow?"

"I am not sweet on anyone, Mr. Grout. Furthermore, he is not gay."

"Gay?" He sputtered, his face going red. "Who said he was gay?"

"You did!"

"I said no such thing!"

This time I sputtered. "Yes you did. The day you asked Nikki to give me his name and number. Then you said it again right now."

"I did not!"

"The 'fairy' artist," I reminded him. "More specifically, you called him the 'fairy artist with the faggot name.' "

"Yeah! Doing art is a fairy thing, but that doesn't mean the person is . . . is . . . homosexual. Hell, woman, what kind of a mind do you have?" He cursed. "Hell, no wonder he left early."

Thankfully Nikki chose that second to appear, not that there was anything else to say. I probably did cause him to leave early, even if it had nothing to do with sexual preferences.

"Can you believe my party?" she said.

Nikki might as well have been dancing on air for as much as her feet touched the ground. She was starry eyed and dreamy.

"They loved me."

Howard put his arm around her, but she danced away.

"They adored me." She headed for the stairs. "I'll be in the Junior League before you know it."

If only she knew.

Howard and I watched her go, and I wondered what I would do now. I was losing possibilities faster than I was gaining them.

"Oh, dear," I said.

"What's wrong now?" Howard asked.

"Nothing. Just perhaps none of the women who were here tonight are . . . good enough to sponsor Nikki."

"Good enough? Hell, any one of them would be great if they have a say."

"But—"

"No buts about it. That Alberta Bentley is going to sponsor Nikki."

"Were we at the same party?"

Howard chuckled in a way that reminded me of the kind of man who could break kneecaps . . . and get back what was left of my money. "Don't you worry about Alberta," he said.

"What do you mean?"

"I gave her husband twenty-four hours to convince his wife of the wisdom of her support—that is, if he wants the campaign contribution he was here to squeeze outta me."

Howard looked at me, waggled those brows, and said, "You're not the only one around here who knows how to be subtle."

Chapter Twenty

BLOW ME OVER WITH A FEATHER. It didn't even take twenty-four hours to get the fourth and even fifth sponsor, which meant we only had one left to recruit. Not that I knew this little morsel at the same time the rest of my Junior League of Willow Creek world did. I found out the next morning at the New Projects meeting.

Pilar was there, as were Gwen Hansen and Lizabeth Mortimer. But it was a meeting for the entire committee that day, which meant that Judy James (wife of Jason—we swear he married her for the *J* in her name) was there, as was Neesa Garvey (wife of Matthew, owner of Garvey Cadillac and Porsche on Travis Boulevard), along with Cynthia Rivers (wife of Dickie) and Annalise Saunders (married to Chris, mother of six). All were rich, bored, and ranked high on the Most Judgmental Members list. I wasn't crazy about the committee, but New Projects was one of the most important since we were the ones responsible for bringing in the crème de la crème of new projects.

Committee placement was all about power. The more prestigious the committee, the more power the individual held. The only committee more powerful than New Projects was Nominating, and it just so happened that my mother was the Sustaining Advisor to that very group.

"Can you believe it? Alberta Bentley is sponsoring Nikki Grout!" This from Gets-around Gwen. "Nikki Grout!" she repeated as if a second time it might make more sense.

The girls were all abuzz about what had unexpectedly (though apparently only to me) turned into Nikki Grout's social success the night before. Talk about spin. I was gaining more respect for Howard's abilities by the hour.

"I heard she was beautiful."

"Striking."

"Totally tasteful."

"And the house? Supposedly amazing!"

Everyone at the meeting was talking about Nikki as if she were royalty who had just come to town. My guess was that Alberta had laid the accolades on thick in order to justify her support.

"If Alberta is sponsoring her she must have been lovely. Can you believe it?"

"Of course," Pilar said with a superior nod. "I knew Nikki Grout was good League material from the beginning. I offered my support well before Alberta did. I've known her for ages. In fact, I spoke with Nikki this morning."

"Really? I would love to meet her!" Annalise said enthusiastically, which was odd since Annalise Saunders was very much a partisan of the too-rich-for-enthusiasm crowd. "And see that house!"

"I'm sure I can arrange something," Pilar offered with a healthy dose of self-importance.

I was pretty much in shock, because:

1. How was I (me, Frede Ware) not the first to know about Alberta's decision?

2. How did Pilar become Nikki's best friend all of a sudden?

3. How was it possible that bribing a politician could work to get a sponsor?

Okay, so a crooked politician shouldn't have been a surprise, and truth be known, there wasn't anything illegal about a man asking his wife to sponsor a woman for the Junior League. Deals were made all the time. It was just the disdain on Alberta's face the night before that threw me.

"And she's gotten her sister to sponsor Nikki as well!"

I caught Pilar looking at me, a hint of a smile lurking behind all that militant severity, and I couldn't imagine what she was thinking. All I knew was that things were getting stranger by the second.

WHEN I WOKE the next morning, the headline read:

NO MORE TACKY ANIMAL PRINTS FOR *MOI!*

I stared at the front page of the Society section of the *Willow Creek Times*, my Bougainvillea china cup, filled with extra strong coffee not tea, held suspended in the air.

"See, I tell you," Nina pronounced from behind me, her finger jabbing at the newsprint picture of Nikki . . . looking remarkably like . . .

"She look juz like you."

And she did. It was disconcerting, to say the least.

In the picture she wore a white cotton sateen blouse and flowing silk skirt. If the photograph had included her feet, I was certain she'd have on sensible one-inch-heel pumps, the skirt and shoes all in "boring" beige. Amazing that after she had fought so hard to hold on to her cheap feathers and god-awful spandex, now there wasn't so much as a hint of flash in sight. Thread by thread, manner by manner, she was learning how to be an acceptable lady of the Junior League. An art in itself, to be sure.

You'd think I would have been proud. Unfortunately, I was just worried, which hardly seemed fair. I ask you, didn't I have enough to worry about already?

The day after the article on Nikki ran, I learned the extent of my protégée's success. Nikki Grout had become all the rage among the ladies of the Junior League of Willow Creek. During the next few days, while I tried to make up more missed Placement hours, fulfill League obligations like the JLWC Thrift Store quotas, and basically continue the charade that everything in my world was as it should be, Nikki went to lunch at the Willow Creek Country Club with Judy James and Annalise Saunders, shopping with Gwen Hansen and Lizabeth Mortimer, and to tea at Brightlee with Alberta Bentley and her sister. With Pilar's help, Nikki was taking over my world lock, stock, and tasteful pearls. Though I couldn't help noticing that Pilar hadn't managed to produce the last sponsor.

Knowing it was time to take the bull by the horns, I bathed and dressed, and at eleven-thirty that morning, I drove over to the Palace without calling. Yet again, I was in for a surprise. Nikki was having a party.

The guests were all girls from the League. Pilar was there, seeming to be ringleader of the affair, though Nikki (dressed in cream slacks, cream silk sweater set, and a single strand of pearls) was holding her own with the group of ladies.

They laughed and sipped sweet tea from fine-cut crystal cups, and ate crustless finger sandwiches from china plates like they had been best friends for a lifetime.

"Hello," I said from the doorway. My voice might have been cool.

The ladies turned and saw me. Pilar flashed another of her peculiar smiles, though it was gone before it settled.

Nikki got wide eyed with excitement. "Frede!" she said, leaping up from the sofa.

"Hello, girls," I said with a smile, as if I weren't ruffled.

"Frede, I'm so glad you came! Pilar said you were busy."

"Did she?" I looked at Pilar and had to wonder if she was really trying to help get Nikki into the League. But if she was up to something else, of the not-good variety, how could Nikki Grout possibly help her?

Nikki pulled me off to the side. "Oh, Frede, can you believe it!" she enthused in an excited stage whisper. "They love me! I'm like a star!"

A star?

She hurried back to her spot on the sofa, plopped herself down between Annalise and Pilar just as Howard entered the room through a set of French doors. He wore scruffy jeans and a Western shirt, his ever-present cell phone in his hand.

"Hello, ladies."

He was his usual loud self and I was surprised that I hardly gave it a thought. In fact, I'm not sure that I would have at all if Nikki hadn't gotten flustered, stammered, then admonished him.

"Howard, please. We're having tea."

A rule I might not have had an opportunity to mention: never, ever criticize your spouse in front of anyone. It is the height of bad manners, and something no one wants to witness—though everyone is happy to gossip about it afterward. Regardless of what your spouse does, just smile, think of it as marital spin, then discuss the issue in private at a later time.

Howard looked confused at first, but he looked downright hurt when he stepped over to his wife to apologize, then leaned close to kiss her cheek. "Sorry, muffin."

Nikki gasped, clearly, finally, remembering the rules. "Howard, not in front of the ladies."

Taking a startled step back, Howard's face was a mask of surprise, making him look like a bulldog puppy that had gotten whacked on the nose with a newspaper. I hate to say it, but I felt horrible for my tacky lawyer.

"We'd best go, girls," Pilar announced, setting her cup on the coffee table.

The girls stood in unison, like synchronized socialites, and Nikki walked them out. Howard stopped next to me and we watched them go.

"Hell, Frede, what have you done to my wife?"

I wondered the same thing.

Chapter Twenty-one

THE FOLLOWING WEEK the JLWC was closed down for Easter vacation. It would be a week without committee meetings, a week without Placements. The only League-sponsored activity during that time was Retreat—a day of relaxation at a place called the Spa just outside of town where Ambitious Leaguers went to meet the most promising prospective new members. It was also the place where Ambitious Leaguers cultivated power.

I had never been to Retreat, not because I didn't have every intention of going far in the JLWC, but because I didn't need to. I was already a part of the most important circles within the League.

As to Retreat and the potential benefits of showing off Nikki, surely I don't need to remind anyone of the whole "dog farting" incident at her dinner table. Why take chances? The best way to gain Nikki's sponsors was by hosting small, intimate gatherings. And perhaps coercion. It had certainly worked with Alberta Bentley.

But, yet again, I digress.

The point is, for me, Easter vacation was a week without League obligations, not to mention a week without Nina since she always went home for the holiday. Being a good Catholic, Nina was all about Easter. I, as a good Episcopalian, was all about finding the perfect Easter bonnet to wear to church on Sunday.

Nina rarely took time off since her family didn't do nearly as well with her autocratic manner as I did. Clearly they hadn't learned the art of ignoring her. Regardless, this meant I was left to my own devices. I don't know about you, but idle time is *très* bad because it gives me too much of an opportunity to think.

Between the Friday when Nina left for vacation and Easter Sunday, I had a total of nine days to fill. Never in my life had I been at a loss for what to do.

For half a second I considered signing up for Retreat, then shuddered at the thought of all that power-bonding. Instead, I plunged into the kitchen, though two hours later I had nearly burned the house down, not to mention, I had a mess that I had little choice but to clean up myself.

On Saturday, I drove to San Antonio and shopped with credit cards. At noon, I took myself to lunch. At one-thirty, I went to an art exhibit in La Villita. By four in the afternoon, with seven days and eight hours left until the break was over, I was bored and getting antsy. So I did the only thing a sensible (read: crazy) woman would do. I decided there was no time like the present finally to have a look at my artist's art. And I do mean art. Well, maybe not, but I wasn't admitting that at the time.

To my credit, I called first. But as usual, he didn't answer. After the third try, I decided it wouldn't hurt anyone if I made a trip over to his abode to see if he was at work in his studio. I had a job to do, after all. A show to put on. Decisions to make. It's amazing how the mind can rationalize the most irrational behavior. Not only was it beyond bad manners to show up unannounced at anyone's home, but showing up at a man's home unannounced was the height of unacceptable behavior.

Regardless, I bathed, powdered, and dressed, thinking that at any minute I would come up with something better (smarter) to do. It was after eight that evening, the sun going down, a chill promised in the early spring air, when I made my way out of The Willows. When I crossed over the railroad tracks into South Willow Creek, I swear the drum of my tires sounded very much like *bad, bad, bad, bad.* I was so distracted by the thought that I nearly ran over one of the protestors.

I slowed down to get a better look at what was going on. There was a big sign that said GENSTAR DEVELOPMENT—A ONE OF A KIND REAL ESTATE OPPORTUNITY. I had to wonder who in their right mind would intentionally buy new in this part of town.

I remembered Nikki saying something about Sawyer being involved in construction. Could he be involved in GenStar?

Immediately I dismissed the thought. He was an artist, undoubtedly starving given his (former) elusiveness, not to mention his address on the wrong side of town.

When I arrived at Hacienda Jackson, I pulled through the open gates to find an array of old trucks and Jeeps parked around the fountain. Either Sawyer was hosting a Texas Hunt Club meeting, or he was having a party.

I decided it was a party when I noticed those sorts of trailer-park tiki lanterns lining the way to the front door. Arriving uninvited on my artist's doorstep for a good (lame) business reason was one thing. But crashing any sort of *soirée* was something else altogether.

I would have put the car in reverse and gone home like the proper girl I had been my whole life had someone not knocked on my window.

Yes, I jumped. (I was in South Willow Creek after all.)

Standing outside my car was an odd man dressed in strange clothes, with his arm hooked over an even stranger woman's shoulders.

"Come on," they called to me. "We'll go in together."

As if we were best friends.

If only you could have seen them. The woman wore multicolored peasant attire with jewelry dangling here and there. I couldn't see her feet but I would have guessed some sort of canvas-and-rope sandals. (Not JLWC appropriate, though God knows Delman flats would have been a fashion disaster with that *ensemble.*)

Her hair was long and loosely curled, done up with all kinds of glittery butterfly clips holding it in a loose twist. While I never would have been friends with this sort of woman, I have to say she was pretty for someone who looked as if she did her shopping at a flea market.

The man wasn't much better. He had thick black hair, as straight and shiny as a clear night sky, pulled back into a ponytail at the nape of his neck. He wore a bright white, high-collared (think Byron) shirt with full sleeves under a paisley waistcoat. I could just make out a gold watch fob looped into his pants pocket.

This wasn't just another world I had driven into, it was another time period altogether.

I buzzed down my window.

"What did you bring?" the woman asked.

"Bring?"

The couple laughed, then opened my door. Can I be blamed for not leaving after they pulled me out of the car, insisting I go inside with them?

"Don't worry," they added. "Everyone always has extra. There will be plenty."

"Besides," the woman said, "Sawyer provides most everything anyway."

"Everything?"

I couldn't imagine what they would have plenty of for what I was guessing could only be a bohemian get-together of decadent debauchery. (Give me an inch and I'm as imaginative as the next person.) I felt equal parts trepidation and anticipation. Which can be the only reason to explain why I didn't stiffen when they came up on either side of me and hooked their arms through mine.

We walked along the brick path, framed by the orange glow of tiki light. "By the way, I'm Burns, and this is Ceta," the man said.

Before I could introduce myself, they laughed again, over what, I couldn't say, and pulled me inside.

I had wondered about the interior of this house with its rust-colored adobe walls and modern art in the courtyard. The minute the rough-hewn front doors were pushed open I stepped into a world so far removed from my own I felt I had traveled to a foreign land. The ceilings were high, with a loft overlooking the main room. It was everything I would never have or approve of, but was oddly striking. A mix of old and new, inside as well as out. Old leather furniture and modern pieces made from metals.

There are four ways of decorating:

1. With taste—think my house

2. With flash—think (parts of) Nikki's Palace

3. With trash—think those homes decorated by delirious people who actually believe it's a coup to find some "treasure" in a junkyard

4. With no rules—that would be my artist's minihacienda

Nothing matched or coordinated; it was a startling mix that assaulted the senses. A person could lose themselves for hours making their way through the treasure hunt of a home, like making their way through a museum, each piece demanding attention. It should have been a mess. It should have insulted the senses. But it didn't, especially the nine-foot-high painting that dominated the south wall of the main room. It was a portrait, a self-portrait of my artist done on a textured cream background, his figure slashed out impressionistically in black coal and rust-colored gesso paint. He was wild in the rendering, with overlong dark hair raked back, shoulders broad, hips narrow, his dark eyes staring back at me.

I couldn't look away even when I felt the artist come up behind me.

"It's . . . something," I said, without turning around.

"Something?"

Yes, I, purveyor of all things art, stood there talking like a stammering schoolgirl, but I was trying to keep my head. The painting was amazing.

"It's as good as the rest of your work I've seen," I clarified.

"As in the one piece in the Grouts' hallway?"

"That would be it, though there is all that sculpture scattered around your yard which I have to assume is yours."

He laughed, this time a not unpleasant sound, then he turned me around. When he did, that shock of wildness I had viewed on the hanging canvas stood in front of me.

Very simply, he radiated physical power. His face was all hard planes, handsome if intimidating, nothing soft about it. He wore a black T-shirt that revealed tautly corded arms, tanned the color of caramel, and jeans that hugged his hips in a way that made me wonder how I ever thought he was gay.

He looked me up and down as if he were deciding if he wanted to buy. Then his mouth rode up at one corner and he stepped back to get a better look. When he did, one of his brows rose in amusement.

I think I might have left out one teensy detail. True, I'm bad about that, but when I had shopped earlier I might have made an unforgivably improper purchase (okay, more than one) at Saks. When I decided I needed to see my artist's art on the wrong side of town, and what with Nina unavailable to chastise me, I had dressed in said improper attire.

"Jeans?"

What could I say? I shrugged.

I wore tight, flared jeans, a sheer white silk tunic top (its neckline embroidered with shimmering metallic beads), a camisole underneath, with high, wedged heels that belonged on Fast Girls at Willow Creek High. While Nikki was turning into me, I was rapidly turning into Nikki.

His smile widened, my heart fluttered (really), and he nodded. "You should wear jeans more often. You look sexy as hell."

There are a lot of compliments I expect. *You are stunningly beautiful. You have a smile that lights up a room. Your pearls are flawless.* But *You look sexy as hell* isn't one of them. While it was new and not unappreciated, it was nonetheless awkward.

"Yes, well . . ."

His mouth rode up at one corner. "You like 'yes, well' a lot, don't you?"

"Yes, well . . . I mean, yes, ah, well . . ."

Good God, can you say pathetic?

He just chuckled, raked his hair back, then offered a reprieve. "So tell me, what can I do for you?"

Have sex with me now.

Just kidding. I didn't really think that, at least not at the time.

"I came here to discuss the show."

"The show, huh?" He didn't look convinced.

"Really, I did. Well, perhaps not entirely, though I do need to see your work so I can decide which pieces to exhibit."

He shoved his hands in his jean pockets and studied me for a second. "If my art is only part of the reason you're here, what's the other part?"

In polite society we don't have much opportunity to practice deflecting direct questions because proper people know not to ask them. While I was getting more practice than ever before, I still wasn't particularly good at it. I just stared.

That grin of his crooked even more and his voice took on a sort of teasing tone. "Admit it. You're here because you can't resist me."

My mouth fell open.

The artist chuckled again, then reached out and touched the tips of those strong fingers to my chin, pressing up, closing my mouth. "Don't worry. Your secret is safe with me."

I might have sputtered. "That's ridiculous." Or not. "I was having a bad day, and I didn't want to stay at home."

Like that was better.

He laughed out loud, completely at ease in his roughhewn, high-ceilinged, no-decorating-rules world. "I'm crushed," he said. "But good news, you've come to the right place. I've got the perfect cure for a bad day."

With the confidence of a man used to getting his way, he took my hand and pulled me back to the kitchen. Yes, the kitchen. But who was I to cast stones, given my attire and my uninvited status.

I smelled food the minute we entered. There were eight people sitting around a large butcher-block table, drinking wine, talking and laughing. I realized that this was all about a meal. No sign of decadent debauchery. (A temporarily bad girl could only hope.)

As best I could tell, Sawyer was hosting a traditional meal. Though it turned out to be anything but traditional . . . and couldn't have been more different from the one Nikki and Howard had hosted less than a week earlier.

I was introduced (I use the term loosely) to an assortment of "his friends" as Frede. Just Frede.

Two of the other guests did a sort of double take at my name and they started to say something, but Sawyer cut them off.

"This is Marcus," he continued.

Marcus was a tall, elegant man dressed in a vintage black suit, white shirt, and a narrow black tie. A bowler hat hung on the back of his ladder-back chair, an ornate cane leaning next to it.

"He tells us he's a professor," Sawyer said in a conspiratorial voice, "but we suspect he's really a method actor getting into a part, that or he's getting really bad clothes advice."

The group laughed, firing off several teasing, less than complimentary comments about Marcus's attire.

Next came Hill, the computer-geek, pocket-protector type that had become all the rage in Austin during the tech craze in the late nineties. "Hill was my roommate at UT. More recently, he's a patient man who puts up with this crazy bunch."

Indeed, Hill looked wholly out of place with the crowd.

Sawyer moved on. "This is Burns." Aka the man I had met when I pulled through the front gates, not to mention yet another man without the benefit of two names. "He's a sorry artist like me. But he's lucky enough to have the beautiful Ceta as his better half."

The woman from the courtyard blushed. "Always the charmer," she mock-chastised Sawyer.

After that there was Zelda, then a man introduced as Quirt Quincy.

"We call him 'Q Squared,'" Sawyer added. "We swear his name is actually an alias and he really works for the CIA, but he denies it. It's either that or his parents weren't thinking when they named him."

Several NC hoots followed.

Next came a playwright named Mabel, then finally, Santo—and he looked like a saint, or at the very least, a cherublike man who appeared not to have a close relationship with the sun. Everyone loved Santo. "Hello," he said softly.

It was a veritable gaggle of odd ducks and I had zero business being there.

"Welcome, Frede," Santo said.

"Thank you, but really, I shouldn't have intruded." Finally, proper Frede was showing her face. "I'll come back another time."

A chorus of protest came from the table. Sawyer leaned back against the kitchen counter, his arms crossed on his chest. He looked even more amused. I considering telling him he should expand his repertoire of expressions, but decided that might bring out the only other emotion I had seen on his face. The brooding macho thing. Or had it been disdain? Either way, I'd take my chances with amusement.

"Stay!" Burns insisted.

"Yes, please do," Ceta added.

"Tell her not to leave, Sawyer," Santo requested with polite insistence.

My artist just looked at me with a knowing smile. He didn't ask me to stay, but I swear there was a challenge in his eye, as if he didn't believe for a second that I would.

We know me and challenges.

"Thank you," I said. "It's nice of you to include me. Can I help with the cooking?"

Everyone gasped.

"No one cooks in my kitchen but me," Sawyer said.

I gave him a look that said, *Are you sure you're not gay?* Sawyer just laughed and Santo found me a chair. Marcus poured me a glass of dark red wine, served in one of the mismatched glass jars. Not only am I not a big supporter of Jars as Glassware, but I'm generally a champagne drinker or, at the very least, white wine. But Sawyer was watching.

"Thank you," I said, taking the Bonne Maman jam jar filled with red table wine.

Sawyer winked at me, then turned to the stove.

Indeed, everyone but *moi* had brought something. Loaves of crusty bread in long brown paper bags, blocks of cheese, olives, wine. Lots of wine. On a very large iron stove the host had an assortment of mismatched pans. No matching cookware for Mr. Jackson.

I felt as if I were in a novel, probably Hemingway, dining in Paris with a group of disheveled expatriates and rich, touring American women. I was getting farther from my world by the sentence.

The kitchen had a primitive look to it, though the stove happened to be Viking and the refrigerator Sub-Zero, telling a different tale, the kind that involved no starving, either physical or monetary.

Hmmm.

Conversation was loud and opinionated. (Politics, religion, personal details of the most private kind.) Sawyer chopped, cooked, and banged pots with an abandon I felt sure he used when he created his art, all the while making his friends laugh and responding to their good-natured ribbing and accusations with ludicrous (if distracted) threats to their health. I resigned myself to the fact that there wouldn't be much "business" happening that night, and I sat back and sipped my jar of wine.

I'm not sure how much time passed, but once he placed an assortment of earthenware plates and bowls on the table, the guests weren't shy about digging in, reaching, taking, half standing to serve themselves any number of dishes, helping each other to whatever they happened to have a spoon in. Sawyer pulled up a chair with a scrape, then waited for me to take my first taste of a caramelized goat cheese tart he set in front of me. In fact, the whole group went still and waited with him. Talk about pressure.

Politely I took a bite, then was appalled when I barely held back a
NC sigh of pleasure over the taste.

The guests cheered. "Success! She loves it! You're a genius, man!"

Sawyer half stood and took an exaggerated bow, all to more cheers. When he sat down again and looked at me across the table (his friends busy talking, eating, and laughing) I felt verra warm, that heart of mine fluttering again.

After that there was mozzarella, basil, and what had to be home-grown tomatoes, marinated in a vinaigrette. Then more bread. More olives. More wine. Followed by an osso bucco that melted off the bone, served in a sauce that he really should have considered submitting to the Junior League of Willow Creek Cookbook Committee.

Santo talked about his poetry and wasn't fazed when Quirt took one of the poet's works-in-progress and made it into a crude rhyming tangle. I would have sworn Quirt did it more to get at me than at Santo, since it was the poet who looked at me and mouthed, *I'm sorry*. But I shocked us all when I giggled, hiccupped, then recited a crude little ditty of my own. I blame it on the wine.

From there things went from loud to louder, worse to appalling. They talked about their work, their hopes, their dreams, Sawyer having a surprising ability to make each of them feel as if they could achieve anything they wanted to. The conversation was as fraught with unfortunate feelings as it was fascinating, like a train wreck that was hard to look away from. Who knows how long that would have gone on if, apropos of nothing, Marcus hadn't turned to me and said, "I can see now why you're the muse that got our friend painting again."

I blinked.

"You're Sawyer's muse?" Santo asked, more animated than he'd been all night.

"Like you didn't know from the second she got here," Marcus said with a scoff.

"I didn't! I mean, really, when Sawyer talked about his muse he called her the—"

"Santo."

You can imagine who cut him off, all smiles gone. And let me tell you, Sawyer Jackson with that chiseled face doing the whole South of Safe thing was a sight to see. Very much like the painting in the main room.

Santo looked sheepish. "Sorry. He didn't really call you anything bad." He grimaced. "Not too bad, at least."

Sawyer rolled his eyes. "Yeah, that's better."

My enjoyment level was plummeting, though everyone else thought it was enormously funny.

Quirt whistled, looking me over. "Yep, I can see it. I can see you being his inspiration." He lifted his glass. "To Sawyer's muse!"

This, I liked, even if it was weird. I had never been anyone's muse before, at least that I know about.

Sawyer shook his head and gave in to a laugh. "Yeah, she pissed me off so bad that I had to have someplace to vent. Painting was as good an avenue as any."

More laughter . . . from everyone but me. I didn't like that part nearly as much.

Mabel had gotten up from the table and put on some country-western music. There was a patio outside the kitchen and Ceta started to dance, by herself, with a glass of wine in her hand, those peasant skirts swishing. Burns joined her. The rest of the group followed, leaving me alone with the host.

"Well, I guess I should be going," I said.

Sawyer tossed his napkin on the table, then stood and took my hand, pulling me up.

There are some men who just walk into your life and have a way of changing all the parameters, or so I had heard. Standing in that kitchen was the first time it ever happened to me. So when he said, "Let's dance," is anyone surprised I let him tug me out onto the makeshift dance floor and was immediately caught up in a Texas two-step?

"Come on, loosen up," he teased.

I started moving to the music. Step, step, swish. I am better at a three-step waltz. I have a Little Miss Debutante certificate to prove it.

"You can do better than that," he said.

All I can say is that the challenge thing must have kicked in, that or I was going to have the same sort of hangover I'd had after Nikki's Spiked Tea party. Whatever the cause, something took over and my steps loosened up, my swishes got swishier. I had just gotten the hang of it when the music changed.

For a second we stopped and moved apart when a Garth Brooks ballad started to play. It was the kind of song that required a great many body parts to touch. Sawyer looked at me for a second, that grin crooking at one corner, then he extended his hand.

Well, what was I going to do? Really. At that point even the ladies at Little Miss Debutante would have said it would be rude to say no. Okay, maybe not, but I was in the mood to dance.

He guided me easily, the sound of his boots sliding over hardwood in a rhythmic swish just below the music. With every turn we took, his thigh slipped between my own in a way that was hard to ignore.

"So, where did you learn to cook like that?" I managed.

"I spent a year living in a small village in Italy after I graduated from college. The place was short on fast food and pizza delivery." He pulled me closer and I could feel him smile into my hair. "A man's got to eat somehow. Cooking seemed the only viable option."

I had a hard time putting this man, who was so at ease with his friends, together with the one who had slammed the door in my face when I asked him to show his art in my gallery. No question the rugged Marlboro man had been dangerous to notions of my propriety. But this man with his easy, crooked smiles and boyish charm was, well, far more dangerous and could easily be hard to resist.

I dismissed the thought from my head.

"What took you to Italy?"

"Art."

Just that.

"Art?"

"Yep."

He danced me through the others, his hand spread against the curve of my lower back, and I forgot about what I should or shouldn't be doing. When we came to the edge of the porch, he grabbed a light jacket and tugged me out a side door, then down three wooden steps to the yard.

It was a picture-perfect night with a full moon and a touch of chill in the air. We walked through the yard and I assumed we were going to his studio.

"So. I'm your muse." I felt a wide smile on my face.

He didn't say anything, though I sensed his amused shrug.

"Little ol' *moi* got you painting again?" I persisted, and even I could hear the NC *Yeah, I'm bad* subtext.

"I thought all you society types at least pretended humility."

We had come around the side of the house, and I could see the studio. Instead of being insulted, I laughed. "The wine made me do it."

I caught sight of one of his wry grins. "Maybe," he said.

"Maybe, what?"

"Maybe you got me painting again."

I cocked my head when a thought occurred to me and my brain did nothing to edit it. "What stopped you in the first place?"

We walked a few more steps and I could tell he considered his answer. "Hard to say. Life. Things turning out differently than I expected."

Then he stopped and I forgot all about muses, reasons, or seeing his art. He leaned back against the abode wall and my pulse went from normal to erratic when his gaze drifted lower to the neckline of my inappropriate tunic. Insanity mixed with the wine and I had a very real wish to do plenty that I knew I absolutely positively should not do.

Run, I told myself.

Move away from the man.

You're married, even if it was to a lying, cheating, missing piece of scum who was breaking the bank.

I looked at his mouth instead.

I was barely aware of the chill until he swung the jacket around my shoulders, tugging the collar up to warm me. When he was done, he didn't let go. Proper had always come easily, like a knee-jerk reaction in a doctor's office to a little rubber hammer. But not that night.

I felt his knuckles slide down my neck, across my collarbone, then lower. Alarm bells were going off in my head, and call me common all you like, but I couldn't seem to do anything other than wonder what it would feel like if he kissed me.

He considered me for a second, his dark eyes verra dark, his palms brushing down my arms. "This probably isn't such a good idea," he said.

I sort of sucked in my breath, feeling saved and disappointed at the same time. "You're right."

Of course he was right.

But when he started to move away, a *très très* bad thing happened. My fingers curled into his shirt.

He went still and studied me. "Hell," he said, then kissed me.

My eyes closed, and I inhaled, as if I had been waiting for this since the day I had probably really known he wasn't gay. He pulled me between his thighs and suffice it to say there was plenty of kissing, lots of hands going to places they had no business going. But as it turned out, in the end, I was nothing if not a woman of strictly proper upbringing. At the very last second before things got too carried away, I uncurled my fingers and pushed at his chest.

He loosened his hold, just enough so that I could duck away. "Fabulous party! Thank you for inviting me," I said, then walked away as fast as I could without looking like I was running.

I made it to the corner of the house before he called out. "Frede."

Even though I shouldn't have, I hesitated.

"I hope your day got better."

Crooked smiles, boyish charm, and now, kindness. I managed a nod.

"I'm glad," he said. "Good night then."

He pushed away from the wall but didn't follow me. He continued on, then disappeared into his studio.

After a second, I hurried back inside the house. I set a record for saying polite good-byes to the other guests, then was out the front door. I didn't catch my breath until I had pulled out through the hacienda gates. I liked proper. I wanted proper. I didn't want what I was willing to bet would be great sex with a man who looked like he knew how to make a woman sing hallelujah. I'd stick to mesquite-grilled lobster tails. Really.

Chapter Twenty-two

IT WAS CLOSE TO MIDNIGHT when I got home, and the minute I walked in the back door the phone rang. For reasons that even I can't imagine, I assumed it was Sawyer.

Answering at the little desk in the kitchen I felt like a teenager getting a late-night call from a boy. "Hello?" I said.

"Fred."

I sat down hard, my keys jangling against the wooden desktop.

"Fred, are you shocked?"

"Gordon?" I stammered. "Where are you?"

He snickered into the phone. "Sorry, can't say." Then he laughed sort of maniacally. My husband.

"You've been drinking!"

"Just a little . . . or a lot." He laughed again. "How's it going?"

"Not so good, as you can imagine."

"Yeah, I bet. How does it feel to be poor?"

Can you say left hook to the jaw out of nowhere?

"Sucks, don't it," he added with another laugh.

He didn't say words like "sucks," and I had never seen him drunk. "Gordon, tell me what's going on."

"What's going on? You have no money, that's what's going on. Though I know you—I bet you haven't told anyone other than that lowlife Howard Grout. Yep, I know all about him trying to track me down. He's a pain in the ass, let me tell ya." He slurred the words. "But forget it. Just throw in the towel. Stop trying to uphold the ol' reputation. Eventually everyone's gonna know. Then you're gonna have to be the Not So Fabulous Frede Ware."

Blood pounded in my temples, and I felt hot all over. "Tell me what you've done with my money!"

He sobered. "Face it, Fred. Your money is gone. *Adios. Hasta* Las Vegas, baby."

"Gordon!" I practically shouted into the phone at the same time as in the background I heard, "Gordon! Who are you talking to?"

I knew it was Miss Mouse.

He turned away from the phone. "No one important, sweetheart." He came back on the line. "Gotta go. Nice chatting with you," he finished with a laugh, then hung up.

At first I was too stunned to do anything but stare at the receiver. Then I dialed the operator. I wasn't sure what would happen. I got someone who said that I should dial *69 to see if the number was traceable. When I did as instructed, all I learned was that the number was unavailable.

After hanging up, no matter how hard I tried, I couldn't sleep. I paced, upstairs, downstairs, the kitchen and study. What if Gordon was right that the money was gone? Not to put too fine a point on it, but I was the girl with the charming personality, the fabulous good looks . . . and the money. I had the disconcertingly uncontemplatable thought that maybe my personality and good looks were made charming and fabulous by my money.

Thankfully, I didn't have to wait until the acceptable hour of nine A.M. to call my lawyer. At five minutes after seven the next morning, he showed up at my door.

"Howard?"

He looked like he hadn't had so much as a sip of coffee. In fact, he looked like he hadn't had so much as a wink of sleep either. His hair was askew and he reeked of smoke.

"What happened to you?" I asked.

He groaned and ran his hand over his face. "My wife has lost her mind and started buying me new clothes. Said mine weren't classy enough."

For the first time I noticed he wore a short-sleeved polo shirt (purple that stretched precariously across his stomach) tucked into pleated khaki pants, with a grosgrain belt and boat shoes. Not exactly Howard Grout–wear.

Regardless, I couldn't imagine what lack of sleep and smelling like an ashtray had to do with his new (and not particularly becoming) style.

"Hell, she won't even let me wear socks! Said no one wears socks with these pansy-ass slipper shoes. She read it in some highfalutin magazine, for chrissake!"

He sounded gruff and put out, but even I could see it was a cover for hurt feelings (yes, my lawyer) by this unexpected change in his wife.

No question I could understand why he wouldn't be happy. For one, he was wearing purple prep clothes. For another, the only reason the whole thing had started was because he'd been trying to help his wife fit in and be happy. Clearly a case of no good deed goes unpunished.

Oddly, I hated to see him upset, I did. But sue me, a suddenly sensitive pup dog wasn't going to find my money. I wanted my shark back.

"The shoes aren't bad," I told him, trying to sound sincere. "In fact, they're great. Really great." I chucked him on the shoulder and gave him what I hoped was an enthusiastic smile. "You and Nikki are great."

He snorted, then drew himself up. "Don't worry about me and Nikki. You've got bigger problems. That bastard husband of yours divorced you. That's why I'm here."

If there had been a chair close by, I would have sat down hard. "What?" Not that I minded being divorced from my good-for-nothing husband, but how could it have happened?

"I just got a copy of these. Divorce papers. Based on the date, you signed them months ago."

I practically ripped the pages to see the signature. The minute I saw it, dread shot through me. "Where did you get this?"

"I set up a poker game with a few buddies who work at the courthouse. We play pretty regularly, and I figured if anyone in town had heard something about your husband, it'd be them. Sure enough, I was right."

"Judges leak information?" I asked indignantly.

"Hell, no. I play cards with the clerks. They're the ones who really know what's going on in a courthouse. After about a six-pack apiece, I started fishing. Subtle. Patient. Then bingo. One of the guys mentioned the divorce papers that had just come in. The hardest part was waiting for hours until the game broke up so I could press him for more. It wasn't easy to get a copy, but I had to have it so you could tell me definitively that your husband is out there forging your signature."

Forging my signature? I cringed.

Even wearing boat shoes and no socks, Howard Grout let nothing get by him. I knew my shark was back when he went on tilt. "You mean to tell me that that is your signature?"

"Well, ah, yes."

To say he started in on a rant to beat all rants would be an understatement. But I barely heard because, one, I felt light-headed with what I suspected was massive amounts of stress, and two, I felt suspiciously as if I might do something utterly weak and completely un–Frede Ware–ish by passing out. Though, excuse me, you might pass out, too, if you had signed your own divorce papers without even knowing it.

Howard's voice finally pierced my shock-clogged brain. "How the hell does a woman in this day and age sign a document without knowing what the hell she is signing?"

Said out loud, it sounded even more idiotic than it had when flitting silently through my head. I wasn't sure how to explain. "I trusted him," I managed.

Pathetic, I know, especially given the more recent developments that had come to light regarding the state of my union.

Howard muttered and cursed.

"In my defense, I didn't sign things so easily when we were first married." As if this made it better. "It just . . . sort of got to that point. For the first few years I read everything." And I had. "But then, over time, I started reading less and less, until it got so that he would explain what the papers were, then I'd read the cover sheet, glance at the first page of the document"—I cringed again—"then I'd flip to the back and sign."

I realized then that Gordon could have slipped anything behind the first few pages and I would have been none the wiser—and apparently hadn't been. "As I said"—my voice sort of wavered—"I trusted him."

For a relatively smart woman, I felt ill with my stupidity. It didn't matter that I knew more women than not who signed all sorts of documents their husbands put before them after little more than a brief explanation and cursory glance. I felt light-headed as I remembered all those stacks of documents Gordon had brought in over the years.

"What else did you sign?" Howard asked.

I hadn't a clue, but I was *verra* afraid I was going to find out soon enough.

That's when I said we needed to go to the police.

Sure, say it's about time all you want. But as we know, I was raised to believe in the sanctity of privacy at all costs. But desperate times called for desperate measures. Unfortunately, Howard didn't agree.

"Damn it, woman, you said yourself that you signed the papers, so there's nothing the police can do unless we can give them something to suggest theft or fraud. Like I said, Gordon losing money you put him in charge of is stupid but it's not a crime. And divorcing you isn't a crime either, especially since you signed those papers too."

When I wasn't convinced, he took me down to the precinct personally, whipping through the Willow Creek streets like he owned them, giving little notice to things like stop signs and speed limits. (Clearly he had graduated from the Frede Ware School of Driving.)

WCPD headquarters was downtown behind the Municipal Courthouse on the east side of Willow Creek Square. We walked into a hive of activity, Howard actually holding my elbow with a firm grip, criminals handcuffed to chairs, phones ringing, people yelling. It was really NC, though I was in the mood for a little yelling myself after Howard got us in to see a sergeant friend of his and all I got was confirmation. "Unless you can provide some evidence that he really did steal your money, and not lose it, there isn't a crime," the man said.

"But he just took it, moved it without my knowledge."

"I'm sorry, Mrs. Ware. But even you admit you gave him control of your accounts, and you signed the divorce papers. Even if you say you signed them without knowledge of their contents, it's still not a crime since it's your responsibility to read what you sign."

Thank you for pointing that out.

To Howard's credit, he didn't say I told you so when we got back in his car. He drove me home. "Something's there, I'm sure of it," he said.

"I'm going through your bank records check by check, and your itemized phone bills line by line. Gordon isn't that smart—somewhere he's made a mistake. I just need to keep looking. Plus, I'm going to figure out a way to flush him out from wherever he's hiding. Then we'll really get somewhere."

THE NEXT DAY, refusing to give in to lesser emotions (like panic or daydreaming about Sawyer Jackson), I got up and started going through the JLWC membership roster. Whether I liked the changes happening in Nikki or not, a deal was a deal and I was still one sponsor short. But how to go about getting the last, I didn't know.

The phone rang at nine on the nose.

"Frede, it's Lalee Dubois."

Lalee (short for Laura Lee) was the sitting president of the JLWC. She was eight years older than me, and had written one of my recommendations when I went through sorority rush at Willow Creek University. She had the confidence of a trust fund heiress and the charm of a Cinderella castle built from marzipan candy. She would have been too sweet to take if she hadn't had the disconcerting habit of saying what she thought when she thought it. No editing between brain and mouth. A very big no-no in my world. In fact, it was a wonder she had ever become president of the League. Regardless, I adored her.

"Hello, Lalee."

We exchanged pleasantries before she asked, "So tell me. Who is putting the group together for Nikki Grout? You or Pilar?"

What? "I am. Why do you ask?"

"That's what I thought, though I just had a call from Pilar and she's bringing Nikki to Retreat today, so I thought I might have gotten it wrong."

Pilar was taking Nikki to Retreat?

As I mentioned, Retreat was a one-day power affair disguised as a day of relaxation. Each member who went was allowed to bring one guest, someone they wanted the other Ambitious Leaguers to have an opportunity to meet and get to know.

Every League does it differently, each holding different types of events. But every potential sponsor wants a way to see how her potential candidate is viewed by her peers. The functions had started back in the days when "blackballing" was de rigueur and a single vote could keep any woman out, and no one wanted to get stuck sponsoring a dud. It can make a person look very bad if she sponsors someone everyone hates.

The JLWC had Retreat, and we could put on such an expensive affair because we had money to do it, plus we allowed very few guests to attend.

If Pilar was taking Nikki, the new flavor of the month, it was possible that she was using her in hopes of winning attention for herself. But then I remembered Pilar's strange smiles and I had to wonder if she'd heard about the unfortunate "Winnie and her flatulent dog" story and her motives were less pure. All I can say is that the concern I'd had before was growing.

While we know I had about as much interest in attending Retreat as I would in attending a NC half-price sale at Neiman Marcus's Last Call (if it didn't fly out the door during First Call then I don't want it), given my mounting concern I decided that there was no time like the present to make an appearance.

With only twenty-five minutes until it began, I threw on clothes, pulled my hair back, then headed through town. The Spa at Willow Creek was just west of the city limits, a sprawling compound of rolling hills and wooden buildings that were built to appear rustic, but weren't. I'm all about spas, but I tended toward a trip to the Velvet Door in town when I wanted a massage or facial.

Entering the Spa that day was like entering a large committee meeting at Brightlee—only in pseudorustic environs. A quick survey told me that there were thirty women in attendance, ten of them guests.

"Frede!" Lalee enthused when she saw me.

We did the one-side air-kiss thing.

"I'm glad you came," she said.

"Don't you look wonderful!" I told her.

Lalee was lovely, a hard worker, and a perfect president—despite her blunt habits, or perhaps because of them. Though now that she was coming to the end of her tenure, there were whispers that we would have to pry the gavel from her hands. I said that was ridiculous because I happened to know she was going to be next year's sorority alumna advisor at

WCU, plus her own daughter was nearing the debutante years. And everyone knew there was nothing quite like the debutante season in Willow Creek for consuming your time.

"Pilar and Nikki just walked in," she said, then looked around before continuing. "Rumors are getting stronger by the day that Pilar is trying to consolidate power. I'd be careful if I were you."

The fact is, presidents are chosen by the Nominating Committee at the Junior League of Willow Creek, not elected. A standing Nominating Committee was chosen by the preceding Nominating Committee, allowing the line of power to hold for decades. But every once in a while, one or two new people came in, gained friendships and alliances, getting themselves on the committee under the assumption that they understood the unspoken "rules" of succession, then undermined the system by bringing in their own friends, the chain of power broken, switching tracks, wrest away by the "upstarts."

I had to wonder if that was what Pilar was trying to do. While Pilar had lived in Willow Creek her whole life, bar one stint up north, her family had never been a part of the power set. If she became president-elect, then president after that, an upstart would indeed be taking over.

Let me just say that my life might have been consumed with a missing husband, missing money, and a new-rich, newly full-of-herself woman I had promised to get into the League, but anyone who thought I was going to roll over and let *what may* just happen was gravely mistaken. Most especially Pilar Bass.

"Pilar, sugar!" I enthused. "Just look at you in all your casual black!"

"What are you doing here?" Pilar wanted to know. "You weren't signed up."

So much for formalities or her earlier displays of faux friendship.

"I didn't want to miss out on all the fun, sugar."

It didn't look like she believed me, not that I wanted her to. All I needed to do that day was participate in the events, smile, and let everyone there remember who they were dealing with. Most especially, Pilar. Simple enough.

Pilar's friend Eloise came up, distracting her. "Pilar! Everyone is going on about what a coup Nikki is!" she gushed, then noticed me. "Oh, Frede!"

Eloise looked like (a pre–Tom Cruise, pre-glamorous) Nicole Kidman. She wore a white blouse, khaki skirt, and white Keds with ankle socks. Her hair was a naturally curly, strawberry blond and pulled away from her face with a ribbon. She was sweet, kind, said nothing but the nicest things about everyone, and was by far the fluffiest egg in the JLWC basket.

"Hello, Eloise, how are you?"

"Wonderful! Just wonderful! This is so much fun! Do you realize this is the f-i-r-s-t time I have ever sponsored anyone? The first time I've ever come to Retreat!"

"Speaking of which," I said, "I don't think I've had a chance to thank you for joining my group to sponsor Nikki."

"Your group?" Eloise looked at Pilar, her pale forehead lined.

Pilar's smile was brittle and forced.

Nikki strode up then, and if her behavior at her secret tea party (however unintentional the secret had been) had been a surprise, her behavior at Retreat was a true shocker. She entered the room looking more like a Junior Leaguer than even me. "Hello, Frede."

Her always enthusiastic demeanor had disappeared and she now spoke elegantly, as if she had been practicing every night in front of the mirror.

"How are you?" she asked, with the sort of plastered-on kindness that screams, *I don't care!* My neighbor was taking to haughty disdain like a duck to water.

I knew success (especially of the sudden kind) had a pesky way of filling a person with their own perceived importance. But who knew that success could go to Nikki's head so quickly, especially since she was still one sponsor short . . . and lived in a partially tacky pseudopalace with a man whom good society only went to in the most dire of circumstances.

Snootiness seemed premature.

"Ladies!" Lalee announced. "It's time."

We moved into the restaurant where we were served tea. Herbal. Hot. No sugar. The morning wasn't off to a promising start.

Lalee opened the meeting with a short introduction of each of our "guests." After the introductions were made, we had an hour to get to know each of the women before we moved on to the tolerable part of the event. The actual spa.

I listened to each woman's chatter with half an ear, smiling and nodding politely. Nothing worse than a group of wannabes bragging, but trying not to sound like they are. The fact is, it's an art form, and not one of these women was good at it, though I overheard Nikki wax on in a way that could make people forget she had grown up in a trailer park and was married to white trash. As they say, success breeds success, and Nikki was changing right before my eyes, her triumph solidly planted in her head.

Finally the power-bonding session was over and it was time to move on. But any hope of actually enjoying Retreat quickly died. I'm all for going to the spa, but yoga? However, I was already there, and leaving before it was over would do more damage than if I hadn't gone at all.

I hadn't thought to bring any sort of exercise clothes, so I was forced to make a quick trip to the gift shop and purchase some soft cotton pants and a T-shirt that said, *OMMM SO HAPPY—WHEN I'M AT THE SPA*.

I know, I know, but I persevered.

We were herded into a large room and were greeted by a thin man who didn't seem to know how to speak louder than in a whisper.

"Mr. Sensitive," I heard one woman remark—and not kindly.

We were divided into two groups of fifteen, each group facing the other on mats, Pilar dragging Nikki to the opposite side from me. Once we were lined up, we were given rudimentary instruction on yoga.

Lessons learned:

1. I am not particularly flexible

2. Dog positions should be left to pets

3. Our instructor, with what was left of his straggly blond hair pulled back into a ponytail, should have been shot for bad taste

"Oh, my Lord," I groaned to Lalee who was doing some sort of twist next to me.

"Just breathe and you'll loosen up," she instructed.

I was breathing, though not easily, and I finally had to straighten. Across the mat, the other girls were not doing much better than me, though Press Wellesley (married to Weldon Wellesley the fourth—the gangly heir to the Wellesley Oil Company fortune, a man who had never been able to get a date in his life until he went away one summer and conveniently returned with the voluptuous Press) was twisted like a pretzel. Lalee straightened and saw who I was looking at. "I swear she's a former stripper and Weldon Three"—*as the father was called*—"paid for her credentials. Was a debutante in Dallas, my backside."

Which was the sort of Lalee Dubois shocker I had come to know and love. Though, in truth, it wasn't a shock that Press was less than proper JLWC material. She had hooker written all over her, though the kind of hooker that had been made over with more money than even I had—please God, don't let it really be all gone.

"Lalee," I teased, "you verra bad girl."

She rolled her eyes. "She is one of the upstarts who is joining forces with Pilar. I swear, we have NC trash coming at us from every direction. Before long, if we aren't careful, we're going to be no more exclusive than the First Baptist Women's Social Club with their advertisements of 'We Turn No Woman Away.'" She scoffed.

I glanced across the mat and saw Pilar whisper something to Nikki. Pilar saw me look, and when she did, she gave me a smirk and a wave.

This really really couldn't be good.

No sooner had we stretched (or performed something that passed for it) than our instructor had us sit on the floor. "Now, ladies, we are going to meditate."

"For how long?" Press wanted to know.

"An hour."

An hour?

"Excuse me," I said with my best smile.

"Yes, Miss Ware," he said softly. And I'm not talking gay Santo soft, I'm talking about a straight man who has spent too much time getting in touch with his inner sensitive side. I'm not all that great when women try to share their feelings, and I sure don't want to see a man do it.

"When you say meditate for an hour," I asked, "what exactly do you mean?"

Mr. Sensitive looked confused. "Ah . . . I mean . . . we are going to meditate for an hour?"

"You mean just sit here? And do nothing?"

Lalee chuckled, and whispered for me to stop. Like I was joking!

"Meditation allows you to empty your mind, Miss Ware. A pathway to peace and harmony."

I would have walked out if I hadn't remembered why I was there, plus every woman there was staring at me.

"Wonderful," I said, my smile not quite as easy. "I'm all about peace and harmony."

We dutifully sat on the mat, crossed our legs in the lotus position, put our wrists palm up on our knees and got started.

"Close your eyes."

Great.

"Relax."

Puleese.

"Let your thoughts go."

That's going to happen a lot.

"Excuse me?"

Everyone's eyes popped open and they looked at me.

Oops, I might have said that last bit out loud. But I'm no fool. I glanced behind me.

Mr. Peace and Harmony started showing tension around the mouth. "Let's begin again."

Close your eyes. Relax. Let your thoughts go. Whatever.

I focused. I started making serious plans to get Nikki's last sponsor. I wasn't about to let Pilar win this one.

To that end, I would invite the entire Nominating Committee over to my house for tea. On my upturned fingers, I started counting off how many that would be. I got to four when I had a vague sense that something was wrong. Opening my eyes, I about leaped out of my skin when I found Mr. Sensitive squatting in front of me, and he wasn't looking all that sensitive anymore.

"Relax . . . your . . . mind," he ground out.

I raised a brow, giving him my best Frede Ware "look," which had him scurrying back to the front in seconds.

Thankfully, that took up a good five minutes, and given all the earlier distractions, we were left with little more than forty-five minutes to meditate. One or two guests were actually good at it, or pretended to be, while the rest of us started whispering to each other. Mr. Sensitive gave me one last glare—like I was the instigator—then strode from the room.

LUNCH CAME NEXT, a time for more power-bonding. And we might as well bond because the food was deplorable, starting with more herbal tea. I was running on zero caffeine and no sugar and I had started to feel like I could happily murder someone. I glanced around for Mr. Peace and Harmony.

The meal consisted of tofu "chicken" salad, which not one of the women ate. Lalee leaned close. "New management. I think we'll have to go to the Velvet Door next year."

A year too late as far as I was concerned.

After lunch, I thought things were finally on the upswing when we headed for the locker room and the promise of a true spa experience. Everyone had signed up for different things. Manicures, pedicures, reflexology. I had chosen massage.

In curtained stalls to maintain modesty, everyone designated for massages undressed and pulled on robes. When I came out, suitably wrapped in terry cloth from neck to ankle, I was assigned to Olga.

I have a tolerance for all people, but I swear this woman was a man. I would have said something when I met her in front of a strange tiled room, but before I could get a word out, she pointed at me as if I were the devil, and barked, "Naked!"

I glanced around in confusion. "Pardon me?"

"You, naked!"

Well, I wasn't and wasn't about to be. I was wearing the robe like a good Junior Leaguer, so I was lost.

"You! Get! Naked!"

Now let me say, she spoke with a very heavy accent (not to mention she spoke in exclamation marks) and all I could think was she was making demands using her native tongue, which were difficult to understand. She couldn't possibly expect me to get naked. I knew all about massages, and they were done on padded tables, in warm rooms filled with scented candles, with towels covering every inch, only one body part at a time revealed for ministration. It did not involve, Naked!

"I'm sorry, sugar, but I'm just not understanding."

She harrumphed, marched over to me, then whipped the robe off my back before I could say, *Are You Insane*.

I gasped, was too shocked to cover myself, then was herded into what turned out to be a shower in the shape of a hallway. "What on God's green earth are you doing?"

She turned a fire hose on me and I had to grab two handles attached to the walls to stay upright.

Well, it was hugely embarrassing, and when I heard a chorus of shrieks race through the halls, I realized that more than one Leaguer was getting a hose-down she would not soon forget.

My mind was pretty numb to the rest of the day of relaxation. All I remember was that after the deluge ceased, I was bundled back into the terry robe, then led off to the warm padded table I had anticipated, but the massage was nothing like anything I had ever experienced.

"Cleanse!" she bellowed.

Wasn't I clean enough? Only it turned out that her specialty was a form of massage that manipulated the organs in order to "cleanse" them. Just know that I haven't had another massage since, and may never again.

We were a battered group when we piled out to our cars. It probably wasn't safe to drive, and I found it hard to care when Nikki gave me an air kiss, swore that we would get together soon, then went off with Pilar and Eloise.

THE FOLLOWING DAY, my body, the one that was supposed to feel newly polished and peaceful, felt the ravaging aftershocks of Olga's therapeutic massage. I could barely get out of bed, though when Sawyer called and invited me to an exhibit in Kerrville, I jumped (with a groan of pain) at the chance. Olga must have rubbed sense out of me along with everything else.

When he pulled up the drive, I didn't wait for him to come to the door. He was still in the car when I hurried out, his hair ruffled from the wind, his dark sunglasses making him look mysterious.

"Sexy," he said when he got a look at yet another of my JLWC Unacceptable *ensembles*.

"There will be none of that," I said with an attempt to look stern as I climbed into the car, ignoring the heat that had rushed to my cheeks.

The show, of sculptures made from natural Texas products, was all the rage and everyone who was anyone was seeing it. I would have gone weeks ago had it not been for the "unfortunate incident" and its fallout dominating my days.

Sawyer drove to the show with quiet assurance, taking turns and shifting gears with the efficiency of a racecar driver. Once we arrived, I walked along with Sawyer from piece to piece, those alarm bells ringing in my head, but there I was regardless. "Tell me about you," I said, standing in front of a horse carved from driftwood.

"Nothing to tell."

"Everyone has something to tell."

He looked over at me, a grin beginning to appear. "Not me."

"I hear you were quite the bad boy when you were young."

"Who told you that?"

"Nikki."

"Nikki loves to talk," he said with a wry grin. "Speaking of Nikki, how's the Junior League stuff going for her?"

I thought of the recent excursion to the Spa. "Fine." Or not.

"For her sake, I hope so."

I glanced over at him. "The two of you seem to be really good friends."

"Yeah. She was always a sweet kid. Lived in a bad situation but still managed to smile. You got to love that. When I moved back to town, she was the first person to come by." He chuckled. "I hadn't been home more than a week and the place hadn't been lived in for close to a year before I got there. When she saw what a mess it was, she left, then came back with two maids, a gardener, and she was wearing old work clothes. I told her I could get the place cleaned up on my own, but she just brushed past me and started barking out orders." He laughed, remembering. "The place would probably still be a disaster if she hadn't stepped in. Housekeeping isn't high on my list of best qualities." He shook his head. "When it was done, a week later, all of us exhausted, I said I didn't know how to thank her. She said, 'Sawyer Jackson, that's what friends do for each other.' So, yeah," he finished, "she's a good friend. I'm happy as hell she found Howard. I've never seen two people who belong together more than they do."

There was that reminder again, of that . . . that thing Howard and Nikki shared—the protectiveness, the "we're in this together" notion, or something. At least that had been the case before Nikki started making inroads into the Junior League.

Feelings tried to surface, but I shook them away.

"So, is it true?" I persisted, changing tracks.

"Is what true?"

"That you were a bad boy?"

He shrugged. "Depends on what you consider a bad boy."

"Did you drink?" I probed.

"Maybe."

"Smoke?"

"A little."

"Fight?"

"Once or twice."

I must have snorted. He laughed and shoved his hands in his jeans pockets, tipping back on his heels. "Okay, maybe more than that. But the way I saw it, I didn't have much choice."

"Why?"

"My father taught me that it was dishonorable to pick a fight—though he said I could defend myself."

"So you defended yourself a lot?"

"I had to. I liked art instead of football. Fortunately I got real good at defending myself. My dad didn't necessarily see it that way." He smiled in memory and shook his head. "Hell, I miss the guy."

"Where is he?"

"He died two years ago. My mother died shortly after."

"I'm sorry."

"Yeah, so am I. I spent too much time traveling, living here and there, always thinking I'd have plenty of time to spend with them."

"Is that what you meant when you said life had turned out differently than you planned?"

He debated for a second. "Yeah, something like that."

"I'm really sorry."

"Don't be. I'm one of the lucky ones. I had parents who lived a good long life. They loved the courses they taught at the university, loved me, loved each other and weren't afraid to show it."

My Danger Man was from a happy family? "Then where does all that angst in your art come from?"

That mouth of his hiked up at one corner. "Who said I had any angst?"

"Then what do you call the scowls, slashing art, not to mention slamming doors in perfectly nice people's faces?"

"How about aggressive happiness."

Next thing I knew I was laughing, enough to make people turn to stare . . . including a woman I hadn't noticed before. Not good.

"Frede?"

My smile was instant. "Marcia!" I pealed.

Marcia Travers was a powerful Junior Leaguer, chairman of last year's Christmas Fair. She gave me an air kiss, then held me at arm's length.

"Frede, you look simply . . . not like you!"

She seemed pleased, and not in the "I'm so glad you're broadening your horizons" sort of way—as could be expected given my denim-clad hips and thighs, not to mention the four-inch stilettos I had added on a whim.

"Thank you!" I said with plastered-on enthusiasm, panic trying to take hold. "What with all Gordon's adventures, I was feeling a little blue missing him." I needed a flow chart to keep track of my mounting secrets: my adulterous husband, my missing money, my divorce that I didn't want anyone to know about yet. If the League had to know I was divorced, then I needed to be divorced with scads of money. "So I got myself out of the house and came to see this amazing exhibit."

"That's right, I heard Gordon was in New Guinea." She patted my hand and clucked. "You poor thing. I can't imagine how horrible it would be to have a husband who preferred traveling over being with me."

For a second I thought I must have heard incorrectly.

She clucked some more. "Though let me tell you, I wouldn't mind if my Walter left me in peace now and again. What with him always wanting my attention, bringing me flowers, showering me with candy, it can be exhausting. So consider yourself lucky, I say."

I couldn't do much more than stare at her utterly fake and insincere smile before she turned her attention to Sawyer.

"And this is?" She raised a brow.

Under the definition of "Having a Bad Day," I'm sure mine was listed as the perfect example.

My brain scrambled, weighing options. Then I did something beyond bad. I glanced at my artist and said, "I'm sorry, what is your name again?"

I know, I know, I should be shot because Sawyer is dreamy, plus, beneath his Marlboro man exterior he's kind. But I had to get Marcia off the scent of scandal. Besides, could anyone really blame me for being in a not-so-nice place after Marcia's sugarcoated jab?

Clearly Sawyer could, since his jaw started doing the angry-clench thing. But if Marcia noticed anything was awry, she didn't let on. Instead, she surprised me when she said, "Actually"—a wicked glint in her eyes—"I know who he is. Sawyer Jackson. Elusive artist. Prodigal entrepreneur. And the Jack part of JackHill Technologies."

A single moment passed before I swung around to face him, my mouth very probably hanging open. "You are the Jack part of JackHill?"

I vaguely remembered the stories from nearly a decade ago when two students at the University of Texas had started a video game production company in their dorm room. One had been a computer major, the other an art major. Between the two of them they had created the games, drawn the animated game strips, then executed computer programs to bring them to life. I thought back to Hill, the tech geek from Sawyer's dinner party. Sawyer Jackson and the tech guy Hill must have been that team.

"The JackHill who went public," I demanded, "then sold to MicroSystems for a bazillion dollars?"

If Sawyer had been less than pleased when I pretended not to know his name, he looked even more irritated over this development. "'Bazillion' would be an exaggeration," he said tightly.

I couldn't believe it. My starving artist was really a bazillionaire—and he wasn't happy that people knew it! I was stunned.

Marcia, on the other hand, was beside herself trying to get close. But Sawyer was having none of it. He politely (if firmly) excused himself and walked out.

I had heard the rumors that the guys from JackHill—on the Fortune 500 list by accident—had no interest in publicity. So much so that each had left the country for years after they sold the business.

I thought of his explanation of living here and there, then him saying that he had stayed away too long. I realized he must have stayed away to keep out of the spotlight and, in the process, missed the last years of his parents' lives.

Marcia went on about JackHill for a good five minutes more before finally departing. But once the coast was clear, I couldn't find Sawyer anywhere. Thinking I had been left to fend for myself, I would have asked the gallery personnel to call me a taxi if I hadn't finally found Sawyer sitting outside on an arty, roughhewn bench.

"I thought you left." I might have snipped.

He looked at me in exasperation. "What the hell could you be pissed off about?"

True, I was the one who had been rude and perhaps owed him an apology for pretending not to know him. But I couldn't get the words out.

"Nothing's wrong." More snipping.

Actually, I wasn't quite sure what was making me act so irrationally. Sure, there was Marcia and her catty comments. But more than that, there was something about the idea of my starving artist as a bazillionnaire that I couldn't get my head around. Though why it mattered I couldn't say. You would have thought I'd be thrilled.

He muttered something that I would have sworn wasn't nice, guided me to the car, then drove me back to Willow Creek in glaring silence.

The skies had been dark all day and he had snapped on the car's old canvas and vinyl top before we left Kerrville. It started to drizzle when we pulled into my drive. I opened my door before he turned off the ignition.

"Damn it, Frede. Look at me."

I swiveled to face him and his expression was as stormy as the clouds in the sky. Every trace of easy humor was gone.

"What is going on with you?" he demanded.

"I said, nothing."

"Stop acting like a child."

A child? Okay, so maybe I was, but who was he to point it out?

I got out of the car, and if he'd had a respectably solid door, I would have slammed it.

Perhaps it could be argued (successfully) that I was acting crazy. But that didn't loosen the tangled knot of frustration I felt over . . . well . . .

everything, and I couldn't find my way through to polite behavior to save my life.

I strode toward my front door and I could feel his anger building, coming off him in waves. I expected at any second that he would fly up behind me to demand an explanation or, better yet, to apologize for calling me a child.

Just the thought jarred me out of my melodramatic stupor. Him, racing after me. A heated argument. And where do arguments frequently lead? To making up.

I forgot about JackHill because I can be just that shallow. I knew a potential dramatic moment when it was staring me in the face. While I frown on dramatic moments (don't laugh) this was one I have to admit I was looking forward to.

Slowing down, I pulled my key from my purse. I took forever to unlock the door despite the crack of lightning that flashed through the sky. Finally, I turned around . . . just in time to see him drive away.

If you think for a second that I was going to run after the man, you are mistaken. I don't do desperate any more than I do big hair in the rain. Or so I told myself.

His car roared off and I told myself to make a cup of tea. I walked through the house, went to the kitchen, but then kept going to the garage. I couldn't have been rational when I got into my Mercedes, then waved at Juan, nearly hitting the electronic arm as I raced out of the exclusive enclave.

Chapter Twenty-three

I WAS DRIVING *très* fast when I left The Willows, faster than I normally would since reckless driving by a woman is vulgar, especially in the rain.

NC or not, I flew through town, trying to catch up to Sawyer. He must have been driving worse than me since I got to the south side of town without catching a glimpse of him.

I shouldn't have kept going since chasing anyone, especially a man, was the height of unacceptable behavior, but I had left good manners behind days ago.

I flew over the tracks, the roads deserted no doubt because of the rain, then arrived at the hacienda without seeing so much as a brake light in the courtyard. I was concerned he hadn't gone home. That or he had a bat cave and had disappeared inside.

Hoping for the bat cave, I pulled through the gates and stopped under a canopy, then was out of my car and at his front door clanging that ridiculous bell loud enough to alert the lesser half of Willow Creek.

This time when no one answered I rang repeatedly until my efforts bore fruit. The door whipped open and my artist stood there looking less than welcoming.

I had to force myself not to take a step back. "So, you have a bat cave," I said.

The line of his mouth tightened and he stared at me in a way that I knew meant his patience was *fini.* "What do you want?" he said.

I blinked. "I . . ."

Then nothing. His anger had a way of rattling me. I didn't know what to say. Me, Frede Ware, at a loss for words. It was a growing trend I didn't like at all.

"I'm busy," he said, then slammed the door in my face.

Yes, again.

That rattled me right back to myself. I'd had just about enough of people being rude to me (the irony of this wasn't lost on *moi*, given my most recent rude behavior at the gallery, in the car, in my driveway). I banged the door open.

"You can't keep slamming doors in my face!"

He didn't stop. He continued on through the house. I followed him all the way to the back door, where outside, the rain was coming down even harder.

He kept going. I came to a dead stop on the threshold and watched him head for his studio.

Well, what was I going to do? I'm beautiful in a put-together sort of way. I'm pretty when I dress up, stunning even, but I'm realistic enough to recognize that my spectacular good looks come about from my clothes, my demeanor, and my hair. And I don't have good rain hair. While I don't use nearly as much spray as my mother, I'm no slouch in the hair spray department. And hair spray and rain don't mix. Which was why I came to a halt at the back door and didn't go any farther.

I mean, really, if I was going to have some big nonacceptable dramatic scene with Sawyer Jackson, the least I could do in the situation was look my best.

But then again, if I didn't follow him, I wouldn't have any sort of scene at all.

I experienced a true Scarlett O'Hara moment, stamped my foot, said something about not going to go hungry again for good measure, pulled a brush out of my handbag, and ran it through my hair to de-spray it as best I could. Then I headed out.

The rain hit me like a bucket of water. While the first part of April is way warmer in Central Texas than it is in say Outer Alaska or even Omaha, the rain was surprisingly cold. It also shocked some sense into me, the kind that should have turned me around, gotten me back in my Mercedes and heading home. But that only occurred to me much later.

As I stood in the rain, all the years of my mother's rules were gone. I didn't care about the Junior League or acceptable behavior. I headed across the wet grass, my not-so-sensible spiked heels sinking into the mud that bubbled up between the bright green blades, and I could feel my blouse stick to my skin.

I was so absorbed in the surprise of not thinking about manners (not to mention the concentration it took to keep my balance in those heels) that I didn't realize he was standing right in front of me until I slammed into the solid wall of his chest.

"Oh."

"What are you doing out here? You're getting soaked."

Even angry there was a trace of Protective Guy.

"Yes, well."

"Is that all you can ever say?" he said.

"Well, no. In fact, what I wanted to say was that I know your show is going to be a fabulous hit."

I agree, it was a completely inane response.

He looked at me strangely, as if he weren't quite sure what stood before him. Then he cursed. The word, or rather words, do not need repeating here. Just know that they were beyond common, and an utterly unforgivable use of profanity strung together like a string of uncultured pearls.

"Go back to your tight-ass world, princess."

My mood was every bit as bad as his, but was I resorting to profanity and insults? *Non.* I had every intention of talking like a civilized adult.

"Don't you think you're overreacting," I said.

"*Me* overreacting?"

He sounded like a lion with a thorn in its paw, all about roar and indignation.

"Really, Sawyer, there's no need to get emotional."

He kind of arched back and groaned. "Emotional? God forbid anyone show emotion."

And he said he created from aggressive happiness. Scoff.

By now we were both soaked well and good. He looked (unfairly) great, like one of those models in a Calvin Klein jeans ad, clothes soaked through so you can make out the muscles under the shirt, dark hair raked back by his hands. I felt a teensy bit on the self-conscious side, not wanting to look like a dead rat and all, and I didn't dare run my hand through my hair for fear of it getting stuck.

He focused on me. "What the hell is wrong with you? After you pretend you don't know me, you come barreling after me like a madwoman?"

True. But what could I say. "You're . . . you're . . . rich!"

That caught him off guard, and quite frankly, me too.

He stared at me through the rain. "First you're mad because I'm not gay. Now you're mad because I'm not poor?"

Adrenaline pumped through me as it all sank in and realization of why I was acting so crazy hit me like a bucket of Outer Alaska rain. "Yes! I'm the one who's supposed to have money. I'm the one who's supposed to be doing you a favor! Not the other way around! I don't need to be saved!"

The words froze in the air between us. Then he shook his head. "That's insane. Nobody is saving anyone. This isn't about favors."

"Yes it is! Now I understand why you don't show your work! You don't need to. Because you're rich! You're only showing with me because you . . . feel sorry for me, or think I'm amusing, or . . . or . . . whatever!"

Okay, so maybe the adrenaline wore off and my voice warbled at the end. Maybe my eyes started to burn.

"Hell," he said, but this time he said it kind of nice. "You make me crazy. You make me do things that are insane."

I tried to smile. "What's a muse for if not to inspire you to new heights?"

He half groaned, half laughed, and his voice was hoarse when he added, "But you're married."

Oh, that. "Did I forget to mention that Gordon divorced me?"

Talk about a walk on the blunt side, not to mention that it was supposed to be a secret.

But then the next thing I knew, he said, "Ah, hell," and pulled me into his arms. Yes, just like that.

It was incredibly romantic, all hands and touching and inappropriate tingling. Very much a soundtrack moment.

I'm not sure what would have happened next if I had been wearing sensible heels. Given the precarious stilettos I had actually worn, when I moved just so, I slipped (you can call me Grace) in the mud.

I felt all that strength of his trying to keep me upright. But it wasn't enough. We fell to the ground, Sawyer landing on top of me, his weight supported on his elbows. We stared at each other, then our mouths slammed together.

We rolled and kissed until he picked me up and carried me into the house. At that point (or at any, really) a sense of right or wrong should have kicked in. But no such luck. I wanted whatever was coming in the worst sort of way.

Sawyer carried me through the house, then up a wide staircase to the loft. His bed was there and he set me down—not on it, there was all that mud—and began undressing me. He smiled when he saw my not-so-proper bra and panties. Nothing Agent Provocateur–ish, mind you, but certainly not a plain beige lace.

"You're beautiful," he said.

He was ultra close, circling behind me, and I could feel his breath against my ear.

"But I knew you'd be beautiful."

I'm all for compliments and I was enjoying the moment. It was after he stripped away my underclothes then turned me around and really looked at me that I felt uncomfortable.

He took my hand, and yet again didn't go for the bed. He took me to the shower.

This was all incredibly awkward, but he didn't seem to be bothered in the least. I won't go to the jealous place, but rest assured, this man knew his way around the seduction arena.

He turned on the faucet, and when I suggested that perhaps a bath, with bubbles, might be even better, he only laughed again.

Next thing I knew I was in the shower, warm water beating down on me. With the artist. I can only hope my mother never reads this.

Who knows how long we were in there, but once we were out and dry, he handed me one of his dress shirts. I pulled it on and felt very sexy, I must say. It practically swallowed me and I felt all jittery when he buttoned me from halfway down. After he rolled up the sleeves to my forearm, he pronounced me perfect.

"But you already knew that," he added.

"Don't tell me you're going to start in on the insults again."

"Never."

He looked me over, and my whole body tingled in anticipation of what was coming, namely the bed and what would happen in it. But my artist was nothing if not unpredictable.

He pulled out a sketchpad.

This might be romantic to some people, but as I could imagine Nikki saying, I had a scratch that needed to be itched.

"Lie on the bed."

This wasn't how I imagined it would be. When I hesitated, disappointed that I wasn't getting the movie-version romance treatment, he gave a mock sigh, picked me up (I squealed) and threw me on the high mattress.

But that was it. Just me. He didn't follow. He didn't sit down next to me. He pulled on a pair of jeans (worn, the kind with metal buttons, the top one undone) and sat in an overstuffed leather chair a few feet from said bed and started to sketch me.

Giving in to the no-sex treatment, I tried my best to look glorious, all the while using the opportunity to ask some questions. His answers were short and distracted, the charcoal pencil never stopping. When I inquired about JackHill, he said they had developed their first game as a fluke, and were as surprised as anyone when kids on campus couldn't get enough of it. So they had created more games, things building from there until MicroSystems had bought them out. When I asked why he still lived in South Willow Creek instead of something in a better part of town, he stopped drawing, looked at me with one of his irresistible smiles, and said, "The hacienda is my home."

Oddly, I really couldn't imagine him anywhere else.

I started to ask another question, but he cut me off. "You've had your quota. Now let me work."

Well. Sniff.

After posing fabulously for a good fifteen minutes sans any sort of communication, I got bored and at some point fell asleep. I know I was asleep because I remember dreaming, of him, then waking, and he was there, kissing me, his fingers smudged with charcoal.

His lips felt verra nice on my skin and I wondered what could it hurt to lose myself to touch and taste and the sorts of sounds that were not on any JLWC Approved list. So I did. We did. For quite a long time.

When it was over, he kissed me, rolled off the bed, then started drawing me again. This time he looked at me differently. Really looked, as if he saw more than all the practiced perfectness. I couldn't imagine what the finished product would look like. What I did know, however, was that it wasn't going to be a piece of art anyone could use for decorating.

Chapter Twenty-four

I WASN'T FEELING GUILTY when I raced home the next morning. Really. Though while I was newly divorced, technically I was still a lady, and last I heard, all the things I had been doing through the night weren't listed in any book of proper behavior I had ever read.

I drove myself to Chez Ware and did my best not to think about it. Though it was a tad on the *compliqué* side to ignore completely when I pulled up to the garage and Nina (clearly having had enough of her own family, or they of her) came flying out the back door from the kitchen.

I knew from the look of her disheveled hair and terrorized face that something was amiss. Though I just about killed her with shock when she got a good look at my attire—warm-up pants and an oversized T-shirt borrowed from Sawyer.

"Wha you doing, Missy Ware? Where you been?" "Been" pronounced like the legume, bean.

Probably because I didn't want to think about where I had *bean,* I thought instead about bean dip, bean soufflés, bean tacos. None of which were a part of my diet, but I far preferred to think of food than the answer.

Then she gaped at me. "You have sex."

"Nina!"

She crossed her arms. "You no can have sex, Missy Ware."

Remember, I was raised never ever to discuss s-e-x. I knew this. My maid knew this. But there she was like a sex-detector, accusation written all over her face.

"Stop!" I said.

"You stop! You stop have sex."

She went off with a bunch of Spanish, none of it (as usual) complimentary, and I knew she knew sex had occurred with my artist. Not that I would ever admit it.

"Nina, really." I swished my hand.

More uncomplimentary Spanish combined with words like "Beelzebub" and "sinner" followed while she held up her hands in the sign of a cross. At me! Like I was the devil.

"Where I've been or what I've *bean* doing isn't your concern."

Nina sniffed. *"Bueno."* Though I could tell she didn't mean anything close to good. "If you no want to say to me where you been, then you say to lady in house."

Blood running cold, and all that. "Someone's inside?" I had gone straight back to the garage, bypassing the front drive.

"*Sí*. Missy Winnie, she say."

"Winifred Opal?"

Nina looked pleased that she had finally ruffled my perfect calm. "That ees the one."

"Inside the house? My house?" There might have been a tiny bit of hysteria in my voice, which pleased Nina to no end. But I knew that because Winnie lived in The Willows she could easily arrive at my front door unannounced.

She nodded. "Now you change your song."

"Tune!"

"Wha-ever."

Nina trying to be hip. Good Lord.

"Don't worry," she added. "Nina take care of Missy Ware."

Which of course I knew. She had been bailing me out of trouble for as long as I could remember, though I always paid for it afterward.

There was the time I broke my mother's favorite Oriental vase when I was four and a half. Nina had worked magic with Super Glue. To this day, my mother still doesn't realize that the fine line isn't really part of the clinging-vine pattern painted on the porcelain.

A few years after that, when I was seven, there was another episode with the son of a visiting Junior Leaguer who asked me to play doctor. I had never played before, but I was always up for a new game. While his mother and mine sat downstairs having tea, I had my first lesson in male anatomy. I might have been naïve, but I wasn't stupid. When he asked to "see yours too," I told him the game was boring. He might have argued, but Nina came flying into the room and about died of shock (at the time I assumed she had never seen a penis either) before bustling the *patient* back into his clothes and downstairs just before my mother entered in a puff of perfume and pearls.

She stopped dead in her tracks, her smile freezing as she looked at me. "What have you been doing, Fredericka?"

No one had to tell me that doctor was probably not the kind of game my mother would approve.

"Nothing, Mother." Formal, even back then.

"Where is the boy?"

"What boy?"

She looked around, frowned then shrugged. "I'm going into town to Brightlee for lunch. Be a good girl."

That was then, this was now.

"When did Winifred get here?" I asked my maid. "What did you say? Why in the world did you let her inside?"

Nina went on about how Winifred marched inside the minute the front door opened, announcing she had to see me. Nina tried to get her to leave, saying I was still sleeping, at which point Winifred called up the stairs.

Nina shushed her, and had her sit in the living room while she bought some time. Upstairs "supposedly waking me," Nina saw my Mercedes wheel up to the garage like an angel sent from heaven. Nina flew down the back stairs, out the kitchen door, then started herding me inside, instructing me to pretend I had just woken up.

Given that I don't do the whole emotion thing, I quashed the urge to fling myself at her and tell her I loved her forever.

I took the back set of stairs up to my bedroom where I quickly pulled myself together.

"Frede," Winifred said as I entered the living room.

"Winifred, what a surprise."

"I've changed my mind."

"About what?"

"I am willing to sponsor Nikki Grout for membership into the Junior League of Willow Creek."

I should have been thrilled since the hard part of my job was done. I had all six sponsors and, barring a catastrophe, Nikki would get in. I had lived up to my end of the bargain, but I felt no sense of accomplishment.

"Great!" Think fake enthusiasm. "I know Nikki will be thrilled."

"Yes, I'm sure she will be. She is just the sort of new blood we need in the League. She wants to do good for the community. And now that she is giving up animal prints . . ."

Ah, the excuses we make up to allow ourselves to change our minds without feeling weak. Nothing like sudden success to have every Tom, Dick, and Winnie jumping on the bandwagon to offer support.

ONCE WINIFRED LEFT, I returned upstairs and took a long bath. After dressing in a proper outfit of silk and pearls, I started to head for Palace Grout. But I couldn't take Nikki right then. So I called.

"She's not here, Frede," Howard told me. "She's gone over to that Pilar's house again."

He didn't sound any happier about his situation with his wife than he had when he had arrived on my doorstep dressed in boat shoes.

"When she gets back, tell her that Winifred Opal is on board. We have all six sponsors."

Howard sighed. "Great." Then a sort of huff. "I mean, that's great."

It was the first time I realized that the single word "great" could mean different things based on the intonation in which it was spoken.

"You held up your end of the bargain." He hesitated. "Funny, but I'm not sure if I thought you really would."

Excuse me?

"But that's another story. For now I need to get the business with your husband finished. I got a tracer on that call he made. He's in Mexico. That much I know. One way or another, you'll have his ass on a platter, Frede, that I promise."

He hung up, and I stared at the phone. Everything was coming to a head, I could feel it.

Over the next few days, I told myself to stay away from Sawyer Jackson and the wrong side of town. When he called, I had Nina tell him I wasn't there. When I called Nikki, she was never available and I knew something wasn't right. I just had no idea what it was.

I concentrated on putting the finishing touches to my big show, telling myself that I was worrying for nothing, everything was going to work out. How could it not? It was me and my life we were talking about.

The day of the exhibit was fast approaching when I finally broke down and drove to South Willow Creek. I couldn't have been more surprised to find Nikki's car in the courtyard.

Sitting there, my fingers curled around the steering wheel, I wasn't sure what to do. Me, me Frede Ware, master of confidence in every situation (except during sex with my artist), hadn't a clue what to do. Before I could decide, Nikki came out.

"Frede!" she enthused in the overly polite and insincere way I had practically invented. I had never seen conceit go so quickly to anyone's head, and I had to believe Pilar had something to do with the drastic change.

"I can't wait for your big show," she chimed. "Sawyer's painting up a storm, doesn't want to be disturbed. He told me to go away! Can you believe it?" She laughed prettily. "I'd love to stay and chat, but I've got to meet Pilar and the girls at Brightlee for lunch. *Ciao!*"

"Nikki," I said, stopping her.

She looked back at me.

"Sugar," I said, "I'm not sure what is going on, but I'd be careful of Pilar, if I were you."

I remembered back to the years growing up with Pilar and her need to be in charge, the tension in her mouth when something good happened for me and not her. The meanness she showed when something didn't go her way.

It was in our sophomore year when our little group finally fell apart. We had survived Nikki finding out I had money. We had slogged through Nikki's mother being an embarrassment because she had worked first at the ice-cream shop, then as a maid. But we couldn't survive boys. At least when it was the one Pilar loved, who happened to love me.

His name was Steve Barker, a senior, a football star, and the most popular boy at Willow Creek High. At the beginning of our sophomore year Pilar became his tutor in math. He teased her like a little sister, called her "P," and it was the only time I have ever seen Pilar . . . well, soft. Hard to imagine now, I know. When Nikki had teased her that she was in love, she vehemently denied it, gave all the reasons why she wasn't. (Jock, lack of brains, slobbered over by all the girls.) I hadn't told her that he called me most every night, despite the fact that I told him I only liked him as a friend. Not only did I have no interest in the callow youths of Willow Creek High, but Pilar was in love with the guy.

But he was nothing if not confident. When he came up to our lockers and asked me to the Winter Formal, before I could turn him down, Pilar walked up and didn't give me a chance.

"You asked her to Winter Formal?" she said, her mouth tight.

"Yeah," he said, smiling. "Tell her to say yes, P."

Pilar went very still, tension riding through her. Of course, our football player was oblivious, and just kept smiling at me.

"Aren't you sweet," I said. "But I can't."

"You can't?" His orthodontist-perfect smile disappeared. "Every girl in school would die to go with me. Damn"—he turned to Pilar—"you'd go with me in a heartbeat."

I can only think he had been hit in the head one too many times.

Pilar gritted her teeth. "Yeah, Frede, you should go with him."

"I can't—"

"No," she insisted. "You have to go."

"There, it's settled," Steve announced. "I'll pick you up at seven."

He walked away.

"I am not going," I said.

"What?" Pilar bit out. "You think you're better than everyone else? Think you can throw your money and your name around and get whatever you want?"

The truth is, she made me so mad I went.

But by the Monday after the dance, after the corsage, after the photos, after kneeing him in the groin when he got fresh in the front seat of his parents' Cadillac, I regretted the whole thing. When I arrived at the lockers I was ready to apologize. Nikki and Pilar were already there.

"How was it?" Nikki squealed.

Pilar slammed the metal door closed. "Yeah, how was it?"

I told them just how awful it was, partly because it was true, and partly because I wanted Pilar to know that it wasn't special, and that I was sorry I had gone. "The highlight was that I met Katie Squires."

"The head varsity cheerleader?" Nikki asked with awe.

"Yes, she was great."

Pilar scoffed. "Like she even noticed you. You're pathetic, Frede. You think you're so perfect, better than everyone else. Well, you're not. You just always managed to make people think you are."

"Pilar," Nikki said. "That isn't nice, and it's not true."

"Just shut up, you little hen wit. Stop playing Pollyanna."

Nikki and I could hardly believe it. I pretty much just stared. But what made matters worse was that Katie Squires walked up to us.

"Hey, Frede."

"Hi, Katie."

I introduced her to my friends and Katie couldn't have been any nicer.

"You know," she said, looking at me, "I was thinking you should try out for junior varsity cheerleader. What do you think?"

Pilar (in all her budding liberal blue-state, debate-team prowess) interjected something about the fact that girls who dressed up like perky hookers displaying themselves for the titillation of boys were a disgrace to all our activist forebears who fought to gain equal rights for women everywhere.

I weighed my options:

1. manage the byways of our little group's increasingly complicated difficulties, or,

2. wear perky uniforms and get the attention of an entire football team and a stadium full of fans.

The answer seemed clear. I closed my locker, walked away, and joined the cheerleading squad.

By the end of our sophomore year the three of us hardly saw each other. Pilar had become an ambitious debater, and Nikki had hooked up with a group of girls who thought the grunge look was something worth aspiring to.

All those years later, standing in Sawyer's courtyard, Nikki looked at me in all her Frede Ware attire, but didn't say anything.

"I just think you have to be careful of Pilar. That's all. And maybe," I added, "you're being a little . . . you know, mean to Howard."

Can you believe it? Me defending my neighbor. Not to mention being direct.

Nikki pulled her shoulders back. "Pilar told me you would rain on my parade."

I admit it, I gasped.

She sighed. "Sorry. But really, Frede, Pilar likes me and she's including me in all kinds of stuff. Just leave it alone."

Was she right? Was it possible I was jealous that Pilar and Nikki had become good friends again? The whole girl-friendship waters could be so hard to navigate.

She left, and I told myself to do the same. Instead I walked through the courtyard to the front door. When no one answered, I let myself in. And quite frankly, after the snippy comments and turncoat behavior I had just experienced, can you blame me?

The house was quiet as I walked through to the back door, then across the yard to the studio. I stopped when I saw him. As always, he looked wild and like he hadn't slept in days, as he painted with all that aggressive happiness he talked about.

He wore jeans with a blue cambric shirt untucked and unbuttoned, paint streaks marking it all. Canvases leaned against the walls, some big, some small. I knocked on the doorframe.

"I said go away!"

"Sorry, but I've gotten into a bad habit of not doing what I should."

He stopped and whipped around, paintbrush still in hand, paint flying off the bristles. His eyes were dark and intense, and I thought for a second that he was going to yell at me. But he smiled in a way that made my blood burn through my already tastefully blushed cheeks.

"Do you still want me to go away?"

Who knew I could be coy.

"Hell, no."

He threw the brush on the palette in a splatter then walked over to me. I was in his arms before I could remind myself that this wasn't why I had come. I almost believed it too.

"God, you're a sight for sore eyes. Ever since you sent out the invitations for the show this place has been crawling with people. Every time I turn around someone else wants to see my work. Is it too late to cancel?" he said against my neck.

"Too late," I murmured.

"Hell." But he laughed, then swept me up.

He didn't carry me to the house and his loft. There was too much impatience for that. In a matter of seconds, clothes were strewn in a trail across the paint-spattered cement floor, then we were doing things on my artist's worktable that didn't involve art. I won't go into details, but suffice it to say that I forgot all about Nikki, the show, and even my missing money.

Chapter Twenty-five

MY SHOW, Hildebrand Galleries Presents Impressions by Sawyer Jackson, arrived on a *fabu* night with a brilliantly clear, star-studded sky. Everyone who was anyone had RSVPed *oui,* and the gallery was filled with a satisfying mix of glittering jewels, stark white walls, and my artist's paintings.

I had worn a stunning (if I do say so myself) midnight-blue, full taffeta skirt that held a slight shimmer, with a white wraparound blouse, and plenty of my evening-appropriate (albeit fake) jewels. Sawyer arrived ten minutes before his art was set to be unveiled. He looked amazing as he made his way through the crowd, sexy in his black three-button suit, blue shirt, and no tie. He headed straight toward me with a look in his eye that was a little more friendly than was appropriate for a public place—especially since I was standing next to my parents. As a preventive measure (why take chances?) I stuck my hand out and shook his like the proper business lady I was pretending to be.

Sawyer raised a brow. My mother looked at me oddly. My father sized up the man.

"So you're Sawyer Jackson," my daddy said.

I made the official introductions as the two men stood little more than a foot apart. They were both tall, well built, and protective. In short, they hated each other on sight. I was relieved when my mother excused herself, and dragged my father over to talk to a congressman who had just arrived.

A smile ticked up at one corner of Sawyer's mouth. He was completely unfazed by my father's glare (or my handshake) and he ran his finger down the sheer organza of my sleeve. "You look great," he said.

I was caught on dual prongs of loving compliments and not about to allow any sort of public . . . anything. I stepped aside with a laugh that anyone watching would consider nothing more than friendly.

He chuckled in that way he had that went straight down my spine. "And your hair."

Earlier I had gone a little crazy and curled it.

"It's sexy as hell."

"You think everything is sexy," I said, trying to act stern.

He just laughed some more. "I'll behave," he said, then glanced around the gallery. "A friend of yours came by the studio today."

"A friend? Who?"

He nodded toward the far corner of the room. When I followed his gaze I was confused. "Pilar Bass?"

"That's the one."

Pilar stood with a group of other girls from the League, each of them sipping champagne out of Baccarat crystal flutes.

He nodded his head. "She wanted to see my work. Hell, I didn't even know she was there until I found her in my studio waiting for me. Said she was chairman of some new projects committee and wanted me to be her next new project."

I blinked. Pilar was going behind my back trying to finalize the New Project? First, Nikki. Then the New Project. Or was she trying to add Sawyer to her list of coups.

My heart started doing the rapid-beat thing, and all the concern about Pilar I had been feeling congealed into a hard knot in my chest. I didn't like it at all.

The gallery director interrupted. "Carlos hung the last painting." She was out of breath, and not her usual calm self. "This is crazy. I hope it works."

"Peggy, are you okay?" I asked, but she was already gone, hurrying up to the Plexiglas podium.

"Attention, please!" she said.

The crowd quieted down and she welcomed the mayor of Willow

Creek. Anticipation was high as Mayor Jameson strode to the front of the room, then spoke eloquently about the gallery, Sawyer, and the dedication Willow Creek felt to the arts.

"With no further ado, I present Impressions by Sawyer Jackson," the mayor finished, pulling away the first drape.

Gasps rolled through the room, but I was looking at Sawyer. His expression went from dark to stormy. He was verra verra angry, though I couldn't imagine why.

Turning, which I shouldn't have, I saw it.

I might have staggered back a step, Sawyer reaching out to steady me, as I stared at a painting I hadn't seen before, the last one Carlos must have hung. And let me just say, no wonder Peggy was anxious.

"Good Lord, Fredericka," my mother choked out. "Tell me that isn't you."

If only I could have. But words were beyond me even if I had wanted to fabricate some sort of story—though what sort of story I could have come up with to explain the small but distinct gesso painting of me, sans any sort of JLWC-Acceptable clothing, is hard to say.

Sawyer's tension radiated through the room. "Fuck." Which, as I recalled, was exactly what we had been doing just before the pose Sawyer had captured that now hung on the wall for all of Willow Creek to see.

I stared at the painting with morbid fascination, couldn't seem to look away, though all I could think about was the fact that I had known I was going to regret following Sawyer out into the rain that day. Between the rain and then the shower, not to mention nary a hot roller or bottle of hair spray in sight, my hair looked awful. Too flat. No bounce. Just raked back and wild. Yes, wild. Though thank goodness Sawyer had painted me in his shirt, even if it was mostly undone and coming off my shoulders. Which reminded me of what I was looking at: a scandalous painting of me, me Frede Ware, wild, NC in all my near-nakedness, that gaudy crystal and fake gold bracelet on my wrist.

I think I saw stars, and not the good kind.

Everyone was whispering and I wondered if I willed it hard enough could I make myself disappear. Which was ridiculous. Even I didn't have that much power, not to mention that said power was rapidly dwindling. That said, I reminded myself of who I was. Fredericka Mercedes Hildebrand Ware.

I raised my chin.

I pulled my shoulders back.

I exuded every ounce of poise I had ever possessed.

No one there was going to see me as anything other than in control of the situation—which was a tad *difficile* to do staring at that painting.

My mother fanned herself. "Thurmond, I think I'm going to faint."

My father was frozen to the spot in a fit of fury. "Where's the motherfucker who tainted my little girl?"

At first I thought he had said "painted" my little girl. Which would have been preferable. But the correct word registered at the same second my father added, "Get me my shotgun. I'm gonna kill that son of a bitch!"

It's safe to say I hadn't seen my father that angry since I was eight years old and had invited our gardener and his family to join us at the Willow Creek Country Club for crab legs and martinis. I've never been quite sure if my father was upset about the gardener or that at eight I was inviting people out for drinks.

Standing in Hildebrand Galleries, I was certain we would have had a felony on our hands had my mother not insisted my father take her home. I wasn't sad to see them go. In fact, I wouldn't have minded if everyone there had disappeared. Alas, I was stuck with a gaping throng of the better residents of Willow Creek to whom I was trying to sell art.

Sawyer was every bit as furious as my father, though his was directed at Pilar.

When I turned and saw her, she just smiled.

"Oops, bad me," she said in a perfect mimic of *moi*, her militant hair swinging, her smile so satisfied.

She strode over to us, one of my Baccarat crystal stems clutched in her hand without an ounce of grace, and added, "Mr. Jackson, sugar, I hope you don't mind that I borrowed the painting from your studio. How could such . . . art go unnoticed?"

I thought Sawyer was going to pick her up and break her in two, but he was a gentleman, after all, and managed to restrain himself. Though barely. Not that I spent a lot of time contemplating Sawyer and what he was going to do. Despite my blond hair, I was smart enough to understand my miscalculation. What I understood in that moment was that I had been miscalculating since that day I accepted Pilar's demand for friendship in Miss Lait's first-grade class. Pilar had always meant to be the Queen Bee. It had never worked out that way, but over and over again, she did whatever she could to fight to stay on top. And she had never played fair.

I shook the memory away and tried to concentrate on the problem at hand. But I really really didn't want to think about it at all. I'm all for blinders when the need arises—which undoubtedly explained why I was in the situation in the first place, both with the painting and with my missing money.

Pilar, unfortunately, wasn't finished yet. She stepped closer, and added, "I knew something was up with you, Frede. I just couldn't put my finger on what it was. Though it seemed only prudent to find out. I can't tell you all the questions I asked Nikki. What the two of you talked about. What kind of places you went to. On and on." She groaned as if it had been a misery. "When she told me what an amazing artist Mr. Jackson was, I didn't give it much thought other than he sounded like an interesting prospect for my Art Stars project. But then she went on about how the perfect Frede Ware was enamored of his work, and how he wouldn't show with anyone but you—which made me determined to get him for Art Stars. I wasn't about to let you be the only one getting credit for the launch of a new artist. Though little did I know what I'd find when I went to see him!" She laughed with delight. "And to think, I have Nikki to thank for it."

Nikki stood a few steps away in her proper silk and pearls, her eyes as wide as the front portal windows on the double wide trailer she grew up in.

"Oh, Frede," she breathed.

"Yes, 'Oh, Frede' is right," Pilar said, turning her attention on Nikki. "And by the way, did I mention that I'm not going to be able to sponsor you, after all? Oops, or Eloise either. Can you ever forgive me," she said with complete insincerity.

The blood drained from Nikki's face as she absorbed the news. She had been used by Pilar Bass. All those lunches and teas, shopping trips and Retreat had been nothing more than a way to get information about me. Nikki had always been sweet and believed anything and everything people told her, so I could hardly blame her for not understanding sooner. But when Pilar had shown up at my house like some light at the end of the tunnel saying she would sponsor Nikki, there was no excuse for me not understanding that the light had really been a train.

"I guess," Pilar added, "you won't be getting into the League after all."

As was Nikki's habit, she ran from the room. Howard, walking in late, followed her right back out the door.

After Pilar's job was done, she departed and so did a few of "my friends" from the League. But a whole lot more people stayed.

With little choice Sawyer talked to the remaining guests, but I could tell that what he really wanted to do was make everyone go away. I stood with a confident smile, while underneath I was having a pesky little problem breathing.

The surprise of it was that by the end, my show was a huge hit, every painting except the one of me sold. Scandal might not do much for my standing in the JLWC but it did a whole lot for making money. Especially when it involved the elusive bazillionaire Sawyer Jackson of JackHill Technologies.

It was late when the last of the guests and staff had gone. I don't think I had moved more than a foot since the painting was revealed. Sawyer came up behind me as I stared at the gesso image.

"Hell, I'm sorry," he growled.

"It's not your fault."

"I should have realized something wasn't right when I found her in my studio."

"If it hadn't been the painting it would have been something else. She finally got her chance to show Willow Creek, and more importantly, the Junior League, that the perfect Frede Ware isn't so perfect. She certainly won't have competition for president now."

"Damn it."

I searched for a fabulous smile, found a close approximation. "Hey, don't worry about it. More importantly, thank you for doing the show." Good manners at all costs.

He looked at me oddly. "Are you okay?"

"Me? I'm fine. Better than fine." Surely no one can blame me for lying.

Two long beats of silence passed while he studied me, then he cupped my chin and forced me to look at him. "It's going to be all right."

"How?" Weak, I know, but the word slipped out.

"You just survive, like the rest of us."

As I backed away, the words blurted out. "I don't want to be like the rest of us!"

"But you already are, you just pretend you aren't. Everybody hits bumps in the road, including you."

I admit it. My mood wasn't the greatest, but hello, I had just experienced a major trauma and I would like gigantic points for having held it together with a huge dose of Frede Ware charm. But even I have my limits. "How is that supposed to make me feel better?"

"Frede, your life wasn't so perfect before this happened. You just pretended it was. Fuck it," he said. "Life is too short to care about bullshit reputations."

This was probably true, but it was so outside my frame of reference that I could only stare at him. Which could be why I was unprepared for his next words.

"Let me help."

As has already been established, I didn't need help. I didn't need saving.

I ignored the voice in my head that was laughing.

"I'm falling for you, Frede. I want to be there for you. Let me help you get through this."

I hadn't bargained for more of his kindness. And I especially hadn't bargained for the startling thought that maybe I was falling for him too. Sex was complicated enough. But potential love?

The fact of the matter was, the last thing I needed was another complication in my life. Granted, it would have been helpful had I thought of that before our single (okay, single-ish) episode of sex. But my brain was back (nothing like the shock of scandal to clear the head) and I needed to put distance between us until I could get my life back in order.

He—the tall, dark, and sexy in-control man—reached for my hand, but I stepped away with a polite smile. "You are so sweet, and . . . well . . . thanks for sharing."

What was I supposed to say? Clearly not that, given the expression on his face after I said it.

"I tell you I'm falling for you and all you can say is, 'Thanks for sharing'?"

Mr. South of Safe who had so inappropriately attracted me in the first place surfaced and his jaw started ticking. Not that I was afraid. Quite the contrary. I wanted to drag him back to the office and let him have his way with me. Which was *très* bad, and could not happen.

I debated.

Nope, couldn't happen.

"I'm sorry, but it's late," I said, "and I think it's best that you go."

Our eyes locked, his jaw cementing.

"Sawyer, please just go. I need some time to think, time to figure things out."

"That's it?"

"Ah, yes?"

Tight-lipped and grim, he gathered his things. "I don't need this."

Like I did?

He headed out, his steps pounding on the hardwood floor.

"Thank you," I called after him.

He stopped at the door and turned back. He looked verra angry and hugely sexy. Yet again it was all I could do not to run after him, demand he take me home and do all those things he was so good at doing. But I held myself in check. "I'm truly sorry about all this." I gave him a little go-team rah-rah fist in the air. "Though congrats on a great show!"

I think he cursed.

My smile was luminous if strained. "When I get things figured out, I'll call you. Just give me some time. We'll talk then, okay?"

"No need. I'd say we're done here."

Ouch.

As he walked away, I watched him go. Standing there, my heart twisting in a way I didn't like at all, I held myself together with all the award-winning poise I was known for, telling myself that it was for the best, adding that things couldn't possibly get any worse.

Chapter Twenty-six

I WAS WRONG.

When I woke the next morning and walked into the kitchen, the phone was ringing. Nina stood there, her arms crossed, one brow raised, her sensibly shod foot tapping like a metronome wound too tight. Talking to whoever was on the phone seemed preferable to enduring a download of castigating Spanish from my maid, so I answered.

"Hello?"

"Have you seen the front page of the *Willow Creek Times*?"

I should have stuck with Nina. "Mother, really, didn't anyone ever tell you that you're supposed to say things like 'hello' and 'how are you' before you launch into discussion?"

"Don't be flip. And stop avoiding the question. Have you seen the paper?"

I hadn't. But when I glanced over at Nina, she smirked and held up the front page like a contestant on a game show flipping up a placard. Had I been sixty-five with a heart condition, I'm sure the headline would have killed me.

THE DEVIL IN THE JUNIOR LEAGUE

And guess who was cast in the role of the Devil. *Moi.*

As much as I shouldn't be, I'm all for front-page attention, but only when it's of the kind that says how fabulous I am. This article was lacking any mention of fabulousness. It (read: I) became the talk of the town overnight. While good society might not talk about sex, they have no problem talking about a scandal.

The newspaper also ran a photo of the infamous painting of "Fredericka Mercedes Hildebrand Ware, daughter of Thurmond and Blythe Hildebrand, granddaughter of Charles E. and Felicia Hildebrand," like an announcement for my debutante ball.

The only good piece of news was that the photo of the painting didn't run with the piece. Instead, at the bottom of the article, there was a single line: "(For photos, see page 6.)"

You can imagine that if nearly naked art is frowned upon for use in tasteful decorating in Willow Creek, nearly naked photos of supposedly proper ladies certainly can't appear on the front page of the *Times*.

"Mother, my other line is ringing. I've got to go." I didn't have another line, but she didn't know that. "We'll talk later. Love to Daddy!"

But when I hung up, Nina was waiting.

"I tell you no sex!"

"Nina, really, it's just art." I scoffed a little.

"Theese no art." By then she had flipped to page 6 and was waving it in my face.

"Call it what you will," I said, "but it's not like I wanted anyone to see it."

"Then how theese happen?"

My maid was like a pit bull, and once she got something between her teeth, she didn't let go. She finally dragged the details out of me regarding the "successful" art show that had turned me into a devil, and how Pilar had known to seek out the painting in the first place.

"Nikki?" she gasped. "Missy Grout do theese?"

I shrugged and poured myself a cup of hot tea, added cream and sugar, then stirred, the gentle clink of silver on china soothing me.

For the next few days, I held it together remarkably well for a newly ruined woman. Granted, people avoided me like the plague. The phone was silent. No one came to call. While I wasn't crazy about being a pariah—albeit a stunningly beautiful pariah—at least I didn't have to see anyone.

Nina didn't have it as easy. She, unlike *moi,* had to leave the house. Groceries to buy, dry cleaning to take, cleaning supplies to replenish. At the HEB supermarket, the other maids wouldn't shop in the same aisles with her. The postman started pushing our mail through the slot instead of coming around back for a cup of coffee. Even the yardman barely said hello. Nina and I had become the outcasts of Willow Creek. Though that didn't deter Nikki.

Three days after the article ran, my neighbor showed up. Her hair was still tastefully dark blond and she still wore the pearls, but she had on a pair of khaki pants that were tight, a white T-shirt (also tight), and flowered Keds. This was a far cry from animal prints and stilettos, but a T-shirt and Keds weren't exactly proper Visiting Attire.

As they say, water seeks its own level, and Nikki was inching back to her old self.

Nina didn't want to let her in, saying as much with her nose thrust high in the air.

"Nina, I'm just as sorry as sorry can be," I heard Nikki say in the entry hall.

I appeared at the top of the steps. "Let her in, Nina."

Why, you ask? Truth to tell, I was getting bored with all my seclusion and pariah-ness. A visit from Nikki was better than watching yet another TiVoed episode of Don Juan de Tango with Nina while I told myself all the reasons I had no business going to see Sawyer and feeling slighted that he hadn't so much as called. Like I was that easy to get over.

I descended the stairs.

"Frede, I'm so sorry," Nikki said. "I never should have told Pilar anything about you and Sawyer."

"Nina, could you make us some tea?"

They both were surprised, but Nikki wasn't about to let me reconsider. She slipped past my sentry and followed me back to the sunroom.

We sat at the same table where I had taught Nikki manners only weeks earlier. "So, tell me all that is going on in town."

She gaped. "I can't believe you aren't going to yell at me or something for what I did!"

Me, yell?

Nikki leaned forward, her eyes wide. "I feel just awful about this mess. What with the painting and me being so gullible that I believed Pilar really wanted to be my friend again when she got all those ladies to lunch and shop with me. I got carried away by all the attention—so carried away that I couldn't see it wasn't real. It's embarrassing to think about what a snoot I turned into. I just don't know how to make it up to you."

"No need, and no need to say another word about it."

I could tell she wasn't going to let it go, so I took a countermeasure. "Have you seen Sawyer recently?"

Actually, I hadn't planned to ask that, but fortunately I said the words with an admirable amount of nonchalance.

"Sawyer? No," she said. "I've left a few messages, but he hasn't called me back. I know he must be furious at me too. Have you seen him?"

"No, I haven't."

"This is just terrible."

I could tell she still wasn't going to let it go, so I tried something else to distract her. "More importantly, how are you and Howard doing?"

It did the trick. She shook her head and sighed. "Can you believe it? I acted like a hoity-toity bitch but he still loves me. I really am the luckiest girl alive. And he has been nothing but wonderful since I told him I won't be getting into the Junior League."

"I'm sorry about that." Part of me even meant it.

"After what I did, how can you even be thinking about that? If I hadn't screwed it all up, I'd be in." Then she sank a little in her chair and wrinkled her nose. "Can I ask you something?"

I wanted to say no.

"You didn't really want to get me into the Junior League, did you?"

How was it possible that I, as a reasonably smart woman, could keep stepping into these awkwardly direct situations? But there it was, her question laid out like bone-china cups and silver spoons on the sideboard ready for a ladies' tea.

"Nikki . . ." I hadn't a clue how to respond and I wanted to kiss Nina when she entered with the tea.

"Okay, don't answer that. But I know it's the truth. The thing is this, at any point you could have gotten out of your deal with Howard—and yes, I know he made some kind of a deal with you, I'm not blind—by telling him: *See, I tried, but it didn't work because your wife can't open her mouth without embarrassing herself*. But you didn't. You turned me into a lady no matter how hard I fought it. And I'll always be grateful for that."

This was getting *très* uncomfortable.

"I just want to say thank you, Frede, and that I'm sorry for being such an idiot to be taken in by Pilar. But don't you worry, somehow I'm going to make it up to you."

"Nikki, you don't owe me anything."

She pushed her cup away and stood. "Sure I do. No one else in town might be speaking to you—"

For the record, let me just say that it is one thing to know something intellectually, and something else altogether to hear someone say it out loud.

"—but I helped create this mess, and I'm going to help you clean it up. You're stuck with me. When it's all over and you've got your life back in order, if you'd rather not have me for a friend, you can kick me out then."

She left and Nina appeared in the doorway so suddenly that I knew she had been there the whole time. We looked at each other. "Drama queen," we stated in unison.

AS MUCH AS I wanted control of things, controlling time was beyond even me, and Wednesday came around with the inevitability of a Texas Belle favoring big hair and lipstick—which meant I had a choice to make. Continue to avoid other people, or suck it up and go to the New Projects Committee meeting. I went for three reasons:

1. There was the whole bored thing, and at least my arrival would set off fireworks—if only I weren't the cause.

2. I was still maxed out in the Missed Hours department. If I missed any more I risked getting kicked out of the League on a technicality that more than a few people would be ready to leap on after my latest "unfortunate incident."

3. I had to adhere to my "pretend you didn't make a mistake and eventually everyone will believe it" policy.

I dressed with care in a pale blue silk shirtwaist and my pearls. Then I put my best Ferragamo-clad foot forward and marched into League headquarters.

I got a glimpse into the committee room before anyone saw me, and I could see that the entire group was there. I think I might have already mentioned that with the exception of Pilar, the women made up the wealthiest of the entire League. They were sitting around a conference table, talking up a storm. I thought the meeting had already begun. Unfortunately, that best foot of mine froze just outside the doorway when I realized the meeting hadn't started. They were gossiping. About me.

There were a lot of things that wouldn't have surprised me, such as:

1. How could she have done it?

2. Where was her husband through all of this?

3. Her parents must be appalled.

No such luck.

"Good Lord, if I had thighs like that, I wouldn't be caught dead flashing them around."

"Did you see those breasts? I swear they can't be real. She's obviously had them done."

"Done badly!"

Badly? They're real!

"And that hair?"

Great, the hair.

"Flat, like she just fell out of bed and didn't bother with so much as a single hot roller."

"Imagine, Frede Ware not looking fabulous!"

This got a laugh.

"What if she comes to the meeting? What will we say?"

"How can she possibly show her face after that spectacle of a show?"

"Rumor has it that she hasn't left the house since it happened."

"If she does come, we won't say a word to her face. I'd sooner die than hurt her feelings."

There was a short slice of silence, before more peals of scoffing laughter.

My heart pounded, and before I could turn tail and run, I entered the room. *"Bonjour!"*

The committee members swiveled around and were struck dumb by my entrance, though Pilar found her voice soon enough. "Well, well, look who's here."

I smiled and entered with my head held high. "Aren't you all just the sweetest things?"

Gwen Hansen and Lizabeth Mortimer blushed. Pilar did not.

Judy, Nessa, Cynthia, and Annalise just stared at me.

I sat down at the table, crossed my ankles, and pulled out my Frede Ware notepad. "You were saying?" I prompted.

The ladies shifted uncomfortably. Pilar snatched up her notes and flipped them open. "No one has come up with a good idea for our new project," she said. "So I think we should seriously consider my idea of Art Stars."

She went on about her brainchild. It was a real bore of a meeting, but I smiled and even took notes like a good little Girl Scout. It was in the middle of Pilar's boast about how Art Stars was truly inspired that Cynthia leaned forward and blurted, "I just have to know. Is Sawyer Jackson as amazing as he looks?"

The meeting came to a grinding halt. Pilar's mouth fell open.

"Yes, yes, tell all," Lizabeth added. "The photo of him that ran in the paper was unbelievable!"

After which the girls lobbed questions at me like alternating ball machines on my fabulous, though currently unused, tennis court.

"How tall is he? He looked tall in the photo."

"Please tell me he isn't short."

"And muscular? I bet he has amazing muscles."

"Though not too muscular!"

It was all a girl could do to keep up.

Pilar screeched and shook her head like a dog shaking off water. "Ladies! She posed naked!"

The questions stopped and all eyes turned to Pilar.

"Technically, sugar," I said in my most mannered voice, "I wasn't totally naked."

Gwen leaned forward, waving her hand like a schoolgirl. "That's right, Pilar. And look at all that art in the museum. Hello. Naked everywhere."

A defender in Gwen. Who would have expected it?

Pilar glared. "We're not talking about . . ." It was as if the words were stuck in her mouth, before finally spewing out: "Classic art! We are talking about this woman, this woman sitting right here, one of us, who posed for an artist."

But I could see the girls were still with me.

"All but naked," Pilar added, "and no doubt that shirt didn't stay on for long. And she is married!"

The girls sighed. Even Gets-around Gwen grimaced. "There is that," they conceded, clearly disappointed that they would have to move back to snubbing me and weren't going to get to hear a single detail about Sawyer Jackson.

They looked at me. "Sorry."

I just smiled, a true Oscar-worthy performance. "Don't worry about it. I'm not." I wish.

Pilar turned her glare on me, and started to say something. Thankfully, my phone rang and I cut her off. "Hold that thought, sugar."

She fumed. I ignored her. Though I didn't have to try to ignore her for long once I answered the call. A blast of words came over the airwaves.

"Howard, I can't understand a word you said."

I listened again, shock racing through me. "You found Gordon?"

I realized my mistake. But if anyone else realized it, they didn't let on. The committee members were too busy staring at Pilar, who had gone white in the face.

"Pilar, honey," Lizabeth asked, "are you okay?"

I didn't wait for answers. I had bigger problems just then.

"Ciao, ladies, I've got to run!"

I wheeled out of headquarters parking lot, too lost in thought to wave at Blake. The Willows came into view in record time, and I barely got a hello off to Juan before dashing through the opening gate.

I wheeled up my stunning brick drive and raced through the front door and found Howard and my maid standing in the great room just off the foyer.

"Where is he?" I blurted.

"Darlin', calm down."

"I am calm!" Or not. "Where is he?"

That's when I became aware of the voice. My heart just about stopped in my chest. I walked like a stiff-legged, wide-eyed, terrified *America's Next Top Model* contestant toward my husband's study. When I pushed open the door, I found Gordon standing behind his desk, smoking a cigar as he talked and laughed on the phone as if he had never left.

Chapter Twenty-seven

GORDON WARE RETURNED TO MY HOME and my life with all the confidence of Russell Crowe in *Gladiator*—though Gordon lacked that medieval, preplumbing look of no bath. Whatever, it wasn't quite the image one would expect from a skulking skunk of a man, but maybe that's just me. If he was worried that he had stolen, then lost and/or squandered, my money, he didn't show it.

"Fred," he said grandly. "Look at you. Just the same. Blond, beige, and boring."

Insults on top of theft?

I saw a very bright, tacky shade of red and felt the need to take a sharp instrument to something besides his photos in my society photo albums. "Where is the money?"

He shrugged. "What money?"

"My money! The money you stole!"

"Tsk, tsk. I have paperwork that says otherwise, and more paperwork that shows that I lost the money. Can you believe it? I lost the money. Now it's gone."

He practically sang the words. I started to launch myself at him, but Howard caught me.

"Now, Frede," Howard said, "you don't need an altercation on top of everything else."

Gordon laughed. "You must be the infamous Howard Grout. God, you've been a pain in the ass, chasing me across the Caribbean and Mexico. Though I should have realized that about you after the fits you gave me when I tried to keep you out of The Willows."

Howard's face got that really dangerous-to-know expression on it, but he held himself in check. "I'm not finished with you yet," he growled. "And remember, you didn't keep me out."

Gordon just laughed some more then stepped around the desk when the doorbell rang. "Good, they're here," he said.

"Who's here?" I asked.

He walked around me and headed out of the study. He tsked at Nina when she only stood there, rooted to the spot.

When he opened the front door, a group of unkempt men with grizzled faces entered. I had the startling thought that he had hired thugs to dispatch my blond, beige, boring self to a landfill rolled in one of my antique Savonnerie carpets. Though behind the thugs, two county sheriffs entered. This was not looking good.

"What the hell?" Howard demanded.

My sentiments, exactly.

"Movers," Gordon explained.

Movers? "You can't have anything, Gordon."

"Nothing? Now, Fred, play fair. And besides, I don't want just anything. I want everything." He handed Howard a thick stack of papers. "I guess you didn't realize that this is my house, not yours."

My poise deserted me. "That's a lie!"

Howard did some speed-reading then looked at Gordon. "You bastard, you've been working on this for months."

My ex-husband shrugged. "What can I say?"

Howard turned to me. "It's the divorce settlement. It states that he gets the house."

"We had a prenup!"

"This supersedes anything that came before it. And given the date, it's another document you signed months ago."

Based on my unfortunate signing habits, I could have signed away my whole life without knowing it—and based on everything we were learning, I had.

Talk about a lesson in needing to read every line of every document your supposedly devoted husband puts in front of you. And people wonder how rock stars end up getting bilked of their fortunes. I nearly fainted at the thought that I could be included in a category of people who wore leather, pierced body parts other than ears, and had really bad hair.

I saw those stars again.

The movers started up the stairs. It was like I went deaf—stone-cold deaf and dumb. I could barely hear over the ringing in my head. I could see Gordon, Howard, and the deputies arguing. I caught words like "judge," "injunctions," "I'm going to kick your sorry ass." But the outcome was still the same. I was being evicted from my own home.

Nina was beside herself.

"I told you I'd get rid of you one day," Gordon said to my maid.

She swung her handbag at him. He caught it. "Not this time."

In under an hour, all my clothes and Nina's were boxed up and loaded into a U-Haul truck that sat like an ugly orange scar on my beautiful red-brick drive. When the movers were done, Gordon handed me the key. "Have at it, babe."

I would have had at his head if things hadn't gone from bad to worse when Janet Lambert strolled in, wearing brand-new Chanel from head to toe, more movers coming in behind her carrying the entire line of Louis Vuitton luggage.

Minnie stopped, struck a pose, looked around, then said, "Is she gone yet?"

I WOULD LIKE CREDIT for having held on to my dignity and brave façade through a great deal—missing money, scandalous paintings, women insulting my thighs. But Miss Mouse moving into my home was more than even the fabulous Frede Ware could take.

In a stupor, I somehow got to Palace Grout where Nina's and my bags were unloaded into the guest cottage out back. As I sat at the Grouts' kitchen table, Nikki and Nina clucked around me. Howard was there, though he looked far happier than I thought he should.

"He took the bait," he said, apropos of nothing, as he pulled a great many things out of the refrigerator.

"What?" we all asked in unison.

He smiled as he slapped a slice of bologna on white bread. He topped that with American cheese, smashing the bread together, then took a bite, sans condiments, sans cutting the sandwich in half, sans plate or any other evidence of civilized behavior.

"What are you taking about?" I asked.

With his mouth full, he explained. "Like I told you back when we found out about the divorce papers, I needed a way to flush him out of the bush. But how, I kept asking myself." He was pacing, eating, and explaining. When he noticed me staring at the sandwich (my disgust eluding him) he extended it. "You want a bite?"

Ugh. "No, but thank you."

"Suit yourself." He resumed the pacing and took another bite. "Fortunately, the answer hit me just like I knew it would. It had to do with your house. I remembered Gordon trying hard as hell to keep me out of The Willows. Kept going on about me ruining the neighborhood, about how it was a crime for me to live next door to his fine fancy home." He chuckled. "It didn't take a brain surgeon to know he was fond of that place." He waggled his brows. "So I decided to spread a rumor—"

Nina and I gasped.

"—around Mexico and the Caribbean," he clarified, "not around here."

He rolled his eyes at our relief.

"I put it out there that as your lawyer, I was having you sell the house."

"But I'm not selling!"

"Of course not. But if I was right, he didn't want that house sold, and the only way he could guarantee it didn't happen was to come back here himself." He smiled. "Like I said, he took the bait. Everything is going according to plan."

"Plan?" I might have screeched. "Getting me kicked out of my own home was part of your plan?"

If Howard was concerned about my outburst, or if he even noticed, he didn't let on. "Frede, I'll get your house back. That'll be like taking candy from a baby. A woman getting kicked out of her own home? Hell, I'll have fun taking that one to court. But in the meantime, we've got Gordon in town acting like an asshole. No question about it, he's up to something bigger than just divorcing you and stealing your money, I can feel it. Which is why we need him back here—so we can force his hand."

As if this were supposed to make me feel better.

For the next few days Nina didn't leave my side. I sat in the guesthouse kitchen, my elbows on the table. If I'd had a bowl of soup I would have slurped it. "Nina, what are we going to do?"

She looked at me in the most tender way, then stroked my hair like she used to do when I was a child. "I dohn know abou you, *chica,* but I got a nice 401K."

Which was completely insensitive and made me laugh so hard that I cried.

After that, other than getting acquainted with improper table manners, I did a lot of sleeping in those ratty pajamas I had saved from college. It was that or turn to massive amounts of alcohol since every time I woke up it was to more bad news.

On Thursday, the *Willow Creek Times* ran the headline WARE AND NEW WIFE, the announcement of their marriage.

On Friday, Gordon made the newspaper again, this time in the Society section. THE WARES GO CLUBBING, a very unfunny twist on my ex-husband and his new wife's launch at the Willow Creek Country Club.

On Saturday, my mother called.

Lying flat on my back with the covers pulled up to my chin, I propped the cell phone against my ear.

"Have you read the newspaper?" she asked.

I debated.

"Fredericka, answer me, yes or no."

"Can I take No for a thousand, Alex?"

She said something about how I was a trial beyond words, though she then proceeded to come up with plenty of those supposedly elusive words to tell me just that. But, as ever, I wasn't in the mood to discuss my predicament with my mother. It was hard enough to read about Gordon and that woman leading my life, picturing them in my home, socializing with my former friends—and even harder knowing that everyone I knew had to be reading the same pitiful tales. I couldn't imagine showing my face at Brightlee ever again.

"Just tell me," she said, "is it true that you are living in Howard Grout's guesthouse and that your good-for-nothing husband has divorced you and is living in your home with some . . . some . . . woman."

"Yes."

Just that, but it was enough to set my mother off on a rampage about my being the first Hildebrand ever to get a divorce, and worse yet, I didn't have a serious bone in my body.

"It's a disgrace, I tell you."

A welcome surge of indignation shot through me. I sat up, the covers falling to my waist. "Mother, I'm plenty serious"—*sort of*—"and would you rather me be married to a man who got a vasectomy without ever telling me, stole my money, and ran off with that woman?"

To say she was stunned put it mildly.

"Good Lord, Fredericka, why didn't you tell me?"

I didn't want to mention my parents' own financial concerns—I wasn't that serious.

"Mother, I've got to go."

"Fredericka, you need to come out to the house right now to discuss this with your father and me."

"Sorry, Mother, but I'm swamped, busy, snowed under with all I have to do. We'll do it another time."

I hung up, and when the phone started ringing again, I fell back into the tangle of sheets. All that indignation had worn me out.

I dragged the satisfyingly plush feather pillow over my head, though I nearly cried over the thought of my own satisfyingly plush feather pillows at my former home. But I put it out of my mind and willed myself back to sleep.

I'm not sure how much time passed, but at some point Nina entered the bedroom, whipped open the guest cottage drapes, found a vacuum cleaner, and started vacuuming. Not that she was interested in cleaning, mind you. It was her most effective way of forcing me out of bed.

"You wake, Missy Ware?" she asked over the whirl.

"No."

"Oh, discúlpeme."

I snorted.

She sniffed indignantly and ran the sweeper right up to the bed. "Eet time you geet up."

"Easy for you to say. You have a 401K."

Abruptly, she locked the vacuum in an upright position, snapped it off, then ripped my covers back. "Enough alreeedy."

I think she might have been watching more than Mexican reality shows since she had been picking up an awful lot of American slang lately.

"Go away," I told her, wrestling the covers back over my head.

She made a lot of noise, rumbling her displeasure. "Wha theese, you? Are you dog who roll over to play corpse?"

"Play *dead*!"

"Wha-ever."

I groaned into the pillow.

"You no dog, Missy Ware. You a fighter. Geet up," she said, yanking the covers completely off the bed.

"No, thank you." As ever, polite.

"You mother ees here."

That got my attention. "But I just talked to her."

"Three hour ago," she said with not a little sarcasm. Have I mentioned how unbecoming sarcasm is?

Throwing the pillow aside, I sat up and gave my maid a look of wide-eyed innocence. "Tell her I'm not here."

"Too late."

"Tell her I'm on the phone . . . or in the bath. Bath is good, tell her I'm in the bath. She'd never walk in on me if she thought I was naked."

"No can do."

"Nina!"

"You hurry. She on her way from security gate."

Glaring, I threw on some clothes and made it out of the bedroom just in time for my mother to sail through the door like a ship.

"Hello, Mother."

She raised a brow and looked me over. If she was appalled that my hair was pulled back in a tangled knot and my clothes were wrinkled, she didn't say it. But who had the energy to make themselves presentable when their secrets were making headline news? After all the trouble I had gone to, everyone knew that my husband had left me for another woman and I had been kicked out of my own home. In a matter of days I had gone from Scandalous Woman to Wronged Pity Case. And let me just say, neither category is particularly popular at the Junior League. Though at least no one yet seemed to know I had become money-challenged.

"No French?" was all she said.

I managed to laugh. "I've decided to take up Chinese."

Blythe Hildebrand looked me over, a very considering look as she absorbed. I expected some cutting remark but none came. She called out to her driver, then she walked past me, straight into the tiny kitchen.

An aging Rado entered carrying two big bags.

"Miss Frede," he said, and would have tipped his cowboy hat if he'd had a free hand. "I'm awful sorry to hear about the pickle you're in."

I had the urge to hug him. "Thank you, Rado."

From the bags, my mother produced groceries and an assortment of goods she thought I would need. It was as close to a hug as my mother was going to give.

I realized just how wrecked I was when I felt my eyes start to burn and my throat tighten over this small kindness. Thankfully Blythe Hildebrand didn't touch me. I would have been a goner had she so much as smiled at me.

But of course she didn't. She turned abruptly and started giving instructions about the groceries. Finally she was finished and I thought she would leave.

"Nina, I would like a glass of tea."

My maid and I didn't react at first.

"Sí, señora."

"Fredericka, sit down."

I felt like I was a child again and I twirled my glass on the table.

"Fredericka, stop playing with the glassware."

"Sorry."

"Sorry? Just sorry?"

It sounded like a trick question. "Sorry . . . ma'am?"

She glared.

"Sorry . . . you . . . came all this way and I don't have any cucumber sandwiches?"

"Fredericka, you haven't said word one to me about that . . . that painting."

"Oh, that." I had hoped the more recent fiascos that had come to light in the newspaper would have made her forget about the show. "No question, I'm definitely sorry about the painting."

"I've never been more embarrassed."

"I know, and I really am sorry."

"How could you have done something so common?"

I didn't think she wanted to hear about how sexy Sawyer Jackson was, or about getting caught in the rain, and how one thing led to another, then ta-da, I was on display for the whole of Willow Creek.

Instead, I went for a conservative, "I wasn't thinking?"

She glared for half a second, then surprised me when she shifted in her seat. Uncomfortably. My mother doesn't do uncomfortable. Ever.

"Life has the uncanny ability to throw us curve balls."

I could no more imagine my mother using baseball analogies than I could imagine anyone throwing my indomitable mother a curve ball. Regardless, I really didn't want to head down that path. "Did I mention how sorry I am about the painting?"

With a frustrated sigh, she took both of our glasses, set them aside, leaned forward, and put her elbows on the table. Elbows on the table! "Listen to me," she said. "Life isn't always easy. Take me, for example. Your grandmother hated me on sight."

I barely swallowed back the nearly blurted, *You knew that?*

"When your father brought me home, Felicia Hildebrand set out to make me miserable. She fought me at every turn, but I never gave up. Sure, I loved the life your father promised, and no question I did things wrong along the way. But I love Thurmond Hildebrand, and I fought hard for my place in his world. It wasn't easy, but I didn't give up." She looked me straight in the eye. "The problem with you is that you've never had to fight to fit in."

I really wasn't in the mood for a "Frede Ware as Spoiled Princess" lecture. But my mother was nothing if not full of surprises that day. She reached out and cupped my chin. "You are still that girl who fits in. You've just hit a bump in the road."

To think Sawyer had said almost the exact same thing.

"Now people are trying to undo you, which means you don't have time to sit around and pretend everything is going to be okay. You have to fight for what you want. Gordon might have taken your money, he might have installed that trash in your home. But you're a Hildebrand, and even a Pruitt. We're a tough breed and we fight for what we want. Stop hiding, Fredericka. Go out there and show Gordon and the rest of Willow Creek what you're made of." She stood up from the table. "Though please, first put a roller or two in your hair, apply some lipstick, and change out of those deplorable clothes."

MY MOTHER SAILED out much as she had sailed in. I sat at the table and felt a stir of something besides exhaustion as two things occurred to me:

1. I could count on my mother not to disappoint in the criticism department.
2. She was right—about how I looked and about being tougher than Gordon Ware.

Who were he and that rodent woman to come in and mess up my life? More than that, with sleep finally cleared from my brain, it occurred to me that Howard was right. Something was up. Gordon had returned to town and was living the high life—and the high life took money.

I got out of bed and walked over to the windows. I didn't think for a second Gordon had gone to Mexico and struck gold in the last two months. In fact, I had to wonder if he had lost my money as he claimed. Siphoned, yes. Somehow made to look like his, no question. I just needed to survive while Howard kept hunting.

Which stopped me cold.

Would Howard really keep digging now that it didn't look as if Nikki would get into the League?

I felt a shiver of apprehension, then pushed it away. Somehow I would find a way to get her in. That was the bargain. On top of that, it was time I started doing something to help my situation. Namely, start doing some messing of my own—with Gordon's head—and pray that he would start getting nervous and make a mistake.

With my feet firmly back underneath me, thanks to my very own mother (who would have guessed?), I felt my old confidence resurface.

"Nina!" I called out.

Of course, she was right there.

"Draw my bath. I have things to do, places to go, and people to make nervous."

She nodded her approval. "Wha you want to wear?"

I smiled at her. "Don't worry about clothes, sugar. I'm going to borrow something from Nikki."

I mean, really, at that point what did I have to lose?

WITH THE SORT OF EXCITEMENT normally reserved for opening day at the Junior League Christmas Fair, I headed for the Willow Creek Country Club. It was April, and the club had opened the pool for weekend use until the end of May, which was the official start of the summer season.

On Saturday afternoons at four, women and children left the pool to get ready for evening events. The men—after they finished golf, and before they went into the Men's Grill for a few hands of cards—swung by the pool for a little dip. I felt like a little dip myself.

The country club was north of Willow Square, built a hundred years ago, and was harder to get into than the Junior League—though mainly because the initiation fee alone was more than the average person made in an entire year.

I pulled through the limestone-and-wrought-iron gate entrance. The main clubhouse stood at the center, underneath a sprawl of willow and live oak trees. The tennis courts and golf course were to the west, the pool to the east. I steered through the circle drive then parked in a reserved spot at the arched entry to the pool.

Beeping my car locked, I sashayed through the main gate into the open-air cabana building that housed the locker rooms and Snack Shack. The tanned, teenage lifeguard who manned the front desk about fell over backward in his chair at the sight of me. I wore a pair of Nikki's finest, tightest spandex pants over my bathing suit, a low-cut top, stiletto heels, and hair so big it looked like a puff of cotton candy. I'd show Gordon blond, beige, and boring.

I signed in with a flourish (prayed the lifeguard wouldn't check to see if I was still a member since I had no idea where that stood) then made the long strut across the deck to the only chaise longue I wanted. The one next to the golfers.

The pool was sparkling blue, empty, and inviting on such a hot day. Not that I ever got in the pool, mind you.

I saw Gordon laughing with the group, the men welcoming him back like a long-lost best friend. Which, of course, was the case. By virtue of his more advanced age, Gordon had had a head start on me as a member of Willow Creek society. As we know, the only thing Gordon had lacked in being an important part of the better circles of our town was his own money. Now, it would appear, he had some, making him more popular than ever.

The gaggle of men joked and drank beer out of wax paper cups. Everyone drank out of wax paper cups at the pool—kids with sodas, men with beers, women with white wine on ice with plastic tops and straws attached to make people think they were drinking sodas too.

It didn't take long before the men saw me approach.

"Holy mackerel," Leo Fraser said with an appreciative whistle.

"You said it," Rob Bateman added.

A whole chorus of crude appreciation, the sort that was totally unacceptable, and just what I wanted.

"Hello, boys," I said, waggling my jeweled fingers at them, my jangle of bracelets falling down my arm when I waved.

Gordon's mouth hung open, and he just about had a coronary when I peeled off the spandex and revealed my bathing suit. Nikki, bless her heart, had just bought it for summer, and sacrificed it to me for the good of the cause. It was the very definition of an itsy-bitsy polka-dot bikini. For all the silk and sweater sets I wear, and despite what the girls of the New Projects Committee said, if I had competed for Miss Texas, I would have won the bathing suit competition hands down.

I lowered myself onto the chaise and stretched out. Acting like a woman of lesser virtue was a whole lot more fun than I ever would have imagined, though perhaps that was due more to Gordon's shock than the catcalls.

"For mercy's sake, Fred, cover yourself up."

I looked over at him, pulled my rhinestone sunglasses down my nose with my perfectly manicured hot-pink nail, and asked, "This is your business, why?"

He sputtered, his male *compadres* getting a good laugh.

I leaned back and prayed I wouldn't burn too badly given my aversion to the sun. But I was a woman on a mission, and if a sunburn was the price I had to pay, so be it.

The men talked to me as I pretended to care about sunbathing. I continued to answer with the sort of practiced nonchalance that men can't resist. Gordon got angrier by the syllable.

Fortunately, it didn't take long for my ex to have enough, which I was extremely thankful for, mainly because I could feel my silky skin start to burn. With a tension that only I recognized, he walked over to me and leaned close. "You've always been spoiled, but I'm done being the fabulous Frede Ware's husband. I'm the one with money now, not you. I'm the one who is important now. So cover up, give it up, and get out of here."

Witty? Who knew.

I turned on faux surprise. "Are you sure you're the one with the money? Maybe I forgot to mention that Howard Grout has found some dreadfully interesting info from our financial records?"

He hadn't, but Gordon didn't need to know that.

If he sputtered over my lack of attire, he about expired over this news. But then he pulled himself back together. "There is nothing to find."

"*Au contraire.* There's a lot to find. Namely, that after you stole my money you didn't lose it."

He laughed, a bitter sound that got his friends' attention. With effort he smiled, though the smile wasn't for me. He looked me in the eye and said, "Prove it."

I cooed, stood, covered up, then blew kisses to the men. But just before I departed, I whispered in Gordon's ear. "I plan to."

MY SECOND FORAY into messing with Gordon arrived with news and a decision. Miss Mouse had joined the Garden Club, and I decided that there was no time like the present to make an appearance at their general meeting. I wasn't a terribly active member, but in for a penny, in for a pound, as they say.

Organizations like garden clubs and ladies' guilds are frequently used as stepping-stones for women without connections to try to get connected in hopes of one day being asked to join the Junior League. It made my blood run cold to think that Minnie might one day succeed in taking my place in Willow Creek society. But I wasn't about to let that happen.

I dressed, this time in respectable cotton, and headed for the Garden Club monthly meeting. When I entered, the women went quiet. I was getting used to bringing a room to a dead stop, but when the women parted like the Red Sea, I came face-to-face with none other than my ex-husband's new wife.

The Garden Club president stepped forward with a stammer. "Frede, how good to see you. I think you know Miss Lambert."

"It's Mrs. Ware," the woman interjected, using a voice that she must have learned from Greta Garbo on the Turner Classic Movies channel.

I turned on haughty and headed for a seat. The other members saw a scene brewing and hurried in behind me. I might have been on the outs, but I was providing the sort of entertainment that was better than anything on television.

The president called the meeting to order, went over a list of the day's business, then finished up with, "Today we are focusing on planning our annual fund-raiser. Do we have any ideas?"

There were the usual suggestions: flower sales and silent auctions. Nothing particularly inspiring.

I was so lost in thought about Gordon's new wife living in my house and the possibility that she might actually one day break into my world that I didn't hear her suggestion at first.

"Jewelry donations?" the president asked.

My head popped up.

Janet stood, kind of waved hi to the audience, and said, "Yes, if each of us donates a single piece of jewelry, we can sell it or something and raise a ton of money. Simple. Easy. No fuss, no muss," she finished with a hopeful laugh.

Everyone stared at her.

"I think it's a grand idea," the president said. "Frede, what do you think?"

I sliced her a smile. "I think it's a fabulous idea. Though if I were you, I'd be careful of your new member's donation. I've recently learned that the Ware jewelry is paste."

It was a little mean, and a lot childish, but I have to admit that I couldn't muster up any guilt. I tried not to be pleased when Minnie went beet red to a chorus of snickering gasps, but I couldn't seem to help myself when I remembered that only days before she had stood in my foyer acting like she owned the place.

My guess was that within the hour Gordon would hear about the encounter, which meant that my work there was done.

I arrived back at the Palace Grout guest cottage and found Nina making tea in the little kitchen. I sat down at the table and was grateful for the glass she served. But as pleased as I was about my earlier endeavors, the truth was, I realized I needed a break if I was going to make my ex truly nervous.

I hadn't been back to the cottage twenty minutes when I heard the clip of somewhat sensible heels burst into the guest cottage. "Frede!"

"I'm in here, Nikki."

She came running and stopped in the doorway to the kitchen. "You'll never guess who's here?"

She had a strange look on her face, part incensed, part angry, and part determined.

"Who?" I asked.

A woman stepped from behind her. "Hello, Frede."

My spine went stiff. "Pilar?"

Not exactly who I expected to come for tea.

Chapter Twenty-eight

"WHAT DO YOU WANT?"

No, not the perfect, indirect form of communication that I had been raised to believe was sacred. Call me twelve and still living in junior high, but really, could anyone expect me to be nice to Pilar Bass? Gordon might have stolen my money, kicked me out of my own home, and planted white trash in my place, but Pilar was the one who had launched me into the world of Number One Topic of Discussion.

Nina stood beside my chair, and I knew with one word she would have taken after the dourly clad woman with her handbag.

"Frede," Nikki said, "you have every right to kick her out. I tried to do it myself." She scowled, as if remembering that I wasn't the only one who had been betrayed by Pilar. "But that's the past, and she told me some things that I think you need to hear."

Nikki had always been the forgiving type, though the ability to let bygones be bygones had never been high on my list of best qualities—probably because no one gave out awards for leniency.

"Really?" I enthused with all my practiced charm. "Talk? About how you stole a painting from Sawyer's studio?" Which reminded me that I still hadn't heard from the man. Not that I had any business thinking about art, artists, or the sorts of things that I had come to understand were why women would be partial to Brazilian waxes.

Pilar didn't flinch. She stood there in her dark hair cut severely at the shoulders, the blunt cut of bangs across her forehead, blue eyes beneath those horn rimmed frames like ice beneath glass. The only reason I knew she wasn't completely at ease was that when she slid her hair behind her ears, her fingers shook.

Interesting.

"Or would you like to discuss how you had the painting hung in my gallery at my big show for all of Willow Creek to see?"

"That's not why I'm here."

"Then why?"

"Gordon."

My eyes narrowed. "Gordon?"

"Yes. I came here to talk about how to kick his sorry ass."

Not the language of a lady, and certainly not what I expected from Pilar, but it got my attention.

I debated for a few seconds, trying to understand what sort of game she could be playing now. "What do you mean?" I asked carefully.

"I sneaked the painting into the show for Gordon."

There was a lot of blinking going on. "What?"

She pulled her shoulders back, raised her chin, and began her sordid tale. "Six months ago, Gordon said he loved me and wanted to marry me. The only problem was you."

Nina let loose with a whole slew of uncomplimentary Spanish. Nikki sighed. Pilar and I stared at each other.

"You . . . you had an affair with my husband too?"

I knew Gordon had been the most popular husband with the ladies of the Junior League, but an affair with Pilar on top of one with Janet Lambert?

She shifted on her feet. "Well, maybe." She looked embarrassed. "Okay, yes. But I swear he said he loved me."

I was in shock. "I don't understand?"

She took a deep breath, then launched into a tale that had to have come straight out of a twisted Eugene O'Neill play. "He came to me and said that if I could ruin your standing in Willow Creek, he'd finally be free to marry me. He believed I was the only person who hated you enough to get it done." She scoffed. "He said he was tired of playing second fiddle to you, tired of you holding the power, tired of everyone thinking of him as Frede Ware's husband. He said it was time he was king."

Nina and I looked at each other and grimaced.

Pilar shook her head. "He said I'd be his queen."

King and queen? She looked embarrassed to say the words, and why shouldn't she. It was embarrassing to hear.

But Pilar plunged ahead. "I didn't have a clue how to accomplish it. You've always been untouchable. It was frustrating, seemed impossible, but I kept looking. But no matter who I talked to, no matter how many times I took Nikki to lunch or shopping, no one ever said anything I could use against you. At least that's how it seemed. Then Nikki told me about the artist, and I didn't want you getting all the credit for finding someone new, so I went over to see his art." She wrinkled her nose. "You know what happened after that."

"Your infamous trip to Sawyer's studio where you saw the painting."

"Yes." She closed her eyes. "At first I was stunned. Then I admit it, I was happy, delirious with it, so delirious that I wasn't thinking straight when I took the canvas." She looked back at me. "It wasn't until Gordon returned married to that Lambert woman that I realized he was using me. I was a fool to have fallen for it. But, what can I say, Gordon could charm the habit off a nun."

That was God's own truth, not that I forgave her, or felt one bit better about her. But at least I finally understood why she did it. Though really, what was I going to say.

"Yes, well, I'm glad we got that out of the way. Nina will see you to the door."

She was dismissed, but she didn't disappear. Nina started for her.

Pilar leaped out of reach. "Wait! Gordon can't get away with this."

"I know that. And I'm working on it."

"Then add this to your info-gathering. Why would Gordon Ware hook up with, or more unbelievably, marry someone like Janet Lambert?"

Nina stopped mid-stride. Nikki looked confused.

"I might not be as beautiful as you—"

This isn't a lie, though I swear, if she'd put a little curl in her hair, swipe on a bit of mascara and some blush, she wouldn't be half bad.

"But I'm a whole lot prettier than Janet Lambert."

True, even without a stitch of makeup.

Then I shook myself. "What's your point?"

"Why, I ask you, would he hook up with someone like that woman—a woman who has absolutely no connection to the world he is from and cares so much about?"

"I take it you have an answer?"

"Call it a suspicion. I think she has something on him, something that is forcing him to stay with her."

My mind raced. I remembered my shock that Gordon would have an affair with someone like Janet Lambert in the first place. Then, after he had denied knowing her, they left the country together and ended up getting married. It hardly made sense. "Are you talking about blackmail?"

"She is."

We whipped around and found Howard standing in the doorway.

He walked into the kitchen. "I think Pilar is on to something. I just learned that Gordon met Janet when he hired her to do accounting work for him."

"See!" Pilar said. "I knew something had to be up. We just have to find out what it is."

"We?" I asked.

"I want to help."

I bristled. "Ah, yes, I know how you help. No, thanks. Had my fill of that."

Standing from the chair, I would have left if Pilar hadn't stepped in front of me. I raised a brow.

"Look, I was wrong to sneak that painting into the show. And the fact is, who was I to get you in hot water over your painting when I was . . . with your husband. But let's face it, I can help."

"I said, we're dealing with it." I might have been curt.

"Hold on, Frede," Howard said. "I want to hear what she has to say."

Nina shrugged. "I agree. At least leesen to her ideas."

"Just listen," Nikki confirmed.

I studied Pilar, hated that I actually wanted to know what she was thinking. "All right. What do you propose?"

"A little reconnaissance at the woman's home in Twin Rivers might bear fruit."

More blinking as I remembered the rundown house I had visited when Gordon first left.

"You want to break into Janet Lambert's house?" Howard all but bellowed.

"Break into?" Pilar scoffed. "No. Just visit. When no one's home we show up and go in, and have a look around. Files, boxes, closets, whatever. She has to have something on him, something incriminating. And I bet it's inside that house."

"I think eet good idea," Nina announced.

"I do too," Nikki added with a nod.

Pilar looked me in the eye. "How else do you propose we break Gordon's balls?"

"Absolutely not," Howard stated clearly. "I will not have my wife, my client, and the rest of you committing a crime." He looked directly at Nikki. "There will be no breaking and entering, do you understand?"

She looked from me to Pilar, considered for a second, then back. "Yes, sweetie doll, I understand."

"Good." He gave each of us a glare. "I'll handle it. I'll find out if there's anything out there. And that's final."

After one last hard look at us, he left.

We waited until we heard his Cadillac roar down the drive.

"He's right, of course," I said.

"No question," Nikki agreed.

Pilar shrugged her shoulders and looked at us as though we were wimps.

I glanced at Nina. After a second she asked, "Who gonna drive?"

Which is how two members of the Junior League of Willow Creek—one in good standing, the other not so much—plus a former trashy wannabe, and a maid, all dressed in black, headed two towns over to make an unexpected visit at the Mouse House.

The big Texas sky was dotted with stars and a moon so big that we might have been smart to wait for another night. But who had time. When I had tried to get Nina to stay at the cottage, she stuck her bottom lip out and said, "I going." Plus she promised to bring her handbag.

"You neva know what you might run into," she added.

Her use of the deadly handbag might come in handy. So she was in.

Nina drove us along the back roads in her Ford Focus in hopes that we would blend in better with the NC environs once we got there. She parked one street over from our destination, in front of a row of narrow, two-story white clapboard houses, both sides of the street lined with cars that were no different than the Ford.

"Nina, sugar, are you sure you haven't done this before?"

She just smiled. "I tell you I good to come."

We hurried through yards, had a run-in with a not-so-pleasant dog that will not soon forget the scolding Nina gave it, before ending up in Janet Lambert's backyard. No lights were on.

The house was a tiny bungalow affair, yellow clapboard, the paint peeling. There were lots of overgrown weeds in the yard.

"What if she sold the house?" I suddenly wondered.

"No way. She's no dope," Pilar whispered. "She's smart enough to keep a backup plan."

Which was probably true.

We squinted through the windows, steering clear of the side of the house where I had run into her neighbor on my earlier visit.

"No one's home," Nikki announced.

We went to the back door, trying not to look obvious. "Now what?" Nikki asked.

Pilar pulled out a nail file.

"I thought that only worked in the movies," Nikki said.

It must have been true, because Pilar had to move on to a credit card, which didn't work any better.

"Now wha?" Nina wanted to know.

"Step aside, ladies," I said.

"What are you going to do?" Nikki hissed into the quiet night.

I glanced around the yard, made sure no one was watching, then I lifted the ancient welcome mat. Standing, I produced a key. I figured an accountant like Miss Lambert would be predictable.

Nina nodded her compliments.

"Thank you," I responded politely.

I led the way and we entered the kitchen. Once inside, we paused to listen, but there wasn't a sound. Indeed, no one was home. We found some old mail on the counter addressed to Janet Lambert. There was even a credit card application or two addressed to Janet Lambert Ware. It made my jaw clench, but on the other hand, at least it was safe to assume she still owned the place.

We divided up the house and started our search. I was appalled by the tiny house. I mean, really, a woman who had plastic on her furniture was now living in my home, sleeping on my sheets, sitting at my dining room table, taking baths with my bubbles. There was cracked linoleum in the kitchen, a sculpted red carpet in the bedrooms, with a burnt-orange shag in the living room.

"No lights," I instructed.

Opening our own handbags, each of us pulled out a flashlight we had dug up out of pantries and tool drawers.

The bungalow consisted of kitchen, living room, one bath, and two bedrooms. I took the kitchen, rifling through drawers, cabinets, even the bread box. As much as I hated to do it, I rummaged through the trash can.

Once I had completed the kitchen, I moved on to the bath. Not that it did any good. I searched every nook and cranny, working my way toward the living room where the four of us ended up to discuss what we found.

"Nothing," Pilar reported.

"Not a thing," from Nikki.

"No luck," I added.

"Nada," Nina announced.

I swallowed back disappointment.

"Damn." Pilar sighed.

"Now, girls, don't give up so easily," Nikki said.

"She's right," I agreed. "Let's go through the house one more time. We have to have missed something."

We split up again, and made a second round. I even tried tugging at the corners of the carpeting in each room to see if I could find anything underneath. We were back in the front room ten minutes later.

"Nothing."

"Not a thing."

"No luck."

A pause before, "Where's Nina?"

We raced from room to room and found her in the main closet.

"Look at theese!" she exclaimed.

"What?" we asked.

She held up a half-dozen 1950s-era handbags, three in each hand. "They are *muy bonito*!"

"That's it? Handbags!"

"Theese hard to find."

If I had been disappointed before, I felt a truly unladylike need to do damage at the sight of those handbags. "Errr," I cried, banging the wall for emphasis.

Which is how we found the file cabinet in back of the hideous faux oak paneling.

"Look!" Nikki cried.

I stared inside the dark hiding place, dizzy with the promise of incriminating evidence. Within seconds, I was rifling through the files, and seconds after that, I gasped.

Pilar leaned closer. "What did you find?"

I couldn't begin to explain. Instead, I displayed the file to show the contents.

My cohorts took one look and were as stunned as I was.

"Jesus Lordy," Nikki whelped.

Nina muttered in Spanish.

Pilar looked up at me, then after a second, she smiled. "I'd say we hit the jackpot."

"We better get out of here, and now," Nikki said.

But before we could get the files closed and the atrocious paneling back in place, we heard a car door shut out front.

Nikki peeked out a front window, shrieked, then came running back. "It's the police!"

"Dios mio." Nina crossed herself.

"Lordy, what do we do?"

Pilar froze, clutching the folder like Lot's wife.

I kept my head. I tugged the folder free, put it in my own oversized shoulder bag, and guided the girls out of the room. "We'll simply leave the way we came. And fast."

But when we were hurrying toward the back door, we could see a young police officer through the window walking along the side of the house.

"Sheet!" Nina whelped.

"Oh, my God, we're going to jail," Pilar moaned.

The woman doesn't blink an eye while suggesting a little breaking and entering, but the minute things go bad she falls apart.

"Just stop it right now," I said. "Everything is going to be fine. Just follow my lead."

Chapter Twenty-nine

"POLICE! OPEN UP!"

We had gotten the kitchen light switched on just before the young officer made his way around the side to the back of the house.

Pilar had lost her military bearing, her face blanching even whiter than usual, and she shook like a hula girl on the dashboard of an NC lowrider in South Willow Creek.

"Pilar, sugar, answer the door."

She stammered, nothing coherent coming out.

"Pilar!"

Experiencing some sort of Helen Keller moment, she squeezed her eyes closed, extended her arms, and stumbled across the room to do as I asked.

"Officer?" she said, her voice trembling.

The young policeman was surprised by the sight of her.

"Officer, what can I do for you?" I asked, distracting him.

Nikki and I sat at the table, with two (plastic—but a true lady makes do) teacups in front of us, napkins in our laps. Nina stood by the stove holding the teakettle, smiling like Vanna White.

"What's going on in there?" he said, standing on the threshold.

"We're having tea, officer," I answered with the kind of manners that had earned me more than one of my Little Miss Debutante awards.

"Tea?"

"Of course. Why don't you come in and join us? Nina, another cup, please."

He entered, and instinctively started to take off his hat, then seemed to realize what he was doing. "Ma'am, we got a call about someone breaking in here."

I could see it was going to take more than good manners to get out of the predicament. "Why, officer, does it look like we've broken anything?" I asked, smiling my big Frede Ware smile.

He was dazed by the wattage that I hadn't turned on so high since I went to the jeweler and found out my jewels were paste. I flashed my fake pink diamond at him. I might be wearing the only black clothes I owned (a dress reserved for funerals) but between my fake ring and my pearls, there was no mistaking me for anything but a lady.

"Please join us," I persisted. "I know how hard men of the law work."

I had turned up my accent to High Southern. Nina groaned and muttered something about me going Scarlett again.

"Nina, get this handsome young man a cup of tea."

The officer looked like he didn't know what to believe. His partner came in behind him, his firearm extended. "What the hell—"

"Oh, my." I preened.

Nina rolled her eyes.

Pilar hadn't moved from the behind the door, as if she had gone from Helen Keller to Boo Radley.

"What's going on here?" the older officer demanded.

"I don't know," the young one said. "I knocked, they answered, then invited me in for tea." He grimaced apologetically. "I guess the neighbor was mistaken."

"Ah, the neighbor. She is a nosy one," I supplied with a tsk. "Always going on about something. I bet she calls regularly to complain."

"Well, true enough, she does," the cute one added.

The other, not-so-cute one, wasn't as easily convinced. "Let me see some identification."

Not the response I had hoped for, and Nina and Nikki had joined Pilar in her dumbstruck stance. Buying time, I rummaged around in my handbag, my brain racing trying to come up with some sort of plan. "Nikki, Pilar, show the officer your driver's licenses." I glanced back at the officer. "Nina, there, is my maid."

The girls managed to get their licenses out. When he was done with them he turned back to me and extended his hand. "Now you. And I don't have all night."

Yet another man who could use a lesson in manners. But I held that back and decided there was no help for it. I extended my own, my brain still racing, though answers wouldn't come. A lesser woman would have started to sweat.

"Fredericka H. Ware. From Willow Creek." He grinned like he was a regular Sherlock Holmes and had just tracked down his first serial killer. "The house is registered under the name Janet Lambert."

"Of course it is!" Think, think, think.

His eyes narrowed. "Then what are you doing here?"

That's when it hit me. "I've come over to pick up some mail, air the place out, make sure everything is as it should be. I'm sure you heard that Janet is now Janet Lambert *Ware*." I gestured toward my license. "And as you've already seen, I'm Fredericka Ware."

He scowled, trying to make sense of what I was saying.

"She's my . . . sister-in-law."

Nikki squeaked.

"Sister-in-law?" the officer said.

I stood, walked over to the counter, and gathered the mail. "See." I extended the stack.

He shuffled through. "Janet Lambert Ware."

Then I held up the house key we had found under the mat. "Janet and I, we're close, really close, and now that she's living in Willow Creek and so busy with her new husband—you might have seen them recently in the *Willow Creek Times*—I do my best to help out whenever I can."

"Ah, well . . ."

He looked like he didn't know what to believe. "I don't know about this."

"What should we do?" the young officer asked. "Take 'em in?"

Pilar started to shake even more.

"Well, I guess so—"

Which was the moment Howard walked in the back door. All traces of purple, polo, and pansy-ass boat shoes were gone. "Hello there, officers." He looked at each of us, and let me just say, the man wasn't happy.

"Who are you?" the older one demanded.

"Grout. Howard Grout," he said.

There was a pause before the young one said, "The Howard Grout?"

"The lawyer?" his partner wanted to know.

As has been mentioned, my lawyer was notorious for his victories. He was also notorious for being someone whom no one in his right mind would mess with.

"Yep. One and the same. I just came by to see the ladies—"

"Yes," I interjected. "Howard is my neighbor in Willow Creek, and of course you've already met Nikki, his wife." I looked at Howard. "I was just explaining about me being Janet's sister-in-law."

Talk about surprise. But Howard is made of sterner stuff and didn't so much as blink an eye. He also didn't confirm my teensy misrepresentation. He might be a shark, but not a lying shark, apparently.

"Officers," Howard said, "if there's a problem, I'm happy to come down to the station with you, and we can discuss what has gone on here. Like, Did you have a warrant when you entered the premises?"

"They invited us in, Mr. Grout," the young one blurted. "For tea!"

The suspicious one glanced from one to the other of us, then at Howard. I could see his brain spinning, weighing his options, deciding if it was worth getting involved with the pit bull attorney, three society ladies, and a maid. "I'm thinking we've made a mistake here tonight. We'll just be leaving now."

They actually tipped their hats when they left.

"I can explain," Nikki said the minute the door shut.

Howard didn't look to be in the mood for explanations. As soon as the patrolmen got in their squad car and drove away, he led us back through the yards to the Ford without a word. His Cadillac stood out on the dark street, parked one car down from ours like a peacock.

"How did you find us?" I asked.

"I didn't become *the* Howard Grout by letting people pull the wool over my eyes. When I got home and no one was there, I drove over here and looked for the car." He turned a hard look on his wife. "You said you understood."

"Well, yes, sweetie doll. But understanding and complying are two different kettles of fish."

Howard groaned, Nina laughed, and Pilar just wanted to get out of there. I was happy to go since I had the files in my handbag.

TWO DAYS LATER, I arrived at the Junior League of Willow Creek headquarters. Live oak trees spread their branches like long moss-covered arms over the parking lot that was filling with Cadillacs, Mercedes, Volvos, Suburbans, and a few lesser vehicles that I couldn't name. It was ten twenty-five in the morning, the New Projects Committee meeting scheduled for ten-thirty, and the sun already starting to burn.

I had dressed with care, not in my usual JLWC-approved attire. Though don't think I had on a single feather. I wore a tailored linen jacket with a mandarin collar, white pants (tight and slightly flared), a linen handbag, and a pair of black patent leather shoes with silver Ben Franklin buckles. The *ensemble* might sound strange, but I was the epitome of sophisticated elegance.

The minute I walked in, the buzz of chatter went silent. And I don't think it was because they were admiring my clothes. The biggest surprise was that I walked in with Pilar, Nikki, and Nina. The group was astounded because: (1) after the complete embarrassment my life had become, I kept showing my face, (2) I was with Pilar, and (3) Nikki was there at all. They didn't mind Nina because they no doubt assumed she was headed for the kitchen.

I'm all for grand entrances, but this was disconcerting given what I was about to do.

I experienced my own frozen Boo Radley moment, but then Nikki came up to me and said one thing. "I'm with you a hundred percent of the way."

"Me too," Nina added.

It was completely sappy, then was compounded the moment Pilar joined us. She looked nervous and uncomfortable and filled with regret. "I'm here too, that is, if you all can forgive me for what I did," she said.

We had gone from sap to high sap, and it hardly seemed the time for a girlfriend moment, but I have to admit that the whole thing was ridiculously nice.

I smiled back, nodded my head, and said, "It's time, girls."

Nikki, Pilar, Nina, and I swept into the meeting room.

"What's going on?" Gwen wanted to know.

"We have a short presentation," Pilar explained.

"Presentation?" Annalise demanded. "We don't have time."

"We are going to make time," I countered.

Their eyes narrowed at me. "The last person we need to hear from is you."

"Pilar?" I said.

Our committee chair hurried to the front of the room, and lowered the viewing screen. Nikki turned up the PowerPoint slide presentation Howard had put together after we showed him what we found in Minnie's house. Nina dimmed the lights.

There was a lot of muttering and whispering.

"Ladies, I present to you my ex-husband . . . and his affairs."

As soon as the first slide flashed on the screen, confusion was replaced with a chorus of gasps.

"Oh, my stars, that's Annalise!"

"With Gordon Ware!"

"Naked!"

The gossip started like a flash fire, racing through the committee. Annalise sank in her seat. Then I flashed another photo up on the screen.

"It's Gwen Hansen."

"With Gordon Ware!" repeated like a tired refrain from a really bad song.

The room was in a rage as gossip turned to Gets-around Gwen. But the room went dead silent when the women finally realized where this was going. I had a photo of every woman there with my husband, compliments of Janet Lambert and her files, each one caught in what I can only call a compromising position. Gordon Ware had slept his way through the entire New Projects Committee.

Most everyone has a secret they don't want people to know about. Some people work harder than others to keep their secrets . . . well, secret. You don't have to look further than me and my missing money or my mother and her less than stellar roots for proof. As it turned out, every committee member there had a secret of her own—more specifically, those compromising positions with my husband.

Gordon knew about secrets, and he knew that my friends would rather die than let it get out that he had been popular with them for more than exaggerated compliments.

From notes we found that Janet had taken, not long after she started doing accounting work for my husband, they started an affair. And not long after that, she became suspicious that he was seeing others besides her. Which was why she started following him, taking said photos, and began taking notes. If he was going to have sex with her and screw her, she was going to document it.

That much I knew, handed to me in the form of copious (if increasingly vitriolic) notes written by the Mouse. But as Howard had pointed out once we had returned to the Palace and I showed him the files, while sex with another person's spouse can ruin a person's reputation in Willow Creek, it's not a crime—at least not anymore. What wasn't clear was why Gordon had succumbed to Janet Lambert's blackmail. There had to be more to it, a piece that was missing, and I was certain the women sitting before me could fill in the blanks.

"We all know about the unfortunate turn my life has taken recently."

They harrumphed.

"Well, one look at these photos and I'd say it's safe to say that I wasn't the only one betrayed by Gordon Ware and Janet Lambert. What I'm hoping is that we can put our heads together and get to the bottom of what the two of them have done."

The plan seemed perfect. Only, things didn't go quite as I had hoped.

"How dare you, Frede Ware!" Annalise said, leaping up from her seat.

"Yes, how dare you do such a thing?"

"But—"

The women turned on me, me Frede Ware.

Pilar was stunned too.

But Nikki wasn't. She flipped on the lights and marched up to the podium.

"I cannot believe my ears," she snapped, her fists planted on her hips. "I thought you were supposed to be ladies. I thought you were supposed to support one another. But no. All you've done is gloat and carry on and blame Frede for no reason."

"No reason?" Cynthia called out. "Frede Ware is no lady!"

"How can you say that?" Nikki asked.

"What kind of a lady has that kind of painting done and displayed?"

Nikki glared. "What kind of a lady has an affair with someone else's husband?"

The room erupted again.

"Ladies!" Nikki found the president's gavel and started banging it. "Ladies, the fact is Gordon left and divorced Frede long before she ever posed for that painting. And Frede"—she looked right at me—"I'm sorry, but it's time everyone knows the truth. Enough with secrets to save face. He stole your money. I've been trying to be nice and not mention that I figured it out, but I just can't sit back any longer." She turned back to the ladies. "My gut also says that he stole money from the rest of you too."

The women went still.

"See, what did I tell you," Nikki said. "Annalise, is it?" she called out. "How much did Gordon Ware get out of you?"

"Ah, well." She flushed.

"Come on, Annalise. Tell us how much."

"A hundred thousand dollars."

"That's all?" Neesa James bleated. "He took me for two hundred and fifty!"

The numbers started spilling out, growing to a not inconsiderable amount. Gordon had charmed them all, charmed them out of money, each of them too embarrassed to admit that they had fallen for him—none of them wanting to be in any way associated with a scandal since we know how well those go over in the JLWC.

"Now, ladies, I ask you," Nikki continued, "what are we going to do about it?"

That shut them up. They swiveled back into their seats, ankles together, hands in laps.

"You mean to tell me you're going to let him get away with it?" she demanded.

Quiet reigned, though everyone knew that soon more members would start arriving at Brightlee, and no one could be certain what I would do given my very determined appearance there that day. Not that I would have shown anyone else the pictures. I am a lady, after all. But none of the committee members could be sure of that.

After one more long second Annalise stood. "What do we need to do?" she asked.

Nikki nodded then turned to me. "Frede, I believe you have something to say."

I said quite a bit, and by the time we left Brightlee, I had put together a nice fat file that I presented to Howard. After he read through the contents, he whistled. When he looked up at me, he smiled. "Darlin', I knew I loved the Junior League."

Chapter Thirty

AFTER THE SUCCESS we'd had at the New Projects Committee, Nikki and I sat at the Grouts' dining room table with Howard going through page after page of my bank records for the last year. Pilar would have helped, but really, I wasn't interested in her seeing the details of my financial life.

"The key," Howard explained, "is to find listings in Frede's bank statements that match the ones from the ladies of the Junior League."

We went line by line, check by check, transaction by transaction. It took hours and was tedious work. Over time, between the collection agencies that had managed to track me down through my cell phone, and the lack of headway we were making finding any matches in my bank statements, I hate to admit that I started having to work *très* hard to keep my poise intact and my confidence buoyed. And I had a sneaking suspicion that there was more to my challenged optimism than simply my husband's betrayal and my missing money.

In a line of thought that was completely unlike me (proof in itself of my following supposition) I felt as if I were changing in some way that I was trying mightily not to recognize. My blinders might have been ripped off, but I still had a trusty pair of rose-colored glasses. How many times had I told myself that my life was going to be just as fabulous as it had always been once I got my money back? But somehow I didn't quite believe it anymore—much less understand why I felt that way.

Through it all, Nina prepared meals (having commandeered the

Grouts' kitchen, relegating their staff to positions beneath her), kept us fed, provided plenty of coffee, and stayed up with us despite her fluttering eyelids.

"Nina, go to bed," I said.

"No! I stay."

It was just as I started on a new printout, Nikki barely awake, Howard barreling through coffee like his stomach was made of steel, that a single word leaped out at me.

"I found it!"

Everyone looked.

"BioBast!"

"Now we're on to something," Howard said, leaping up to look over my shoulder. "I knew a connection had to be there."

What we had learned from the New Projects committee members was that while each of them was having an affair with my husband, Gordon had charmed them into investing in "a once-in-a-lifetime opportunity" called BioBast. He had told them that the investment was so secret, so exclusive, that they had to sign nondisclosure agreements in order to invest. Once he had their money, however, he lost interest in them. While a Junior Leaguer Scorned in Willow Creek wants revenge as much as any other woman, there isn't one I know who would want it at the expense of their reputation, even if money was involved. So when their BioBast statements started showing extraordinary losses, not one of them dreamed of doing anything about it. As they saw it: Money lost. Secret kept. Face saved. I certainly understood the logic.

"It's time to research BioBast," Howard said.

The next day, late, Howard walked in while Nikki, Nina, and I were in the Grouts' kitchen. He looked worn out but determined.

"What did you find?" I asked, trying to act calm.

"BioBast is incorporated in Mexico and operates just over the Texas border in Nuevo Laredo. But I haven't been able to find anything else. It's damn near impossible to get detailed money information out of anyone when transactions are across borders. Plus, I don't believe BioBast really exists."

"Doesn't exist?"

"Yep. But I've got to find proof. So I'm driving down to Mexico to see what else I can learn."

My cell phone rang. I glanced at the display and found the same "Unavailable" that had popped up again and again recently, which had turned out to be a slew of collection agencies. As had become my habit, I went with my new policy and ignored the call. Then something worse happened. The Grouts' telephone rang. Nikki picked up.

"Hello?"

She cocked her head while she listened. "You're looking for Fredericka Ware?" Glancing over at me, she smiled apologetically, then mouthed, *Bill collector.*

I tried to hide my cringe, but Nikki must have noticed. "Sorry," she said. "Wrong number." Then she hung up.

Silence (of the embarrassed variety) settled in the room. Nina muttered. Howard cursed, then started out of the kitchen, but I stopped him.

"You know that drive to Mexico you're making?"

He eyed me.

"I'm going with you."

Crazy, I know, but I didn't want to think about betrayals or scandals or collection agents who had proved immune to my charm. All I wanted to think about was fixing my life. And while I was all about being positive, it was harder and harder to sit back and watch my husband run around town like the king he wanted to be. Worse than that? I had to hear about his Queen Mouse. It seemed the perfect time to get out of town, even if it was only for a quick jaunt to the border.

"Suit yourself," Howard said. "I'm leaving first thing in the morning."

THE NEXT DAY, I was actually surprised when I found myself with my lawyer (in a nondescript tan car I had never seen before) flying down 1-35 at the crack of dawn.

Sitting next to Howard, silently recounting my situation, I tallied all that was wrong.

1. My ruined reputation

2. My missing money

3. My artist and his ability to write me off so easily

On the plus side:

1. I was going to regain my reputation once I straightened this mess out

2. I was going to find my money

3. I would go to see my artist and force him to listen to my explanation

All would be well. How could it not? My melodramatic musings about blinders and rose-colored glasses had to have been brought on by hormones or low blood sugar, or . . .

I couldn't quite come up with any truly plausible excuse, and it was actually a relief when we hit the border crossing and the long congested lines to get across the International Bridge. Anything so I didn't have to think about what was really wrong.

After a stop-and-go drive for a good thirty minutes, we were waved through into Mexico. We drove through crowded, narrow streets, past El Centro and the yellow and white adobe façade of the Church of the Holy Child, its tall steeple guarding over the central plaza. Howard had some scribbled directions he wasn't really using, proving he had been down there before.

The farther we went, the less civilized the areas became. But I was too caught up with the idea of the pieces of my looming revenge falling into place (finally) (surely) to worry. Though my worry quotient went up a tad when we rounded a bend, hit a stretch of gravel road, then Howard slammed on the brakes. "We're here."

It was a little before eleven A.M. and we had stopped in front of a virtually windowless and grimy cinder-block building in a very bad part of town. The sun was already blazing this far south, baking the dirt and gravel that surrounded the structure. The building looked like it housed the kind of business that easily could have sustained the huge losses Gordon claimed BioBast had experienced. Though someone was making some money since there was a brand-new Lincoln Town Car parked out front.

Regardless, successful or not, the place did look like an open concern with its BioBast sign emblazoned across the front, an employee parking lot with cars off to the side. Howard stared up at the sign as if he couldn't believe it.

One of the best things about confident men is that they believe in themselves so completely. The down side is that said confident men have a hard time believing they are ever wrong. And let me just say, there was a whole lot of wrong staring my lawyer in the face if it was important for BioBast to not exist.

"Looks like BioBast exists after all," I said unnecessarily.

He just stared some more.

I wasn't sure how BioBast's existence hurt my cause, but I could tell from the expression on his face that it did. My mood was not improving and I wished I had stuck with the bill collectors back home.

But Howard was not so easily deterred. He pulled up next to the Lincoln and turned off the ignition. "You coming?" he asked, opening his door.

I glanced around the nearly deserted, exceedingly downscale neighborhood. Was I coming? Hello.

We entered the building through a single metal door, the paint peeling, and found a quaint if dated reception area replete with a real live receptionist. More proof that BioBast existed.

"*Hola,*" Howard said in Spanish.

"Hello," she answered back in heavily accented English.

"I'm interested in learning about BioBast," he said.

The receptionist whipped out a four-color brochure filled with handsome people looking industrious while wearing surgical masks doing who knew what. I couldn't imagine any sort of sanitary anything going on in the building, much less the neighborhood, but who was I to judge.

"Hmmm," he said, flipping through the pamphlet. "This looks interesting. Can I talk to the manager?"

"I don't know. Señor Vega is very busy. Do you have an appointment?"

The door opened and a small, ancient Mexican man appeared. "Who are you?"

"Señor Vega?"

The man glanced from the receptionist, to me, then Howard. "*Sí.*"

"I'm Howard Grout—"

"I'm busy." He started to close the door.

"I'm working with the Mexican government on a potential scam involving BioBast."

My lawyer said it so convincingly that I wondered if he really was working with the Mexican government. Who knew, maybe he played poker with them too.

"What's this scam? There is no scam here. You have the word of Pedro Vega!" he finished proudly.

As if to prove the point that there was no scam and a business really did exist, the phone rang, an employee came out of the back with a stack of files, and some sort of delivery person came through the front door. A lot of Spanish transpired, files were dropped off, deliveries signed for, then Howard and the manager stared at each other.

The fellow with the file walked over to an industrial time clock, pulled out what even I knew was a time card from a long rack of cards, punched it, put it back, then headed out of the building.

"I'm busy," Señor Vega said. "I have a business to run." Then he disappeared behind the office door.

"Let's go," Howard said.

"Just like that?"

Taking my arm, he led me outside into the relentless sun.

"We came all this way for that?" I persisted.

He wasn't even fazed. "We're not done yet."

I headed for the car, then stopped when I realized Howard wasn't behind me. He had walked over to the employee parking lot. A rundown guardhouse stood outside the chain-link fence that surrounded the small lot filled with several cars. When Howard approached, the guard came out.

If I hadn't known better, I would have thought the two men were best friends. For a few minutes, they talked, laughed, nodded, before Howard finished up with a slap on the man's back, then ambled over to me.

"What was that about?" I asked.

"Just checking things out. Had a little chat with Fernando."

A few lines from the Abba song started up in my head, and I almost didn't catch it when he said Fernando had been a guard there for twenty years. "And he's proud of it. He said he and his two nighttime deputy guards, Pizarro and Norberto, attend to the building twenty-four hours a day."

But that was all he said before he guided me back to the car.

We wheeled off, making our way through an assortment of streets (dirt, gravel, tarmac). It was well after noon by the time we stopped in front of Palacio Municipal, a fortlike building with arched columns running across the front on both levels of the two-story structure.

I could have done with lunch and a cold glass of sweet tea, but when I suggested as much, Howard said we didn't have time. He pulled two dollars from a money clip and bought two meat empanadas off a disreputable-looking street vendor. Not really what I had in mind, so I thanked him and said I was on a diet.

Howard shrugged and then made short work of both of the small pies. "Mmm-mmm," he said when he was done.

"What are we doing here?" I asked.

"Finding out who owns the BioBast building."

It took us forever to work our way through the masses of humanity that filled the municipal building to get to anyone of importance. While I waited, Howard talked to this official, then that official. I couldn't make out a word he said, though it was easy to see he was working his wiles with the staff—namely with a discreet transfer of money from palm to palm. Whatever. But after over an hour of palm-greasing, then another hour of waiting on a hard bench in the main room, we were finally led into a small room with nothing more in it than two wooden chairs, a table, and a thick document. Howard pored over it like a theological student poring over an ancient copy of a King James Bible.

"Interesting," he said finally. "Very interesting."

"What?"

"The building is registered to our friend Pedro Vega of Vega Industries, not BioBast." He stood. "Come on, let's go."

A clerk was waiting when Howard opened the door. More money was exchanged, then the tome and the clerk disappeared. When we walked outside, the sun was on the wane. We got into the nondescript vehicle and retraced our path, not to the border crossing but to BioBast.

It was four-thirty when we arrived, but instead of pulling up to the front as I expected, Howard slid the car into a spot across the street and down a ways from the building.

"Howard, really. What are we doing?"

"Have a little faith in your lawyer," he said with a wide grin. "Besides, if I'm right, this shouldn't take long."

Sure enough, at five minutes after five something happened. The front door of BioBast opened and the receptionist and Pedro Vega himself exited. But no one else exited before Pedro padlocked the front door.

My perfectly smooth brow furrowed.

Howard chuckled. "I knew something wasn't right."

Sure enough, something wasn't right. The manager had locked the front door, but the parking lot was still filled with cars. With little more than a wave at Fernando, Pedro and his receptionist got into the black Town Car and roared off.

"There must be a back door," I said, though by then I was too excited that maybe we were actually learning something of the helpful sort to get too worked up over employee-rights abuse.

Howard didn't respond. Sitting low in our seats, we waited another five minutes, then another after that, then the next thing we knew our Abba-inspired guard came out of his little guardhouse, locked up as well, then pulled the big gate shut and padlocked it. All twelve cars were still inside.

"Bingo," Howard said. "What did I tell you? All isn't as it appears."

As soon as Fernando departed with no sign of his secondary guard staff arriving to take his place, Howard got out of the car. After a quick glance up and down the road, he strode calmly to the chain-link fence, pulled something out of his pocket, then picked the lock with impressive swiftness, before slipping inside.

I experienced a massive mix of nerves as my lawyer went from car to car, peering into the interiors, snapping pictures with the tiniest camera I had ever seen. I jerked around in my seat to see if anyone had come out on their porches or were peering out their windows. When I turned back, Howard had moved on and was climbing up a bunch of crates stacked up against the grimy building. After peering inside through a high window, he started taking more pictures.

My heart was pounding, but that was a cakewalk of enjoyment compared to what happened next. The sound of barking dogs erupted.

"Oh, my Lord!"

Howard must have thought something similar (but probably said something very different) because he leaped off the crates, then came running for the gate. I've never seen such a barrel of a man move so quickly, though I guess a pair of matching Doberman pinschers hot on your trail could get anyone moving fast. But what truly amazed me was the look on my neighbor's face. I would have sworn he was enjoying himself. I was convinced of it when he raced through the gate just before the dogs got him, and he crashed the gate closed with a laugh. Yes, a laugh.

When he returned to the car, he was out of breath and grinning. "I guess that was Pizarro and Norberto," he said.

I wasn't amused. "Funny. You could have been . . . wounded." Then were would I have been?

"I wasn't, doll face, and let me tell you, it was worth the jog. BioBast doesn't exist, just like I thought." He preened a little. "This is a fake front. And now I have proof."

"What are you talking about?"

"Inside, there is nothing but a big empty warehouse with a few old crates that say 'Vega Industries.' And those cars in the lot? Junk. No steering wheels. No seats."

I shook my head in confusion. "I don't get it. We saw people come in and out of the place. The delivery guy, the file guy."

"All part of the scam in case someone like you or I showed up. When millions of dollars are involved, you can afford a few extras for your play."

Call me what you will, but I still didn't understand. "But you told me BioBast was incorporated. How can it not exist?"

"Any fool with a few hundred bucks, the ability to fill out a form, and someone to answer a phone can incorporate. People do it all the time, at least crooked people. They set up fake businesses, get people to invest in them, send out bogus statements to the investors, then carry or wire the money to offshore banks to launder it. It's hard as hell to track that kind of trail, and investors rarely regain their investment. The reason people rarely get their money back is that they can't find the trail."

I squinted as if that would help me understand. "We found the trail to my money?"

"Another piece of it. First, there's the nonexistent BioBast. Second, there's my new friend Fernando. If he's been a guard here for twenty years, what has he been guarding since the nonexistent BioBast is a 'new' company according to their very own brochure? My guess is that he's been guarding Vega Industries. And third, there's our man Vega himself."

"Mr. Vega is going to lead us to my money?"

"If my gut is right, at the very least, he's going to point the way. Now I just need to dig up everything I can on Pedro Vega and Vega Industries."

"That's it, more digging?"

"Yep. At least for me. But there's something else you can do when we get back."

"What?"

"Turn up the heat on Gordon even more."

Chapter Thirty-one

IT IS SAID THAT STANDING ERECT is one of the most determining differences between man and beast. Last I looked, Gordon Ware hadn't dropped down onto all fours, but he still wasn't human. Thankfully, though, he had started to have some very human emotions. Namely he was getting verra nervous.

As Howard, a few ladies of the Junior League of Willow Creek, and I secretly prepared to bring Gordon down, it was my job to ensure that Gordon stayed off kilter. Is it so bad that I enjoyed myself?

In truth, I was happier than I should have been (though maybe it was really simple relief that we were finally making appreciable progress) but I couldn't quite get any noble sentiments going. There was no rationale of, I was righting wrongs, or helping women everywhere. In fact, the last time I had been so inappropriately happy was when my artist was doing things to me that are better left unmentioned. Which reminded me of Sawyer.

I couldn't seem to help myself when I got into my car and drove to South Willow Creek. I bypassed the usual crowd of protesters at the construction site. I slipped past the Easter-egg-colored houses with their peeling paint. But when I arrived at the hacienda, the gates were shut and locked.

I got out of my car and peered through the windowlike insets in the big wooden gates. The house was completely dark and the grass inside the courtyard was unmowed. No one had to tell me Sawyer was gone.

There's a pesky problem with creative types. They're moody, lean toward the dramatic, and when they say they're falling for you and you respond with things like "thanks for sharing," they take it personally. I say, move on, get over it. Based on the totally dark, unlived-in hacienda on the outer edge of South Willow Creek, I'd have to say Sawyer wasn't of a like mind.

Then I saw the wooden signs, leaning up against the adobe side, stacked like canvases, partially covered by a big blue tarp. But I could see enough to make out one word. "GenStar."

It wasn't a surprise that my bazillionnaire must indeed have something to do with the development, based on what Nikki had told me. The surprise was that if he did, then surely he would come back. I'd get my chance to explain. But just explain, I told myself. That was all I wanted so I could stop feeling maybe a little bad for having been so rude to him.

Until then, I had a bigger job.

On Tuesday morning, I called Beau Bracken at the *Willow Creek Times*. It was time to call in my favor. He was happy to help.

On Wednesday, the headline read: FREDE AND FRIENDS DO DINNER.

The article was about Pilar, Nikki, and me at the opening of the newest restaurant in town, the piece accompanied by a photo of the three of us. I cut it out and dropped it in the mail to Gordon just in case he wasn't getting the newspaper.

On Thursday, the *Times* ran: THE LADIES OF THE LEAGUE

It was an article about an organization that sticks together through thick and thin to do "good works" (aka or to make people pay), accompanied by a photo of me back in the center of the JLWC.

On Friday night, the busiest night at the Willow Creek Country Club, Pilar, Nikki, and I made an appearance.

As a rule, ladies don't go to dinner at the WCCC without male escorts—preferably of the husband variety. But while Howard could have joined us, when we stuck our heads into his office to say we were going, he was on the phone. Based on his tone of voice, the call sounded like the kind that preceded trips in trunks to uninhabitable marshlands in New

Jersey. I decided we should go ahead without him. While I didn't approve of his method of practicing law, I saw no reason to deter it.

We arrived at the WCCC, each of us dressed in proper attire, making the sort of red-carpet worthy entrance to the main dining room that would have done a movie star proud. Everyone turned to stare, and this time it wasn't because I was still a pariah. It was because it just so happened that Gordon was there, dining with his new wife.

There isn't a lot of divorce going on in Willow Creek, at least in the better parts, so the members of the club were all eyes and ears. But I wasn't there to make a scene, I just wanted to *be* seen, by Gordon who I had learned would be dining there that night.

The girls and I strode toward our table, smiled and waved, air-kissed, and made sure everyone noticed us. We were nearly to our destination when we just happened to pass Gordon's table. Pilar and Nikki kept going, but I stopped. You could practically hear the gasps as the entire dining hall, guests and wait staff both, inhaled.

"Why, Gordon, sugar, what a surprise," I said.

At the pool, he had been full of sneering bravado. But I could tell Howard's plan was starting to wear on him. His eyes darted around the room, then he forced a smile. Janet hadn't learned manners and she showed her common roots by glaring.

"You remember Pilar, don't you," I said, gesturing to the table where my friends were seated.

He looked. She waved.

"You've probably heard by now that Pilar and I have reconciled our differences."

His jaw started to tick beneath his plastered-on smile.

"And surely you've heard of Nikki Grout, Howard Grout's wife?"

Nikki nodded her head.

I smiled big for my audience, then lowered my voice and leaned close. "Remember when you told me I'd have to prove you stole my money and didn't really lose it?"

His hands curled around the napkin in his lap.

"I just wanted you to know that it's happening, one step at a time, one nail in your coffin with every new piece of information we learn." I straightened, then added, "I think you're going to look *fabu* in prison stripes."

I swear he went white.

Continuing on, I joined my friends. We ordered champagne, made a toast, ate a sumptuous meal of Steak Diane, au gratin potatoes, broccoli florets, and cherries jubilee. Two hours later when we arrived back at the Palace, Howard was waiting for us.

"Hold on to your hats, ladies. We hit pay dirt."

I doubted Howard was familiar with the Categories of Men, so I assumed he was referring to success of the make-Gordon-weep variety.

"What did you find?" I asked.

"I found out how Gordon is paying for his lavish lifestyle."

"How?"

"I had an interesting call with your banker friend—the one who let Gordon evaporate your account without thinking that maybe, just maybe, he should have said something to you? While that isn't a crime, it's probably not great for business if that kind of news got around to the wealthier residents of Willow Creek who he loves to do business with."

"What did he say?"

"After helping our charitable banker see the wisdom of sharing, I got him to let it slip that the Bank of Willow Creek gave Gordon a personal loan for his living expenses."

My heart sank. "If he had to borrow, then the money really must be gone."

Howard just smiled. "Darlin', you can't get a loan unless you have collateral."

"What? What did he put up?"

You would have thought it was Christmas, as excited as Howard was. "GenStar."

I went very still. "The construction site in South Willow Creek?"

"One and the same."

"You're kidding! But doesn't Sawyer own that?"

"Sawyer? Hell, no, he was one of the protestors."

I blinked. Did that mean it was possible Sawyer wouldn't come back after all? That I'd never have a chance to explain? Or that I might have fallen for an NC tree-hugger type?

"But even better," Howard continued, "after some further persuasive digging"—spoken in his Guido-the-enforcer voice—"I learned that GenStar is a wholly owned subsidiary of a company called JR Holdings."

I could tell it was good news from the expression on his face, but I had no idea why.

"And guess who else JR Holdings owns?" he added.

"Who?"

"Vega Industries."

A beat passed before it registered. "The warehouse in Mexico where BioBast is listed!"

"One and the same."

"But what does this mean?" I asked. I might be able to use words like "appreciable" at a whim and discuss concepts like opposable thumbs, but I couldn't make heads or tails of what my lawyer was telling me.

Howard grinned. "Through a twisted path that Gordon hoped to keep hidden with a whole lot of smoke and mirrors, all that money of yours and the girls that went into BioBast was the money Gordon turned around and used to buy the GenStar land." He chuckled. "Who would have thought that any good lady from the Junior League would own property in South Willow Creek?"

My head spun. My money had been right under my nose the whole time, most especially every time I flew over those railroad tracks to Sawyer's hacienda.

"And word on the street," Howard continued, "is that your ex is having a fancy party tomorrow night to announce his plans for the property and to raise even more money. I think it's only neighborly if we were there."

DESPITE MY RECENT FORAY into "unfortunate incidents" (a plural situation by then) I had been privy to several Big Nights. Nikki's coming-out party. Sawyer Jackson's big show. And now this. One hundred fifty of Gordon's not-so-close friends attending a *soirée* to beat all *soirées*.

Given that I know everyone in town, including caterers and wait staff who hire out, I heard about every detail of Gordon's big party, from the golf-ball-sized servings of beluga caviar to the type of red wine he planned to serve. It was all I could do not to spoil my own big surprise by calling up and telling Gordon that the red was a mistake, both for his party and my gorgeous Oriental carpets, all of which were in the beige family of colors. But I held back.

The party was scheduled to begin at eight that evening so the guests could see the sunset through my floor-to-ceiling windows that faced west. Howard, Nikki, Pilar, and I were ready. Nina was at the wheel of my Mercedes. My parents were in the car behind us, and we met the caravan of Junior Leaguers at the foot of my fabulous red-brick drive.

We had to proceed slowly because Gordon's guests had parked along the narrow length, a whole slew of Rolls-Royces, Bentleys, Mercedes, BMWs, Cadillacs, and, God forbid, Hummers. On top of that, there were media vans, press cars, and I even recognized a few state senators' and congressmen's black limousines. Clearly Gordon thought he was on the verge of achieving his dream of independent importance and financial success. He was in for a surprise.

My not-so-little entourage swept up the red bricks, flustered the valet attendants, parked, and marched to the front door. I hushed my group, then clicked the door open quietly. I could see that my grand room was filled with an assortment of people. The first person I made out was my sister-in-law Edith, looking proud as punch. Nothing like the return of the prodigal son, along with money, to bring back the love.

If I'd had any doubt about what I was about to do (which I hadn't) the sight of her would have banished it.

I recognized some of the politicians and even a reporter or two. But the biggest shock came from everyone else who was there: a group of strangers dressed up in the gaudiest mix of oversized diamonds and flashy Dolce & Gabbana you have ever seen.

The barely clad, generously endowed women were seated in rows with their tar-thick mascara, bright red lips, and skin so taut and shiny that they looked like inflatable sex dolls someone had overfilled. The men weren't much better with their white suits, alligator-skin shoes, and plenty of gold chains, circa 1977 and the beginning of the disco craze. It was a regular gathering of Euro and Latin American types who have far more money than taste.

Gordon Ware stood in front of the crowd, smiling for photographers, Miss Mouse sitting next to him.

"I present to you," he said in his overly satisfied way, "a GenStar Development: Estancias of Willow Creek, an investment opportunity for an unparalleled experience in housing. It will be extraordinary, an address you will be proud to call home."

Before he could reveal the architectural model, we made our entrance. And it really was grand, causing quite a commotion.

"What the hell is going on here?" Gordon demanded.

At the sight of *moi*, Minnie leaped up. "Get out of my house!"

Now, I ask you, is that any way to treat a guest in her own home?

"You can't be here! Call security! I'm going to have you arrested for trespassing."

"I think my name is on the list. And oh, look, I have a key!"

Her eyes narrowed. "Gordon, make them leave."

"Frede," he warned, though he did it through a forced smile as the cameras flashed. "What are you doing here?"

Better than that, I noticed that he had started to sweat.

I did a little smiling myself as I strode to the podium. The only reason he didn't physically keep me away, I'm sure, was that my daddy and Howard followed in my wake. Plus, my mother was there, and we know how Gordon feels about my mother.

"Ladies and gentlemen"—so it was a stretch—"indeed, Estancias of Willow Creek is going to be an unparalleled experience. What Gordon is here to tell you about is an amazing site that he has begun preparing in South Willow Creek." Just the term "South" got people stirred up with worry.

I kept going. "Who knew, but it turns out that a few of my friends from the Junior League and I are the largest investors in the property."

The guests looked confused. Gordon gaped at me.

"Actually, we're the only investors so far, but we are nothing if not pleased to join in with my ex-husband to introduce this new development, especially since . . . drum roll, please . . . it's just been approved that Estancias of Willow Creek will be next year's New Project for the Junior League."

Annalise, Gwen, and the girls cheered.

The guests' confusion only got worse.

Edith looked like she was going to pass out.

"Like hell it is," Gordon hissed, but when he lunged for me, my daddy stood in his way.

"It's going to be a development to be proud of, I assure you," I continued, unflustered. "A tract of land that will be developed into a housing project for the needy."

"The needy?" A whole lot more choking echoed through my high-ceilinged home. The new Mrs. Ware had to be restrained. It wasn't pretty.

One after another of the guests stood, their expressions bewildered, their accents thick.

"Estancias is supposed to be filled with mansions!"

"An exclusive enclave!"

"With gold gates and coats of arms for each of us!"

"What is going on, Ware?"

Gordon seemed to be on the verge of having a coronary, and couldn't get words out. Since I am nothing if not helpful, I continued. "Did he say that?" I asked with an indulgent smile.

Everyone in town had wondered what kind of development could possibly go up in South Willow Creek. It wasn't zoned for retail or industrial. And who would knowingly build a home on the wrong side of the tracks—at least the kind of home that would turn a profit for a builder? The audience there in my grand room answered the question. The sort of individuals who wanted a prestigious Willow Creek address but didn't have a clue about what was considered right or what was considered wrong in our exclusive world.

"What he meant to say is that this is going to be a wonderful project, one well worth your investment dollars. And rest assured, your money will be in good hands. As it turns out, I am the single largest investor in the project"—I curtsied this time—"and I have appointed my father as director of the development, while my lawyer, Howard Grout, has graciously accepted a seat on the board."

When my father waved at the crowd, Gordon leaped away and grabbed my arm, then dragged me out of the room before anyone could react. Thankfully, we didn't get very far before my daddy and Howard circled him.

"You can't do this," he bit out.

"Of course I can, sugar," I answered, sweet as pie. "You used my money, and the money of my friends at the Junior League, to buy the land."

"You can't prove that!"

"We already have."

This from Howard, who stepped forward and handed him a stack of papers. Gordon only needed to read the top page. He was a lawyer himself, and while we know he didn't practice much law, he was smart enough to understand. But just in case . . .

"Howard tracked the money," I explained, "once we found out where to look. He followed your pesky little path from BioBast to Vega Industries to JR Holdings, and finally, to none other than GenStar."

My father stepped forward. "I'm going to set you loose in a cotton field, give you a head start, then set after you with my shotgun. Not sure anyone would miss you."

"Daddy," I said fondly. "I'm thinking that won't be necessary. I feel certain that Gordon is going to turn over the property without a fuss."

"Like hell I will."

"Oh, dear." I looked at Howard. "I guess we'll have to do this the hard way then." I shrugged innocently. "We'll just go back in there and explain to your guests and all those scary media and government types that you might have a teensy problem overseeing the project from jail—which is where you will be if we let the Texas State attorney general know that BioBast doesn't exist." I pulled an exaggerated breath, then blew it out. "Though who knows, maybe all those people sitting in there won't mind. Do you think?"

His face went purple, veins standing out in his neck like red lines on a road map. "Fred," he spat.

I ignored him and turned to my lawyer. "Howard, if people *do* mind, what are we looking at? Fraud? Racketeering? Treble damages because our little Gordy here had the brainchild to send bogus statements to the good ladies of the Junior League through the mail?" I looked at my ex. "Really, Gordon, I would have expected better from you."

His knees buckled. Thankfully there was a chair behind him. I wanted revenge, but I didn't need any actual blood.

"What's wrong? You're looking a tad peckish. Though I guess the prospect of spending the next ten to twenty years with a boyfriend named Big Bud might make anyone look a little green around the gills."

He dropped his head into his hands. I swear I thought he was going to cry.

I turned to Howard and my father. "It sounds like the guests are getting restless. Can you go in and calm them down while Gordon pulls himself together?"

We were left alone, and Gordon groaned. After a second, he looked back at me. The tears dried up like a spill of water on West Texas tarmac. I could see the wheels in his brain start to spin, and when he spoke he looked sheepish—not easy to do when he already looked like hell.

"I'm sorry, Fred," he said with the hopeful eyes of a practiced innocent. "I swear I am. I didn't mean for this to happen."

"Have you forgotten all the papers you tricked me into signing months before you ever left? Makes it hard to explain away as an accident."

"Well, there is that," he lamented. "And okay, I might have gotten a little carried away. But GenStar was going to be my ticket, Fred, you understand that, don't you?" He groaned. "It was going so well. But then Janet got all those pictures of me with everyone." He cursed. "Then she found out about BioBast. What could I do?"

It was one of those rhetorical questions, but I took a stab at answering anyway. "Not get into the situation in the first place?"

He grimaced. "I swear, Fred, I wish I could do it all over again. We all make mistakes."

I had said nearly the same thing to my mother. The thought surprised me.

"Let me make it up to you," he said. "Now that the pictures are out and you know about BioBast, I'll send Janet packing. I'll turn the whole project over to you and the League just like you want. Then we'll make this work big-time. Together. It'll be just like the old days."

His speech was impassioned, and I remembered those first days when I met him in the Willow Creek University Law Library. "Are you saying you want me back?"

"Yes. I never stopped loving you."

"You mean it?" I breathed.

He started to relax. "Fred, we're meant to be together, always have been. Neither of us really wanted to get a divorce."

"You are so right, Gordon. I don't want to be divorced." I smiled my big Frede Ware smile and felt a whole lot of completely inappropriate satisfaction. "But I'd rather be divorced than married to you."

I turned away and felt a great many less than noble but extremely satisfying emotions as I left Gordon in stunned defeat.

I walked back to the grand room and the podium to speak to the confused masses. "Ladies and gentlemen, I hope you will join me and the Junior League of Willow Creek to help those who are less fortunate, by investing in what truly is a once-in-a-lifetime investment opportunity."

One man stood. "There's not going to be a golf course?"

"I'm afraid not."

"No condos?" from another.

"Sorry."

"No fancy nineteen-thousand-square-foot mansions?"

"Not going to happen."

The gathered guests glanced among themselves, then practically ran each other down trying to get out of the house. The truth is, flashy Euro and Latin types don't think a bunch of sweater-set do-gooders are appealing any more than we think of them as perfect fits for the JLWC. So when the last guest had gone, my little group of friends, my family, and the Junior Leaguers realized we had our New Project.

The girls let up a shriek of joy, Howard twirled Nikki. And Gordon sat stunned, as if he couldn't figure out how it all went wrong.

Janet Lambert fumed, then couldn't believe it when the movers I had hired arrived to pack her bags.

"You can't do this!" she insisted. "It's our house. We have papers that say as much."

"Oh, yes, I forgot. Howard?"

My lawyer stepped forward and extended yet another document, this one the deed to my home. "Sign here, Ware," he said.

"He is not going to sign that!" Minnie yelped, then focused on *moi.* "You signed everything away!"

"True, bad me. But I didn't perpetrate a fraud. Gordon did. And if I'm not mistaken, you did the books for said fraud. Oops, bad you."

Her mouth pinched, a truly unbecoming look on anyone.

"And unless you'd rather my goodwill disappear and I go ahead and let the authorities know about the fraud of BioBast, then I suggest Gordon jump right over here and sign his heart out."

Like the defeated man he was, Gordon slunk over, took the pen and signed the papers.

The Mouse glowered, and did little more than watch her Louis Vuitton come back down my stairs.

When the movers were done, I extended a key. "It goes to the U-Haul out front," I said, then looked at Gordon. "I'm sure if you ask nice, your wife will give you a ride."

Chapter Thirty-two

I HAD DONE IT. Okay, so I had done it with *beaucoup* amounts of help from my friends, and more importantly, from Howard Grout. But my life was back in order. What else mattered?

That was the thing. As I had suspected when I was sitting at Howard's dining room table going line by line through my bank statements, something else did matter, something that stirred just below the surface like an obnoxious Psychology 101 work study problem. But the answer still eluded me.

Thankfully, I had plenty to do to keep my mind occupied. I threw myself into:

a. finalizing details of the League's New Project,

b. selling the newly successful Hildebrand Galleries, and

c. moving Nina and myself back into Chez Ware.

But the shine was off the fabulousness of my home. Neither of us wanted to be there, so we started contemplating our options for the future. After a few days of Nina's sitting at the kitchen table using a blunt-nosed, eraserless, three-inch golf pencil to write up a pros-and-cons list of her options, my maid turned in her dishtowel.

"What do you mean, you quit?" I was stunned. "You can't quit."

"You no need me, Missy Ware. I too old to be running after you anymore." She smiled. "Besides, I going to Mexico to try out for *Bailar Mejicano*."

"You're going after Don Juan de Tango!"

"So sue me."

I laughed and gave her a big sweeping hug, though I couldn't imagine my life without her. But during the days it took her to pack up her life and make arrangements to leave, she sat me down and launched into one of her Spanish diatribes—this time directed at me. She went on about how she wasn't one to give advice (insert sarcastic snort here) but that she couldn't leave without telling me that it was a big world out there, bigger than Willow Creek. Speaking rapidly in her native tongue, she went on about how I had spent my whole life living in Willow Creek, even attending college in town.

What was I supposed to say to that? True, and this matters why?

Even though she clearly wasn't interested in an answer, neither was she finished with me yet.

"Missy Ware, I think you afraid to leave."

Me, afraid? Of anything?

"Go, Missy Ware. See what ees out there. Go someplace that isn't so easy. So safe."

I dismissed my maid's words out of hand—at first. But over the next few days as Nina finalized her plans, I couldn't get the words out of my head.

That's when I couldn't keep reality at bay any longer, the truth bubbling to the surface like rich crude oil. I had been saying I didn't need help, that I didn't need saving. But who was I kidding? Apparently only myself, since men had been running my life and/or saving me since I was born. Of course I had made it worth their while with my charming personality and stunning good looks. But was Nina right? Was I afraid of life outside the comfort of my little world?

The day after I sent Nina off on her quest for Don Juan with detailed instructions on How to Get Her Man, I was surprised by what I understood I had to do. Now that my blinders were gone and my rose-colored glasses crushed ruthlessly under Nina's sensible heel, I knew things had to change.

I called my mother, though Blythe Hildebrand didn't begin to understand the changes I told her I was going to make. My father was too caught up in his new job running the land-development business for the League to realize things were any different. Nikki and Howard couldn't believe what I wanted to do, but they supported me in every way they could. Which reminded me that I still had one last debt to pay.

"Mother, I need your help."

"What's this? You're actually coming to me for something?"

"Yes, I have a favor to ask."

When I told her, at first she hemmed her annoyance. Then she sighed. "Fine. I'll take care of it."

As only my mother could do, in twenty-four hours she put together Nikki's sponsor group. Me, my mother, and Pilar were a given. But she brought in Lalee Dubois, plus one of her closest friends, and Annalise Saunders. It was an impressive group, a power group, that would serve Nikki well in her future at the JLWC.

Only when I knew that the package was complete and accepted in time for the deadline did I call Nikki.

"Are you sitting down?"

"What's going on?"

"You're getting into the League."

I swear, I heard her squeal of delight all the way from next door.

"Are you sure?" she asked.

I filled her in on the details, and told her that she would receive an official invitation in the mail. "You'll be introduced at the May meeting."

"That's just days away! Will you be there with me?"

"I wouldn't miss it for the world."

As soon as I hung up, Juan called up from the front gate. "Miss Dubois is here to see you."

Lalee arrived with the incoming president and the secretary of the Nominating Committee. With Nina gone, I had to scramble around to serve tea. But I was getting more proficient by the day.

"We're here," Lalee began, as I served them tea and petits fours in the sunroom, "to ask you to become our next president-elect."

I sat up even straighter. "After all that's happened?"

"The fact is, you have been trained for this job since birth. And the truth is, the Estancias Housing Project is a coup."

"Quite the coup," Constance added.

"We are getting more publicity out of this than we've had in years. While we certainly don't want a lot of publicity, this is just the kind that will help us bring in even bigger donations."

"From politicians and corporations," the secretary said.

"Exactly," Lalee continued. "And we believe you deserve to be rewarded for that."

See, people really can't resist me for long.

I felt a smile and I understood in an instant what my answer would be. "I love that you asked, and part of me wants to say yes—"

"You're saying no?" they asked in unison.

"Yes, I'm saying no. At least for now. But there is someone who would be great for the job."

And we all know who that was.

"Pilar Bass would be perfect."

THE MAY GENERAL MEETING was the last meeting of the JLWC year and was always well attended—one last chance to show off or brag until September. Not only would the new Provisional Class be presented, but the new president-elect would be introduced. When I arrived at Brightlee I smiled when I saw Pilar sitting on the dais with the incoming officers. She flipped up an excited wave when she saw me. Pilar, giddy. I swear.

Nikki sat in the front row with the rest of the Provisionals, and when she saw Pilar wave, she whipped around and waved as well. What was I going to do, ignore them?

I waved back.

After Pilar was introduced, along with the new slate of officers, there wasn't a lot of business to take care of before the Provisionals were announced. Lalee took out the list of names. "It's my pleasure to introduce our incoming Provisional Class of the Junior League of Willow Creek."

As their names were called, each woman stood to give a polite and/or nervous smile. When it was Nikki's turn, she stood, turned around and waved to the crowd like a beauty pageant contestant. She got the biggest round of applause of the entire class.

Afterward, our little group of three went back to the Palace. Howard was waiting. "How'd it go?"

"They loved me!" Nikki enthused.

He picked her up and twirled her around. "I knew they would, sweetie doll."

When he set her down, he led us to the kitchen. Why bother to point out all that he does wrong anymore, and quite frankly, what does it matter? Especially since he did something so very right. He pulled out a bottle of chilled Dom Pérignon from a silver bucket.

"I started making a big batch of Cosmos for you gals, then thought, nah, ladies should have champagne."

Howard Grout might turn into a proper gentleman yet.

He popped the cork to our cheers, and after he poured, he gave his wife a toast before he added, "I'll leave you ladies to celebrate."

He started to leave, but Nikki raced after him. "I love you, Howie." Then she kissed him on the lips in the tackiest display of public affection I have ever seen. I got teared up at the sight.

"To Nikki," I said, when she returned, "and Pilar."

We toasted, and Nikki laughed. "My guess is the Junior League of Willow Creek is never going to be the same!"

Can you say understatement?

Chapter Thirty-three

IT WAS A CRYSTAL-CLEAR June day with a startlingly blue sky when my plans for my new future were finalized, the same day Sawyer Jackson walked back into my life.

I was at the dedication ceremony for the Estancias Housing Project, the protestors now supporters. The media was there, along with senators and congressmen. The development would be the largest nongovernment-sponsored low-income housing project in the state. The atmosphere was festive with music and speeches, before we took ceremonial shovels to the dirt. Everyone clapped with polite enthusiasm.

Once the speeches were done and the site christened, the crowd started dispersing. It was as I headed over to Howard and Nikki, who were waiting for me, that I saw him.

He leaned back against that death trap of a car, his ankles crossed, his arms folded on his chest, his sunglasses covering his eyes. He looked just as dangerous as I remembered.

When I got close, he pulled off his sunglasses and hooked them over the collar of his black T-shirt. "Frede."

I'd like to say I felt nothing, zip, zilch. Sure, I wanted the chance to explain why I had been less than mannerly to him, but that didn't mean I wanted all those overly feelingish feelings he had an uncanny ability to make me, well . . . feel. But that was the thing about Sawyer Jackson. He was everything I shouldn't want but, surprise, surprise, did.

I felt the old, perfectly improper stirrings at the sight of him, all tall, dark Marlboro man, and it would have been *très* easy to race across the last few steps of uneven, preconstruction earth and throw myself at him. But it's me we're talking about.

"How've you been?" he asked.

"Never been better. Even better, in fact, since all you protestor types approve of the new project."

He still leaned up against the car, and he seemed to consider my answer. "You heard about the protesting then?"

"Yes. Nikki told me."

A smile curved on his face. "Golf courses, mansions, and luxury vehicles would have ruined the neighborhood." But then the smile was gone. "I heard about what happened . . . with your money, with the land. Nikki told me."

"That Nikki, always talking." Though at least I didn't have to explain it all myself. "But"—I cleared my throat—"that is no excuse for how rude I was."

The grin resurfaced. "So, we're back to formal."

I remembered the night of Nikki's dinner party, the first time he said that. "We never left."

Which made us both laugh.

Nikki hurried over. "Sawyer, do you mind taking Frede home for us?"

"Nikki!"

Her cheeks were flushed, her eyes wide with excitement. "I'm so sorry—"

For the record, she didn't look sorry at all.

"—but I just remembered Howard and I have to drive to . . . San Antonio."

"You can drop me off first."

"Ah . . . we have to go now. No stops. Sorry!" She hurried off.

Short of getting one of the construction workers to take me home, I was stuck. Everyone else was gone.

"A little transparent, don't you think?" I said.

Sawyer raised his hand like the Boy Scout we both knew he wasn't. "I had nothing to do with that."

"I bet." But it got me in the car.

We whipped through the streets without a word, and I admit it, when we got to my house I asked him in. Not that I was going to let anything happen, really.

"Would you like some tea?" I asked.

He glanced around. "Where's Nina?"

I told him about my maid's foray into the world of television, about her quest for Don Juan de Tango. He followed me to the kitchen, and if he thought this was odd he didn't let on. I was feeling quite proud of myself when I put the kettle on to boil while he told me about his travels, the museums, the way he lost himself to art.

I could have told him a thing or two about losing yourself in order to forget, but I didn't, not because old habits die hard, but because I didn't trust myself. When it came to Sawyer Jackson and *moi,* I never seemed to do what my brain knew was right.

After pouring the water, I let the tea steep, then poured in the sugar. When I turned around his expression was speculative.

"I wish you had told me what was going on," he said.

Just like that, all dramatic and Cary Grant–like. I felt a little thrill, which is a very bad sign.

He didn't let up. "If you'd said something I wouldn't have been such an ass." That smile of his surfaced as he stepped even closer and the thrill got worse. "Let me make it up to you."

"Now, Sawyer, there's nothing to make up." I swatted at his arm, though somehow my hand stopped short of a full sweep and ended up on his sleeve. Which must be why he pulled me to him.

Well, what's a girl to do? When he lifted me up, I let him carry me out of the kitchen and up the stairs. It was all very Rhett Butler–ish, and the most soundtrack-worthy moment of my life.

When it was over, far too many hours later, I left him sound asleep in a tangle of my nine-hundred-ninety-nine-thread-count sheets.

I pulled on clothes and went downstairs. The doorbell rang just as I stepped into the entry hall and I almost didn't answer.

"Frede! Everything is done! Congratulations!"

The woman stepped inside and handed me the paperwork. I glanced through the stack.

"Mmmm," she said.

I raised my head and found her looking up the stairs.

"Who is this?" she asked.

Sawyer had come to the top of the stairs. The sight of him, dark hair raked back with fingers, no shirt, jeans hanging low on hips, made me question all the plans I had been so painstakingly making. No surprise there.

When I didn't answer, the woman was smart enough to say she had to go and she'd talk to me later about making arrangements for the closing.

Sawyer came down the stairs. "You sold the house?"

"I did."

He considered me for a second, then nodded. "I have a proposal for you."

"Proposal?"

"Come stay with me, for as long as you want. We'll start over and take it one step at a time."

His offer was beyond tempting, what with the good sex, charming grins, and, heavens, he even cooked. And no question I had been saved from my bad judgment and idiotic signing habits and could continue on in Willow Creek with life almost entirely as I had known it. But there was still that pesky problem of my needing proof that I was truly strong, that I wasn't afraid. And more than that, how could I explain to him, or anyone, the growing excitement I had begun to feel at the prospect of stepping out of my world and proving to myself that I didn't need things to be easy and comfortable, that I could go out into the world beyond my backyard and succeed there too.

All I can say is that something was pulling at me, like the other end of the rainbow pulling at Dorothy. Maybe I'd find a green witch and strangely dressed monkeys, but I had to take the chance.

"I think I could fall for you, or maybe I already have," I told him. "But it's time I stopped letting other people take care of me."

"Frede—"

"If I come stay with you, that's what I'd be doing. It would be wonderful, amazing . . . but easy. It's time I find out what I'm really made of. And I can't do that here in Willow Creek."

• • •

DAYS LATER, he was there when I was ready to leave. I had gone Inactive in the League and sold or donated whatever else was left of the Chez Ware furnishings. Sawyer stood in the front drive with my parents, Pilar, and the Grouts.

Once the situation had finally penetrated my father's blueprint- and construction-soaked head, he announced he wasn't happy about my leaving. But despite his threats not to be there, he showed up, wrapped me in one of his all-encompassing embraces, and said, "I always knew you deserved the world. I shouldn't be surprised that you're going out there to get the whole damn thing for yourself."

My mother didn't agree, but she looked stoic and resigned. She didn't hug me, but she did hold me at arm's length. "Don't stay gone for long."

Before my mother could step away, I couldn't help it. I wrapped my arms around her. "I love you, Mama."

I was fast acquiring a taste for sap.

When I turned to Nikki she launched herself at me, holding tight, making me promise that we'd be friends forever. Even Pilar ran over and made it a group hug.

Howard just smiled, and when I pulled away, he said, "Thank you for all you've done for my Nikki."

"It was a two-way street. I thank you too."

The bargain I had struck with Howard was paid in full. What can I say, I gave my NC neighbor a hug.

Then there was Sawyer, that dark hair ruffling in the early morning breeze, his black T-shirt just tight enough to show off his broad chest without making him look like he worked in a hair salon. I felt shy. Me. And when he slid his palm back along my jaw, I gave in to the first public display of affection of my life. I kissed him good-bye, ignoring my mother's, "Well, I never."

He pulled back, but only slightly, a grin curved on his mouth. "On the night everything went wrong at the art show, you asked me for time. Now I'm smart enough to give it to you. Go do what you have to do, but know that I'm not done with you yet. Not by a long shot."

One of those completely inappropriate and no doubt non–Gloria Steinem–approved thrills shot through me. I barely managed to tear myself away from all his sexy dangermanness and get into the car. But in the end, I knew I had to do it.

They were lined up when I finally turned the ignition, Nikki leaning into Howard, Pilar standing close to them, my mother with her chin held high, my father looking wistful, and Sawyer confident . . . always confident. It was a picture-perfect postcard moment, and I gave my best parade wave as I drove down that long, redbrick drive.

Driving away was the most difficult thing I have ever done. I still find it hard to believe that I left my family, my friends, and my artist. But who knows? As they say, you can take the girl out of Texas, but one day she'll have to go back. Besides, until then, sexy artists are always in high demand at any gallery. And let me tell you, there are an awful lot of art galleries in New York City.

Yes, that's where I am. Me in NYC. Can you believe it?

Nina was right. No surprise there. I had to go someplace that wasn't comfortable. As I see it, it's the perfect place to prove myself. I'm going to flatten my hair, find an amazing job, and read everything that is put in front of me word for word, then I'm going to turn myself lose on the city that never sleeps. They're going to love me. How could they not? Because, accent or no, family connections or not, changed in ways I'm only beginning to comprehend, I know one thing for certain. I'm still me, me, the fabulous Frede Ware.

Turn the page for a sneak preview
of Linda Francis Lee's new book
The Devil at the Debutante Ball
coming in winter 2008 from
St. Martin's Press

DENIAL \DE-NI-AL\ N (1528): one small word crammed with three tiny syllables that quite frankly causes great big problems in a whole lot of lives; a word, like most, with multiple meanings. 1: refusal to admit the truth 2: negation of logic, and 3: (my personal favorite) the reason I got tangled up in what I now refer to as The Debutante Mess.

Granted, I had been around etiquette, manners, and the waltz since birth. And true, I had made my own bow to society eleven years earlier in one of Texas High Societies' premier social events. So on the surface there was no reason I shouldn't have gotten involved. But I had left Texas to get away from all of that.

Actually, I left Texas to get away from my mother's, let us say, larger-than-life personality and her renowned beauty she never let anyone forget; my sister Savannah's obsession with babies and her inability to have one; and all the complaining I had to endure over my sister-in-law's lack of obsession with babies and her apparent inability to stop having them.

But as Michael Corleone in *Godfather III* said, *Just when I thought I was out, they pull me back in.*

My name is Carlisle Wainwright Cushing, of the Texas Wainwright family. More specifically, I am a Wainwright of Willow Creek. My mother is Ridgely Wainwright . . . Cushing-Jameson-Lackley-Harper-Ogden. I kid you not.

Given my mother's predilection for divorce, is it any surprise that as an adult I had become a divorce lawyer?

It had seemed a natural choice given that, as the only truly practical person in my family, I had been dealing with the dissolution of my mother's marriages in one way or another since I was in ruffled ankle socks and patent leather Mary Janes—-and not the Manolo kind.

To be specific, it was my mother's pending dissolution of her most recent marriage that initially dragged me back to my hometown from Boston, where I had moved three years earlier. Then, once back in Texas, like Alice falling down the rabbit hole, I slid along the slippery slope from divorce court to the debutante court, all because I couldn't say no to responsibility. Or so I told myself.

See? Denial. Whitewashing the truth, a sleight of hand with reality until even I believed the convoluted excuse for why I had gone home.

But I'm getting ahead of myself.

"Carlisle is here," announced the woman who swore it was her face that had launched a thousand ships, "to deal with my pesky divorce situation."

My mother sat at the head of the formally set dining table, perfect in her cashmere and heirloom pearls.

"She is?" my sister asked.

"You are?" my brother demanded.

Even Lupe, our longtime family maid, who was serving her famous veal cordon bleu, froze for half a second in surprise.

"Have you lost your mind?" I stated in a way that was far more direct than any self-respecting southern belle would ever be.

Ridgely Wainwright-Cushing-Jameson-Lackley-Harper-Ogden shot me, her youngest child, a glare. But I wasn't the same eager-to-please girl who left three years earlier. I returned my wineglass to the formally set dinner table and smiled tightly.

"Mother, could you join me in the kitchen? Please?"

"Not now, Carlisle. We are in the middle of dinner. Lupe, the veal looks divine."

"Mother."

She wore the cream cashmere sweater set with cream, wool flannel pants, bone low-heeled shoes, her shoulder-length blond hair elegant and swept back with a cream velvet headband. She held her own wineglass in her perfectly manicured hand as she studied me over the length of fine linen, sterling silver, wafer-thin crystal, and tasteful fresh flower arrangements made of white roses, light pink peonies, and lavender hydrangeas. After a second, she nodded. My mother was more perceptive than her porcelain china doll exterior would lead the average onlooker to believe. She understood without having to be told that Miss Never-Make-a-Scene Carlisle Cushing was feeling a whole lot like making a scene. She probably followed me out of the dining room more out of surprise than anything else.

As soon as we stepped into the service galley of stately Wainwright House, the dining room door swinging shut behind us, I stopped abruptly just outside the kitchen and turned back, bringing me face-to-face with my mother.

"Oh!" she squeaked.

"I really am not in a position to stay here and help you with your divorce. I have a job, remember? In Boston."

She only peered at me. "Dear, have you put on weight?"

I might have pressed my eyes closed and counted to ten. I definitely wondered how I had ever allowed her to trick me into coming back to Texas.

"And your skin, it looks dry, terribly dry. I don't like to brag, but you know I'm famous for my youthful appearance. But I look this good because I take care of myself, Carlisle. Don't the pilgrims sell moisturizer?"

On principle, my mother is not fond of anyone who lives north of the Mason-Dixon line. In her personal dictionary, she refers to New Englanders\new eng-land-ers\ n (1620) as 1: The Pilgrim People (or assorted variations) 2: Yankeefied 3: Pantywaist Thurston Howell the Thirds.

I ignored her criticism and maintained focus, not easy to do when she was looking me over like a judge at a beauty pageant. "The only reason I am here is because you called me saying you were having an emergency."

Tension settled around her eyes. "This divorce mess is an emergency. And if you don't clear it up then I swear to goodness it is going to be the end of me." She pressed her delicate hand to her chest. "Darling, really, I need you."

To be completely honest, to say that my mother was larger than life would be an understatement. She should have been a stage actress, probably would have had it not been for the fact that as a direct descendant of Texas founding father Sam Houston himself, the great-granddaughter of the fifth Duke of Ridgely who arrived in Texas in the late 1880s, Debutante of the Year when she took her own bow more years ago than she was willing to admit, and with more money than even Ross Perot, she didn't do such base things as act on stage. Instead, she acted her way through life until I'm not sure anyone (including my mother) knew who she really was.

That said, I love her, am a good daughter, just as I love the rest of my family, though is it any surprise that I have found it easier to be a good daughter when I'm not living right in the middle of my mother's theatrics?

I was twenty-five when I came to this realization, at which point I did the only sensible thing a sensible girl could do. I opened the big atlas in the Wainwright House study to the double spread of North America, closed my eyes, and took a stab at the map. My finger landed in the Atlantic Ocean, but it was reasonably close to Nova Scotia, Maine, and Boston. Not wanting to be referred to as a Canuck, and having no clue what anyone actually did in Maine other than wear plaid flannel and fish for lobster, I packed my bags and headed for the Baked Bean capital of the world, landing in a city with a great many people who had more onerous ancestries than I.

Even better, not one person in Boston knew my name. Which meant, I realized, on a not-so-sensible intake of breath, that I could be anyone I wanted, namely a New Me \new me\ adj n (2005) 1: not Sam Houston's descendant 2: not the duke's great-great-granddaughter 3: not even Ridgely Wainwright-Cushing-Jameson-Lackley-Harper-Ogden's youngest child.

Moving to Boston had been quite a feeling. Freeing. And given my Texas accent, when people stereotypically assumed I was white trash, probably inbred, ignorant, and undoubtedly poor, well, I didn't do anything to set the record straight. I let them assume the worst.

I know, it sounds terrible, and if I could do it all over again, believe me I would. Not that I minded being considered that Texas girl from the wrong side of the tracks. But something that seemed like an adventure at twenty-five had a way of coming back to bite me three years later.

Though that was the least of my concerns just then.

"There are plenty of attorneys who can deal with this, Mother."

"Yes, just like that one I had for my last divorce who bungled everything so badly. Do you think for a second I am going to trust anyone else but you?"

My mother's last attorney had done such a horrible job with the divorce that one Mr. Lionel Harper (husband number four) had become a line item on the family accounting ledgers. Not to mention that the lawyer had been a publicity hound and our family had been in the news more in the ten months the negotiations raged on than in the previous ninety-nine years of Wainwright history.

"We can't have our family name disparaged, dragged through the mud. Yet again. You are a Wainwright, even if you choose to live elsewhere."

"I can't stay in Texas. Whether you believe it or not, I really do have a job. A good job." And I did. I had a great position at Marcus, Flint, and Worthson, one of the largest and most prestigious law firms in Boston.

"Pshaw. You have a job using the law to make a bunch of those Kennedy types mind their p's and q's. I say tell them to start pronouncing their r's and find a new attorney. You are needed here, with your family, to make that sniveling Vincent Ogden rue the day he ever decided he didn't want to be married to me."

Tension settled around my eyes this time, not that there wasn't truth in what she was saying. If anyone could make anyone rue anything, it was me. I had gotten more than one of my clients out of sticky marital predicaments.

But, again, I lived in Boston.

I loved it there, loved the surprise of four true seasons, the lush green Boston Common in spring, picnics at the Hatch Shell listening to the Boston Pops in summer, the stunning orange, yellow, and red of autumn, and skating on the iced-over Frog Pond in winter.

Also, it just so happened that I was engaged. Not that my mother knew this, and not that I was about to tell her right there in the service galley amidst the dessert china and coffee cups ready for the next course. But I was engaged to the extremely amazing Phillip Granger, a lawyer at my firm who had a warm smile, laughing blue eyes, and a kind soul that I wrapped around myself like a cashmere throw in winter.

There was just one problem. He wanted me to set a date for the wedding, and, well, even I couldn't set a date until I told my mother that I was getting married, but the minute I told her (after she had recovered from the stupefying shock that I was marrying a Yankee, that is, if she did recover) she would dive headlong into the sort of traditional wedding plans she would expect. I had no interest in showers and teas and all the prewedding niceties my mother wouldn't see as negotiable. I planned to have a sensible, low-key civil affair, which would definitely kill my mother, bringing me full circle as to why I had yet to set a date for the wedding.

But there had to be a way to convince her that what I wanted to do was the best thing for everyone involved. Which was the only reason I didn't simply walk out of Wainwright House, get back on a plane, and return to Massachusetts. Instead if, say, I stayed, just for a little while, not dealing with the divorce so much as helping my mother find a decent lawyer, it would give me a little breathing room from a certain unset date, and time to figure out how to tell my mother I was getting married and not have to succumb to all that a large Texas wedding would entail.

"This is what I'll do," I said.

In copious detail I mapped out exactly how I would facilitate the process. I would help her find a lawyer. But there would be no other involvement.

"Well, that's fine, dear. Though before you do all that . . . organizing, I have to meet Vincent at his lawyer's office first thing in the morning. Come with me, talk to your stepfather. Vincent always liked you. Maybe you can talk some sense into him. If not, turn on all that unladylike killer charm you are famous for and scare him a little."

I wasn't sure if I was flattered or insulted.

"If there has to be a divorce," she added, "then convince him it should be done quickly, quietly, and without a lot of fuss. Then depending on how the meeting goes, we'll think about getting another lawyer."

Sure enough, first thing the next morning, my mother's driver Ernesto drove us through the craggy live oaks, rolling green hills, and the perfectly kept streets of town, past the main square, alongside Willow Creek High, then the university, to the offices of Howard Grout, Attorneys at Law, LLP.

Howard Grout was a notorious lawyer who had gotten Fredericka Ware (a daughter from another of Willow Creek's oldest families) out of a sticky predicament last year. In court, I had heard he was meaner than a junkyard dog and he only hired lawyers who were cut from the same cloth. Not that this worried me, but it was good to know these things going in.

The offices were nice in that *new* nice way meant to announce in bold letters that they had made it without the help of old money. After working out of his home the previous year, Howard had opened up shop in one of the best buildings in town. While the exterior was traditional limestone blocks, inside everything was made of glass, steel, and jutting granite sculpture. There wasn't an inch of dark walnut wood paneling, mahogany desks, or oil paintings at Howard Grout, LLP, to be found.

Dressed in an Armani power suit that, thankfully, I had brought along, I had pulled my shoulder-length light brown hair back into a sleek ponytail. Never one to go far without my baby-soft black calfskin briefcase, I held it at my side, my black, low-heeled Chanel pumps the only minor indulgence I allowed myself.

My mother followed in my wake (a rare occurrence in itself) looking stunning, her blond hair perfectly done, her makeup easily camera ready, her nails a demure shade of barely pink that matched her lip color. She also wore her usual strand of Wainwright pearls around her neck.

We walked down the long wide hallways of marble flooring bisected by plush oriental runners, the walls lined with modern art. At the end of the hall a Schnabel filled the space.

"Who is that?" I asked the receptionist.

"Who?"

"The woman in the portrait." I gestured toward the broken crockery forming a mosaic portrait, a signature Schnabel piece.

"Oh, that. It's Mrs. Grout."

"Nikki?"

"Yes. Mr. Grout had it done as a surprise." The girl shook her head. "He said it was like a mast on a ship, or something. Their good luck charm when he opened the doors. I don't know about you, but I've never seen a picture painted on a bunch of broken tea cups and saucers."

Howard Grout appeared out of an office. "Did I hear someone talking about my Nikki?" he said grandly.

"Mr. Grout. I'm Carlisle Cushing."

"Of course you are. And this is your mother. Prettiest lady in town, next to my Nikki, mind you."

My mother smiled like a coy schoolgirl. "Now, Howard. Aren't you just the sweetest man."

He chuckled and slapped his big round belly that lay beneath the three-thousand-dollar Italian suit. "We both know that's a baldface lie. I'm a lot of things, Ridgely darlin', but sweet ain't one of them."

He bid us good-bye, then barked out orders to some unfortunate soul in another office.

We continued on, my mother speaking to most everyone we passed.

"Isn't that a lovely blouse you're wearing, Lisabeth. Though you might consider blue next time. Pink really isn't your color."

Lisabeth stared, pretended the comment didn't bother her, then ran for the bathroom mirror just as soon as my mother was out of sight.

"My word, look at you, Burton Meyer. Looking younger and younger every time I see you. Is that hair dye you're using? Or have you given in and gotten Botox?" She kissed his cheek. "Whichever, you look just as handsome as any man your age can look, sugar."

Burton Meyer stammered.

"Morton Henderson, your sweet Mabel must be quite the cook for all the weight you've gained." She patted his round belly, which no other soul in all of Willow Creek dared do, given his reputation as a bloodthirsty litigator. "Don't you worry, though, I won't breathe a word of this to your mother. I know how she and Mabel don't get along."

Ridgely left her usual trail of destruction in her wake, like a hurricane racing through town. Anyone with half a brain got out of her way.

When I led my mother into the designated conference room, my stepfather was waiting.

"Hello, Vincent."

Vincent Ogden was a fit man with reddish brown hair tamed within an inch of its life on top of his head, and a well-trimmed beard and mustache. He wore a tweed jacket and cuffed slacks, a white dress shirt but no tie. He looked as if he just stepped out of the faculty lounge at Willow Creek University.

"Carlisle," he acknowledged, then with little more than a glare at my mother, he turned away and started to sit down at the conference table.

"Typical," my mother said. "Sits before a lady does."

"Lady? In your dreams! A lady knows how to treat a man!"

Technically, a woman knows how to treat a man, not necessarily a lady. But I kept that to myself.

My mother raised her chin. "When you turn into a real man, let me know. I was married to a milquetoast."

"I'm no milk toast! You're a shrew and it's just easier to lay low than have to deal with your theatrics on a regular basis."

"*My* theatrics," she shrilled. "If ever there was a drama queen in my house, it was you."

"Yeah, your house. Your money. Your everything!"

I had seen it before, dueling jabs.

"Mother, Vincent, please."

Not that it did any good. They went back and forth, each insult worse than the last, until the conference room door opened. Thankful that opposing counsel had finally arrived, I turned around with my best professional smile. But this time I stiffened and sucked in my breath like an actor overacting in a really bad play.

"Jack?"

"Hello, Carlisle. I heard you were back in town."

His voice was deep and smooth, with hints of fond amusement. Okay, "fond" might have been overly optimistic. Either way, I was so stunned at the sight of him that my muscles refused to take signals from my brain.

It had been three years since I saw Jack Blair last, though he didn't look any different, unless even more dangerously handsome counted as different. To say we hadn't parted on the best of terms might be the most accurate statement I've made so far.

He wore a blue sports coat and a tie, barely done, and gray slacks. A far cry from the traditional suits back in Boston, but also a far cry in the opposite direction from the black leather bomber jacket and 501 jeans he had sported before.

He still had those same broad shoulders and narrow hips, still had the same dark brown hair and brown eyes, not to mention the crooked smile that made him look like the angel he wasn't, and never had been. Not that Jack had ever tried to be an angel.

I shouldn't have been surprised that he had gone to work for Howard Grout. Jack was an all-purpose attorney, going wherever there was money to be made. He was also my first love.

The first time I ever met Jack Blair I was a precocious freshman in high school. I had placed out of Algebra I and Geometry and entered Algebra II on my very first day of high school with the sort of arrogant pride that showed just how oblivious I was to how kids really work. I had dressed with care that day, wearing a starched white button-down shirt, a green plaid skirt, green knee-high socks, and penny loafers with a brilliant shine. Walking into class before the bell rang, I was quite pleased with myself until I realized the room was filled with juniors who stopped what they were doing when I entered.

"Hey, babe, kindergarten is a block away at Willow Creek Elementary."

"Call the Geek Squad. One of their members has gone missing."

I ignored them and found a seat. Unfortunately, it was at the back of the room.

The desk was like nothing I had seen before in my days of learning, a black-topped table for two with high wooden legs. You can probably guess who walked into the class and into my life and sat down next to me. Jack Blair.

The teacher hadn't arrived yet, and it didn't take a math whiz to see that the girls adored Jack, some of the cooler boys wanted to be like him, and every squeaky nerd in the class was afraid of him. I fell solidly into the Adore Him at First Sight category.

"Hey," he said, ambling up to the table in a T-shirt, jeans, and workmen boots that could have used a good tying.

He was disheveled, as if he had gone straight from bed to class, but his smile gave my heart its first taste of internal gymnastics.

"Mind if I sit here?" he asked.

Did I mind?

Would you please?

Could I bronze the chair afterwards?

"Sure," I said with remarkable cool considering the calisthenics going on in my chest.

He collapsed into the chair with a groan, then proceeded to fall asleep. He didn't so much as move a muscle when the bell rang and Mr. Hawkins walked into the room.

The petite math teacher with his relic Elvis pompadour, shiny suit, and pencil-thin black tie went on about something, though I could barely focus given the, well, god sitting mere inches from me. Until that moment, I can safely say that I hadn't given "boys" a thought. My only interest was in school and making excellent grades on my way to becoming an even more excellent lawyer. In the scenario in my head, there was no room for romantic entanglements. I'd leave that up to my mother, sister, and brother—all of whom seemed to be obsessed with the opposite sex, their lives altered as a result of it.

No doubt it was because I was working so hard to ignore the amazingly muscled and tanned arm lying on the desktop next to me that I didn't realize Mr. Hawkins' monotone voice was getting closer by the syllable. When the teacher slammed his yardstick against our table I nearly had a heart attack, though Jack barely moved. He sat up, yawned, and gave the teacher the same crooked smile he had given me. "How ya doin'?" he asked the man.

The teacher seemed at a frustrated loss, words working themselves to the surface until he bit out, "Not so good."

"Sorry to hear it. Life's rough, no question."

I thought Mr. Hawkins would explode.

"I've heard about you, know all about how you slide through class, getting A's because you're the star quarterback."

Quarterback?

All that easy charm evaporated, though I could tell Jack was trying not to show it. Clearly there was more beneath the surface of My Heart's Desire than easy charm.

"For a change, you're going to have to do the work." The man sneered. "Now sit up and pay attention."

Everyone watched as Jack sat up with a shrug as if not embarrassed in the least, while I felt heat burn in my cheeks from all the stares.

Mr. Hawkins returned to the front, passed out books, and gave us our first assignment just as the bell rang.

I did my best to forget Jack Blair until the next day, when he returned to class and sat down at my table again as if that were his seat.

"Hey," he said with a cheerful grunt, and promptly put his head on his arms and fell asleep.

Mr. Hawkins started class, going a hundred miles an hour. The barrage of words came fast enough to make me only partially aware of my neighbor as I worked to solve for *x* and *y* in case I was called on.

It was after I finished a particularly difficult equation that Mr. Hawkins whipped the yardstick down on his own desk, jarring the entire class, with the exception of Jack.

"Mr. Blair," he bellowed. "The answer, please."

I still don't know why I did it. But I kicked him under the table, bringing him upright. I'll never forget the look in his eyes when he glanced at me. By day two, my adoration had turned to dumbstruck love. Who would have guessed.

"Mr. Blair," the teacher repeated. "The answer?"

It wasn't hard to realize that Jack walked a fine line. One slip over to the other side and there would be hell to pay. Mr. Hawkins was looking for an excuse to get rid of him. And hello, I was madly in love, and not thinking about consequences. So I did the only thing a love-struck math whiz could do. I wrote the answer on the corner of my paper so he could see.

Jack looked at it, then me. He debated for a lifetime, then shrugged. "X equals 3,458."

You'd have thought the teacher would have been pleased and let it go. No such luck. He was furious. And his fury was directed at me.

Mr. Hawkins bore down on us like a tornado headed for Kansas. I realized right then that I was going to be kicked out. For cheating. Me, Miss Never Get In Trouble. Me, Miss Obnoxious Do-Gooder, was going to get kicked out of class.

The heart attack that had been threatening was knocking at the door. And Jack Blair knew it. With what I swear was a curse, he locked eyes with the approaching storm, cursed again, then smiled. Yes, smiled.

Slowly and with great relish, he tore off the edge of paper holding the answer, then put it in his mouth and ate it.

You really can't make something like that up.

Mr. Hawkins went crazy, screaming, threatening to kick us both out for crimes ranging from disrespect to cheating.

"Go ahead, send us to the office," Jack said, the tone a taunt.

I whipped my head around to look at him, mouth agape with a look of Are you crazy?! I had never been sent to the office in my life.

He just chuckled, burped, then added, "What are you gonna tell them, that you kicked us out because I ate a piece of paper and she watched?"

Mr. Hawkins glared, fumed, but knew when he was beaten. Muttering, he retreated to the front.

The next day Jack showed up for class and didn't fall immediately asleep when he sat down.

"Thanks for yesterday," he said with that heart-stopping smile.

I fumbled around in my normally large vocabulary and came up with, "Oh, well . . ." and that was it.

He reached into his jacket and pulled out a plastic egg, the kind from a bubble gum machine. "Here."

"What is it?" I breathed.

"I'm not sure. But it came out of the machine and, hell, figured it was the least I could do." Then he promptly went to sleep.

I knew on sight that whatever was inside was nothing more than a silly gesture, but still, my heart beat wildly. And when I cracked it open, a plastic ring with a strange blue plastic "stone" fell out. Jack didn't so much as move when I whispered thank you, and he certainly didn't notice when I slipped it on my finger.